Beyond the Badge: Finn

Blue Avengers MC
Book 2

Jeanne St. James

———

Credits:
Photographer/Cover Art: Golden Czermak at FuriousFotog
Cover Model: Caylan Hughes
Editor: Proofreading by the Page
Beta Readers: Alex Swab, Author BJ Alpha and Sharon Abrams
Logo: Jennifer Edwards

———

www.jeannestjames.com

Sign up for my newsletter for insider information, author news, and new releases:
www.jeannestjames.com/newslettersignup

———

———

Keep an eye on her website at http://www. jeannestjames.com/or sign up for her newsletter to learn about her upcoming releases: http://www.jeannestjames. com/newslettersignup

Author Links: Instagram * Facebook * Goodreads Author Page * Newsletter * Jeanne's Review & Book Crew * BookBub * TikTok * YouTube

Terms Used

PLCB - Pennsylvania Liquor Control Board
LEO - Liquor Enforcement Officer and/or Law Enforcement Officer (used for both)
PSP - PA State Police
The Plant - a place away from stations/barracks/etc. for law enforcement/a task force to conduct clandestine criminal investigations.
Plant Manager - in charge of wiretapping/transcribing calls
Bid - prison sentence/jail term
MC Chapter - The national club with a national exec committee (President, VP, etc.); Ex: Deadly Demons MC
MC Charter - Each charter is run independently, does not answer to a mother charter or a national chapter; Example: Blue Avengers MC
Sled - biker slang for motorcycle
A-Cert - Wire-tapping certification
TFO - Task Force Officer

1

UC/UCO - Undercover Agent/Officer

Printing - the outline of a concealed carry gun showing through either a shirt or garment that the person is wearing

AUSA - Assistant US Attorney

RICO - Racketeer Influenced and Corrupt Organizations Act

Thrust stage - a stage that extends into the audience on three sides and is connected to the backstage area by its upstage end.

Adonis belt - the V-shaped muscle that runs diagonally from the hip bones to the pelvic region.

CW - Cooperating Witness, unpaid

CI - Confidential Informant, some are paid

Stash vehicle - a place to store their supply of drugs for dealing.

Re-up - to refill one's drug stash

Fruit of the poisonous tree doctrine - Extends the exclusionary rule to make evidence inadmissible in court if it was derived from evidence that was illegally obtained

Probable cause (PC) - a legal requirement that reasonable grounds must be met before a police officer can make an arrest, conduct a search, seize property, or get a warrant.

Character List

BAMC (Southwest Regional Charter):

Axel Jamison - *President* - Sergeant, Shadow Valley PD
Shane Fletcher (Fletch) - *Vice President* - Trooper, PA State Police
Antonio Alvarez (Rez) - *Sergeant at Arms* - Officer, Southern Allegheny Regional PD
Aiden Cross - *Secretary* - Corporal, Southern Allegheny Regional PD, Nash's (DAMC) husband
Mike Miller - *Treasurer* - Officer, Pittsburgh PD
Daniel Finnegan (Finn) - *Road Captain* - Officer, Southern Allegheny Regional PD
Bradley Lennox (Nox) - Officer, Shadow Valley PD
Colin Crew - Senior Special Agent, DEA, Tri-State Task Force Leader
Owen Decker - Trooper, PA State Police
Danielle Montgomery (Monty) - Corrections Officer, SCI Greene

3

Timothy Frasier - Liquor Enforcement Officer, PA State Police
Roland North - Lieutenant, Pittsburgh PD

Other Tri-State Drug Task Force Members:

Luke Rodgers - DEA Special Agent
Luis Torres - DEA Special Agent
Ian Butler - Corporal, PA State Police
Ken Proctor - Officer, Uniontown PD
Carl Powers - Trooper, PA State Police
Sam Kruger - Corporal, Greensburg PD
Warren Reynolds - Corporal, PA State Police
Don Mullins - Narcotic Detective, Pittsburgh PD
Nova Wilder – FBI Special Agent, Organized Crime Division

Others:

Melina Jensen (Mel/MJ) - Manager at The Peach Pit
Mitch Jamison - Former BAMC President, Axel & Zak's father, retired from Shadow Valley PD
Bella – DAMC born and raised, Axel's wife
Valerie (Val) - Decker's adopted niece
Liam & Laney Jamison - Axel & Bella's twins
Nash - Cross's husband, Member of Dirty Angels MC and the band Dirty Deeds
Sapphire - Mel's best friend and hostess at The Peach Pit
Saint - Deadly Demon in charge of The Peach Pit
Ringo, Popeye, Mutt, Chubs and T-Bone - Prospects working at The Peach Pit

Playlist

Finn and Mel dance to the following songs:

Hot in Herre - Nelly
Burn It to the Ground - Nickelback
Closer - Nine Inch Nails
SexyBack - Justin Timberlake
I Like the Way You Move - BodyRockers
Yeah - Usher
Candy Shop - 50 Cent
Low - Flo Rida
American Woman - Lenny Kravitz
Earned It - The Weeknd
Body Party - Ciara
Dark Horse - Katy Perry
You Can Leave Your Hat On - Joe Cocker
I See Red - Everybody Loves An Outlaw
Partition - Beyoncé
I Feel Like I'm Drowning - Two Feet
Love to Love You Baby - Donna Summer
Perfect - Ed Sheeran

Chapter One

"WHAT THE FUCK!" Finn screamed at the ninety-six inch TV. "That was clearly holding! You refs are fucking blind!"

"Jesus, dude, you're going to stroke out," Monty warned as she bumped his leg with her knee.

He lifted his legs out of the way, but only enough to allow her to squeeze by on her way to the other couch. "Seriously, you couldn't go around?" He dropped his boots back onto the scarred and battered coffee table.

"I could've. But I didn't." The twenty-six year old prison guard sank down onto the empty couch to his left, cracked open a can of IC Light and took a long swig.

Three large couches were set up in a U and he was sprawled out on the center one so he could see the Pittsburgh Steelers game perfectly. This afternoon they were playing the Baltimore Ravens and he hoped his team gave their rivals a bad spanking.

Finn wrinkled his nose at the beer she was drinking. "There's better beer in the fridge."

Danielle Montgomery rolled her green eyes. "If I wanted another brand, I would've grabbed another brand, genius."

"I wonder about you sometimes," Finn informed the only female member of the Blue Avengers MC.

"Well, I wonder about you *all* the fucking time."

Finn pointed the top of his beer bottle at her. "Do men like that short hair of yours?"

Her dark hair was kept pretty damn short, but then keeping it that short helped prevent the max security inmates from grabbing a handful and wrenching her around by her hair.

"Do men like that short hair of yours?" she echoed.

Finn grinned and flapped his eyelashes. "I do get my fair amount of the male gaze."

Monty almost choked on her crap beer. She pounded her chest and coughed. When she could talk again, she said, "I heard gingers are spicy."

"I'm super spicy. Do you want a taste?"

"*Eww.* No. You're an asshole. I don't like spicy asshole."

"To know that means you've tasted one."

"I do get my fair share of the male gaze," she echoed him.

"Do they tend to wear orange jumpsuits and identify as an inmate?"

She grabbed the pillow tucked in the corner of the couch and whipped it at him.

He laughed and ducked. Snagging it from where it landed on the couch next to him, he tucked it behind his head. "Thanks. I've wanted that pillow for the past fifteen minutes but was too lazy to get up and grab it."

Monty shook her head.

"Can you two shut the fuck up? I'm trying to watch the game," Nox bitched from the couch on the right side of the large U.

"That's right, we're crashing in Nox's living room right now since he's made himself at home here," Decker said as he joined them, dropping on the couch next to Nox and throwing a beefy arm over the man's shoulder.

With a scowl, Nox shrugged it off. "If you need to cuddle, go do it with Monty."

Decker glanced across the TV area and asked, "Monty?"

"Don't even try it," she warned.

Nox finally sold the home where he and his late wife had lived. Since that house held too many memories for him, a deal had been struck that after the closing, he'd take the equity and use it to finish the second floor of The Plant as an apartment. This way he could live upstairs at the clubhouse, something he'd already been doing anyhow. However, he was still in the middle of working on his new digs.

The floors were now refinished, the plumbing and bathroom fixtures installed, the walls and trim painted, and the primary bedroom framed out. Eventually Nox would build a second bedroom, but that would be the last thing on his long to-do list. A kitchen was his next priority.

He was still sleeping on a damn cot up there. But at least he moved it from the third floor—since that was now home to the Tri-State Federal Drug Task Force—to the second floor, where he had more privacy.

Since the apartment wasn't completely habitable yet, he was using the first floor of the Blue Avengers' church as his living room and kitchen until appliances were installed and his place was furnished, since he ended up donating all the furniture he'd owned with his late wife.

"What's going on, fuckers?" Antonio Alvarez called out, appearing from the back hallway.

"You're missing the game," Finn informed their club's sergeant at arms.

Rez shook his dark head. "I was listening to it on the radio on my ride over. I'm not sure I want to watch this slaughter." Keeping his eyes glued to the game on the huge TV, he stepped behind the curved counter in the back corner of the common area and grabbed a cold beer from the fridge. "Fucking dirty birds!"

A grumble went up from all of them at the nickname they called the opposing team.

"What do you expect? They're always tough to beat," Axel Jamison said, also coming from the rear of the building since they only used the rear or side door to come and go from The Plant, their club's church.

"Did you just get off shift?" Monty asked the BAMC president.

"Yes, unfortunately. I came straight over."

"Where's Bella?" Monty asked about his wife. "With the kids?"

"No. She's doing something with the Dirty Angels sisterhood. I think they're all planning some fundraiser for Ellie Walker's foundation."

The Walker Foundation was a worthy one. It had been created to provide prosthetic care for amputees who couldn't afford it, since her husband was a vet who'd lost his lower leg while serving.

"Who's got the twins?" Rez asked.

"My parents. My dad's dropping them off here soon," Axel said, joining them over by the TV.

With beer in hand, Rez shouted, "What the fuck!" at the TV when he came over to stand at the end of the couch where Finn had his ass planted.

Finn flung a hand toward the big screen and bitched, "Right? They're playing like shit. They might as well just forfeit this fucking game and go home."

"Don't count them out yet," Nox grumbled.

"There is no way they're pulling off a W with this shit show," Finn told him.

"Where's Fletch when we need him?" Rez asked. "He probably didn't do his ridiculous pregame routine." He twisted his face and flapped his arms around, almost spilling his beer as he emulated Fletch that time they caught him doing his superstitious ritual. Now the state trooper only did it where no one could see him.

"Guess it's not so ridiculous if you think it helps," Monty huffed and shook her head.

Finn grabbed his phone from the cushion next to him. He texted their VP:

> Hey, asshole! Did you do your Steeler's pregame ritual? If not, you better do it. They're playing like they belong in the Pee Wee League!

The reply came within thirty seconds.

> Like I'm going to fucking tell you that. I don't want to be blamed for this embarrassing loss.

Finn quickly texted back:

> Too late. Your fault. You didn't do it because you're embarrassed to look like an idiot in front of the FBI.

> You mean Nova, you dumb fuck?

Fletch's response had Finn growling as he tossed his phone back onto the couch and shouted, "Don't fucking run it! Pass it! Pass! Pass! *Nooooooo!*"

"Yo, arm-chair coach, you're going to burst a blood vessel and I don't want to have to replace you on the task force," Crew yelled as he emerged from the room where their executive committee met.

"Were you upstairs?" Axel asked him.

"Yeah, I was checking to see who's up there already since we have a task force meeting."

"And?" Decker asked.

Crew answered, "Powers is up there transcribing some calls and Torres is listening to some dirty talk."

"Dirty talk?" Monty asked, her dark eyebrows raised. "I should've become a cop. That sounds like fun."

"He's listening in on wiretaps. It can be boring as fuck. In fact, ninety-nine percent of the time it's a snooze fest."

"Transcribing those fucking calls are even worse," Nox mumbled.

"We're all taking turns doing it," Crew said. "Because, yes, it fucking sucks."

"Anyone else up there?" Rez asked.

"Not yet. Reynolds, Butler and Rodgers can't make it. Kruger and Mullins will be here after the game."

"Yeah, that was dumb to schedule a meeting on a Sunday," Finn told the task force leader.

"It was actually smart." Crew tapped his finger against his temple. "How many of us are already here on Sunday? If not for a club run, then for football?"

Finn couldn't argue that point, so he didn't. Instead, he downed the rest of his beer and watched the next play.

And of course the Steelers got a penalty! When he whipped his empty beer can, it pinged off the TV, leaving some splatter behind.

"Hey!" Monty yelled at him.

"What the fuck are you doing?" Nox asked.

Jamison shook his head. "You want to replace that monster out of your own pocket?"

"This season is fucked!" Finn yelled in frustration.

"It's only the first game of the regular season. You know it takes them a bit to get their shit together," Crew reminded him.

"Yeah," Decker agreed. "They're always better the second half of the game and the second half of the season. It's the Steelers way."

It sure seemed to be. They always spiked his blood pressure.

"Aww shit. Better straighten your asses up," Rez announced. "The old guard just walked in."

"That means little ears are in the building," Jamison reminded them.

"They're almost twelve, Jamison. And they're around bikers all the time, especially since you *live* in a neighborhood full of them. You don't think they hear worse shit than what we say?" Decker asked.

"But you all are supposed to be upstanding citizens," their president reminded them with a completely straight face.

Not one person in that room didn't laugh.

Even Mitch Jamison chuckled as he escorted his grandchildren into the common area. "I wish it was different, but it isn't. They might hear it but that doesn't mean they can repeat it until after they're eighteen. It's the Jamison family law."

"Eighteen? Good luck with that," Nox grumbled.

"Hi, Dad!" Laney ran up to her father and practically tackled him. "How was work?"

Jamison wrapped his arms around his twelve-year-old daughter, squeezed her tight and planted a kiss on the top of

13

her head. When he straightened, he smiled down at her. "Work."

She giggled and pulled free, then fist-bumped Crew on her way over to throw herself on the couch next to Monty, grabbing the potato chips from the table and shoving her hand deep into the open bag.

Hell, those chips were probably stale. Finn had no idea how long they'd been sitting out on the table with the bag gaping open. Around there it could be weeks.

"Grandpa was yelling at the radio on our way over here," Laney stage-whispered to Monty, then pulled out a fistful of greasy BBQ chips and shoved them into her wide-open mouth, orange crumbs falling all over her shirt and clinging to her lips.

"I'm not surprised," Monty stage-whispered back, giving her a wink.

"Liam, are you going to come give your old man a hug hello?" Jamison asked his son.

"I'm too old for hugs, Dad." Liam plopped down on the couch next to Nox and rested the soles of his sneakers on the edge of the coffee table. "Can I have a beer?"

"Absolutely. Grandpa will get one for you. Right, Pop?" Jamison asked his father, Mitch.

"Sure! Maybe there's some root beer left in the fridge. Liam, go check. I'm sure your sister wants one."

"Then she can get one herself," Jamison's son mumbled.

"And you can take your feet off the furniture," Mitch told him.

"Finn has *his* boots on the table."

"That's because he's rude. Don't be rude like this a—" Rez caught himself in time. "*Animal.*" He came around the front of the couch and kicked Finn's feet off the table.

Finn shot Rez a silent *I'll-get-you-back-later* promise, planted his feet on the floor and sat up.

"All right. I'm out of here," Mitch announced.

"Bye, Grandpa!" Laney shouted.

"See you kids later." Mitch glanced around the common area and added, "*All* of you children."

Jamison's old man disappeared back the way he came from, shaking his head as they all shouted, "Bye, Grandpa!" in unison.

"He needs to dust off his bike and come along on our next run with us. It's been a while. I'm sure he misses it," Crew said to Jamison.

"Mom made him sell it."

"What the fu— *freak?*" Decker shouted.

"Grandma said he's getting too old and brittle and he needs to be careful now and not die. 'Cause if he dies, then he can't help her with the grandkids," Liam announced with his nose buried in his cell phone.

"That's not how she said it," Jamison said with a sigh.

"That's what I heard."

"He's getting older and she doesn't want him getting injured, that's all."

Laney added, "She also said she doesn't want him cracking open his noggin even though it might knock some sense into him."

"That I believe."

Liam raised his eyes from his phone. "See? I don't lie, Dad."

"That I don't believe," Jamison said dryly.

"Mom said small fibs are okay," Laney said.

"I think you both need your ears cleaned out."

"You sure these two are your kids, Jamison, and not Finn's?" Monty asked with a laugh and tucking a long red strand of Laney's hair behind her ear. Both of the twins had hair close to the same red as Finn's, so it was an ongoing joke. Just like Finn always busted Monty on her short hair.

He pitied the teasing the twins probably encountered at school since he'd gone through a shitload about his own red hair and freckles when he was younger. Now he took it in stride. Even when his MC brothers called him Heat Miser or one of the many other nicknames they came up with.

"Mom didn't have sex with Finn," Laney announced with a serious tone. "I asked her."

"You did what? When?" Jamison asked, his expression a bit shell-shocked.

Laney shrugged. "A million years ago. She said we take after Aunt Ivy."

"And that's true."

Finn grinned at Laney. "I mean, you *could* be mine. But we'll pretend you're not so I don't have to pay the same crazy amount of child support like Crew pays for his kids."

"I don't mind paying for anything my children need. I do mind paying for my ex's lifestyle."

"Yeah, but you pay a ton," Finn said.

"Kids cost a lot," Decker mentioned. He would know since he was raising his four-year-old niece, Valerie.

"They're worth every damn penny. Now, the ex on the other hand..." Crew let that drop since children were in the room.

"Exes are exes for a reason," Finn stated.

Crew came behind the couch where Finn was sitting and shoved him in the back of the head. "*Phew*, the sage wisdom coming from that pea-brain of yours."

Nox groaned loudly. "Can we watch the d— *darn* game in peace?"

"Yeah, you all are really annoying," Liam said. "It's hard

to concentrate on the game."

Finn dropped his head and covered his mouth with his hand so the kid couldn't see him smirking.

Jamison moved behind his son and plucked the cell phone from his fingers. "Now you'll have no problem concentrating."

"Dad!" Liam reached up to grab it back but his father moved out of reach.

"I'll hold onto this for a while. You'll get it back when I think you deserve it back."

"Dad!"

Jamison shrugged. "Do you want to go home, or do you want to hang out here for the game?"

Liam huffed sharply, crossed his arms over his chest, and slouched down.

Damn, the kid was now looking more like Nox's son.

"I thought so." Axel went and sat with Monty and Laney. "Okay, who wants to make bets to see if the Steelers can turn this damn game around."

"I'm telling Grandpa you said damn in front of us," Liam threatened.

"He's heard me say worse to his face."

"You have?" Laney breathed with her eyes wide. "When?"

"That's a story for when you're older."

———

Unfortunately, the Steelers did not turn the game around. It was a hard and depressing loss and Finn was currently drowning his sorrows with a cold Yuengling Lager.

Jamison and his kids had left a while ago. Monty a half

hour ago. And the only people left at church were his BAMC brothers also working on the federal task force.

Crew's salt-and-pepper head popped out from the club's meeting room doorway. "Yo, assholes! Task force meeting. Upstairs. Now."

"Everybody else here?" Decker asked as he and Rez played a game of foosball.

"Yeah, waiting on you turds."

"Where's Nox?" Finn asked.

"Doing something up in his place. I'll grab him on the way." Crew's head disappeared and Finn heard the side door slam a few seconds later.

"Duty calls, boys," Finn announced, downing the rest of the beer and tossing the empty into the recycle bin.

Once they got upstairs, Decker, Finn and Rez settled into empty seats around the long conference table. Like normal, as task force leader, Crew sat at the head of the table. They were joined by Torres, Kruger, Mullins, Powers and Nox. Nine out of the fifteen-member task force team.

It was rare that all of them were able to gather for a meeting, especially if someone was undercover, like Fletch and Nova, or doing surveillance.

"All right," Crew started, his gaze scanning the occupants of the table. "Since Fletch and Wilder are still deep under-cover, I have them on a conference call along with Butler and Reynolds. I've been meaning to have this meeting to give you the latest updates on the investigation. I met with leaders of the two other groups and this is what we know so far between the wiretaps, the UCs and the surveillance, so pay attention.

"We have three major players involved with this trafficking. That we know of, anyway. A Mexican cartel as the supplier, the Deadly Demons MC as the transporter and La Cosa Nostra as the distributor. More specifically, the Russo crime family out of Pittsburgh. That's the organization funding the whole operation.

"Here's what we've learned so far, some info confirmed, some not. Russos are buying five kilos of 'ice' a month from a cartel. The DEA in Texas is working on discovering which cartel, but if any of you get wind of who that is, get that info to me ASAP. Of course, they're using code and haven't mentioned the names of the players in any of the wiretaps so far. The Demons are calling the supplier Los Malos MC. We know for a fact Los Malos MC, or even a cartel by that name, doesn't exist. They're only using it to throw off anyone listening."

"Sounds like they may be smarter than we thought," Decker said.

"Maybe," Torres said. The DEA agent and "plant manager" sat to Crew's left. "But we'll figure it out eventually. With all the wiretaps between the three groups, not one has slipped and actually named the Russos or the cartel... yet."

Crew picked up again there. "Whether they're smart *enough* is questionable. They can't even figure out when they're being tailed. That's how we discovered where the majority of that meth was landing. The pipeline breaks down like this... The Demons have a member who's a long-haul trucker and they're using his rig to transport the bricks of meth for the Russos. Side note: even though the rig's in this biker's name, we think the MC paid cash for it. Group one slapped a tracking device on the rig and are setting up more surveillance to notify the DEA in Houston when it's on the move so they can try to identify the cartel. But since they tagged the rig, it hasn't gone anywhere near the border. What we assume is, once a month the Demons are transporting it from the southern border into West Virginia by mixing it in with legitimate loads of cilantro so it goes undetected.

"Once the load shows up, the MC takes one kilo as payment. By taking it in that method, they're making more money than being paid outright in cash because of how they're cutting it up and selling it on the streets. Then the Demons are using various methods to deliver the remaining four kilos to one of the Russo lieutenants. From what we can tell, the Russos are paying twelve thousand per kilo wholesale. The second it hits Pennsylvania, that value doubles."

"That's a hell of an investment," Finn muttered.

"Exactly. But remember, that's only the uncut value. We can safely assume the Russos are then turning around, breaking it down into half and quarter kilos and selling them to street-level dealers. Those dealers then break it down even further by cutting it with filler. Our guess is the Russos are making about two hundred and forty grand when they sell it to the low-level dealers. That's a hell of a return on their original investment of twelve K."

FBI Special Agent Nova Wilder's voice came from the speaker phone sitting in the middle of the table. "And why they most likely got involved in this business venture."

"You didn't catch wind of any of this shit while you were undercover with the Russos?" Finn asked her.

"No. There could've been some low-level dealing but my guess is once Frankie, the former underboss, took over, he decided to expand on that. I do know his father wanted to stay out of the drug business. But now with Frank Sr. out of the way, Junior is now boss. This has to be a new venture for them. If they were moving this amount, I can't imagine I wouldn't have gotten even a slight whiff of it."

"Agreed," Crew said. "This flow of meth only recently hit

the DEA's radar, spurring them to establish this task force to squash it. Fletch, you want to add anything from your end, since you're dealing directly with the Demons' Uniontown chapter?"

Shane Fletcher, a state trooper currently undercover with the Dirty Angels MC spoke next. "The Demons are breaking down their kilo by cutting it with cheap baking soda. They're then distributing it to key players within their MC. Those key players have 'teams' of fellow MC brothers to sell it on the street, in bars, at bike rallies, wherever. Our contact right now is really limited to Wolf and his crew, but we're working on getting in tighter with him."

Crew picked up from there. "Because of this organized effort, the data shows that their club is the fastest growing outlaw MC in the country right now. This all stems back to this hookup with the Russos. Overflowing coffers only makes their MC stronger and is creating a snowball effect by allowing them to expand both sales and territory by adding chapters to their club. But that's not all. They're also buying up businesses in PA and Ohio to launder money and expand retail sales. Think backdoor dealing. They're grabbing locations where their customers tend to hang out, like bars, strip clubs, roach motels, used car lots, pizza shops... shit like that. Places with high traffic. Cash comes in, drugs and washed money goes out."

Torres cut in again. "While all of this might make them financially stronger, it also makes them weaker. The more people involved in these enterprises, the higher the chances of their house of cards falling down around them. It just takes one pulled card for it all to tumble."

Crew nodded. "Our three groups are tasked with pulling that card and demolishing that house. But to do it right, we need to take them and the Russos down in a coordinated effort. Especially when it comes time for indictments. It needs to be organized and swift."

"Squash them like the fucking roaches they are." Mullins, a narcotic detective with the Pittsburgh PD, slammed his hand on the table like he was doing just that.

"Anyway," Crew continued, "in the meantime, I have something new we can move on. A few days ago, Rodgers had contact with a CI who bought an ounce out of a strip club right outside of Uniontown. It just so happens The Peach Pit was recently bought by the Demons. Of course that purchase was an immediate red flag. We also heard chatter that they could be using some of the strippers as mules to move product or using them to deal. The info was a bit sketchy on that point. All the CI could tell Rodgers was that he walked in with cash and walked out with an ounce. We need to confirm that's what's happening and who's involved. If it's true and they're also using that location to launder cash, that's another RICO violation, not for the Russos, since they're racking those up on their own, but for the Demons. The more charges we can pin on them and their members, the better to take the whole organization down. And if we take them down, we can choke the flow of meth into PA. Or at least this particular pipeline."

"And that's the reason we're all sitting around this table. So, now what?" Rez asked.

"I'd like to set someone up in the strip club. Maybe not long-term but at least long enough to confirm and document that the Demons are using The Peach Pit as part of their drug business. Whether by selling from there, laundering money or using the girls as mules. Or even all of the above."

"You want one of us to go in as a regular?" Decker asked.

"That's one option I'm tossing around. The other is to have someone work there to get a peek behind the scenes."

"The only female on the team is Wilder. She's already undercover with Fletch and the Dirty Angels," Finn reminded him. "Are you planning on pulling her, or bringing someone new on board?"

Crew shook his head. "I'm not pulling her. I want Fletch and Nova to stay put. While we can't bring in anyone new because of the budget, I have another idea."

Wilder's voice came through the phone. "That's good, because I would say no to stripping."

"Yeah, I would nix the idea of Nova stripping, too," came from Fletch.

Nox groaned. "You're not using Monty, right? She won't go for that, either."

"Not Monty," Crew confirmed.

"Then who you got in mind for that fucking job?" Finn asked with a smirk.

Crew's gray eyes landed on him.

The second the task force leader also smirked, Finn knew he was fucked.

Chapter Two

Panic swept through Finn. "Undercover as a manager or bouncer or something? Because if so, I'm good with that."

"No." Crew's smirk turned into a full-blown shit-eating grin.

Fuuuuuuuck. "Then what?"

Don't say stripper.

Don't say stripper.

Don't you fucking say stripper.

"As an entertainer."

An "entertainer." *Riiiiight.*

Calling them stripes didn't change a leopard's spots. *Goddamn it!* "What the fuck? There's no way the Demons bought a male strip club."

"And you'd be right. They didn't."

"You want me to strip in drag?"

Rez snorted. "Is that even possible?"

"He'd just need a wig. And fake tits," Decker answered. "I think he has the tucking down pat."

Crew shook his salt-and-pepper head. "Not in drag,

dumbasses. Think one of those all-male revue shows. Like in Vegas."

"Like Thunder From Down Under?" Finn asked.

Crew jabbed his finger toward him. "There you go."

"No." *Just no. Fuck no.*

"We all have to do what we have to do," Nox reminded him.

Finn stared across the table, surprised at the grin spreading across his normally steely-faced club brother. At least Nox was finding this whole thing amusing. The man had been in a deep depression ever since his wife died almost a year ago. Any sense of humor he'd had in the past—which had never been abundant to begin with—had disappeared.

"You think this is funny?"

Nox's grin disappeared and was quickly replaced with a straight face. "Fucking hilarious."

Well, *hell*, it might be worth taking the assignment just seeing some life coming back to the widower. Even if it was at Finn's expense.

He turned his attention back to the man at the head of the table. "No."

"You're perfect for it."

"How's that?" He cleared his throat when his voice cracked.

"Dude, I'm sure you stare at yourself in the mirror for extended amounts of time. If I was in the shape you are, I'd volunteer," exclaimed Powers, a veteran trooper with the PA State Police.

Finn doubted that.

"He probably maintains it by secretly swinging around a pole," said Kruger, a Greensburg PD corporal.

"Yeah, your pole." Finn blinked. "Wait." With a shake of

his head, he closed his eyes and sucked in a deep breath. This whole thing had scrambled his thoughts.

Decker snickered. "You got something to tell us, Finn? You know we're all accepting here. If you need assistance coming out of the closet, we're here for you."

"Fuck off," Finn told him.

"Your outstanding physique and your lack of identifying tattoos aren't the only reasons I picked you."

Finn had an inkling about the other. "Pick someone else."

"Nope. Everyone else has other shit to do. And you're perfect for this assignment."

Crew was loving every fucking second of this. *Bastard.* "No, I'm not," he grumbled.

"I'm sure your mom can give you pointers."

"My mother was never a fucking stripper. She's a dance instructor."

"Right and she taught you all the moves," Crew reminded him, pursing his lips and wiggling his shoulders.

Like he could forget the first twelve years of his life. *Sure.*

Rez twisted his head toward Finn. "What moves?"

"You didn't know?" Decker asked their club's sergeant at arms. "He let it slip one night that his mom took him to her dance studio every day and he was heavily involved in the classes."

"Against my fucking will. As soon as I was old enough to stay home by myself, I got out of going."

"But admit it, you still know how to move," Crew said, amusement making the corner of his eyes crinkle more than normal.

Asshole. "Of course. The ladies never complain. But I have a natural gift for horizontal dancing, not vertical. How about you just send in some of us as customers. We go in, observe and maybe even do some buys."

"Like I said, I'll most likely plan that, too. But this isn't a long-term assignment, brother. It's only to get behind the scenes and customers aren't allowed in the back. Dancers are."

"That's true. Most strip clubs have some sort of bouncer keeping patrons out of the area where the women dress and hang out," Rez said. "Count me in. I'm willing to go in as a customer."

"I'll probably take you up on that. With your tats, you'll blend in perfectly with the clientele," Crew told him.

Alvarez was the most tattooed member out of both the Blue Avengers and the task force. Luckily, the Southern Allegheny Regional PD, where both Finn and Rez worked, didn't have any limits on tattoos. Rez even had them on the back of his hands. That wouldn't fly with some other departments.

"You just want to watch women shaking their tits and ass," Nox called him out.

"Damn right! And on the feds' dime, too. Do you blame me?"

Decker raised his hand and bounced in his seat. "Oh, pick me. I want in, too."

"What about Val?" Crew frowned. "Your mom won't mind babysitting longer than normal? We might be talking some late nights here."

Decker had been raising his four-year-old niece since not long after she was born. Ever since he took Valerie from his drug-addicted sister. But he had no help except for his elderly mother. Since she wasn't in the greatest health, she could only deal with the active little girl for a limited amount of hours a day.

"If she can't do it, I'll find someone else to help out."

"You should just hire a full-time nanny," Nox told

Decker. "Stop being such a cheap ass and putting your poor mom to work."

"She loves spending time with Val," Decker exclaimed.

"Yeah, as a grandmother, not a substitute mom."

Crew cut in on Decker and Nox's conversation. "Let's get back on track. Talking about nieces and nannies aren't it."

"Yeah, let's," Finn cut in, "since I'm not liking this whole idea. How the hell am I getting in the door if they only have women working the poles?"

"Did you miss the part where I said we'll be using an all-male revue as cover?"

Finn needed more details than what the man was giving. "But are we creating one?"

Crew shook his head. "Not needed. Got a buddy whose brother runs a group that tours. They book at bars, strip clubs, parties, wherever, for one- or even two-night performances. I already checked with him and he's on board. Especially after my buddy showed him your pic, Finn. He's down a guy due to an ACL tear, so he needs you to fill in. He said if you like it and you can dance well, then he might even be interested in hiring you full-time."

Decker snorted next to him. "Something to fall back on if this cop gig of yours goes belly up."

"Get the fuck out of here," Finn muttered, dropping his head and shaking it.

"It's the perfect cover to get behind the scenes and only Nick will know you're undercover. No one at the club will or any of his dancers. Since your mom still has her studio, you can use it to get limber and practice some signature moves. In the meantime, I'll make contact with Nick, the owner/manager, and have him reach out to The Peach Pit and offer their services. Their male entertainers usually make a fuckload of cash and so does the venue. Because of that, I can't imagine whoever's running The Peach Pit will turn them down. The Demons seem to be all about raking in the green."

"You're going to have to shave your body," Decker warned him with a smirk.

At the other end of the table, Rez snorted. "He probably waxes. Do you think he's naturally hairless like a naked mole-rat?"

"I think mole-rats might have a few stray hairs," Decker claimed.

Finn didn't even know what a naked mole-rat looked like. He didn't want to, either.

"So does Finn, around his asshole. Unless he gets that waxed, too. Do you?"

"How the fuck would you know what my asshole looks like?" Finn asked Rez. "Anyway, I don't fucking wax."

Decker coughed out a, "Bullshit."

Finn surged from his chair and reached for his belt. "Do you want me to prove it to you?"

A bunch of shouts rose around the table. "No!"

"Fuck no!"

"Sit down."

"We don't want to see that ginger-rimmed hole."

Crew's next words got caught up with his laughter. "All right. So, that's solved."

"No, it's not," Finn insisted.

"It is. I'll make contact with Nick and let him know you'll be his newest stripper. I'll let you know where and when to meet up with him so he can teach you their routines. Think up a good fake name in the meantime."

Jesus. "I'm only doing this once, right? If so, I don't need to learn any fucking routine."

"You need to make sure you blend in with the rest of the

guys. I think they all do some group dances in addition to their individual routines."

"Sounds like you went to watch them, Crew," Mullins said with a laugh. "Did you take a wad of ones with you? Play a little dollar bill hide-and-seek with those swinging banana hammocks?"

"I watched a couple of their videos on the Peckers website," Crew confessed with a shrug. "For investigative purposes, of course."

"Peckers?" Finn's voice cracked again. He had to clear his throat to bring it back down an octave. "You said *Peckers?*"

"That's the name. Well, officially it's Peckers All-Male Revue."

"Finn's going to be a Pecker!" burst from Decker as he slammed his hand on the table and laughed so hard he fell forward, almost cracking his forehead on the conference table.

"He already is," Rez confirmed.

"Not just a Pecker. A redheaded Pecker! I heard it's a rare species." Crew squawked loudly, sounding like a sick bird.

Torres hooted. "This is pure fucking gold."

He was so glad everyone was having a good laugh at his expense. "I quit," Finn grumbled, rising to his feet again.

"No you don't. Sit down," Crew ordered.

"I do. This shit isn't funny. You're just fucking with me, right? With this whole thing? I'm being punked?"

Crew's laughter quickly faded away. "Wrong. Need I remind you that you agreed to be a team player when you accepted this assignment?"

"Being a team player shouldn't involve me taking off clothes in front of a bunch of horny women..."

Wait. Hold up a damn minute.

"Look at the smoke billowing from his ears," Decker hooted, whacking Finn on the back. "Someone grab the fire extinguisher!"

"He might be glitching. Push his reset button," Kruger suggested.

"The fucker just realized he'll have a captive audience of drunk, horny women staring at his freckled package," Rez announced, wiggling his pinky in the air.

"Waving cash at him, too," Powers added

"That he won't be able to keep. No double-dipping," Crew reminded them. "All right, is there anything else we need to cover? Any new info or discoveries?"

"Wait. I didn't agree to this," Finn said weakly.

"You don't have to agree to a particular assignment. You agreed to join the task force. You want to remain on it, or do you want to leave and head back to doing patrol?"

He sank back down in his chair and scrubbed his hands over his face. He needed to wake up from this bad fucking nightmare.

"I think I like freckled Pecker better than redheaded Pecker," Torres announced.

"Use the fake name of Peter," Mullins suggested. "Peter Pecker."

"You're all assholes," Finn grumbled. "Every fucking one of you."

FINN PULLED his assigned task force vehicle into an empty parking spot behind The Peach Pit. He turned off the Kia Soul and stared at the back of the strip club located right on the edge of Uniontown. The employee lot was full but then, between everyone involved with tonight's performance, plus the regular employees needed to run the club, that wasn't surprising.

When he met up with the traveling entertainment troupe to learn the opening and closing group routines, Nick said the manager of the club would only give them the next two Monday nights in a "take it or leave it" offer. Mondays were the only nights available since the club was normally closed then. The rest of the week was out since the venue only had a single stage, unlike some other larger strip clubs.

The Peach Pit agreed to book two "limited engagement" performances to see how much money it drew before committing to any additional shows.

Finn didn't give two shits about how much money the gigs brought Nick, the owner/manager of Peckers, or even those fucking Demons. He'd get on stage tonight and possibly next Monday and then that was fucking it.

After that... He. Was. Done.

It was bad enough he had to explain to his sixty-four-year-old mother why he was asking for the keys to her dance studio. He made sure the studio was locked down tight and no one was observing him watching male stripper instructional videos so he could break down specific moves while he mirrored them.

Luckily, his mother had a great sense of humor and thought him going undercover as a stripper was hilarious. However, Finn wasn't amused when she also asked for a video of his performance.

That was a big fucking N-O.

"They don't allow cameras in strip clubs, Mom." At least that was how it was the last time he'd been to one. They had to leave their phones at the door and pick them up on their way out. He assumed The Peach Pit had the same policy. If they didn't, he wasn't telling her that. But they'd better, because without that policy, someone could get him on video and if it got out, his cover could be blown.

No matter how much his mother insisted, he refused to give her the name of the club, the company he'd be dancing with or the date of the show. He wouldn't put it past her to show the fuck up with dollar bills in hand. If she did, he would have to leave the country.

Fuck leaving the country, his soul would leave Earth because he'd be dead.

He shuddered at the thought of simulating sex moves, while basically naked, in front of the woman who birthed him.

Blowing out a harsh breath, he unfolded himself from the Kia and retrieved a duffel bag from the back seat full with all the shit he'd need tonight.

With gritted teeth, he pounded on the rear steel door. It took a few minutes for someone to answer it.

"You were supposed to be here a half hour ago, Danny," Nick complained. "I hired you as a favor because my brother said you need some extra cash. Don't make me regret this."

No one regretted it more than Finn.

This Nick dude was the only one who knew he was undercover, but even annoyed at Finn's tardiness, he was sticking with the story. The rest of the dancers only thought "Danny O'Neill" was short on cash and wanted to fill in for the injured Pecker as a side hustle. The couple of times Finn practiced with the group to learn the choreography for the opening and closing acts of the show, Nick had done a good job of not blowing his cover.

He followed Nick down a short hallway and into a huge dressing room full of lockers, couches and a few vanities with mirrors surrounded by lightbulbs. Colorful feathered boas were flung all over the room, as well as discarded platform heels, fancy bras and thongs. He wondered if the dressing room normally looked like a disaster area or if the women who danced the previous night had left in a rush.

"Hurry up and get ready, then change into your first outfit. The show starts in twenty. Make sure you're prepped and know your routines. Just follow Tyson's lead if you forget any of the moves."

Twenty minutes was more than enough time for him to change. Though, he should've gotten here earlier so he could snoop around. He'd have to do that before or after his solo stage act. And maybe even after the show.

He gave Tyson, a huge blonde dude with washboard abs and thick muscular thighs, a chin lift.

His head jerked back when a woman appeared out of nowhere to stand in front of him. "Strip down so I can oil you up."

When he stared at her, her words not quite penetrating his brain, she lifted a bottle of baby oil. "I don't use a lot, just enough to give your skin a gleam and it'll emphasize how cut your muscles are. The women are going to go bonkers over you."

He reached for the bottle but she shook her head and pulled it out of his reach. "No, I do it for the guys so it's applied evenly." She gave him a friendly smile. "By the way, I'm Nick's assistant, Abby. We need to let this soak in a bit before you put on the first costume. Just throw your stuff anywhere, or grab an empty locker."

He glanced around the large, open dressing room and silently greeted the rest of the dancers in various stages of undress. Including him, there were eight dancers in all.

"Where can I get undressed?"

She blinked, then blinked again. "Right here." Her brow furrowed. "You aren't shy, are you? Because that might be an issue since you're going to be stripping down in front of a crowd of a hundred most-likely intoxicated women."

He was far from fucking shy, but still...

"C'mon, strip down, we're running out of time," she urged.

He should walk right the fuck out of there, but with a sigh, he found a locker without a padlock and dropped his bag on the ground next to it. Facing the locker, he unlaced his boots, then toed them off before stripping down to his underwear. He placed each item of clothes in the locker as he went.

When he finally turned, Abby was right there, waiting. She ran her gaze over him with one cocked eyebrow but then stopped on his boxer briefs. "All the way, I have to oil everything but your main asset."

"That would be hard to do since my main asset is my brain."

"*Mmm hmm,*" she murmured through lips pressed together. "Not to those ladies filling those seats out there." She pointed to Finn's bulge. "That's your main selling point. The bigger, the better. Then the rest," she waved her hand in front of him from head to toe, "is the freckled icing on your carrot cake. So tick tock, Danny, otherwise Nick will be pissed if the show starts late."

With a grumble, Finn turned away from her and slipped out of his boxer briefs, tossing them into the locker.

As he reached into his bag to grab a pair of underwear he'd bought for tonight, Abby said, "No, use those or a pair like those for your individual or the closing dance. You need to wear a white jock strap for the opening routine. Everyone's going to be wearing similar construction crew outfits and strip all the way down to your jocks."

Nice. "I didn't bring a jock strap."

36

"Not a problem. I'll grab you one once I get you oiled down."

Great. He curled a hand over his very soft package and began to turn around.

"Stay facing the locker, I'll do your back first."

He mentally sighed.

"Arms down."

He sighed again, this time out loud, but dropped his arms as she began rubbing baby oil all over them. She then moved to his neck, smeared it over his shoulders and down his back.

"Man, you have freckles everywhere, don't you?" Abby murmured as she slathered the baby oil all over his ass cheeks.

Besides being teased for being a redhead when he was a kid, he also had hated his freckles because someone was always making a joke about them. As an adult no one gave a shit, so he no longer did, either. Since there was nothing he could do to change it, he had no choice but to accept them.

Only his MC brothers—and sometimes his fellow police officers at Southern Allegheny Regional PD—busted his balls about it now. Not to be bullies like kids could be, but because it was very normal, and even expected, for them to all bust on each other. Fucking with each other over the stupidest shit only made their brotherhoods stronger. It also helped lighten situations when shit got heavy and dark.

Abby evenly rubbed the oil down his legs. "I'm not going past your ankles since you'll be wearing black rubber-soled boots for your dances. Did you bring a pair?"

"Yeah. Wore them here."

"Turn around."

He clenched his molars together so hard a muscle jumped in his cheek, but when he turned and her eyes immediately dropped to his flaccid cock with raised eyebrows, he said, "I can do the front myself."

"I can do the front," Abby insisted, pushing away his outstretched hand. "You can oil your own front once you get the hang of how much to use. It has to be the correct amount. You don't want to be greasy but you also need that shine."

With a frown, he stared at her. "How'd you get this job?"

She shrugged. "Just lucky, I guess."

He picked a spot over her head on the other side of the room as she rubbed the whole front of him down, coming close to his junk but not touching it.

"You need to trim closer next time. And if you do peek-a-boos with your cock, then you should be bare."

Peek-a-boos with his damn cock.

"I'll take that into consideration," he muttered.

The only peek-a-boos he was willing to do was when it appeared and disappeared as he sunk it into a warm, wet pussy.

When she was finished she rose to her feet and smiled up at him. "Okay, all done. I'll go grab you a clean jock. You'll need to start out in the white tank, black socks, your black boots and break-away Dickies. Also, don't forget to wear a belt. You can grab one of the fluorescent vests near the door on your way to the stage. But give it a few before you get dressed to give the baby oil a chance to soak in a bit first."

She turned and walked back to an open portable trunk in the corner. He continued to stare at a non-existent spot across the room to avoid meeting the other guys' eyes while he stood there totally naked.

He was going to kill Crew.

He was just going to fucking kill him. The bastard was probably sitting at home with his feet kicked up, drinking a fucking beer and laughing about where Finn was and what he was about to do.

Asshole.

Then Abby was back, holding out a jock. "That should be your size. Try it on."

Gladly. He yanked them up his legs and adjusted everything into place while Nick's assistant watched him like a hawk. It was almost as if she didn't think he'd know how to wear a jock strap. Since he'd played baseball all through high school, he knew how to fucking wear one.

"Make sure your VPL is emphasized."

What? "VPL?"

"Visual penis line. The more distinct it is and the bigger your cock looks, the more tips you'll bring in, whether artificially enhanced or not."

Because, yeah, that was his fucking goal, to show off the size of his dick for money. When he went shopping for the underwear Nick recommended, it had been eye-opening.

He never realized such a large selection of bulge-enhancing underwear with ball pouches existed. Actual pouches that separated his cock and balls to emphasize the assets passed onto him through genetics.

"So, if you're not going to dance fully erect, then you at least need to have a chubby."

He didn't remember seeing that requirement in the employee handbook.

Maybe because there *was* no fucking employee handbook. It was possible that Crew had told Nick not to tell him all these details because he would've backed out.

"What happens if I don't?"

"Nick could fire you and the ladies might laugh at you. Nick's in business to make money and you're here to make money, too. The sad fact is, the bigger the dong, the bigger the tips."

Great. "Is there somewhere I can go to... uh... wake myself up?"

Abby flung a hand out. "Just do it anywhere. We're all used to doing what needs to be done before a show. Nobody will care what you have to do to get it done."

Crew will fucking care, when I throat punch him for this.

"We have a laptop over there with porn queued up, if you need it. If not, I can fluff you."

She could what?

He had to have heard her wrong. He looked around to see if anyone else was shocked by that unexpected offer.

Everybody else was minding their own business and doing last minute preparations. Including getting themselves hard since there was only about ten minutes left before they had to hit the stage.

"I think I can manage, but... thanks, I guess?"

"We also have a penis pump available. It's the fastest way to get some girth and length. Once you're pumped up, just tie it off so it stays that way."

He wasn't sure what to address first in this whole turn of events. "Like a communal one?"

She smiled and shrugged. "Use it to pump, not to dump." She turned to walk away but paused. "You brought a cock ring, right? If you didn't bring one, I have some spare Willy Rings."

Christ. Thank fuck he kept where and when he was dancing secret from his mother. Dancing in front of her in a jock strap or underwear that emphasized his dick would be bad enough, but with a damn hard-on?

It would take years of therapy to get over that horror.

"I didn't bring a cock ring, no. I don't need them normally, so I—"

"Not a problem, I'll grab you one of those, too. But you're running out of time, so get jerking or pumping or whatever you're going to do." With that she walked to the other side of the room and dug around in the utility trunk again. He wondered if these Willy Rings were new or shared like the penis pump.

He shook his head and turned back around so he wasn't facing the rest of the guys while he tugged on his cock.

Of course it was going to be fucking difficult to get aroused in a room full of men. And not to mention, one assistant who doubled as a fluffer.

Fuck.

He blew out another breath, braced a hand against the metal locker, closed his eyes, tuned out all the male chatter behind him and began to fist his limp dick.

This wasn't going to work, he was too distracted. Everything about this was awkward as fuck.

Concentrate. You can do this. Just pretend you're at home in the shower or something.

You can do this. It'll be more embarrassing if you can't.

Treat it like a job.

You love your job. You're dedicated to your job.

You only fucking hate Crew.

A tap on his shoulder had him opening his eyes to see a black silicon ring held out in front of his face. "Here you go. I put a little baby oil on it so it slides on easier. Do it when you're still semi-aroused and you're not completely hard. It's easier that way."

He swallowed down, *"I know how to use a fucking cock ring,"* right before it exploded from him.

41

"Again, just yell if you need help, that's what I'm here for."

"I appreciate your dedication," he muttered.

Christ, was he fucking blushing? He had to be. Heat was rushing through him and he was about to break out in a fucking sweat.

"Let's wrap it up here, boys," Abby yelled while clapping her hands together. "I hear Nick getting the ladies riled up and ready to go."

Shit. He slid on the cock ring, pulled his half of a softy through it, rolled it down to the root and then quickly kept jerking on his dick. He squeezed his eyes shut again and replayed the last porno he watched a couple of weeks ago.

Yeah, that one was really fucking hot. That was the exact imagery he needed to get his blood flowing south.

He replayed the two women eating each other out. Then the playful spanking that was hard enough to leave red palm prints. *Yeah, there we go...* He could even hear them squealing and laughing as they chased each other naked around a pool like water nymphs. Their huge tits bouncing, them splashing each other with water, making them slick and wet...

And then the good part...

They get frightened when they hear breaking glass and hug each other while calling 911. Of course, their savior arrives at their door... a cop to assist them...

In his memory, it turned out to be a redhead with a Southern Allegheny Regional PD patch on his uniform.

Because who better to protect and service... *serve* them.

He opened his eyes and glanced down.

Fuck yeah, that did the trick.

Abby shouted, "Let's go, Danny! Hurry up and get dressed."

He tugged the jock strap into place and made sure his

VPL was perfect. Then pulled on the white tank top, the pull-away pants and slid his black leather trouser belt with a Velcro closure he used with his duty belt through the loops.

He quickly tugged on his boots, lacing them up and double-knotting the laces so he wouldn't trip and break his neck on stage.

You can do this.

You can do this.

You can fucking do this.

He slammed both palms against the locker, leaned into his arms and nodded to himself. Pushing off the locker, he flexed his neck to the left and to the right, while bouncing on his toes a few times, then shook out his hands.

Okay, he was ready.

He could do this.

Not just do it, but do it like a fucking pro.

Since he was the last to leave the dressing room, Abby stood by the door holding out a construction worker's vest and a hard hat. He took them from her and shrugged the vest on.

"You'll do fine. A few butterflies are normal for your first time. Then it'll become second nature." She slapped him sharply on the ass as he squeezed past her.

Fuck my life.

No, fuck that motherfucking asshole Crew!

Paybacks were a fucking bitch.

Chapter Three

FINN BLEW out a long breath to settle his churning gut and followed the line of "construction workers" down the hallway. He was the last one to run out onto the smoke-covered stage. When he lined up next to Tyson, the colored spotlights flashed across the stage and the group.

The screaming from the audience was already at a fevered pitch. To the point he could barely hear the background music.

"Come on, ladies! Make some noise!" Nick yelled into the microphone. "The louder you get, the more they'll take off." The manager raised his arms up, egging them on.

They didn't need that encouragement and Finn didn't think they could get any louder.

He was dead wrong. The roar of the women now made the music almost impossible to hear. He hoped that changed once they started their choreographed routine to make sure he hit all the beats. Those points in the songs were one way he'd remember all the moves.

Whistles, high-pitched screams, shouts of "Take it off," "Show us your dicks," "Fuck me!" and even "Marry me!" rose above the din.

He felt like a shaky newborn fawn in the middle of a pack of starving cougars.

He'd practiced this routine every day for the past week at his mother's studio, hoping muscle memory would help him out. But, *damn*, the moves he had to learn weren't the same as what his mother taught in her classes. Not even close.

All eight dancers faced the crowd in a straight line while Nick stood off to the side. The T-shaped stage was what Nick called a "thrust stage." The main stage ran along the back of the club but the end of the T extended out into the area full of tables and chairs.

Packed tables. More occupied chairs lined both sides of the large area, along with booths along the outer walls.

There wasn't an empty seat in the house. Women even crowded the very front of the club closer to the main entrance.

He swore every woman in western Pennsylvania had shown up tonight.

The dancers all stood with their heads tipped down, their feet spread, their arms crossed tightly over their chests, causing their biceps and pecs to bulge.

"Are you ready, ladies?"

Another deafening roar went up.

"Let me introduce you to the men ready, willing and able to lay some pipe!" Nick yelled into the mic. "Make some noise for Apollo!"

The guy at the far end of the line raised his head, swept his gaze over the audience, planted a hand on his hard hat and spun in place, grabbed his crotch and did a body roll from head to hips. He then gave the women a huge smile and a wink.

One by one Nick introduced the dancers. All of them repeating the same moves as Apollo.

Finn braced as Tyson finished his little intro dance since he was next.

"And last but certainly not least, let me introduce our newest Pecker! Say hello to all these wild women, Blaze! Ladies, meet Blaze. He's so hot he'll light the stage on fire with his sexy moves. He also might make you wet... with sweat." Nick fanned himself with his hand.

Grinding his teeth, Finn performed his intro routine.

"It's hard to pick a favorite, isn't it? But by the end of the night, I'm sure you'll have at least one... Make sure to let him know by being generous tonight. Are you ready?" Nick yelled. "Are... you... ready?" he shouted into the mic even louder.

He signaled to the DJ, tucked away in a raised booth in a corner up near the front entrance, and Nick moved to stand farther off the stage where he could watch the routine but the audience couldn't see him.

The colored spotlights began to move with the beat of Nelly's *Hot in Herre*. Thank fuck it was loud enough to over-power some of the women's screaming so Finn could hear the music.

The opening group dance wasn't complicated. It was made up of body rolls, strutting across the stage, hip thrusts, leaping into the air and then dropping to the stage in a dolphin dive before humping the floor.

While they did all of that and more for the first song, Nick and Abby brought out eight chairs and set them in a line as Finn and the guys spread out around the thrust stage, doing their best to keep the women's focus on them.

Once the chairs were in place, the manager and his assistant went down onto the floor and, one by one, picked women from the audience waving fistfuls of cash and assisted them onto the stage. Once all the women were seated, the dancers circled them as a group before standing behind one of the eight chairs.

Closer by Nine Inch Nails began to blast from the speakers. That was their cue to move into the next dance.

In a synchronized move, they all removed their hard hats, placed them on the heads and leaned over their assigned woman, slowly running their hands up her body, from her knees all the way up to her chest. When they clamped their hands over their tits and shook them, the women on stage laughed and squealed.

Finn didn't get why these women enjoyed getting felt up by strangers. On any other normal work day, he'd be taking a sexual assault report.

But, whatever. They paid for this. They gave their consent by buying a ticket, walking through the front door and volunteering to join them up on the stage.

One by one, each dancer removed the hard hat from the woman's head while Nick walked behind the line, collecting them to take off-stage.

With coordinated timing, the strippers removed their vests in a slow but sexy manner, threw them to the back of the stage, then, in an exaggerated walk, circled their assigned chair until they were standing in front of the women.

In a synchronized move, they propped their right boot onto the edge of the chair, did a body roll from head to hips and added two sharp hip thrusts before dropping their boot back to the floor. They then turned around and straddled her thighs.

When Finn's lap dance volunteer did a reach-around,

trying to pull him down onto her lap, he gently removed her hands and placed them back on her own thighs so he could get through the next part of the dance without her interfering.

Or neutering him.

Every move the dancers made was calculated, including slowly sliding their white tank tops up their torsos and playing peek-a-boo with their cut abs and Adonis belts, before ripping the cheap undershirts in half, swinging the shredded fabric over their heads several times and tossing them into the crowd for the audience to fight over.

Once they were shirtless, the women on stage began to get handsy by sliding their hands up and down their oiled torsos, grabbing ass cheeks, some even squeezing the dancers' crotches.

Finn danced as best as he could, all while being groped.

As one, all eight dancers turned and faced the crowd, doing chest and hip pops, as well as hip grinding, along with body rolls and the typical moves most male strippers did. One at a time, they removed their belts, swinging them around, doubling them up and snapping the leather together high up in the air, then they stepped behind the chairs again, hooking the belts around the women's throats, pretending they were going to choke them. They didn't, of course, even though one of the women screamed, "That's it! Choke me, baby!"

Jesus.

They slid the leather sensually over the women's necks before chucking the belts behind them for Nick to gather.

Burn It to the Ground by Nickelback came next on the playlist. They continued to work the seated ladies as they danced, eventually yanking off their tear-away pants and stripping all the way down to their jock straps.

Heavy black construction boots and jock straps was quite

the fucking fashion statement, but it was no surprise that the women couldn't care less. The ear-piercing screams proved they loved every damn second, even though they'd probably give a man the side-eye if he only wore that get-up outside of a strip club.

Nick ran back out on stage and handed each woman a water pistol. The dancers then spun their assigned chair around so the women's backs were to the crowd while the guys faced them.

Still in their boots, they perched carefully on the seat's edge, grabbed the women's heads with both hands and thrusted their man-meat directly into their faces to the beat of the song.

The second they paused and leaned back, the women took aim and shot water at their crotches until the thin, white fabric was soaked and practically see-through.

Not even two minutes later, with water dripping down Finn's legs and puddling at his feet, they spun the chairs around and straddled the women's thighs again but in reverse this time, so both the women and the dancers faced the crowd.

The woman couldn't keep her damn hands off Finn's package. He was afraid if she'd squeeze his nuts any tighter, they'd fucking pop.

He was relieved when Nick and Abby came back out, corralled the wild, and apparently horny as fuck, women and escorted them back to their seats.

During the whole opening routine, a hailstorm of crumpled-up dollar bills bounced off their bodies and landed on the stage.

After dancing for one more song as a group, they all filed off stage, leaving the cash behind. Finn assumed Nick would collect it and the guys would split the tips. Not that he would walk away with any of it for all the effort he was putting into this undercover operation. That sucked, since he'd earned those tips by working up a damn sweat and being manhandled by women not of his choosing.

He was also out of breath since he wasn't used to doing so much damn cardio. That proved he needed to alter his personal fitness routine. Less bulking up and more heart-pumping exercises. And not just the horizontal exercises he did with a female partner.

Back in the dressing room, he plucked dollar bills from his jock strap. His bulge had grown twice as big since his jock strap was jam-packed with soaked singles. He shuddered when he thought about how fucking dirty money was and how it had been stuck to his dick. He'd be scrubbing himself down in a searing hot shower once he got home.

"Those women are fucking crazy," he muttered.

From across the dressing room, Apollo said, "That's nothing, wait until we go out onto the floor. It gets even worse."

As they were toweling off and peeling off their wet jock straps, Abby appeared again. "Great job, Danny! You kept up and synced perfectly with the other guys. Looks like you made a killing, too. You have a bit before you have to go back on stage since you're last in the lineup. Take a breather, hydrate, and when you're ready, I'll oil you up again before you get into your next outfit."

Great. He couldn't fucking wait.

"Apollo, hurry up and get out there. You need to keep those women burning hot."

Apollo rushed to change into the ten layers he would strip away during his individual dance and ran out the door.

Finn was tempted to yank off the cock ring to give his

poor dick a break but then he didn't want to jack-off again to get it re-inflated.

Keeping a cock ring on for a few hours better not do permanent damage. The fucking government would be paying for a pump or a prosthesis if it did.

———

"DANNY, YOU'RE UP NEXT!" he heard from the open doorway to the dressing room. "The rest of you get ready for the closing routine and the meat market."

The meat market? Did he even want to know what the fuck that was?

As he passed Abby, she said, "Since you're last, as soon as your done with your individual routine, get back here as quickly as possible and change into the outfit I'll hang up on your locker."

Yeah, sure. If he survived getting through the three songs he had picked for his solo dances.

He was now dressed as a business man in a black suit jacket that he bought years ago for a wedding and added a tie and dark sunglasses. He still wore his black boots and had borrowed a pair of black breakaway pants. Underneath his dress shirt, he wore another of the cheap white tanks that Abby had an endless supply of since they were easy to tear simply with your hands.

During the opening act, the women had loved that, so he figured he'd do it again. Since his tips would be shared with the rest of the guys, someone should at least benefit from the blood, sweat and endless tears he was putting into this damn assignment.

He had layered a skimpy pair of shiny break-away briefs over a pair of those "enhancing" underwear with the cock sack. He'd been a little alarmed at the purplish shade of his dick when he tucked it into place, making sure his VPL was distinguishable.

If it fell off because of this, he was killing Crew. Then he was shoving his atrophied cock down his club brother's throat.

With one last deep breath, he cleared his mind and ran out onto the stage to the pulsing beat of Justin Timberlake's song *SexyBack*.

Fuck the screaming women. Fuck the money being thrown. Focus on the routine you put together so you don't make a complete fool of yourself.

As soon as he hit the middle of the raised stage, he spun in place and imagined an invisible line drawn from where he stood to the very end of the T that extended into the middle of the club. Putting one foot in front of the other and walking heel to toe—as if he was taking a roadside sobriety test—gave him the desired hip swing, especially when he added a slight bounce on his toes to each step.

When he reached the end of the T, he removed his sunglasses and tucked them into his pocket before slipping out of his jacket, all while grinding his hips. He threw it over his shoulder and did the same sexy strut back, with one hand tucked in a pocket like a business man leaving the office at the end of a long day.

Once he was back on the main stage, he tossed his jacket out of the way, rolled his hips and shoulders, swinging his head from left to right with the music. He bit his bottom lip, then grinned, loosening his tie and lifting it over his head before chucking it off to the side.

The second his fingers went to the buttons of his dress shirt, the women went nuts.

He slipped each button free while moonwalking across

the stage. When he hit one end, he did a Michael Jackson hip move by rising onto his toes and adding a crotch grab that sent the ladies rocketing out of their seats. By the time he moonwalked back to the other side of the stage, repeating the same hip move and crotch grab, he had his shirt completely unbuttoned and quickly slipped out of it, tossing it to Nick standing right off stage.

Then he strutted back out to center stage again in just his pants and tank top, raised his arms up and flexed, kissing one bicep and then the other, before grinding his hips once again in a slow circle. With clenched fists, he pumped his flexed arms up and down, while thrusting his hips.

Like with the opening dance, he leaped straight up in the air, then dropped into a dolphin dive. Once he landed on all fours, he rolled his hips like he was fucking the floor since that seemed to be a crowd favorite with the ladies. He dragged himself across the stage by his hands while pulling his knees behind him in what he hoped looked like a sexy military crawl.

Pull. Hump. Pull. Hump. Pull. Hump...

By the time *I Like the Way You Move* by BodyRockers filled the air, he was back on his feet, shredding the tank top and tossing the remains out into the audience, then flexing his pecs to make them bounce. With one sharp tug, his pants broke away and he tossed them aside to expose the skin-tight shorts he wore underneath. While somewhat similar to boxer briefs, they were much smaller, tighter and a hell of a lot shinier.

He had to admit, they did frame his cock nicely and he might have to consider wearing them on his next "date."

On his way down the T again, he went through all the typical moves he learned and when he got to the very end, he began pointing at a few women, giving them a wink and wagging his tongue at them. Once he had them in a frenzy, he turned around and bent over, giving them a closer view of his ass while shaking it and flexing his thighs.

The decibel level in the club between the loud music and the even louder women made both his ears ring and his temples throb.

He might not only lose his damn cock, he might also lose his hearing, but he pushed on anyway by picking out a woman in the audience, pointing at her, pointing to the side stairs, then crooking his finger at her.

She didn't need any more encouragement to join him. She sprung from her seat and raced over to the stairs at the side of the stage. With an extended hand, he assisted her up the steps. Keeping a tight grip on her, he tugged her to the center of the stage and put his lips to her ear to tell her to stay put.

The brunette was blushing while also laughing as Finn danced around her, occasionally pausing in front of her to grab her hand, slide it down his chest and even over his crotch. But he kept control of hers with his own so she wouldn't go too far or do any damage.

Eventually he got her onto her back on the floor, sliding down her body until they were in a sixty-nine position with him humping her face and doing body rolls over top of her to look like they were fucking. He ended it by tea-bagging her when he ground his balls against her forehead.

She was laughing so hard she began to hiccup as she beat him on the ass like a fucking drum.

Plastering a grin on his face, he bounced back up to his feet, helped her stand, and gave Nick a chin lift. The manager, once again standing off to the side and out of sight from the audience, came back out and escorted the woman to her seat.

Thank fuck Finn managed to time that whole thing perfectly. By that point, the song *Yeah* by Usher began to play.

More roars, hoots, and ear-piercing screams surrounded him as he worked his way back down to the end of the T. Once there, he dragged his right hand diagonally across his torso, then did the same with his left. Hooking his thumbs into the elastic waistbands of both sets of underwear, he wiggled them down his hips just enough to tease them and let them think he was going full frontal.

He worked them back up, then tore away the boy shorts to expose the pouched bikini underwear underneath. Thrusting his hips hard enough to make his erection flop around had the women surging from their seats and screaming to the point he could barely think.

He grabbed his cock and thrusted his hips again. Once. Twice.

Circle. Circle.

Chest pop. Hip pop.

Repeat.

Flexing his arms again, he tightened his biceps to make them bulge, and with an eyebrow wiggle, he slowly licked each from bottom to top.

Then he blew a kiss to a group of women sitting at a table at the end of the stage.

While they were screaming and bouncing in their seats, he turned his back to the club full of rabid women, spread his boots wide and slowly bent forward until his ass was pointed toward them. After flexing one ass cheek, then the other, he reached through his parted legs, circled his ankles, then slid his hands up to his ass before smacking both cheeks hard.

Thank fuck that was his last move and his individual routine was over.

He'd survived.

He only had the closing group dance to get through before he could drive to Crew's place and kill the motherfucker in his sleep.

Chapter Four

HE HATED that they wore military uniforms, fake or not. To Finn, even wearing what was obviously a costume still felt like stolen valor. Or disrespect. But then, he figured it could be typical garb for male strippers. Just like wearing police or firefighter uniforms.

It was true that a man in uniform tended to attract women. One reason why badge bunnies were a thing.

Even so, military costumes were what they wore in the closing routine as they ran out on stage to *Candy Shop* being blasted through the speakers.

They spread out along the part of the stage that extended into the audience, four on one side, four on the other, each of them taking a spot close to the edge. With their heads tipped down, one hand cupping their crotch and one hand planted on their abs, they popped their chests to the beat of the popular song by 50 Cent.

Nick's voice came through the speakers. "C'mon, ladies, raise that money up high! Let these men see what you're offering. The bigger the bill, the more likely you'll get an experience with them tonight you'll never forget!"

That was their cue. Slowly, they raised their faces, whipped the cap that matched their assigned uniform into the crowd and as one, leaped off the stage onto the floor.

Jumping from the frying pan right into the fire.

"If you want to be pecked, wave those dollar bills high, ladies!"

Since Finn really didn't give a fuck about the money, he picked someone who only had a single wrinkled dollar bill flapping over her head but her face was full of excitement. He figured she might not have the cash to attract the rest of the dancers on the hunt for wads of the green stuff. He went over to her since she deserved to have a special night, just like the rest of the women.

As the women tipped them for a chance to remove a piece of their clothing, Abby and Nick weaved through the tables and chairs, picking up the discarded clothing to make sure they weren't taken as souvenirs.

Straddling the young strawberry blonde's thighs, he lowered his body while grinding his hips, but avoided putting all of his weight on her legs.

He didn't bother to take the dollar from her but asked, "What do you want to remove?"

The woman's face was beet red and she seemed to have swallowed her tongue, but when her friend shoved her arm and encouraged her, she finally shouted, "Your pants."

With a smile and a wink, he told her to grab them and pull. She did and Abby came out of nowhere to take the pants from her.

"What else?"

"I only have one dollar left."

"I don't care. What else?" he asked again.

She bit her quivering bottom lip.

"Meg, take off his damn shirt!" her friend screamed at her while bouncing in her seat.

"Your shirt," the blonde decided. Finn could hardly hear her over the loud music.

"Take it off," he urged.

Since the uniformed shirt was fastened with Velcro, it didn't take much for her to tear it from him. Abby appeared like magic and grabbed that, too.

"What next?" he asked her.

"Your tank top," she said breathlessly.

"Rip it off me."

With a high-pitched squeal, she grabbed two handfuls and pulled, shredding it easily.

"There you go, sweetheart." To make the shy woman's night even more epic, he grabbed her hands and ran them over his bare pecs and abs, before cupping her fingers around his cock and thrusting into her palm a couple of times.

Her friends lost their shit to the point they were practically falling out of their chairs.

He leaned over and dragged his tongue up her cheek, drawing a gasp from her. He put his mouth to her ear. "You wet?"

With her bottom lip once again trapped between her teeth, she nodded.

"Good."

"Me next!" her friend screamed.

Finn moved away from the blonde and moved over to her not as shy friend, kneeling in front of her chair and leaning back to grab his ankles and make a bridge with his body. Her friend grabbed his junk, squeezing it hard, then dragged her pointed nails up his bare torso.

That fucking hurt. He glanced down and saw the red

lines she created. Being fair-skinned, it didn't take much to leave marks behind.

Tonight's show was turning these women into animals. All of them. Outside of the club's walls, most wouldn't get away with acting the way they were. Not without the risk of being charged with sexual harassment. Or sexual assault.

They knew in this venue they could get away with normally unacceptable behavior. To them, the dancers were nothing more than meat or puppets performing for singles, fives and the occasional larger bill.

One would think that no one had ever paid attention to them before and they might be sexually frustrated. Either that or tonight was just an excuse to step out of their everyday life, their normal behavior, and let themselves go crazy.

He got it. Sometimes he needed to let off steam himself. But he wouldn't do it in a strip club and if he did, he certainly wouldn't get away with manhandling the strippers. He'd find his ass thrown out onto the street and banned from the club.

Why women were allowed to do it to male entertainers when it was forbidden for men to do the same for female dancers, he'd never understand. The rules should be the same.

But this wasn't his career. This wasn't his job.

Daniel Finnegan wasn't a stripper, Danny O'Neill was. Tonight he was only playing a part.

Possibly next Monday night, too, but he still had to survive these last few songs first.

With a knee spin, he transitioned back into a stand as the second woman was desperately shoving bills down his tiny boy shorts in an excuse to grab his dick.

He pulled away and moved on, working his way through the crowd to Flo Rida's *Low*.

Another woman helped him out of his snug boy shorts

and almost tore off the black thong with the cock pocket he wore underneath. If she took that, too, he'd be wandering around with everything hanging out.

When he paused before another woman, pulled her from the chair, shoved her over the back of it and began to spank her ass, a roar rose up around him and a line began to form.

Fuck.

When he heard *American Woman* by Lenny Kravitz, he knew they were only halfway through the "meat market" portion of tonight's *fun*. Of course, this was the most lucrative time for the dancers. He had to admit every single one of them earned those tips by sacrificing themselves to a bunch of crazed women.

Four more songs and they were done.

Four more.

He could survive this. He could.

He dodged grabby hands when possible and found the quieter, less rowdy attendees in the crowd to approach. But he kept moving, trying to give attention to the women the other dancers ignored.

The Peckers were after tips, not attention. This was their job. It was what paid their bills. Right now, being undercover was Finn's real job and the federal government was paying his salary. That gave him a whole different outlook on how much he was willing to be touched, poked, scratched and bitten.

Not to mention, propositioned. He wondered how many of these women were married and had forgotten that fact tonight.

As he worked his way toward the front of the club, closer to the bar near the entrance, he spotted a blonde leaning back against a wall with a drink in hand. She wasn't screaming or trying to get any of the dancer's attention by waving money over her head.

She also didn't seem to be with a group like most of the other attendees. In fact, she appeared to be alone. Even though she wasn't trying to draw attention to herself, she still stood out.

At least to Finn.

She was wearing black skin-tight vinyl pants, a red sleeveless button-down blouse with enough of the buttons unfastened to show plenty of cleavage, and red three-inch stilettos. Paired with those shiny, narrow pants, her legs looked endless.

Her left arm was completely tattooed in black and gray, in what could be a variety of flowers with a few butterflies mixed in. From the distance, he could make out at least two big sunflowers.

Her loose hair fell well past her shoulders, long enough so the strands reached past her breasts. The thick, blonde curtain was mostly straight but had a little bit of a curl at the ends.

Because of the lighting, he couldn't identify the color of her eyes. The same eyes glued to him as he weaved his way closer to see if she'd flash any money, encouraging him to approach.

During his second practice with the Peckers, Nick advised Finn to only approach women waving money. He'd taken the manager's words to mean it only took a lonely one dollar bill held in the air. If she was doing so, he was supposed to take that as a sign the attendee wanted attention from one of the dancers. If she wasn't flashing money, he had to assume the woman only wanted to observe and not actively participate.

Even though the lighting was dim and he was still quite a

few feet away, he could see the slight upward curl of her bright red lips as the blonde sipped her drink. She continued to hold his gaze over the rim of her glass as he moved closer.

She showed no signs of shyness, but rather unashamed interest and plenty of what he assumed was confidence.

Unfortunately, he was forced to stop along the way when he was grabbed from all angles. He gave the women in his path a few seconds of attention before moving on. However, when it got to the point they'd grab his package or twist one of his damn nipples, he'd carefully extract himself and move on to the next.

Those women were handsy as fuck. They were not only grabbing his cock, they were pawing his ass and trying to shove their hands down his underwear. They'd even hook their arms around his thighs to hobble him and force him to a stop as he tried to worm his way through the chairs.

Trying to get to the blonde was like threading a fucking needle. He wasn't sure if it would be possible to get close enough to have a few words with her, but he was determined to at least try.

He was not a quitter and the blonde was hot as fuck. The way she acted reserved, as compared to the rest of the women tonight, intrigued him. No shaking money over her head to tempt the dancers over to her. No screaming. No outward signs of excitement at all. She simply stood at the back of the audience, quietly observing and not purposely drawing attention to herself.

Despite that, she had caught his. With his eyes set on her, he kept weaving through the packed tables and octopus arms until a woman jumped up from her seat and blocked his path. She wrapped her arms around him, rubbing her cheek over his chest, then licking a line up his damp skin all the way to his ear, where she whispered, "Take me home and set me ablaze."

Jesus fuck. He would *not* be doing that, if he was going home with anyone, it wouldn't be her.

He peeled her arms from around him and extracted himself carefully.

No, it wouldn't be her, it would be...

He glanced back over to the wall where the blonde had been leaning.

She was fucking gone.

Goddamn it.

———

It would take a while for the ringing in his ears to subside, but at least the club was now dead quiet and he could finally string some thoughts together. Once the last song played and the Peckers finished their personal interactions on the floor with the crowd, they escaped backstage and to the dressing room.

The first thing Finn did was roll the cock ring off his poor abused dick. A hiss escaped him while removing it and he no longer gave a fuck about rubbing it in front of Abby or the other guys. He was more worried about getting the blood circulating again to his most important organ.

Okay, second most important organ after his brain, which happened to be throbbing with a damn headache.

One by one, the dancers left after they pulled on their street clothes and packed away their personal belongings.

While he waited for everyone else to split, he found bite marks on his thighs, bruises already forming, scratches criss-crossing every part of him and he swore he had a missing chunk of hair. When he had pulled money from his thong to add to the community tip pot the dancers split, he noticed phone numbers scribbled on some of the bills.

Jesus. More proof tonight had been a complete fucking zoo. The women acted like restless, starving animals and the guys were the raw meat thrown into their cages.

When Finn hung back, he hoped he wouldn't get kicked out before getting a chance to snoop around, since that was the whole damn reason he'd come to The Peach Pit in the first place. The whole reason he'd allowed himself to get molested and manhandled, and not in a way he normally preferred.

Since a room with two showers was located directly off the dressing room, he used an excuse about cleaning up before getting dressed and heading home. Luckily, no one seemed to pay him any mind.

Nick, the only one with the knowledge that Finn was undercover, gave him a chin lift and the warning, "The manager said the rear door will lock behind you. Just make sure you don't forget anything or you'll have to come back to get it tomorrow during regular business hours," before he disappeared for the night.

That wasn't a problem and, in reality, it was the perfect excuse for him to return to the club before next Monday night. That way he could get behind the scenes again, but when a full staff was working, as well as the regular dancers.

Now, about a half hour after entering the dressing room, he finally found himself completely alone. Even though exhaustion weighed on him, he still had a job to do. His real job.

Once again fully dressed in jeans and a T-shirt, he began searching through every locker without a padlock. He found nothing other than what would be expected in any typical strip club dressing room.

He flipped chairs upside down to see if any drugs were taped underneath. He checked inside the toilet tanks in the attached restroom. He dug through every drawer in the mirrored vanities.

He found zero indication that any of the strippers were dealing meth. Obviously, if they were smart, they wouldn't leave evidence behind. It was also possible it wasn't the strippers dealing. Even though he hadn't spotted one Deadly Demon in the club tonight, that didn't mean they weren't around during normal club hours and involved with the backdoor dealing. It could even be the manager. Or bartender.

It could be anyone.

But he couldn't imagine anyone was dealing meth from a Demons owned business without the MC being aware or involved. Whether the confidential informant was right or not about the bikers dealing out of The Peach Pit, Finn also had no doubt the outlaw MC could use the club for money laundering.

It was the perfect business to clean dirty money. And lots of it. The male patrons always had cash on them to attract the dancers' attention, just like the women had done tonight.

Would the MC have to wash all of their drug money? Most likely not, since some of it could be spent anywhere in smaller amounts. However, not all of it could be used for everyday spending depending on how much they were raking in when it came to their drug business.

By expanding into Pennsylvania and Ohio and setting up two additional chapters, along with buying businesses that regularly dealt with cash, were they setting themselves up to start dealing more than the single kilo they got in exchange for the use of their big rig?

That could very well be the case. They might not only be growing their territory but their cash flow.

It made a lot of fucking sense.

While tonight was a bust for him in regards to finding any evidence, the club was bigger than just the dressing room. It was also bigger than just the dancers. He really needed to find a way to get back inside when he wasn't there to dance with the Peckers.

He needed to find a way to make a connection with someone on the inside. Maybe with one of the dancers, if possible. And not as a customer, either, since dancers only pretended to care about the men who tipped them, when in reality, they only flirted with them for one thing.

Cold hard cash.

Any man who believed a stripper was nice to him because she really liked spending time with him was a fucking fool. The same went for the women who jotted down their numbers on dollar bills that had the potential of ending up scattered over the country.

What he needed to do was witness a buy or make a buy of his own. But first he'd need to figure out who was doing the dealing. That might not be an easy feat.

He sighed as he zipped up his duffel. He was ready to call it a night and go home to take a long, hot shower, turn on the replay of Monday Night Football and drink a cold beer or two.

He definitely needed to get off his feet since dancing for an extended period of time in steel-toed boots wasn't ideal. It actually had been torture.

At this point, his plan was to return tomorrow night to speak with the club's manager about retrieving an item he "accidentally" left behind. He had balled up a pair of his cock-pocket bikini underwear and hid it at the bottom of the locker he'd been using.

A clearing of a throat had him twisting his neck to glance toward the dressing room's doorway.

The blonde that he'd wanted to talk to, the one who had fucking disappeared before he got that chance, the one who oozed confidence and not desperation, stood just inside the door.

Holy shit.

"I was just checking to make sure everyone left."

Or was she coming to find him? Could this be a sign? His lucky night?

Whether it was or wasn't... "I don't think they allow customers back here."

"They don't." When she smiled, he was distracted by the little sexy mole above her upper lip. "I'm not a customer."

"Then who are you? A dancer?" Maybe that was why she'd hadn't gone wild like the rest of the women.

When she didn't answer, he asked, "The owner?" knowing full well that the Demons now owned the club. But he was testing to see if she'd mention it. If she had inside information, whoever she was.

She shook her head and one side of her blood-red lips pulled up. "The club manager."

Chapter Five

Mel took a step farther into the room. She hadn't expected any of the male strippers to still be around. She had waited until the rest of her skeleton crew left before making sure all doors were locked and lights were off, starting at the front entrance and working her way into the backstage area.

On her way out to the rear parking lot, she decided to peek her head into the dressing room since she expected it to be a disaster area like it was at closing almost every damn night. When it was, she tended to come in a little earlier than normal to put it back together. But surprisingly, the guys left less of a mess than the women usually did.

Once a dancer was done with her shift, she didn't waste any time hightailing it home. To her significant other, to her kids, to her family. Most of the women the club employed had families to support. Others were college students with classes the next morning.

And some, like with any other industry, simply hated their job. The ladies only danced because it was one way to make decent money as long as they knew what they were doing and at least acted like they enjoyed it.

In the end, stripping was a job just like any other. To be successful, you needed to have talent and know how to work your audience.

She was just as surprised to find the redheaded dancer nicknamed Blaze still in the dressing room as he was to see her. "I didn't mean to startle you. I was on my way to lock up and leave. I didn't realize anyone was still back here."

"You didn't startle me." His head tilted slightly as he slowly and thoroughly slid his gaze from her hair to her red stilettos.

Those shoes were another reason why she was anxious to leave. She couldn't wait to kick off her toe-pinching high heels. She'd do that as soon as she climbed into her SUV.

"Sorry, I didn't mean to keep you from closing up. I wanted to clean up before I left." Even though he said those words, he made no effort to leave.

"You're not." Or at least he hadn't delayed her. Until now, anyway.

She didn't want to be rude but since she didn't know him, she wasn't sure if she could trust being alone with him. She kept a healthy distrust of all men until they proved that they could otherwise be trusted. When working at a strip club, while most of the clientele were nice, some were unhinged. They'd dealt with stalkers too many times. That was one reason, when the club was open and dancers were coming and going, they had security. At least before the Demons took over. She released a soft sigh over that whole situation.

"But I would like to get going soon since this is normally my night off." Maybe mentioning that would get him moving.

His brow furrowed. "If it's your night off, why are you here?"

She shrugged. "Basically, I was told to be here. And honestly, watching you guys dance tonight was a nice perk." Especially since she'd be paid to be here, instead of paying to be here, like the rest of the patrons.

At first she had been annoyed when was ordered to open the club on a night they were normally closed, but since every man in the Peckers All-Male Revue had been hot as all get-out, it ended up not being such a hardship.

She studied the man before her. *Blaze.* His stripper name fit him perfectly. He was so hot he had lit the club on fire.

"Do you normally drink while you work?"

Well, that was an odd and unexpected question. Why would he care? "Not usually. Tonight I decided to enjoy both myself and the show since I was only here to oversee the staff who volunteered to work overtime. It was nice to take advantage of my bartender's mad skills at mixing a mean margarita. I rarely do."

"But the owner's paying for your time, isn't he?"

The owner was more than one "he." It was a bunch of them. She wasn't quite sure whose name graced the club's deed anymore. Not since the Deadly Demons became the new owners. She couldn't imagine the MC had some sort of official corporation or LLC.

She could be wrong, but she tried to not ask too many questions once they came in after forcing the previous owner out.

Even so, why was this dancer so curious about her? She had noticed his interest earlier during the last group dance, despite hanging toward the back of the crowd and purposely not drawing attention to herself.

She knew a dancer's interest usually wasn't genuine and she also wanted the Peckers crew to concentrate on the paying customers.

"Of course I'm getting paid. I don't work for free. Anyway, who couldn't use the extra pay? Isn't that why you do this? Or is this your full-time job?"

"Just doing it for a little extra scratch."

She tipped her head and considered what he said. "More than a little. I saw how much money was thrown on stage during your solo dances. I also saw the amount of money protruding from your," she wasn't sure what to call what the male strippers wore, but whatever it was emphasized the tool they were blessed with, "underwear when you were working the floor. You were a hit out there. You made a killing."

He shrugged his broad, nicely-defined shoulders and a hint of a smile could be seen on his full lips. "Yeah, who knew women liked redheads with freckles."

Since he had done it to her, she didn't feel bad raking her gaze down his body. "Don't act like you didn't know it was due to more than your hair color and those sexy freckles."

The slight curl at the corners of his lips turned into a full-blown grin. "I didn't. Tonight was my first night dancing."

Her mouth dropped open. "No way." She never would've guessed he only started stripping. He'd been damn good and, because of that, it was definitely more than his looks that drew the women.

His eyebrows raised. "I'm not lying. I was desperate for a little cash so I needed an easy side gig. I figured I'd give it a shot. Since you're around this almost daily, do you think my success had to do with my dancing?"

Was he being serious or pulling her leg? "Do you really need that confirmation?" She glanced at how the sleeves of his T-shirt stretched tightly around his bulging biceps. "You work out for a reason other than only your health. Your moves are as smooth as well-greased ball-bearings. But, of course, you knew that, too." She took a couple of steps closer to him and jutted out her hand. "I'm MJ, by the way."

"MJ," he repeated in a murmur while taking her hand and giving it a firm shake. His fingers were long and warm, his grip strong. "Danny."

She grinned. "*Hmm.* I thought your name was Blaze."

Danny chuckled. "Right."

"The nickname Blaze might be a bit cheesy, but it fits you."

"Because you think I'm cheesy?"

"Again, you don't need confirmation from me on why the name Blaze fits you."

His red hair and beard, along with his smoking hot body, were only two things that had caught her attention. He truly did have the natural ability to dance. Some of her own dancers really had to work at it, while it came naturally to some of the others. Even so, it was hard to believe tonight was his first time on stage. But since he seemed to only be performing for extra cash, she wondered what he normally did for a living.

He threw the strap of his duffel bag over his shoulder. "I'll get out of your hair and let you close up."

As he moved closer to the dressing room door, she said, "By the way, Danny, that was really sweet of you."

He paused, barely a couple of feet away. "What was?"

"The way you kept approaching the women with hardly any cash. Unlike the rest of your crew." She had taken notice. It stood out to her even more because the other dancers were focusing on the women with the most money in hand. Mel understood why they would, but every woman in that room had purchased a ticket to attend, so to get a little extra attention could make their night.

Finn shrugged. "I'm new at this. Maybe I'm doing it wrong."

"No, you're not. You made those women's night even more special by getting them involved."

If Mel let the Peckers come back for a few more shows, those women might also return. Whether Danny realized it or not, what he did was good public relations for both the outfit he danced for, as well as the club.

She continued, "Listen, I know what it's like to have your friends ask you to go out with them when you're flat broke and have to scrounge to even pay for your own meal. On one hand you're glad you were included, on the other, you also wish you hadn't been. It can be embarrassing, even stressful. You made tonight worthwhile for those ladies. Even if they only had a single dollar in their hand, you made them feel like they had a fistful of cash."

That was the sign of a good man.

"You're giving me too much credit." He stepped past her and out into the hallway. He paused and tipped his head toward the rear exit. "Come on. I'll walk you out."

"I'm not giving you too much credit. Let me tell you how I know..." She followed him out, closing the dressing room door behind her. "Not all men should be at this club throwing money at women they don't know. Not because it's immoral or anything like that, but because the truth is, they can't afford it. Yet, they love and need the attention they get from the girls. Maybe they're lonely and need the companionship, even if it's paid for and for only a few hours. A myriad of reasons exist why they come here when they can't afford to. But here's the kicker, while one night they may only be able to spare a couple of bucks in tips, if the girls look past that and still shower him with attention and kindness, the next time he comes in with money he *can* spare, you know who's getting it?"

"The dancer who was nice to him." The deepness of his voice rumbled through her. It was the cream cheese icing on his delicious carrot cake.

She ignored that deliciousness and after he briefly moved to the side to let her pass, she continued down the dimly-lit hallway. "You got it. I remind the girls of that all the time. My advice to them is to be kind no matter what. Kindness, like karma, pays, even if it's not in cash."

"Very wise."

She shoved the push bar on the rear door with her hip, opening it and spilling the two of them out into the dark night. She took a deep inhale of the late night air. For mid-September, the temperature was perfect and the humidity low. It made her wish she had spent a quiet night at home on her back deck. While she enjoyed tonight's performance, she also enjoyed her much-needed down time.

"As the manager, I make sure the girls are nice to everyone when it's their rotation on the floor. Of course, if the guy's a complete asshole by being rude, handsy, even verbally abusive, she can avoid him until I can have his ass tossed. Don't get me wrong, being nice doesn't mean being a door-mat." She scanned the rear parking lot, only seeing her turquoise Trailblazer at one end of the paved area and a white Kia Soul at the other.

The car did not match the man. In fact, she didn't know any men who drove a Soul. Maybe he was more in touch with his feminine side than most men she dealt with on a daily basis.

She assumed a lot of male strippers were gay. It could be Danny was, too.

Or she could be completely off-base for both of those theories. She'd never dealt with an all-male revue before.

She stopped in the middle of the parking lot since she would be heading to the left and him to the right. "Welp—"

"I'll walk you to your car."

Again, he seemed like a good man, but her assumption could be completely wrong. "You don't have to do that."

"Of course I don't, but I'm doing it anyway," he insisted.

She thought he was going to put a hand on the small of her back when he lifted it. But he caught himself, curled his fingers into his palm and dropped it back to his side.

Interesting. That respect for her, even as small of a gesture as it was, made him look even better in her eyes. Men should never touch women without their consent first. Not only was it safer for her, it protected him, too.

That was actually one of the club policies Mel had put in place once the former owner promoted her to manager. Touching a dancer without prior approval was a good way for a man to get permanently banned from The Peach Pit.

"Suit yourself," she said with a quick shrug and headed in the direction of her Chevy. However, his next question made her pause at her driver's door.

"How long have you worked here?"

Maybe his interest in her *had* been genuine. If so, she'd need to squash that. "For the last ten years."

Both rust-colored eyebrows shot up his forehead. "I didn't realize a strip club manager would be a long-term career. Especially one worthy of that kind of loyalty."

Most people tended to look down at her choice of employment. Because of that, she normally kept what she did for a living to herself or gave them a generic answer. She usually said she was a night club or social club manager. And if she had to reveal the true details and she received flack about it, they could take that judgment, roll it up into a suppository and shove it up their ass.

Some might think of stripping as degrading, Mel considered it empowering. She enjoyed the time she had spent on stage. She enjoyed working with her fellow dancers. She still did. Only now it was in a different capacity that included support and guidance. "I worked my way up from the stage to management."

When his eyebrows hiked their way almost to his hairline, she noted that his gorgeous hair, besides being red, was full, thick and not receding. Her guess was he was somewhere in his thirties.

"You were a stripper?"

She could see his wheels turning, like he was trying to picture her on stage. "Was. For the first five years. So, when I talk about taking the time to be kind, I speak from experience. Once I discovered it by accident, I made it a habit. I've also pushed that same mentality for the last five years I've been managing the place. I want to see both the girls and the club do well."

Or she did. While she still wanted only the best for the girls, her feelings about The Peach Pit were quickly changing. Though, she hoped the success of the club continued until she could find somewhere else to work. She couldn't afford to be unemployed, even for a short amount of time.

She wasn't worried about her current stable of dancers. They all were skilled and professional enough that none would have a problem finding a job dancing at another club. Maybe even a better one. When the club changed hands, most of them only stayed solely due to Mel.

Some had even declared that if she left, so would they.

"You liked it."

His conclusion brought her focus back to the parking lot.

"I used to love it." And that was completely true. Pole work was great exercise and to get paid to stay in shape? To love your own body and be proud of it? Yes, she loved it back then, but even now she still loved to help the new dancers get comfortable in their own skin, too.

Weirdly, dancing on a pole had been a freeing experience after growing up in a very strict, conservative family. She started stripping to put herself through college because she didn't want to be saddled with debt. She stayed for the money and because she appreciated the art and athleticism behind it. Dancing on any stage, whether while removing clothes or not, was an art form when done right and it built confidence, if you didn't have an abundance of it to begin with.

You were completely exposed on stage. You could hide nothing but your thoughts and your most intimate places.

His brow furrowed deep. "What does that mean?"

Did he really care or was he only showing interest because he wanted something more? "The club changed hands recently. Unfortunately, other things have changed, too."

"By you saying 'unfortunately,' I'll assume it was for the worse."

"And you would be correct."

"Too bad. Especially if you loved your job."

She shrugged like it was no big deal, but to her, it actually was one. If the former owner, Laura, hadn't been chased away, Mel might have stayed until retirement, if she didn't end up buying a club of her own first. Or if Laura had wanted to retire—in her own time and on her own terms— Mel would've considered buying her out and taking over The Peach Pit's ownership, instead, since it was an established club she was more than familiar with. In fact, it was something they had discussed a few times, but that option was quickly thrown aside once the Demons became a dangerous menace and forced Laura to sell to them to save herself. But that wasn't a conversation she wanted to have late at night out in the dark behind the club with a stranger.

"I've been thinking about a change, but until I find something that pays me just as good or better, I have no choice but to stick with it." *For at least as long as I can bear it.* "It's not like I have a great resume since I started stripping not long after I turned eighteen."

"And you're..."

"Not eighteen anymore."

She could see him doing the math in his head. It was time to go before he asked more questions. "Okay, I need to get home."

"You have someone waiting?"

"I do."

He waited for her to explain. She didn't. Again, she didn't know him and she'd already shared enough.

"You okay to drive?"

She smiled at what sounded like genuine concern. "Yes, I nursed my drinks all night. I couldn't hit them too hard and still manage the club with a clear head."

Yes, he seemed to be a nice guy... However, first impressions weren't always correct since they were based on shallow assumptions. She learned that lesson a long time ago, too, just like the lesson about being kind to those who were unable to be generous.

After pressing the button on her key fob to unlock her SUV, she opened the driver's door and climbed in.

As she secured her seatbelt, he leaned in and said, "Guess I'll see you next Monday. I hope the rest of your night is a good one."

"Same to you. And I look forward to next Monday...
Blaze."

She had considered trying to convince Cookie, the
assistant manager, to open next Monday instead of her, but
now she was rethinking that. She could always use the extra
pay, anyway.

She had started an account a few years ago in hopes to
eventually buy The Peach Pit from Laura. Once that opportunity slipped from her fingers, her only choice was to use
those savings to buy or start a club of her own. Right now,
what she had wasn't enough, so doing some extra shifts might
get her there faster.

With a smile that would cause any woman's breath to
catch, he tapped the top of the door frame with his hand,
then shut it for her.

Danny continued to stand there as she started her Trailblazer and pulled away with a wave.

He remained in that same spot until she could no longer
see him in her rearview mirror.

She was surprised to find herself looking forward to next
Monday when she'd see him again.

Chapter Six

Sᴀᴘᴘʜɪʀᴇ ʟᴇᴀɴᴇᴅ ᴄʟᴏsᴇ, so she could be heard over the DJ's loud music, and said in her ear, "Someone's asking for you."

"Who?" Mel turned to face her.

Sapphire straightened and wiggled her eyebrows. "Some hottie. Did you start dating again?"

Her hostess and fill-in dancer already knew that answer. "No."

"Well, the man asking for you just might change your mind."

"I don't even know who it is, Phire."

"But you will, when you go out to the lobby."

Mel rolled her eyes. "Do you know what he wants?"

"You."

Mel bumped her hip against Sapphire's. "You really want my eyeballs to pop out, don't you? Is that why you keep making me roll them so hard?"

The voluptuous brunette's platform heels made her even taller than her five-foot-eight and Mel appear even shorter than her five-foot-five height, not including her three-inch pumps she had worn tonight. While hostessing, her employee wasn't required to wear those shoes, but the men tipped her more when she was dressed to the nines. Like she was tonight and every night Sapphire worked.

The slinky, sequined, *sexy-as-hell* gown Sapphire wore was one of Mel's favorite. The woman's long, elegant back was completely exposed all the way to the top of her very firm ass cheeks, and the V neckline in the front—*Hell*, it couldn't even be considered a neckline—plunged to below her belly button. Her very perky, double-D breasts were only held in place by double-sided tape.

Mel would borrow that dress in a second if it fit her. She didn't quite have the same generous curves like Sapphire, who laughed. "Well, I could use a new set of peepers. My vision's going to shit and it's not like we have medical coverage here."

"If you need to borrow the money for an exam and contacts, you know you can come to me."

The Peach Pit's hostess grabbed her arm and squeezed. "I appreciate you looking out for us, MJ, but you don't have any more money than we do. If Laura was still here..." Her words drifted off on a sigh.

All of them missed the former owner.

Unfortunately, that was water under the bridge. They had to do the best they could with the situation handed to them. At least until something better came along.

If it was up to her, she'd start her own club sooner rather than later and pinch all the girls from The Peach Pit. She had no doubt if she opened up a new place, her stable of dancers would be instantly full and she could then steal the customers, too.

But... If she did that, she might end up with her throat

sliced and dumped in some field or quarry. None of the Deadly Demons she met so far seemed to be good people.

Not a damn one.

Unfortunately, right now, they were all under that MC's thumb.

"Should I let him in or will you be going out to meet him?"

"I'll go out. He's not a Demon is he?" She'd be surprised if her visitor was one since normally they wouldn't ask to see her, they'd just barge right in and get in her face. Plus, Sapphire said he was hot. Mel hadn't seen a "hot" Demon, yet. In fact, everyone she'd met so far was the exact opposite.

"Not even close. He smells good and looks good, too. Unlike those gross, handsy motherfuckers who treat us like we're nothing more than pieces of meat who belong to them."

Mel frowned. "Something new happen that I need to know about?" It wouldn't be the first time those Demons tried to take what they wanted without permission.

"Not to me. And the rest of the girls know to come to you immediately if anything does. I'm talking about the shit we've been dealing with since those assholes took over."

"I'll remind Taint that we won't have any dancers left if he can't control his 'brothers.'" She ground her teeth. "We shouldn't have to protect ourselves from our own boss, or bosses."

"Yeah, well, when Cookie isn't around, Saint's no better than the rest of them." Sapphire visibly shuddered. "I doubt he'll care what you have to say."

Cookie was Saint the Taint's ol' lady. Unfortunately, she was also The Peach Pit's new assistant manager. While Saint oversaw the operations of the club, his woman was supposed to be the acting manager when Mel wasn't around. However, Cookie had no management experience when the Demons slid her into that position, despite Mel's suggestion of making Sapphire her second in charge. Worse, the biker's woman had zero work ethic.

Mel also suspected that Cookie pocketed some of the dancers' tips when they weren't looking.

Saint was the complete opposite of his road name. But then, there was nothing sweet about Cookie, either. Both were arrogant, disrespectful and had a hard, brutal edge to them.

Mel had a sinking feeling that both Taint and Cookie were also selling drugs from the club. That illegal activity alone could get the club shut down and boarded up. Their greed could screw over a lot of people who needed their job.

Including Mel.

"Do you want me to stay here and watch things while you go out there?"

"No. I'm sure it'll be quick. Since I'll be busy with whomever it is, you can continue to man the door until one of the prospects show up."

"*If* they show up. Don't expect miracles."

Whoever was working the front door for the night was tasked with collecting the cover charge, storing customers' cell phones and securing any legal weapons.

Yes, weapons. Knives, guns, whatever. Years ago, after a wife came into the club brandishing a loaded handgun because she was angry her husband was spending their food budget on the dancers instead, Laura had installed a metal detector so that anyone entering the club had to walk through it first. They also had a no cell phone policy so naked pictures of the girls or identifying photos of their clientele didn't get leaked, either. Laura had wanted everyone to feel comfortable.

If someone wanted to make a phone call, they headed out to the lobby to make it. No exceptions.

But she wouldn't be surprised if the Demons eventually got rid of those policies put in place for the safety of both their staff and customers.

She followed Sapphire past the busy bar and through the double doors out to the small lobby. Her step stuttered when she saw who it was.

One side of his mouth pulled up when she stepped out from behind the taller woman.

She didn't know who to expect, but definitely not him. Last night they parted ways thinking they wouldn't see each other until next Monday night.

But here he was.

Not only was "Blaze" standing there, he was looking damn delicious in a forest green short-sleeved Henley that fit his broad shoulders and bulging biceps like a second skin. The rich color highlighted both his hair color and skin tone. His long legs were encased in a pair of jeans so worn that most of the blue had faded away. There were tears at both knees and the bottom of his pant legs appeared slightly frayed over the same black boots he wore last night while dancing. They reminded her of the style of boots the Demons wore. Biker boots.

"He's one of the Peckers," Mel told Sapphire as her hostess moved back behind the counter.

"Oh, then damn, I should've worked last night. Do all of the dancers look like him? If so, I'll make sure to work next Monday night."

She noticed that Danny never even glanced at Sapphire, despite her eye-fucking him. Instead, his eyes remained on Mel.

"What do you need?" She waved him through the metal

detector but he shook his head.

He jerked his chin at the walk-through metal detector. "Got a knife on me. Just needed a word with you."

"Do you plan on stabbing anyone?"

He chuckled. "No."

Since there wasn't a lot of room between the metal detector and the front door—and he was already taking up most of the space—she urged him to, "Step through."

The metal detector certainly did beep when he did so. That made her think he had more than a knife on him.

"Might be my belt buckle setting it off, too," he murmured, but not pulling up his shirt to show her if he was even wearing a belt.

He stopped in front of her, closer than necessary, then his gaze took a slow trip over her from head to toe.

Hmm.

Tonight she wore a black, sleeveless, one-piece jumpsuit that crisscrossed her chest, showed plenty of cleavage, as well as her toned stomach, and also exposed her back. She'd paired it with a simple pair of black "fuck me" pumps and a wide rhinestone belt.

The outfit was simple but sexy and not overly revealing. She preferred that eyes remain on the stage and her dancers, not on her.

However, Danny's eyes were certainly glued to her.

She cleared her throat, drawing his attention back to her face. "So, why are you here?"

It couldn't be just to see her.

"I forgot something last night. Wanted to stop in and grab it. Pretty sure I left it in the dressing room."

Since the girls were in and out of the dressing room, she doubted they'd want some stranger back there while they were changing or getting ready to perform.

"What was it and where? I can grab it for you."

"I'm not sure where. But it's a special pair of underwear that we wear when we dance."

Ah, the ones with a pocket to tuck their penis into, to emphasize that particular asset. The women had gone wild over those last night.

Mel couldn't deny she had appreciated them, too. "Do you know where in the dressing room?"

"No. Mind if I look?"

"Actually, I do. I don't let any men into the dressing room when the girls are in there."

"Understood. But unfortunately, it's one of the only two pairs I have right now and I need to wash them before our next performance."

He only had two pairs? He really *was* new in the business. "You aren't going to buy more?"

"Not until I figure out if this side gig is worth keeping. Those underwear aren't cheap."

"Are you having doubts about dancing?"

He shrugged. "While the money's nice, I'm not sure it's worth the physical damage that goes along with it."

"The women were certainly over-enthusiastic last night." All the dancers were getting touched inappropriately. At least from Mel's point of view. Maybe most of the Peckers didn't mind it because it meant better tips.

"Enough to leave bruises and scratches. Having my body all marked up is not good for business," he finished.

"Not good for your health, either." Especially if he picked up an infection from a bite or scratch. "Do we need to have stricter rules in place for next Monday?"

"Not for me to decide. You'd have to talk to Nick."

"I'll do that." She tipped her head toward the solid double doors that led into the main area. "Come on. You can stand outside the dressing room while I clear it or at least make sure they're decent enough they don't mind you in there."

"They get naked on stage," he reminded her needlessly.

"They do, but to make money. No one gets to access them for free, except their significant others, of course."

He grinned. "Good point. And I'm not going in there to get a free peep show."

Before she could pull the door open, he had pushed past her to open it. As she slipped by him, his warm, long fingers spread over her lower back for a split second, causing a shiver to sweep through her.

She brushed aside her reaction, and on their trek through the occupied tables, she met Raven's eyes to check in with her on stage. Mel received the slightest nod from the black-haired beauty, but it was enough to signal the performance was going well and there weren't any issues. Like one of the customers getting out of hand.

Last night had been much more crowded due to the Peckers' special performance. Tonight's number of occupants was a typical Tuesday night. Fridays and Saturdays tended to be the busiest and when the girls earned the most tips. Sometimes Sundays, too, when it wasn't football season.

She had her most loved and experienced girls work the weekends. Those spots were highly valued and it took a bit for anyone new to work those nights. They usually didn't get that chance until they filled in for one of Mel's more popular girls due to them calling off or having plans.

She didn't need to look over her shoulder to see if Danny was following her. She could feel his presence behind her as they weaved their way toward the back hallway where one of the Demon's prospects stood guard at the entrance. He was only supposed to permit the dancers beyond the velvet rope, unless a customer paid for a private dance in one of the two small VIP rooms in the back. If a customer wanted to book a dancer, they were escorted to the room and afterward, directly back out. They didn't want anyone loitering in the back for the girls' safety.

Ignoring the prospect named Ringo, she unclipped the rope, holding it open for Danny to pass and waiting until she could secure it again.

But he paused and she saw why. With his brow furrowed, he was checking out the biker standing sentry with arms crossed over his chest.

After securing the rope, she grabbed Danny's arm and tugged him down the narrow hallway where it was a little easier to hear.

"That guy works here?"

"Yes."

"You hire bikers?"

"I don't, no. The new owners do."

"The new owners are affiliated with a motorcycle club?"

"You could say that," she murmured, wondering why he cared.

She expected more questions, but surprisingly, he let that drop. They stopped just outside of the dressing room. "Stay here. Let me see who's inside."

After he gave her an answering nod, she opened the door and slipped inside.

She only saw two women getting ready and both were already dressed in their outfits and now sitting in front of the vanities, putting on their "faces."

"Sorry, ladies, I have a gentleman here from Peckers All-Male Revue and he left behind a piece of his outfit. Do you mind if he comes in and looks for it?"

Pepper waved a hand over her shoulder while Chyna shot her a smile in the mirror. "Is he cute?"

Mel pinned her lips together and nodded. As soon as she did, both dancers spun around on their chairs, interest filling their eyes.

"You're married," Chyna said to Pepper.

Pepper bugged her eyes out at her co-worker. "So? That doesn't mean I can't look. I'm not dead. I get stared at all night, what's wrong with me doing a little staring of my own? Especially at someone in the business."

"He'll make it quick," Mel assured them and opened the door, waving Danny inside.

The tall redhead mumbled a thanks, and as soon as he stepped into the dressing room, Pepper released a long, low whistle.

Chyna added on a, "Well, *hellooooo*, handsome!"

Danny grinned. "Sorry for barging in, ladies."

Chyna looked him up and down. There was no shame in her game. "Are you going to be here next Monday night?"

"That's the plan as of now."

"I'll have to come in on my night off," she stated before asking Mel, "Are the rest of that traveling troupe hunks like him?"

Great. Of course Chyna would put her on the spot.

"They're worth watching. They have quite the moves," was the safest way for her to respond.

Chyna *mmm*'d and pursed her lips, dragging her gaze up and down Danny's physique some more.

"Are you single, handsome?" Pepper asked, her eyes flicking from him to Mel and back.

Mel shot Pepper a look and reminded her, "You're not."

Pepper shot back a huge smile. "But you are."

Shit.

Chapter Seven

BUT YOU ARE.

"Thanks for that reminder," Mel muttered.

She was definitely single and with all the hours she worked, she couldn't see that changing any time soon. Until she found better employment elsewhere, she had no time to date.

She ignored the look and the whispers both girls shared, turning back to Danny. "Do you need help looking?"

"No, just give me a minute while I take a quick look around."

"What do they look like?" Pepper asked.

Danny released a soft snort-laugh. "Tiny, shiny and with one of those, you know, pouches."

Chyna asked with all seriousness, "Is the pouch tiny, too?" even though she was kidding.

Danny played along. "I'd have to say that's where most of the fabric was used."

Chyna wiggled her eyebrows and released a sexy, little

growl. "Size is great and all, as long as you know how to use all those inches."

"I haven't had any complaints."

"That's what they all say," Pepper said on a sigh, turning back to the mirror and continuing to sweep blush across her criminally high cheekbones. She kept one eye on what she was doing and one eye on Danny in the mirror.

"How was the turnout last night, MJ?" Chyna asked, also keeping her eyes glued to Danny as he wandered around the large room, thoroughly checking every corner and even peeking under chairs.

"Packed. We sold out last night and we're almost sold out already for next Monday. We might have to bring Peckers in once a month. They're quite a draw." And when she opened up her own club, theme nights like that might be financially beneficial.

"Do you like being a Pecker?" Pepper asked him.

He lifted his head from where he was peering into some of the empty lockers.

"He's new," Mel answered before he could.

"Maybe he needs some pointers," Chyna suggested, giving Mel a pointed look and a sly smile.

Heat crept into her cheeks at Chyna's blatant attempt at matchmaking. "Their type of dancing isn't quite the same. You know that."

Chyna raised a brow. "Close enough."

It wasn't. They hadn't used either of the poles on stage last night. That was one of the main props Mel had always used when she stripped. It was also heavily used by her stable of dancers for good reason. Subconsciously it could be seen as a phallic symbol. Some men mentally put themselves in the pole's place while watching a dancer on stage.

"Found them," Danny announced as he leaned over and

reached toward the bottom of a locker. Once he straightened, he held them up. "Now I can get out of your hair, ladies."

"You can barge in anytime, handsome," Chyna assured him. She arched a brow at Mel. "In fact, give him an open invitation so he can come visit."

Mel shook her head and swatted her hand toward Chyna. "You know men are off-limits from being back here. Normally, anyway. This is supposed to be your safe space."

"And I'll respect that." Danny wished them all a, "Good night."

"See you Monday night. I'll save some of my tips for you!" Chyna shouted as they stepped back into the hallway and Mel closed the door behind them.

"Nice ladies," Danny said with his lips twitching and the corners of his eyes crinkled with amusement.

"Apparently, they're a bit thirsty tonight."

He tipped his head down. "How about you?"

She avoided the sudden intensity in his eyes. "I had my fill last night. Those margaritas were delicious."

"You know what I meant," he murmured.

"I know what you meant," she repeated just as softly.

He stared down at her for a few seconds, then seemed to snap out of whatever thoughts he was having. "Sorry for the inconvenience."

"Don't be. I have to be here no matter what."

"For the girls, then."

"Did either of them look inconvenienced? You seemed to make their evening."

"They see men all night long."

"None like you."

"I'm sure that's not true."

"I guarantee that's very true." She smiled. "I work here, remember?"

He lifted the underwear he had balled in his hand. "I guess I should've brought something along to hide these. Will it be too obvious if I shove them into my pocket?"

"There's a room full of men out there. Nobody's going to be interested in what you're carrying."

He still didn't move to leave. He continued to stand close and study her face. She didn't think it was all that interesting. Now his on the other hand...

When his head dropped a fraction and his empty hand lifted, the air turned static and rippled around them, causing Mel to swallow hard and her nipples to pebble. *What the hell was going on?*

"Well, I need to get back out on the floor. I'll walk you out." To break whatever invisible and unexpected connection was crackling between them, she turned to head back toward the front of the club.

"Hey..."

Her heart skipped a beat when he grabbed her arm and spun her back to face him.

"What are you doing tomorrow night? I'd love to take you to dinner."

As soon as she glanced down at his hand on her arm, he released her. "I'll be here working, what else?" She did her best to act like his touch hadn't affected her, even though her pulse was now pounding in her ears.

"No dinner break or anything?"

She forced herself to concentrate on what he was saying and not on watching his moving lips. But, *damn*, it was difficult. "Depends on if my assistant manager shows up. If she does, I'll be done at seven. That is, if you don't mind a late dinner. Otherwise, I'm stuck here until we close."

His brow dropped low. "Does he or she normally not show up?"

"The former one did, but she left right after the club changed hands. Now I'm stuck with a very unreliable one."

"Why don't you fire them?"

She wished she could. "I can't." Normally, she hired and fired the club's employees. However, she couldn't fire any "staff" the Demons brought in. None of them were even on the payroll. She suspected they were being paid cash under the table, if at all.

"Why not?"

"Because she's Saint's girlfriend." Or ol' lady. Or wife. Or whatever. She really had no idea what their dynamic was. She also didn't care enough to ask for clarification.

"Is Saint the new owner?"

"The club was bought out by one of those," she flapped a hand around, "motorcycle gangs... Or clubs... Whatever they call themselves. Truthfully, gang seems to fit."

"A biker gang actually *bought* the strip club?"

"Commandeered it, more like it." She tried to keep the bitterness out of her answer, but she failed.

And because she did, she saw Danny's spine snap straight and his broad shoulders pull back. She was not expecting that defensive reaction.

"What does that mean?" He wasn't asking a question, he was demanding an answer.

She'd give him an answer but skirt around the details. "It means they forced out the previous owner, whom I loved. Laura started out just like me by becoming a stripper when she was younger and moving into management at another club. The difference between us was, she then bought The Peach Pit. However, with her gone, things have changed and not for the better."

"How did it change?"

"She was working on making The Peach Pit more

upscale, so it would attract a better clientele. She wanted it to be different than most seedy clubs."

"But I thought you were the manager. Couldn't you continue to work toward that?"

"I was helping her do that, but my hands were tied once Laura left and Saint began to oversee the club's operations."

He rubbed his forehead. "Sorry, exactly who is Saint if he's not the owner? I'm confused."

"A biker." She actually hated saying his name. She swore every time she did, it conjured him up. Like an evil hex.

"His actual name is Saint?"

"It's his road name, I guess. I have no idea what name he was born with, nor do I care."

"Sounds like a nice guy."

"Let's just say he certainly is *not* a saint."

"And he was hired by this... motorcycle club?"

"Not hired. He's one of them. So is Cookie, my so-called assistant manager. They also put prospects to work in the club, just like good ol' Ringo there. But at least the prospects show up. Maybe not on time but..." She sighed.

"Damn, they took over, didn't they? I'm assuming none of them worked here before this MC took over."

"No. I never would've hired them. Neither would've Laura. And even if I hired them because they had experience and were reliable, I certainly wouldn't let them wear those vests—or cuts, or whatever the hell they call them—while working. That's not going to attract an upscale clientele."

Danny turned his head and focused on Ringo, still standing at the velvet rope with his back to them.

"His patch only says prospect. What club is it?"

Why was this man so damn interested in the details about The Peach Pit? "Are you well-versed in motorcycle clubs?"

Something ghosted behind his hazel eyes and she wasn't sure what it was.

"Not at all, I was just curious."

"The Deadly Demons." She fought an eye roll at their club name, though she was sure it fit those assholes perfectly.

"Never heard of them."

"You're lucky, then. I hadn't either until they jammed Laura between a rock and a hard place."

"Meaning?"

She glanced over her shoulder at Ringo. The music was loud enough that he couldn't hear their conversation but that still didn't mean she wanted to discuss what went down with Laura when any of them were around. "They just pressured her to sell, that's all."

She barely caught it when his eyes narrowed. If she had blinked, she would have missed it.

"What you're saying is, whether you go to dinner with me is dependent on this woman who's tied to the Deadly Demons."

She sighed. "Unfortunately, yes. If she doesn't show up, I'm forced to work a double." Unless she could get someone she trusted to fill in, like Sapphire. But she didn't like to drop that kind of responsibility on anyone else's shoulders.

Unlike most of her dancers, Mel was single and didn't have children, so it was simply easier for her to stay.

"How about on your next night off?"

She tried not to laugh because she didn't want him thinking she was laughing at him. But sometimes she had to laugh about the whole situation with the club, otherwise she just might cry. "Monday nights are my only night off. And your troupe will be here performing this coming Monday."

"You only have one night off a week." It wasn't a question, it was a growl.

She did the math quickly in her head. "Actually, by the time my next Monday off rolls around, I'll have worked twenty days straight."

"What the fuck."

She agreed with that muttered statement. "We used to be closed on Mondays and Tuesdays, but Taint demanded we be open seven days a week. I negotiated down to six after I convinced him we don't have enough staff for that and they aren't willing to put more on the payroll. He's only willing to fill spots with their prospects, of course. My guess is because they're either not paid or paid poorly. Anyway, because of being understaffed, I convinced them to keep Monday nights closed." She shook her head. She was waiting for that fight to circle back around. She was sure Saint the Taint would eventually put his scuffed boot down and have the club open every night, including holidays.

"Wait. Who's Taint?"

She slapped a hand over her mouth so she wouldn't burst out laughing. "I didn't mean that to slip out. It's Saint. I kind of call him Taint, instead."

His warm chuckle surrounded her like a hug. "Do you call him that to his face?"

"Only in my head."

"Nice." He tilted his head. "It seems like you don't get much personal time at all."

"Not lately."

"That has to be exhausting."

"It is. Add dealing with the public on top of those long hours and..."

He nodded. "Understood. I deal with the public in my day job."

"Which is?"

"A subject for another time. Like at dinner. So... Can I

100

give you my number and you can call or text me if she does show up tomorrow night?"

Good lord, was she actually going to go on a real date with him? Would it even be considered a date? She didn't even know anymore, it had been so long since she'd dated anyone.

Maybe he wasn't interested in her personally but more professionally. It could be he only wanted to pick her brain about stripping. Even if that was the case, it was better than eating dinner alone. Like she did night after night. And, bonus, he seemed open, warm, and well-spoken.

Now she really was curious about what he did for a paycheck, besides stripping.

"I don't have my phone on me. It's stored in my locker. Do you have yours?"

He slipped his phone from his back pocket. A phone he really shouldn't have in the club according to Mel's own policy. But then, she let him walk into the club with a knife, too, so there was that.

When he was ready, she rattled off her number.

After plugging it into his contacts, he lifted his head and tucked his phone away. "I just texted your phone so you have my number."

"Sounds good. I'll text you tomorrow night if she shows up. If not, it'll have to be another time."

"No problem, as long as you agree to come to dinner with me."

Before she could answer, the back door opened and Taint himself strode through it.

"Fuck," she muttered under her breath.

Danny immediately spun around, for the most part becoming a wall between her and the biker. Did he do that on purpose?

She stepped to his side anyway. She couldn't get out of

dealing with the head biker, unfortunately. Not if she wanted to keep her job.

"Who's that?" Danny asked her quietly. His narrowed hazel eyes remaining on the approaching man.

She sighed. "Taint."

"That's him?"

"You should probably go. I need to get back out on the floor."

"Are you going to be okay? You don't want me to stick around?"

A lot more meaning was behind his questions than what he was actually asking. It was a whole vibe. As in, he thought she might need protection.

That was sweet.

But totally unnecessary.

"Can you find your way back out?"

"Sure." He dropped the volume of his voice to the point Mel could barely hear him ask, "You sure you don't want me to stick around for a few?"

"I'll be fine. I appreciate the offer."

He nodded, but that gesture did not match his guarded expression. "You have my number, text me if you need me."

Her brow furrowed. What was he going to do? Go against Taint if the biker stepped out of line? The man had a whole outlaw army behind him. Danny was only one man. A dancer, at that.

Yes, he was built like a brick house, but she knew Taint was packing at least one gun and most likely had a couple of knives on him, too.

"Thank you. And I'll let you know about tomorrow night."

He reached out and squeezed her shoulder. "Text me if you need me. I'll wait in my car for a few."

"You don't have to do that. I'm used to him and I'll be fine. But I appreciate you looking out for me."

"Not a problem." When he turned to face her, his jaw shifted. And for a second, she didn't think he was going to leave. But after another nod, this time with his expression carefully masked, he headed out toward the main area of the club.

Suddenly, Mel felt very alone.

Despite that, she stood her ground as Taint stopped in front of her.

The fucker sucked on his teeth and took his time running his gaze over her. Of course, he paused on her breasts before continuing all the way down to her high heels.

Asshole.

When Cookie wasn't around he was always eye-fucking the girls or trying to touch them.

"Should show your legs more."

And you should go choke on your own dick. "I need to get back on the floor."

As she turned, he snagged her arm and pulled her back to him. "Who was that?" He jerked his chin in the direction Danny went.

Mel glanced down at his hand on her arm. Unlike Danny, Taint did not release her. Instead, he tightened his grip. "He was one of the dancers from last night. He forgot something and came back to pick it up."

She gave her arm a little jerk. A message for him to let her go.

He stared at her for far too long, with a look that made her stomach churn, before loosening his fingers. She rubbed her bare arm where he'd held her. It didn't hurt, she only wanted to brush away the memory of his touch.

"Before you go out there, got business to go over."

Great. What that fucker knew about running a business could fit on a grain of sand. "What about?"

"Fire that fuckin' Chris guy and that other guy... The bouncer. Whatever his fuckin' name is." Saint squinted as he thought.

Like squinting would help him think.

Mel somehow managed to avoid rolling her eyes. She made the mistake of doing it once when the Demons first took over and Saint had actually grabbed her by the throat. Luckily, Chris had stepped in, pulling the angry biker's focus to him instead.

Losing her best bartender would be a major hit for the club. He'd been with her for years now and was the one who volunteered to work last night. He also made her the best margaritas.

The better the bartender was in a club, the more they made in alcohol sales. The more alcohol they sold, the more generous the clientele was with tipping. The Peach Pit would soon be a sinking ship since Taint kept poking holes in the hull.

"The fat fuck that only works weekends. That one. Fire him, too."

Mel gritted her teeth. *Goddamn it.* Willy was a part-time bouncer willing to work weekends. And it was difficult to find good help on the weekends.

The Demons' hostile takeover was destroying this club along with the vision Laura had for it. Mel *really* needed to make finding another job her priority. But, *damn it*, she hated to abandon the girls, even if temporarily. She was their advocate and fought for them when it came to Saint's ridiculous ideas. To him, the girls were not human, only assets to make money.

She shook her head. "We need them, Saint." Desperately.

"Gonna bring in more prospects to replace 'em."

More Demons? *Shit.* "When?" She figured it would happen eventually, but she was hoping it wouldn't be so soon.

Her heart dropped when he answered, "This weekend. Gonna replace anyone who ain't a dancer. These prospects'll be my eyes and ears when I ain't here. And it's gonna save us a shitload of scratch."

Great. More reasons to abandon ship and find a new one. Or build one of her own. Not that she needed any more reasons. Simply the man standing before her wearing a worn black leather "cut" with filthy patches was more than enough.

"You're not paying them?" She wondered if that was legal or if the PA Department of Labor and Industry would have something to say about that.

"Fuck no. We own those prospects' ass. They gotta do what we say or they don't get patched in. So, do whatcha gotta do to train 'em right. They give you any shit, you come to me and I'll straighten 'em the fuck out. Hear me?"

No he wouldn't. He didn't care enough to straighten out any of his prospects.

She pulled a long breath in through her nose and when she released it, she also released a, "Yes."

Mel's lungs seized and she couldn't breathe when Taint leaned down and practically went nose to nose with her. She leaned back trying to avoid him touching her again, or inhaling his rank beer and pot breath, but he dragged his thumb over her bottom lip and whispered, "Good thing you're fuckin' hot and know what the fuck you're doin', otherwise, your ass would be replaced, too."

Mel's stomach churned. Taint's touch gave her the willies, unlike the warm fuzzies like Danny's did.

Danny with no last name.

Shit.

If she was going to accept his dinner invite, it would've been smart to ask that important information, then maybe she could have cyber-stalked him to see if she could dig up some info on him first.

She knew nothing about him except that he danced part-time with the Peckers.

Maybe she'd check in with Nick, the owner/manager of the all-male revue, to confirm their show on Monday night. Then she could find an excuse to ask for Danny's last name.

Yes, that was what she'd do.

In fact, that in itself was a good excuse to get the hell away from Taint. And while in the dressing room, warn the girls that the asshole was in the house.

Chapter Eight

"I just wanted to have this quick meeting to catch everyone up to speed. Anyone who can't be here physically because they're either doing surveillance, undercover work or taking some much needed down time has called in and is on mute unless they have something to contribute."

Finn was having a hard time concentrating on Crew standing at the head of the table on the third floor of The Plant, the Tri-State Drug Task Force's headquarters and the Blue Avengers MC clubhouse. Instead of seeing the task force leader, he could only envision a certain blonde. One who looked nothing like Crew.

Thank fuck.

While he'd reluctantly admit Crew was *kind of* handsome, Finn didn't swing that way. Hell no. His preference leaned toward a bluish-green-eyed blonde who looked smoking hot in that black one-piece *sexy-as-fuck* jumpsuit she wore at the club on Tuesday. He doubted Crew could pull that off as well as MJ.

He'd wanted to take the strip club manager to dinner last night, but she texted him only a few minutes past seven to cancel since she was stuck staying late.

While he expected it, it still pissed him off.

Not the her being unable to go to dinner part—he was determined that would still happen—but the fact that the Demons were taking advantage of her. They'd better be paying her fairly for all of the overtime she was forced to work.

If they weren't...

Shit. There was nothing he could do about that. Except help take down that outlaw club.

Realistically, he should stop being distracted by MJ and pay attention to the man continuing to talk.

"The Demon's Uniontown church is now fully up and running. And as you all know, Powers and Proctor have been sitting on it."

When not on the task force, Ken Proctor was an officer with Uniontown PD, and Carl Powers was a trooper stationed at the Pennsylvania State Police's Uniontown barracks. Both knew that area well. Finn hadn't known either of them before the task force was formed, but both must have pulled the short straw to take turns sitting surveillance outside of the Demons' church. Because he didn't know anyone willing to volunteer to sit in a damn vehicle for long hours at a time, taking notes, video and photos while trying not to be made by the target of the surveillance.

Finn wasn't sure if doing a boring stakeout was better or worse than stripping on stage in front of a pack of horny, unrestrained women.

Powers' voice came through the phone sitting in the middle of the conference table. "They bought a run-down gas station. As much money as they're raking in with drugs and

108

whatever else, I'm not sure why they picked such a fucking hovel. Unfortunately, we can't see much of anything, except for who's coming and going, unless they open the three garage bay doors. Plus, the area behind it has a six-foot fence, so it limits what we can see back there, too."

Nox, sitting across from Finn, grumbled, "It makes sense they would pick an old run-down business. They probably got it cheap and it would draw more attention if they picked a palace."

"Turns out they may be smarter than we think," Crew continued. "By picking such a dump, everyone, including non-suspecting law enforcement, might think the club's still broke as fuck. If suddenly they have a shiny new clubhouse, then someone might sit up and take notice."

Rez hooted out loud. "Jokes on them, the feds already have."

"They bought a dump for the same reason we left the front of our church the way it is. It blends in and anyone driving by wouldn't know that the building is occupied or by who," Decker reminded them.

"Don't give those assholes too much credit when it comes to their thinking skills," Fletch's voice came through the phone. "The ones we've been dealing with are pretty fucking dumb. They have the same amount of brain cells as they have teeth."

"They might have a criminal mastermind or two amongst them but, honestly, I think the rest are doing mental gymnastics and coming in dead last in the intelligence Olympics." Wilder's voice also came from the speaker phone. "None of them will ever be members of Mensa."

"They're not hiding that it's their clubhouse, though," Powers spoke up. "They usually have their bikes lined up out front and they just put their logo proudly on the front of the building. They also go in and out of the front entrance wearing their colors, so they're not hiding it's their church, only that they're suddenly rolling in the dough."

Crew took it from there. "It would be ideal to get someone planted in their chapter or, at minimum, we need to bug their clubhouse since Powers and Proctor can't stake it out long term. I'll work on that now that they're finally settled in at that location."

"Agreed. Doing both would be great," DEA agent Luis Torres said, "but if we only have one option, then planting bugs in their church should be the priority."

"No shit," Nox said. "But if we can find someone to go undercover, they could also plant the bugs. The problem is, who do we have that can infiltrate them and not cause suspicion?"

"Can't be me," Crew stated. "I come off as a badge."

Rez wrinkled his nose. "Yeah, you've got that federal agent funk all over you that even an infant can smell a mile away."

Crew ignored him. "We need someone both young enough and able to pull off being a dirtbag with ease. Preferably someone without a family because whoever does this might be out of pocket for a while, like Fletch and Wilder. Also, we have to consider that whoever goes in as a prospect will most likely be under a huge magnifying glass until they prove themselves. I can't imagine those fuckers aren't paranoid about letting in new recruits, especially now that they're trafficking meth with the fucking Cosa Nostra. They might even be worried about the Russos having the same idea as we do."

"I can't imagine that the Russos trust the Demons and I could see them putting someone on the inside without the club knowing," Wilder said. Out of anyone on the team, she was the most knowledgeable when it came to the Pittsburgh crime family since she had been undercover with them for about a year. "Paranoia runs high within that organization, even amongst themselves. For good reason, too. They're always worried about being taken out, by one of their own or by someone on the outside, or even being brought up on RICO charges. While they might get respect on the inside of a federal prison, they certainly won't get all the luxuries they're used to."

"I can't imagine living every day being paranoid about getting fucked over by someone in your own organization. It has to bug the shit out of them." Nox shook his head. "What a miserable fucking life."

Finn wasn't so sure Nox's life wasn't miserable, either. The loss of his wife had devastated him and he still wasn't back to his normal self. He might never be. Selling their marital home and turning the second floor of The Plant into his new residence had helped, but only somewhat. Even though he'd moved in, he still wasn't done with the construction since he was basically doing it all on his own.

He had turned down most offers of help from the rest of the Blue Avengers. They figured if he needed assistance, he knew enough to ask. But between that and the task force, he'd been keeping busy in an attempt to prevent spiraling to the bottom of a dark pit.

Moving into The Plant was the best thing for Finn's fellow Blue Avenger, especially since someone from the task force was always on the third floor if he needed company.

"Fuck 'em. I hope they're all fucking miserable and develop ulcers from being paranoid. I hope they have insomnia and massive hemorrhoids. Meth destroys a lot of fucking families. So, fuck all of those greedy motherfuckers."

Damn. But what Don Mullins said was true. Being a

111

narcotic detective with the Pittsburgh PD, he'd seen the heartbreak and devastation drug addiction could cause. Something Decker had experienced personally.

Finn floated a possibility out there... "If we put someone undercover with the Uniontown chapter and so do the Russos..."

"Wouldn't that be fucked up." It wasn't a question but a statement by Decker.

He was right. It would be fucked up. Finn added, "That might get sticky as fuck."

"Maybe. Maybe not," Crew said. "The Russos have no clue we know they're involved. Demons don't know that we know about them, either. We just need to make sure it stays that way."

"Or this investigation is screwed," Decker concluded.

"Anyone undercover with the Demons could get screwed if they're discovered," Rez warned.

Not just screwed but actually end up dead.

Crew nodded. "Let me chew on it for a bit. Group one has two TFOs already installed with the mother chapter in West Virginia, and I think they're trying to get at least one more inside. Group three is working on getting one of their TFOs in the new Ohio chapter. We should really do the same. Having someone on the inside would be valuable."

"But nobody sitting at this table or on the other side of that phone line is in their twenties," Rodgers, another DEA agent, said. "We're all seasoned law enforcement. Some of us more than others." He flicked his eyes toward Crew's salt-and-pepper hair that was heavy on the salt. "We've talked about this option at the beginning, it would be easier to send in someone young to be a prospect."

"Even though I doubt there's an age limit, I would guess that someone over, say thirty-five, might draw more suspicion and be watched more closely. The two I saw at the club were in their early twenties. Fletch, have you seen any older prospects?" Finn asked the state trooper.

"No, but that doesn't mean it doesn't happen. We really haven't dealt with a lot of their prospects. Wolf probably doesn't trust them enough with distributing the meth, at least in the amounts that we're buying, until they've proven their worth. On the flipside, I wouldn't doubt he's using them for dealing on the street. This way if they get busted, no big loss."

Crew spoke next. "Since they're expanding territory at a fast clip, my assumption is they need to expand their membership just as quickly. They might not be so damn picky when it comes to increasing their numbers. They can easily weed out prospects before getting them heavily involved in distributing or dealing drugs." He scrubbed a hand down his bearded cheek. "Again, let me take this into serious consideration. I'll have to run this by my supervising special agent first, anyway. I'll schedule a meeting with him."

Powers' voice came from the phone in the center of the table again. "We're seeing mostly prospects going in and out of the gas station. Seems like they are definitely increasing their numbers."

"I can confirm that," Crew started, "since I had a meeting with the leaders of group one and three. The Demons have now successfully set up their new Ohio chapter right on the outskirts of New Philadelphia. While it's small yet with only about four patched members, it has about a half dozen *wet-behind-the-ears* prospects."

"That sounds about the same as the Uniontown chapter," Powers confirmed.

"All right," Crew's gaze circled the table, "that could mean age might not be a factor. However, being able to pull off being an outlaw biker would. Would any of you consider wearing a Demons' prospect cut?"

When no one spoke up, Finn said, "I'd volunteer but you made me a fucking Pecker. Those two prospects and the Demon in charge of The Peach Pit all wore Uniontown patches. So, me going under with them would create suspicion."

"Yeah, I read your report. While we're on that subject, you want to do a quick summary for everyone else?" Crew asked Finn.

Decker snorted. "Actually, we only want to watch a video of you dancing."

"Too bad for you since they don't allow that there." *Thank fuck.* If there was video proof, he'd never hear the end of it. "And if you want to see my cock wrapped in satin, just ask, Deck. I'd be glad to show it to you, though you might get a complex afterward."

Decker chuckled. "Doubt it."

Finn glanced around the table. "Let me just say, I need hazard pay for Monday night. Those women were fucking *brutal.*"

"Thought you loved women manhandling you." Rez smirked. "Aren't you on that type of dating site? What's it called?" He pursed his lips, scratched at his temple and pretended he was thinking, but Finn knew better. Rez didn't have enough brain cells to have a solid thought. "Not Tinder, I think it's called Spankers."

"Damn, does that really exist?" Mullins asked with a laugh. "Is that hookup app available in the Google Play store?"

"Nah, the app is actually called Wankers and it's used to set up dates with his own fist." Decker made a jerk-off motion with his hand.

Crew scrubbed his fingers back and forth over his short hair and sighed loudly enough to catch everyone's attention. "As entertaining as this conversation is, let's get back to business."

"Powers, do you have the names of all the bikers in the Uniontown chapter?" Finn asked.

"Yes, I have a current membership list if you need it."

"Can you email that to me? Like I said, I've already seen two prospects and one patched member at The Peach Pit so far."

"What are their road names?" Powers asked.

"The patched member's name is... get this... Saint. He's like the strip club's CEO or something." *Or something.*

The muttered "fuck" coming from the phone's speaker wasn't a good sign.

"Know him?" Crew asked Powers.

"I've seen him coming in and out of the gas station a lot. He's got an ol' lady that seems to hang around there, too."

"Yeah, her nickname is Cookie. She's the club's new assistant manager, except she doesn't show up for work when she's supposed to. The two recruits are Popeye and Ringo. One was working the front door, the other guarding the back hallway. I'm sure there are more I haven't seen yet. All three had fresh Uniontown patches on their cuts."

Crew's eyebrows shot up his forehead. "They're wearing their cuts in the club?"

"Sure are," Finn confirmed. "They're not hiding shit. At least not who they are, anyway. Any illegal activities, on the other hand..." He shrugged. "None were working on Monday night during the show. Just the manager, who's worked there for a decade, and a few other people, none of the Demons from what I could tell."

"Then how'd you see those Demons you mentioned?" Crew asked.

"I purposely left an item behind on Monday night, went back on Tuesday with the excuse to get it when the club was open during normal business hours. I didn't see any drug deals, but then, I wasn't there long."

"Keep working on getting in the back."

Finn shot the task force leader a look he hoped strongly conveyed his annoyance at being an undercover male stripper. "Do I have a choice?"

Crew grinned. "Fuck no. You've got your foot in the door, now wedge your whole body in."

"We've got one more show there this coming Monday night. Unfortunately, if it's the same staff working then, I might not get shit. I need to figure out a way to get in there during their regular nights when the Demons are around and more of the dancers, in case some of them are involved."

"You have a plan?"

Finn slid his hand down his jawline as he answered Crew. "I just might."

He could see the DEA agent's ears perk. "Yeah? Want details."

Finn wasn't sure if he wanted to involve MJ. His interest in her was solely personal but... taking the club's manager out to dinner *might* provide some perks professionally as a side benefit. Ultimately, the task force was a team and he needed to do his part. That might mean using her, whether he made her aware of it or not.

"I tried to make a date with the manager. It ended up getting canceled at the last minute because the assistant manager, Saint's ol' lady, keeps fucking MJ over and not showing up."

"MJ?" Crew asked.

"The manager."

Crew frowned. "Are you trying to get something going with her?"

He sucked in a breath, thinking that getting something going with her—even personally—might get messy. Especially since his only reason to be at The Peach Pit was to gather intel on the MC using the club to deal meth.

"She's made it clear she's not happy with the Demons. She might be good to get on our side."

But, *hell*... even thinking about using MJ for the benefit of the task force made him cranky. While she would be a good asset to have, he'd prefer not to do it behind her back. While he might be interested in screwing her, his intention wasn't to screw her over.

It could also get messy because if he revealed who he was and why he was dancing with the Peckers and then she ran her mouth...

"You can't tell her—"

Finn cut off Crew. "No shit." He knew how to do his damn job.

Crew dropped his chin to his chest and stared at him for a few seconds before he ground out, "All right. Work her if you can."

Finn had another idea that might work in both his favor and the task force's while avoiding any kind of betrayal of MJ or her position at the club. "Could we turn her into a CI?"

Finn could see Crew's mind working as he stared at him from the other end of the long table. "Do you trust her enough?"

"I don't fucking know her. But my plan was to take her to dinner with the intention of getting to know her better. I could feel her out—"

"He means feel her up," Rez huffed.

Finn ignored him and told Crew, "Give me a week or so to see what I can do to get closer to her. If I think she'd be willing to become a confidential informant, I'll come to you first before proposing it to her. If she's willing, it would be a huge break for us since she's there six nights a week and, with being the club manager, she has her finger on the pulse of everything going on behind the scenes."

"Damn," Crew said, sounding a bit impressed with Finn's possible plan.

"Yeah. Did I already say she hates the Demons? And working long hours is only one of the many reasons. The drugs, if she's aware of it, might be another."

"Seems as though you already made a connection with her."

"Only briefly. From what I saw so far, she seems smart and savvy. She could be valuable for our investigation since she has full access to the club, everyone who works there, as well as the customers. If anyone is going to see shit being peddled there, it'll be her."

"Okay, take her to dinner, do your second Peckers show, and feel her out a bit more before doing anything else. We have to make sure she's not involved in any of the dealing first before we ask for her cooperation. We don't want her giving the Demons a heads up. Once you get a good read on her, get back to me if you think she'll be an asset," Crew instructed.

"You got it."

"All right. The rest of you think about whether you want to go undercover with the Uniontown chapter. If you're willing, I'll need you to start growing facial hair right away. We can get you set up with a Harley and an appropriate wardrobe. Finn, Fletch, Wilder and I are out. So is Reynolds and Powers. You two know why. Torres, too."

"Because I'm also brown," Torres pretended to be

surprised at that fact, "and the Demons only prefer bikers of the mayonnaise variety?"

"That and you're the plant manager. I need you to keep managing the wiretaps, especially if we end up bugging the Demons' new digs." His gaze circled the table again. "But fuck, that disqualifies Rez, too. Even ignoring our ages, that only leaves Decker, Nox, Butler, Rodgers, Mullins, Proctor and Kruger."

"You said someone without a family, remember? Then I'm out because of Val," Decker said, mentioning his four-year-old niece he was raising as his own.

"Fuck me. Then that narrows it down to Nox and Kruger, unless," Crew grinned and shrugged, "someone needs a break from their family. However, assume this UC assignment will be a long one like Fletch and Wilder going under with the Dirty Angels. Once we get you inside, we want to keep you there as long as possible."

Finn couldn't imagine Crew would really want Nox undercover with the Demons. Not right now with where his head was at.

"Look," Fletch's voice came from the speaker phone, "Nova and I have been doing weekly buys with Wolf and his crew. In the meantime, we'll see if we can get friendlier with him, continue to build that trust and maybe score an invite to their new clubhouse. Keep in mind, every time we make a buy, we meet at a different location and he rotates through his underlings for the exchange, so we rarely deal with Wolf himself. That has me thinking they might be just as paranoid as the Russos. But... if we can get them comfortable with us enough to have us over at their church, that may open up the possibility of me or Nova planting bugs. Neither of us are experts at it but I'm sure it's not that difficult and we can find someone who's an expert to advise us. This way if we can't plant someone within the Uniontown chapter, we can at least monitor their activities."

"Good idea. But they might never trust you enough, Fletch," Crew said. "Even so, definitely work on that in the meantime. Because you're right, the only other option would be to break in and plant them."

"And one of us getting caught breaking into their club-house could blow this investigation to pieces," Nox concluded.

"That's a strong possibility," Crew agreed. "We have to assume they have a security system in place. Maybe even cameras. Especially if they're storing meth there."

"That would be another good reason for us to try to elbow our way into their church," Wilder added. "We might be able to see what kind of security setup they have."

"All right. That gives us something to work on. In the meantime, I'll go ahead and work on obtaining approval for one of us to go undercover with the Uniontown Demons. Getting approval to install listening devices or even cameras at that location might take a bit longer. Anybody have anything else before we adjourn this meeting?"

Wilder spoke up again. "I just had a thought. Fletch could start hinting to Wolf about patching over from the Angels to the Demons. He could show interest since the DAMC is totally against dealing drugs. Since his cover story is that he patched over from the Blood Fury, it's not like he has any long term loyalty to the Angels. It could work. That would get us inside their chapter plus inside their church to plant bugs."

"Possibly," Crew said, rubbing his hand back and forth over the back of his neck.

"It's a good plan," Mullins said.

"It's an option, but I'd prefer to leave you where you are

at the moment and only use that as a backup plan. If they would even allow it. The Fury and the Angels are allies, so that story was solid and plausible. The Demons might not want any Angels patching over. They're not allies. From what I understand they're barely even civil to each other."

"True," Fletch said, "but it would mean more numbers for them and less for the Angels. That could be to their benefit if they decide to keep marching north into the Angels' territory."

Crew groaned. "I hope to fuck they don't. Those two clubs going to war might fuck up this whole investigation."

"But if we get someone inside or at least get the gas station bugged, we'd be able to hear if that's in the works," Finn reminded Crew.

Crew's eyes flicked from him back to the phone in the center of the table. "Okay, Fletch, hint to Wolf you might be interested in wearing their colors. Only say you're thinking about it and ask if that's something they'd even consider. However, the more unsure you act about it, the better."

"You got it. I'll float the idea out there and see if Wolf bites."

"All right, that gives us a few different angles to work on. Anybody else have anything?" When nobody spoke up, Crew finished up with, "Meeting adjourned. Let's get the fuck out of here."

As Rez rose from his seat, he announced, "We'll have the game on downstairs if anyone wants to stick around to watch Thursday Night Football and have a beer or two." He twisted his head toward Finn. "Brother, you sticking around?"

"Hell yeah."

Rez smirked. "Good. Since the Steelers don't have any cheerleaders, maybe you can stand-in and show us some of your fancy dance moves." The BAMC sergeant at arms rolled his hips, but not nearly as smoothly as Finn could. "I'm sure we can find something that'll work as pompoms for you."

"He can use his balls as pompoms," Decker suggested *oh so* helpfully.

Finn flipped them the bird. "Both of you... just fuck off."

He headed downstairs followed by laughter.

Chapter Nine

Finn pulled the Kia behind The Peach Pit and didn't bother to waste time looking for a parking spot. In fact, he didn't think there was an empty spot to be found since the back lot was packed. Instead, he parked right in front of the employee entrance and glanced at the time before shooting MJ a message letting her know he'd arrived.

It was kind of late in the evening to have dinner, but he'd gotten an unexpected text about forty-five minutes ago: *Cookie showed up. I'm starving. Have you eaten yet?*

He had, but hearing from her had made him hungry all over again. Just not for food.

One side of his mouth pulled up at his own depraved thoughts as he waited for the solid metal door to open.

It finally did about five minutes later and he was surprised to see the strip club manager in worn jeans, brown leather knee-high heeled boots and a clingy emerald green sweater that fell off one *sexy-as-fuck* shoulder. She must have changed for their dinner date since he doubted she wore that all day inside the club.

A late September breeze picked up her loose hair and swirled it around her head and into her face like a gold tornado.

Finn hopped out of the piece of shit SUV and rushed around to the passenger side to open the door for her. "Sorry it isn't fancy, but it's efficient."

A total fucking lie because it wasn't even that, but he didn't give a shit if it was or wasn't since he wasn't footing the bill to fill the gas tank. However, he'd prefer to pick her up in his own damn vehicle or on his bike. Unfortunately, that was impossible since the Kia was registered to one Danny O'Neill, while his Jeep Wrangler Rubicon was registered to the real Daniel Finnegan.

Unfortunately, for every minute he had to drive that Kia Soul, he swore he lost one more piece of his own fucking soul.

Keeping one hand on the car door, he said, "I'm surprised you didn't want me to meet you at the diner."

She lifted her bare shoulder. Well, not completely bare since it was the arm covered in a full black and gray sleeve. With the sweater's wide neckline, he could now see that the detailed flowery tattoo also extended over her shoulder cap.

He closed his eyes and drew in a slow breath to fight the urge to lean in and trace every one of those damn flowers with his tongue. Not only would licking someone he'd just met make things a bit awkward between them, it might get him slapped in the face or kneed in the nuts.

While settling in the passenger seat, she answered, "It's only down the road."

"Do you normally get in vehicles with strangers?"

When she froze in the middle of pulling the seat belt across her torso, her head spun toward him and her blue-green eyes widened. With a grin, he slammed the door closed before she could escape.

He jogged around to the driver's side and climbed in, shutting them in together.

As soon as he did, she murmured, "With that comment, you're making me rethink this."

"Don't. You have nothing to worry about."

"Said the spider to the fly." Her chest rose and fell as she took a deep breath.

This was not a good start to their dinner date. He shouldn't have planted any doubt in her mind. "Would you be more comfortable taking your own vehicle? I won't be insulted if you do. I get it." *And, believe me, I've seen some shit with my job and that's the reason why that comment slipped out before I could stop it.*

Of course, he had to keep that last part to himself. She couldn't know he was a cop with the Southern Allegheny Regional PD. Just like he couldn't reveal he was a temporary federal officer gathering evidence of drug dealing with the very MC that bought her strip club.

At least, not yet.

He wanted to use tonight's dinner to get to know her better and to see if she'd be a good candidate for becoming a CI. But tonight wasn't all about business. He selfishly wanted to know more about her for himself.

For fuck's sake, he wanted to know *everything* about her. And he hoped to fuck she wasn't involved in the Demons' dirty dealings.

She sighed. "It would be nice to live in a world where women didn't have to worry about their damn safety twenty-four/seven."

"I won't argue that. I saw an online discussion asking women what they'd do if the Earth was devoid of men for a day." Even as a cop, the answers were eye-opening.

"If that happened, the whole day would be heaven on

Earth. We would relax and do things we normally wouldn't. We shouldn't have to be on the defensive all the time."

"Again, I agree. I'm sorry life's like that for you and other women." Even though part of his job was to help protect citizens in his PD's jurisdiction, it wasn't always possible. "Should I start driving or do you want to drive separately?" Despite the interior of the Kia being dark, he could feel her staring at him. He glanced over at her. "I want you to be comfortable."

After a few seconds, she nodded. "The diner's only about five minutes away. Do you have any nefarious plans for me within the next five minutes?"

He fought the twitch of his lips. "I promise going fifteen miles per hour above the speed limit and not using turn signals is as bad as it's going to get."

She grabbed the door handle like she was about to jump out. "Well, damn, you just proved you're a psycho." When she laughed, her whole face lit up.

His grin matched hers. "How about if I use my turn signals and keep it to five above?"

"I can deal with that."

He nodded and shifted into Drive. "You'll have to direct me to where we're going."

"There aren't too many places around here open past nine, so take a left onto 119. Do you know where Walnut Hill Cafe is?"

"No, I'm not from around here."

"Where are you from?"

"Up near Belle Vernon." Of course he had to lie about where he lived.

Just like he had to lie about his name, what he drove, why he was dancing with the Peckers, among other things. He was a walking, talking pack of lies. And he hoped if there came a time where he told her the truth, she'd understand why he did so and not hold it against him.

"How's the food at the cafe?" Not that he was really hungry, but he'd order something so she wouldn't feel self-conscious eating.

"The best. They now know me well in there because whenever I get stuck working a double shift—because of Cookie not showing up—I call in a take-out order."

"Then, would you rather eat somewhere different tonight?"

"No, it's fine. It's good, it's close and it's getting late."

She was right. It only took a few minutes until he was pulling into a mostly empty parking lot in front of the Walnut Hill Cafe. He found a spot by the door and, as soon as he shut off the engine, he hurried to get out and open the passenger door for her.

He offered his hand to help her out and she took it, having a hard time keeping the surprise, tinged with amusement, from her face.

"What?" Once she was on her feet, he closed and locked the doors, reluctantly releasing her hand.

She shook her head. "I've never had a man open my car door for me."

That stopped him in his tracks. "Never?"

"Not that I can remember."

"Well, there's a first time for everything." He made sure to hold open the diner's door for her, too.

Right inside the entrance, a sign directed them to seat themselves. Even though the diner was basically empty, he steered her to a quiet back corner. Before they had even settled into the booth, a waitress appeared, dropping off menus, ice water and taking their drink orders, then she was gone in a flash.

Once they were alone again, MJ stared across the Formica table at him, wearing a pensive look.

"What? Do I have something on my face?"

Her lips curved at the corners. "Besides those *adorable* freckles? No."

He used the back of both hands under his chin to frame his face and batted his eyelashes. "*Aww.* I haven't been called adorable since I was like five or so. And it was by my grandmother. Do you also have tissues and Werther's Originals stashed in all your pockets?"

He hoped she'd find that funny and laugh, but when she didn't, he kept his gaze locked with hers and waited her out. Obviously she was working through something in her head. Not a few seconds later, her expression turned curious. "I couldn't find anything on you."

Well, damn.

No surprise she didn't since the feds hadn't taken a lot of effort building his background. Not like they had with Fletch and Wilder. Because of going undercover with the Dirty Angels, their identities had been well thought out and extensive. In contrast, Finn was only supposed to dance with the Peckers for one or two nights and then bounce. No one expected anyone to dig deep on who he was.

Even so, he was impressed she even gave it a shot instead of blindly agreeing to go to dinner with him. "Do you normally try to dig up dirt on your dates?"

"*Is* this a date?"

He cocked an eyebrow and tilted his head. "Isn't it?"

She shrugged. "It's been a while since I've actually dated. Life's been a bit hectic with working long hours and as you might know, dating isn't easy. But to answer your question, yes, I try to do a little research first. I mean, it would be foolish not to. Just imagine discovering later that I could've easily googled someone to find out they murdered their whole family and buried them out in the woods. Women can't be too careful nowadays."

"But despite not finding anything, you still got in my car and came to dinner with me."

"I had to trust my gut instinct."

"How did you search? I never gave you my last name."

"I know." She shrugged. "I asked Nick."

Damn. She wasn't fucking around. "And he gave it to you?"

"I explained that you wanted to take me out to dinner and I don't go out with anyone I can't google first. I especially don't get in a man's car when I don't have his complete name. My gut instinct is decent, but it's not perfect."

"What if I'm using a fake name?"

She held his gaze across the table. "Are you?"

He gave the best answer he could without outright lying. "My name's Daniel."

"That's the same as Danny, then."

In his case, it wasn't. "Just so you know, having a man's name isn't enough to keep you safe."

"I'm full aware of that, Danny O'Neill. Especially when a man has no online presence." She arched an eyebrow at him. "Not even any social media accounts. That's rare these days. Do you prefer Danny or Daniel?"

Ah, she *had* done some deep diving on him. "Danny's fine." It really wasn't since no one called him that, not even his mother. He preferred Finn, but Danny would work for now. "As for social media, it isn't my thing. Like you, I guard my privacy and don't feel the need to share every detail of my life with strangers."

"What, you don't think anyone would be interested in a photo of your breakfast?"

He huffed. "Everybody knows what a bowl of Fruit Loops looks like. And if they don't, they're not living their life to the fullest."

When she dropped her head, he could only hear her soft laughter since her hair curtained her face. He reached across the table to sweep it out of the way, but caught himself right before he made contact.

He had his balled up hands already in his lap when she lifted her face, wearing a big smile. Big enough to make her eyes sparkle and the corners crinkle. "Fruit Loops, huh? I haven't had those since I was a kid."

"Spoiler alert: somedays I still act like one."

She wasn't the only one who'd done a bit of digging. However, he had tools at his fingertips that she didn't. He had run her license plate through the Department of Motor Vehicles to get her personal details and then ran that info through J-Net, the Pennsylvania Justice Network, to make sure she didn't have a rap sheet or outstanding warrants.

Her criminal record was clean but he now knew her full name, her address, her birthday... *Hell*, most details about her. Even how many parking and speeding citations she'd received since obtaining her driver's license at seventeen.

However, he couldn't tell her any of that. For now, he'd play dumb and wait for her to share her more personal details with him when she was ready. But having that info in his pocket was also a good way to see if she was truthful and trustworthy. Both were requirements, along with being reliable, to be a good CI. *If* she was willing to cooperate.

He was about to give her her first test since he knew the answer before asking the question. "So tell me, what does MJ stand for?"

"They're my initials."

He released a low chuckle. "I figured that, but that

doesn't answer my question. You don't have to tell me if you're uncomfortable." By not pressuring her and giving her an "out" when it came to getting in the car with him or answering any personal questions, he was trying to build a foundation of trust between them. He not only had to trust her, but he wanted her to trust him, as well.

"I only used MJ at the club for the same reason the girls use stage names and you use the name Blaze. For safety and privacy, of course. I don't want any of the customers knowing my real name or hunting me down outside of work."

She pinned her lips together when the waitress brought their drinks and dropped off a basket of warm bread, then asked if they were ready to order. Mel ordered without even glancing at the menu while Finn ordered the soup of the day since he'd already filled his gut earlier at home with a fat, medium-rare steak and a loaded baked potato.

Once the waitress disappeared again, Finn's attention was pulled back to Mel when she grabbed a roll. After ripping it in two, steam rose from the center as she slathered some butter on both halves. Lifting a piece to her mouth, she said, "Melina Jensen. Outside of the club, I normally go by Mel," then her straight, white teeth sank into the soft roll.

He watched her lips as she chewed. A crumb got caught in the corner of her mouth and he once again curled his fingers into his palms tightly to prevent reaching across the table and sweeping it away with his thumb. He bit back a groan when her tongue darted out and the clinging crumb disappeared.

Jesus, he never wanted to be a crumb so badly in his life...

He cleared his throat and shook himself mentally so he could concentrate on their conversation. "Very smart. Should I call you Mel or Melina, then?"

"Mel's fine. Except when you're at the club Monday."

He watched her throat undulate as she took a sip of her iced tea. Fuck the freshly baked rolls, he wanted to taste her throat.

Concentrate, you idiot.

He forced himself to nod. "I have no problem keeping your secret as long as you keep mine."

"Of course. And I appreciate that. Us dancers have to stick together, right?"

"Right," he murmured as a smear of creamy butter was left behind on her bottom lip with her next bite.

Jesus fuck. His cock decided he wanted in on this conversation. Since when did sloppy eating become so fucking sexy?

Because if that was a thing, then all the shirts he owned with food stains meant he was eligible to win the spot for People Magazine's "most sexiest man alive."

He ripped the paper ring off the rolled-up napkin, dumped the utensils onto the table, and reached across the table to wipe her lip. If he allowed the butter to continue to cling there, he was going to launch himself across that fucking table and lick it off.

Again, he had enough marks on his face from his freckles alone, along with a couple of small scars from when he was a kid, he didn't need her handprint from a slap adding to them.

But when he sat back, he did notice her blue-green eyes flare. He showed her the napkin. "You had a smudge of butter..."

"Thanks, but you just could've told me."

"True, but what would be the fun in that?"

"First opening the doors for me, now this... You seem to be a real gentleman."

He snorted and rubbed his hands together. "Then my evil plan is working." And he was somehow pulling it off since no woman had ever mistakenly called him a gentleman.

"Your mother must have taught you manners."

"That's not all she taught me."

Her eyebrows rose. "Do tell."

Shit. He wanted to tell Mel about his mother being a dance instructor since she'd probably appreciate that fact, but he couldn't. She would ask questions, like the studio's name and where it was located. It might be simple small talk but he'd still have to give her false answers once he scrambled to come up with them.

If only he'd met her while he wasn't in the midst of being undercover... Especially in an undercover assignment trying to document the illegal activities of the new owners of her place of employment.

Suddenly the waitress was back, plunking down Mel's large grilled chicken salad and his soup, whatever it was. He never paid attention to what she announced as the soup of the day, he just ordered it.

He glanced down. Minestrone. He tried not to gag. Thank fuck he ate earlier.

He forced down the rising bile and unwrinkled his nose.

"You okay? You're the first person I know to like minestrone. I can't stand it."

"I should've ordered a salad." He needed to turn the conversation back to her and the club, not talk about the food. "So, do you plan on trying to stick it out at The Peach Pit now that the Demons have taken over?"

She swallowed another mouthful of salad. "Unfortunately, right now I have no choice but to stay."

"But you're considering other options."

"Of course. I've been looking elsewhere but well-paying jobs in my particular line of work are scarce. No surprise, right? Unfortunately, being a strip club manager is a pretty small niche and not quite the same as running a restaurant or a sports bar. I could do it but I'd rather not. Anyway... Here's a secret I haven't told many people... I've been saving to buy my own club."

The last part tumbled out quickly, like she didn't want to tell him and hoped he didn't pay attention to it. But he heard it and it definitely caught his attention. "Yeah? One like The Peach Pit?"

"Absolutely. Strip clubs can be a gold mine if managed properly. Some days I just want to walk out when Cookie doesn't show up because I'm exhausted. But then I dig deeper and stick it out because I tell myself it's more money to put aside for my dream."

"I've never met anyone who thought owning a strip club was their dream business."

She speared a piece of chicken with her fork and brought it to her lips. "Then you haven't talked to the right person."

His lips twitched. "Apparently, I'm talking to her now."

"The girls are loyal to me and I'm loyal to them. Luckily, they would go wherever I go. The secret—that really shouldn't be a secret—is treating them right. I'd love to own an upscale club with an upscale clientele where I could offer my employees benefits and maybe even tuition and childcare assistance. By treating them fairly and with respect, the turnover would be greatly reduced," she explained.

"I figured women stripped out of desperation. To make a quick buck."

"Some do, but not all. I didn't and ten years later I'm still at The Peach Pit."

"But you're no longer dancing on stage."

"I could if I had to."

"But you don't," he said more firmly.

"Right. I don't, but if I had to..."

Was she thinking about getting back on stage? "You said you only started dancing to put yourself through college."

By repeating what she told him the other night, he wanted to prove he'd been listening. It was one more way to build her trust.

"That's why I started but not why I stayed." She stabbed at a few chunks of lettuce dripping in vinaigrette. "Believe it or not, I loved stripping. I loved being on stage. I loved entertaining. I even loved interacting with the customers. When you're working for the right club and have a great manager, it doesn't feel like work. I consider pole dancing, whether for exercise or work, an art."

When she shoved the forkful in her mouth and chewed, he kept quiet, hoping she'd continue. He didn't want to sit across from her and keep lobbing questions like an interrogation. He wanted the conversation to be more organic due to showing interest in her and her career. That might lead to her sharing more details about the goings-on at The Peach Pit.

Tonight's goal was to get her comfortable and get her talking.

But once she swallowed her food and didn't continue, he was forced to ask, "What about your family? They didn't mind you working the stage to pay for your education?"

After taking a sip of her iced tea, she considered him over the rim of her glass for a moment. When she set it back down, she said, "I hid it from them for the first couple of years. I lied about where I worked and made excuses about how I could afford my courses. But those two years made it clear, I loved dancing and hated college. So, I never went back for what should've been my junior year. When my parents kept asking why I stopped taking classes, I finally told them the truth at Christmas dinner."

He couldn't imagine that scene... sitting around the

holiday table with family and informing your parents that you've dropped out of college to strip full-time. He was sure that went over well. "How old were you when you finally told them?"

"Twenty. At that point I'd already moved out because I knew my choices, for both my education and my career, wouldn't go over well."

"And it didn't."

She shook her head. "No. My parents are super conservative. That's why I held out telling them until I had my own place." She shrugged. "I figured they'd kick me out. I was right about how they'd react. After my confession and once the initial shock wore off, they treated me like a pariah. Especially since I decided to dance full-time and told them I planned on working toward opening my own club."

"A lofty goal at twenty." He was impressed that she had solid goals at that age. When he was twenty, he was more worried about getting laid and partying with his buddies than his future. He didn't even consider becoming a cop until his mother dug out pictures of her father wearing his uniform and all of his promotion photos.

Something as simple as a shoebox full of old photos had slammed the brakes on his aimless drifting and he turned hyper-focused on becoming a police officer just like his grandfather.

Some of it had to do with the pride his mother had shown when it came to her father and his successful career in law enforcement.

He had wanted to make her proud, too. His path at the time was not and he'd been determined to change it.

So, he understood the determination Mel had to sticking to her path. Others might find it humorous that her goal was to own a strip club. But a successful business was a successful business no matter what that business was.

As long as it was legal.

"Yes, it was lofty and still is, but I saw a glimpse of what I didn't want."

"Which was?" he asked.

"A typical nine-to-five, with rows of restrictive cubicles, time-sucking meetings, answering to the boss of a boss of a boss. You get the picture. Honestly, to me that life would've weighed me down like I was wearing heavy chains. Before the Demons took over The Peach Pit, I felt free and in charge of my own destiny. Even better, not forced to play office politics. Anyway, when I told my parents, I still held a sliver of hope they'd accept my life choices, but I wasn't surprised when they didn't. No matter what, I had to do what I thought was right for *my* future and happiness, not theirs. Or anyone else's."

"Did they cut you off?"

"Not completely. Not at first, anyway. They only had minimal interaction with me for years. Meaning, they only talked to me when it was absolutely important. Like when my grandparents passed. Or when my brother got married. When I became an aunt for the first time. They pushed me to the outer edge of their world and only threw me crumbs to keep me from totally starving. I guess that was one way to keep the door cracked open since they also made it clear many times that I'd be welcomed back home once I was done with my latest 'phase' of acting out."

"Acting out? You made a career choice."

"They don't see stripping or even managing a club as a career choice. They see it as an embarrassment."

He didn't miss the sadness that flashed over her face. There and gone in a split second. Maybe she could hide it on the surface, but he had a feeling being rejected by her parents cut her deep, even though she'd been prepared for it.

"You don't regret it?"

"I do and I don't. But I was aware I'd seal my fate with them once I got my sleeve." She lifted her tattooed arm. "And then my piercings."

She had a small gold ring in her right nostril and her ears were triple pierced. Two in each lobe and one at the top of both ears in the cartilage. Now he was wondering if she was pierced elsewhere.

And if she was, he was curious as to where.

Concentrate, idiot!

"And I really super-glued the lid on that coffin when I told them in no uncertain terms, for me, stripping wasn't a phase and I had nothing to be ashamed about. They, of course, strongly disagreed. I haven't talked to either them or my brother since. I expected to be frozen out by my parents but was surprised about my brother. It turns out he thinks I'd be a bad influence on his 'impressionable' daughters. Even though being body positive should be a good thing and not something bad." She grimaced and set her fork on her plate.

Oh yeah, her family's reaction and lack of acceptance still caused her pain. "Sorry they're like that."

"How about you? You never said what you do for your 'day job.'"

Fuck. "I work in security."

"Like a security guard?"

He'd go with that. "Yes. For a security company that assigns us wherever we're needed, whether it's an event or at a business. The shitty pay is why I was thankful when Nick decided to give me a shot at dancing. Especially without any prior experience."

"Well, you're really good at it. Amazing, in fact." She

pushed her almost empty salad plate to the edge of the table. "You should go out to Vegas and join one of those permanent all-male revue shows. I'd bet you'd rake it in. Especially being a redhead. You don't see too many of those in this business. True redheads, anyway. You'd be a unicorn. Plus, just think, no more cheap polyester uniforms and aluminum foil badges. I bet you don't even get to carry handcuffs or a gun."

If she only knew...

"My two-way radio makes me feel powerful."

That finally pulled a chuckle from her. "What about your parents? Siblings?"

"I'm an only child. My father had a massive stroke and died when he was only forty, so it's been only me and my mother for a long time. We're still close." None of what he just revealed was a lie.

"I'm sorry about your loss." She reached across the table and squeezed his hand. Unfortunately, she didn't linger. "Is your mother retired?"

"She..." *Shit.* "Yes."

He could tell her the truth later if it got to that point. Right now, he had to keep the details of the real Daniel Finnegan to himself.

It was time to refocus their conversation back on the club and the Demons before their time together ran out. He couldn't waste any moments since Monday night was the last valid excuse to go back into that club unless he decided Mel could work well with him and the task force. *And* if, more importantly, she'd agree to it.

"Enough about me. My life is boring. Do you think the Demons will replace you like they did your assistant manager?" *And will that force you back on stage?*

He'd love to see her dance, but he would hate to be in a crowd of men while she did it. Simply picturing her surrounded by horny men, especially if they acted like the women did with him on Monday night, already annoyed the fuck out of him.

And if they attempted to touch her, kiss her, lick her... *bite* her.

Jesus, he'd end up behind bars himself.

He forced himself to unlock his jaw.

Concentrate, asshole. You have a job to do even though you'd rather just do her.

"Honestly, I don't put anything past them. Right now they're firing my best employees." She held up a hand and shook her head, her expression becoming sharp. "Right now they are making *me* fire great employees and substituting them with young bikers with zero work ethic or experience. And because these guys aren't getting paid, from what I understand, they don't give a shit about the small, but important, details. They're simply bodies filling spots."

The MC was digging their claws deeply into that business. The more of their own people they could get in there, the easier it would be to sell meth and launder that drug money without getting caught.

Chapter Ten

Danny's brow dipped low. "Who all have they fired and replaced?"

Did he truly care about what was happening with the club? Or was he only acting interested to get down her pants?

The man was gorgeous, sexy as hell and proved he could swivel his hips in a way that left no doubt he wouldn't be wooden in bed. Plus, so far, he'd been nothing but a gentleman. He didn't need to fake any interest in her job to convince her to drop her panties.

Not that she was planning on doing that tonight. Her thong would stay right where it was.

"Anyone not a dancer. The latest on the hit list were my best bartender and one of my weekend bouncers. They were both reliable and honest, unlike the prospects taking their place. That's one of many reasons I'm frustrated and, even as burnt out as I am, why I still worked last Monday and will work again this Monday. Not to mention, why I bite my damn tongue whenever I'm forced to work a double because Cookie doesn't show up. Unfortunately, I need that damn job too much right now. The only positive out of all the negatives is I can squirrel away the extra money I'm making." At least she was still being paid for all that overtime. But the second she was shorted...

"For your own club."

"Yes. That goal is what's keeping me motivated right now. I normally try to be a positive person but they are making me bitter and full of hate. I'm still pissed that they forced Laura out, then without even a lick of experience in this business, they came in and took over. They want to run The Peach Pit the way *they* wanted to run it. They disregard my suggestions, even though I'm the one with all the experience. None of it makes sense to me since a well-run club in the right location should be a cash cow, but it's like they don't care if the club makes money or not. Why would they want to buy a successful business and run it into the ground?"

The whole situation was just off. When the Demons first took over, she asked both Taint and Cookie about their plans for the club and their only answer was "to make money."

No shit. Who owned a business with the intent to lose money? No one with any common sense. Though, she couldn't argue that both Cookie and Taint were lacking sense.

"Do you think they could be using the club as some sort of front? I would think most MCs are considered criminal organizations similar to the mafia. I mean, I don't know much about them but... Have you *seen* any illegal activity?"

"Besides intimidation?" Mel only had proof of what they did to Laura, anything else she didn't. As of now, she only had suspicions.

His head tipped to the side like a curious Irish Setter puppy. "Intimidation?"

"I never talk about this at the club—for good reason—but

the Demons forced Laura to sell. They started out by trying to get her to pay for protection. When she refused, they made her life a living hell. They demanded she either pay for protection or sell the place to them. Honestly, I think forcing her to sell was the only end goal, not providing protection. Eventually, she had no choice because the threats weren't only against the club, they began to threaten her and her family, too. She kept finding windows broken, both at the club and her home. One night she found a brick with a note thrown through her windshield. Another night she found her tires slashed. And those are just some of the many things they did."

"Did they come out and admit they did those things? Did she confront them?"

"She was not a doormat. The woman was fierce, so she confronted them every damn time. And every damn time they said it wasn't them and tried to convince her that by paying for protection, those threats would stop. Of course, the cost for that so-called protection was more than she could afford. On purpose. Then they so *kindly* offered to take the club off her hands so she could move somewhere safer. That's what she finally did to protect her family because they left her no damn choice. She almost had a mental breakdown from it all." Both her blood pressure and anger spiked just from talking about it and she pressed her trembling hands to the Formica table top.

"But despite all that, you stayed."

"Laura put up a good fight and I don't blame her one bit for finally giving in, but at least she had her husband to fill in the financial gaps until she figured out what to do next. I don't have that safety net, so I couldn't, and still can't, just walk away. I decided to stay and take as much money from them as possible so when I finally leave, it's on my terms."

"Unless they fire you first."

She tipped her head. "And that could very well happen. But if they do, they will not only lose my expertise, they will also lose almost every one of the dancers. For the most part we're a united front. If I'm fired, they will walk out and never come back."

"Are the Demons aware of that?"

"I haven't said anything, but I think some of the girls warned Saint he'd lose his workforce if they lost me. That's most likely why he's slowly replacing the rest of the staff first."

"What about your hostess?"

"I wouldn't be surprised if they pull Sapphire from that position and force her back on stage full-time. It's a shame really, since she's such a good hostess. She knows how to work the floor and does it like a pro. She's good at getting our customers to part with their cash. She can coax a drunk into a car service without a fight. Saint knows Phire and I make a great team and that we keep the club running smoothly, but that doesn't mean he won't eventually replace us both with his own people."

His brow furrowed. "Why would he want to do that? Especially if they don't have the experience that you and the rest of the employees do."

"I have my suspicions." But like everything else, it was safer to keep them to herself. She didn't want to get on Taint's bad side. She had no doubt the biker could get violent. She'd already seen him lose his temper with both customers and the prospects.

He was a walking, talking lit fuse and it didn't take much for him to explode.

"What are your suspicions?" He reached across the table and peeled her hand from the table top to give it a reassuring squeeze. "Do you think they're up to something illegal? Are they doing something that law enforcement should be aware of?"

"My gut instinct says yes. But I'm afraid if the cops find out about whatever it is, they'll shut the whole club down. It's more than only me I have to worry about. It's the girls, too. They depend on dancing to pay their bills and support their families. To pay for their education. Whether some in society agree with it or not, dancing on stage is a job just like any other. It's a legal source of income and they would lose that."

"But if the MC is using the club as a front for illegal activities, that alone could shut the business down. It doesn't matter how well the club is being run. It doesn't matter how much the club is making if it's dirty money."

He was right. But what could she do about it?

Before she could respond, he continued with his voice low and soothing. "Look, I'm an outsider so don't be afraid to talk about whatever it is with me. You can trust me to not share anything you tell me with any of those Demons."

She should pull her hand out from under his because she was distracted by the way his thumb was brushing back and forth over the back of her hand. "I don't know you."

"But you know I'm not one of them. If you need to unload in a safe space, consider me that safe space."

"Again, I don't know you, but I *do* know they're dangerous. That's why I'm careful of what I say when I'm at the club or even in the parking lot. I never know where they are, what they're seeing or listening to. I don't want to be their next target."

His spine snapped straight and he sat back on his side of the booth. "Mel..."

She pulled her hand from his and dropped it into her lap

so she could concentrate. "I'll be fine as long as I don't ruffle any Demon feathers."

"But what if they're doing illegal things and you get caught up in it?"

"I'm going to do my best to avoid that." Mel had no desire to be a part of any illegal activities. None whatsoever. So far, she'd turned a blind eye to anything suspicious as long as it didn't hurt her or her girls. She was only biding her time until she could get out.

But that didn't mean she wasn't worried about blowback from the shit they were doing.

"What if you could do something about them?" he asked. "What if you had the opportunity to find out what they're doing and why they bought the business, beyond the obvious reason, would you?"

Where was he going with this? "For what reason?"

"To get rid of them."

"Like they did with Laura? Hold it over their heads until they're forced to abandon the business?"

"No. I mean... Maybe call a crime tip line or report them somehow with whatever info you have."

She'd have no problem snitching on them if she had solid proof.

She suspected they bought The Peach Pit to use as a base to sell drugs and possibly launder cash. But how was she going to prove that? Worse, what if she was wrong and the Demons found out she was snooping? Or worse, calling in tips to police hotlines?

It could be catastrophic.

"Think about it."

"That's a risk I'm not sure I'm willing to take." She was done talking about the Demons. They had already taken over almost every waking moment of her life. She hadn't planned on talking about them over dinner. Her intention tonight was to forget her job for an hour or so and enjoy the company of the man across from her. It was time to change the subject before she regretted texting him. "You haven't touched your soup. Weren't you hungry?"

"I already ate."

She had been surprised when he'd only ordered a bowl of soup but figured he was on a strict diet to keep his physique for stripping. "Oh, you should've said something. We could've gone to dinner another night."

His hazel eyes locked with hers. "Mel, it was never about the food."

"You have a lot of interest in the club," she murmured, ignoring the implication beyond the words that came out of his mouth.

He shook his head. "No, I have a lot of interest in *you*. Your life just seems to revolve around the club."

He wasn't wrong.

When the waitress came to clear the table and ask if they needed anything else, she broke the invisible hold between them. Before the server could even place the check down, Danny grabbed it and immediately dug out his wallet.

"I can pay for mine. You don't have to pay for the whole bill. You didn't even eat." She never let a man pay for her meal. When they did, they tended to expect something more than just company in exchange.

"Again, it wasn't about the food, Mel."

It wasn't only about the food for her, either.

If only the topic of conversation hadn't been a stomach-churning one. She would have liked to learn more about him than simply discuss herself and her problems. Right now her salad wasn't sitting well.

She met his warm hazel eyes across the table. "Thank you for keeping me company while I ate."

"It was a pleasure. And I'd love to do it again."

So would she.

He ended up paying the bill, despite her resistance again at the cash register, and they headed out. Not five minutes later they were back in the rear lot at the club.

His deep voice filled the Kia. "Are you going back in, or going home?"

"Home. I don't want to go in and give Cookie a reason to leave, then I'll be stuck working another late night. I really need a break and a good night's sleep."

Before he could get out and open her door for her, she did it herself. She leaned back in and said, "Thank you for dinner. See you Monday night, *Blaze*."

His sexy smile lit up the dark interior. "See you Monday night, *MJ*."

He sat in his Kia while she got into her Chevy and he didn't leave until she did.

Everything about him seemed a bit too perfect. And while she was interested, that worried her.

She was already dealing with enough problems from the Demons. She didn't need another headache in her life.

Even a gorgeous redhead she'd like to see dance horizontally.

———

"Yo!" Finn called out to Crew as soon as the DEA agent walked into church. He slipped his mirrored sunglasses off his face and tucked them into the neckline of the Henley he wore under his leather BAMC cut.

Anyone available for today's club run was gathering

downstairs at The Plant. He had sent out the invite by text and they were still waiting on a couple of members. Once everyone arrived, they'd head out with Finn, the club's road captain, leading the formation.

Crew approached him. "What's up?"

"Need to run something past you."

His gray eyes narrowed. "About?"

"Me being undercover."

Crew shook his head. "I already know you fucking hate being a Pecker. Don't need to hear you bitching about it again. Sometimes you're worse than my fucking ex-wife."

Finn sighed. "Not about that."

Crew cocked an eyebrow. "Then, what?"

Finn tipped his head toward the nearby meeting room.

Crew considered him for a full second before nodding. "Got it. Let's go." The task force leader followed him into the room where the executive committee met and closed the door behind them. "I assume this is about the Demons. Talk to me."

"I had dinner with the club's manager last night. Tried to take her temperature on what might be going down behind the scenes at The Peach Pit."

"And? Did she witness shit?"

"I think so, but she held back on giving me any details. I tried to get her to open up about it, but she's worried about speaking out because she knows those Demons are dangerous. Especially after they only got their grimy hands on that club after harassing and intimidating the previous owner. They pushed her out using threats and acts of violence by slashing her tires, breaking windows and who knows what else. I wouldn't put anything past those motherfuckers."

With one hand on his hip, Crew dropped his head and shook it. "Damn."

"Yeah. So, no surprise that Mel's being extra cautious."

Crew's grim expression disappeared and his lips twitched. "Mel, huh?"

Finn purposely ignored his smart-ass tone. Instead, he pointed out, "I noted any info I found on her, including her full name, in my daily report. If you'd read yesterday's, you would've seen she normally goes by Mel, except for at the club where she uses MJ to protect her privacy."

"I'll check it out." His amusement quickly disappeared. "What do you think? Do you want to approach her with the opportunity? More importantly, do you think she'd be open to helping us?"

"I think if I can talk her into it, she'd be a huge asset. It also sounds like she could also use the CI pay. That might help convince her."

"Do you think she's trustworthy?"

He didn't know her that well—yet, anyway—but... "I actually do. She might not like talking about them but she made it clear she hates them. She hates how they're driving the club into the ground and also how they treated Laura, the former owner she was close with. Mel seems to have plenty of motivation to help get rid of them."

"Like?"

Finn shrugged. "In addition to what I just stated, loyalty to the club and her employees. She's been there ten damn years."

"Ten years? As the manager?"

No surprise that Crew had the same reaction as him. Neither figured that working at a strip club was a long-term career choice. "First five as a stripper before the former owner moved her into management. Once she became manager, she retired from the stage."

"She knows the club well, then," Crew concluded.

"She has a close relationship with and is protective of the dancers, too. That could also be to our benefit."

Crew ground his hand against the back of his neck as he considered Finn's proposition. "When would you ask her?"

"If you give it the green light, tomorrow night after the show."

He pursed his lips and tilted his head. Finn waited for smoke to start billowing from Crew's ears. But he got it. As the task force leader Crew had to carefully consider every move the group made before making it. One wrong move or decision could blow the entire investigation.

If that happened, his neck would be on the line. Especially when it came to an investigation involving three large criminal organizations: a Mexican drug cartel, an outlaw MC and the Sicilian Mafia.

Crew finally said, "You'll have to out yourself."

And that could be a risk. "Right. But will it matter? I'll be done with the Peckers after tomorrow night either way." At least he sure hoped tomorrow night would be his last night dancing.

"It won't matter as long as she doesn't run her mouth after you reveal who you are. But it's not definite about your dancing days being over. It'll hinge on her cooperation."

For fuck's sake. "They don't have any more shows scheduled at The Peach Pit."

"But if she says no to helping us and doesn't blow your cover, you might have to convince her to book the Peckers for more shows."

Great. That was reason enough to work extra hard on convincing her. "I'll do that, if needed." *But not willingly.* "However, if she agrees, make sure her CI pay is decent. She's saving up to buy her own club."

"Damn. The woman's got ambitions. If she can wait it

out, she might be able to buy The Peach Pit in a fire sale once we're done with shutting down the Demons."

"*If* she can wait it out. I'll mention that possibility to her since that might be more motivation to assist us. If it was me, I'd prefer that option rather than starting from scratch. I'll play that up since she knows that strip club inside and out. She loves her work. She might even be able to rehire the employees that the Demons are firing and replacing with their own prospects."

"Sounds like they're doubling down by getting rid of outsiders."

"No shit. I expect that more prospects means more dealing for them and more money in their pockets."

Crew let out a loud hoot. "They're not going to start having their ol' ladies and sweet butts dancing on stage, are they? Because I've seen some pics of their women. That will draw a crowd but not the right kind."

Finn smirked. "Let's just say that the dancers I saw working there are hot as fuck. If they replace them with their own women, it'll turn the club into what could be any typical one-percenter biker bar."

"Like the Hawg Wild Saloon." Crew chuckled. "You saw some of the footage that Fletch got from there, didn't you?"

"Yeah. Saw the photos and video. Not my scene."

"It's not Fletch and Wilder's scene, either." He lifted his eyebrows. "But we're part of a team and we all have to pull our weight. No matter what the assignment."

True that. "So, do I have your approval?"

"Yeah. You approach her and I'll approach my supervisor on getting her on the books for providing info."

Finn nodded. He now needed to formulate a plan on how to approach her with this idea. He preferred to ease her into it instead of simply throwing it at her feet and hoping she'd agree.

Crew interrupted his thoughts. "We ready to ride?"

"Not yet. I've got one more thing to run by you first."

"I already said that if she agrees with becoming a CI, you can stop dancing with the Peckers."

"No shit. That isn't it. I have another idea."

"Then spill it so we can get the fuck out of here."

"I've been thinking about this since last night's dinner... I'm going to propose—"

"Already? Congrats!" Crew yelled. "You move quick!"

Finn grimaced. "You're such an asshole."

"I assume you repeat that to yourself every time you look in the mirror?"

"I'm pretty fucking sure your ex was repeating that when she cut your head out of all your wedding pictures." He blew out a breath. "*Anyway,* I figured out a way to keep me behind the scenes at the club without having to get on stage." And getting naked and pawed by a bunch of rabid women.

Crew was still smirking when he asked, "How?"

"When I run the CI opportunity by her, I'm also going to ask if she'd act like we're seeing each other."

"Wait... You mean like playing her boyfriend?"

Fuck, he could already see Crew's mind turning. "Yeah. It'll give me a reason to visit her at the club, and also a reason to hang out there and observe. But the best part is it'll give me access to the employee area to possibly witness any backdoor dealings myself."

Crew slapped his palm against the front of Finn's cut. "Well, damn, there might be something in that pretty little head of yours after all. I always thought you were all looks and no brains. But by you asking her to go steady and giving her your class ring, are you hoping to have a real shot with her?"

Like Finn would admit that to the expert ball-buster. He knew better. "Simply being a team player, that's all."

Crew burst out laughing. "Uh huh. I know you too well, you horny fucker. Look at you trying to snag some... *perks*." He turned serious. "But you know you can't fuck with a CI, brother."

"I don't plan on fucking with her."

"Let me rephrase... You shouldn't fuck a CI if you're her handler, Finn. That could make any possible testimony suspect. The defense attorneys would just fucking *love* to sink their teeth into any inappropriate conduct that occurred during the investigation."

"She doesn't have to report to me."

Crew's eyebrows rose. "Damn, brother, so you *do* want a piece of her."

Finn shrugged. "Right now, I'm just going to try to get her to be a CI and for me to be her fake boyfriend, then we'll go from there. If it gets sticky, we'll pivot."

"Pivot," the task force leader repeated, dropping his chin to his chest and shooting Finn a look. "If there's a possibility that you two might become horizontal dance partners, I don't want you managing her at all. Unless you don't mind putting *everything* you do in the daily reports. Down to the last detail."

Right. "Let me get her to agree first, then we can revisit this. If she agrees to pretend she's my girlfriend, we can have you or someone else on the team be her handler, if you think that will keep things neater."

"Sounds like you *are* interested," he grinned, "*and* you think you can get her."

"I'm not thinking anything except ahead. I'm only considering possibilities."

"Speaking of possibilities, do you think the Demons, especially that Saint dirtbag, will have a problem with you hanging out there? Do you think it'll throw any red flags?" the task force leader asked.

"It could," Finn answered truthfully, "but I plan on playing a very possessive boyfriend. I could act like an over the top jealous motherfucker and pretend I hate her working in a strip club."

"But she's not working the stage."

"No, but even as the manager, she's on the floor and surrounded by a bunch of horny men almost every night. Any insecure narcissist isn't going to like that. That shit would eat away at his psyche. I don't think Saint's ready to replace her, so they might tolerate me hanging around and 'watching' my woman just to keep her working there."

"True." He stroked the wiry gray hairs on his chin. "If you can pull it off, that may work. It could also fucking backfire. Either way, she'd have to agree to all of that first. One thing you neglected to mention... her relationship status. No *real* living, breathing, jealous boyfriend will come out of the woodwork and fuck up your plan?"

"If she wasn't single, I wouldn't have taken her out to dinner."

Crew huffed out a laugh. "Bullshit. I've known you for years now, Ginger Snap. I bet you didn't even ask."

Fuck. He didn't. He only assumed, figuring she would've shot him down about dinner if she was. "Here's another option... If she says no to either proposal, I can go in as a regular customer."

"Yeah, but even regulars don't go in that often, do they?

Even if you go into the club every few days, it'll delay getting the info we need. I don't want the evidence gathering on this portion of the investigation to be dragged out. There's no reason for it and I might need you elsewhere. If she says no to the CI gig, then at least try to convince her to do the fake relationship bit. Make sure she knows it'll benefit her, too. Though, I can't imagine you being anyone's boyfriend would be a benefit."

"You mean like the benefit your wife got by divorcing your ass?"

Crew frowned. "Ex-wife."

"Whether she agrees with the plan or not, we should consider sending in some of the TFOs into The Peach Pit as customers, anyway."

"I'll add that location into the rotation like the pizza shop, Hawg Wild and the rest of the businesses the Demons are buying up. But doing it that way is such fucking hit and miss, especially since they're not dealing the meth out in the open."

"True. But it's easy to hang out in a strip club for hours at a time to observe. Unlike a pizza shop."

"Agreed and more eyes can't hurt. All right... Report back to me after tomorrow night with the results. I just hope she doesn't blow your cover after you tell her who you are."

"I don't think she will."

"You don't know her, brother."

Funny, that was what Mel said to him last night at dinner.

"Your gut instinct will only take you so far," Crew reminded him even though Finn was well aware of that fact.

"I'll make sure to spend as much time with her tomorrow night as I can between sets and after the show. If I get any kind of off feeling about her, I'll scrap the idea."

"Sounds like a plan."

Crew opened the door and Finn followed him out into

the common area. After a quick visual sweep of the first floor, he saw everyone he was expecting to show up was now gathered.

"C'mon," Finn called out to catch everyone's attention. "Let's go mount up. I want to be back here before the Steelers game later."

"About fucking time. We were waiting on you two assholes. Were you diddling each other in there?" Rez asked, making some kind of obscene hand gestures that didn't make sense to Finn and it wasn't worth asking.

"Aww. Were you feeling left out, dickhead?" Crew asked Rez, then he turned to Axel Jamison. "Do we have enough beer and chips and shit for the game?"

"I don't know about you but I don't plan on eating shit. As for junk food, we should have plenty," the BAMC president answered. "I gave Nox money out of the club account to stock up. Plus, some of the guys on the task force keep bringing beer and booze whenever they use this space to hang out."

"Good." Crew nudged Finn with his elbow. "Better cover that flaming hair, Pippi Longstocking. Especially right now while you're undercover as a Pecker. Once you're clear of that assignment, it won't matter who sees your ugly mug and fiery mess on your head and face."

Finn noticed he didn't mention the rest of what they talked about when it came to his assignment. He most likely would bring it up to the task force members if and when it got the green light.

"I'm already ahead of you on that." Finn headed over to the counter where he'd left his stuff earlier and slid on dark wraparound sunglasses, tied a black bandana around his lower face and covered his hair with a black leather skullcap to disguise his very recognizable features. He turned to Crew and held his arms straight out from his sides. "Do I look anonymous enough, Motley Crew? I've been wearing this or a full-face helmet whenever I'm on my bike, whether wearing my cut or not. I definitely don't want this assignment cutting into my riding time."

"Well then... Let's fucking ride!" Decker yelled as he passed Finn and whacked him hard on the back. "Like Rezavoir Dog said, we've been waiting on you two fuckers."

"Let's fucking ride!" Finn repeated in a shout, leading the way.

Chapter Eleven

IT WAS THE SAME SONGS, same outfits and same dance routines as last week. But none of that made it any less freaking hot.

Mel's eyes were glued to the stage the second the dancers ran out and started the opening act. Even though there were eight of them, she mainly focused on one as he moved around the stage, nailing the choreography and expertly "flirting" with the women closest to the stage.

Tonight was another sold-out show. Every seat was full. The noise level in the club had become deafening between the Peckers' DJ and the women making every noise known to humankind. Crumpled balls of cash also rained onto the stage.

If she owned the club, she would put the Peckers on a regular rotation since, apparently, there was plenty of interest.

She was thankful a few of her dancers were willing to work the floor tonight as servers and also to help behind the bar since her new "bartender," a Demon prospect, was not only overwhelmed, but just about useless.

No "just about" about it. His skills were limited to using the beverage gun to fill glasses with pop or water and using a bottle opener to pop off bottle caps. When it came to the moneymakers, like the mixed drinks the ladies in the audience loved so much, he floundered. Big time.

And right now, this crowd was fresh and had fistfuls of cash so they were quite demanding when it came to getting their drink on.

She could help with the basic stuff but, like the prospect, she had zero skills in mixology. That was the reason why Taint firing her best and most experienced bartender had been a major hit for the club.

She had to remind herself over and over that the business's profits weren't going into her pocket, so she needed to stop stressing over it. As long as she was getting paid for her overtime tonight, that should be all that mattered.

It *should* be all that mattered.

But still... She hoped the club stayed afloat until she was ready to leave and was able to take the rest of the employees with her.

She sighed in frustration.

Then she sighed again in sexual frustration as Danny began removing the final pieces of the construction crew outfit they all wore for the first routine. She thumbed away the saliva caught at the corner of her lips.

Damn, that man could move his hips! And when he popped them...

Her core clenched tight.

Her reactions only reminded her that her sex life had been sorely lacking lately and getting some sexual relief was long overdue. Now she just needed to find the right man to do it with.

Maybe one with blazing red hair, expressive hazel eyes, *sexy-as-hell* freckles and a panty-melting smile.

One Danny "Blaze" O'Neill.

Since she had a strict "no customer rule," it was a good thing Danny wasn't a customer.

She squeezed her thighs together as he dropped to the stage in sync with the rest of the dancers. With one hand on his hip and the other holding up his weight, he smoothly rolled his body, humping the floor over and over.

Had someone screwed with the thermostat in the club? She began to sweat as she imagined herself being that floor.

Luckily, she stood as far from the stage as she could get so he wouldn't see her drooling over him.

Sapphire sidled up to her wearing a black leather miniskirt, black thigh-high leather boots, and an overflowing black sequined bra-like top. "That idiot's in way over his head."

"Really? I think he's doing great."

Enough to make *her* panties wet. *If* she'd been wearing panties.

Sapphire snapped her fingers in front of Mel's face and clicked her tongue. "Not *him*, girl. The idiot behind the bar... Spot."

Mel reluctantly yanked her attention away from Danny and her brow furrowed. "Spot?"

Sapphire flipped a hand over her left shoulder toward the bar. "Spot. Fido. Whatever his stupid nickname is."

Mel bit back her laugh. "Mutt."

Sapphire rolled her bright blue eyes. "Mutt. He's useless no matter what his name is."

"You know it's out of my hands."

Phire squeezed Mel's bicep. "I know. It's not your fault. It's those assholes. I'm not sure how much more I can take, MJ."

"I get it. I'm at my limit, too, but we just need to hang on a little longer."

"How much longer?"

"I don't have nearly the amount of money needed to start a club, Phire, even if I manage to get a business loan. You know that. If I did, I would've left when Laura did."

"If those assholes replace my hostess spot with a prospect, I may be forced back on stage."

"Same. And I thought those days were over." Wearing three-inch stilettos almost every night was bad enough but dancing in six-inch platforms? Mel groaned and dread filled her chest at that possibility.

"The tips were great, but..."

"You know how to charm the men, so you still get tipped well as a hostess," Mel finished for her.

"Yes. And the best part is I don't have to work as hard."

"Or get naked." Mel sighed. "I'm sorry. I know you're staying for me."

"And I know you're staying for the girls," Sapphire countered.

"I'll try to talk to Taint again."

Her long, dark brown hair swept across her shoulders when the club's hostess shook her head. "He doesn't give a shit. You'll be wasting your breath."

"I know, but I hate this feeling of helplessness. It might not do any good but in my heart I'll know I at least tried."

Phire gave her a quick hug. "I'll go help the girls take drink orders and then make sure that Muttly is making them correctly."

"I'll keep an eye on him, too," she murmured and

watched her hostess snake her way through the packed tables, stopping along the way to collect empty glasses and take drink orders.

Mel turned back to the stage just as the Peckers finished their opening dance and filed off the stage—no longer wearing anything but jockstraps—to go change for their solo routines.

Mel decided now was a good time to head over to the bar to check on Mutt's malfunction and make sure he was referencing the Bartender's Bible she'd given him. Not that it was helping...

Mel didn't think anything would help except to rehire her former bartender.

Her step stuttered and she almost stumbled on her heels when she noticed three large men stuffed around a small table in the back corner. They were tipping back bottles of beer and seemed to be joking around since they were elbowing each other and laughing.

While she liked her customers to enjoy themselves, she didn't want any of the Peckers to feel uncomfortable, especially if the trio was making fun of them.

She hadn't been aware that any men bought tickets for tonight's special event. They *could* be gay or bi or... simply assholes.

She was determined to find out.

She detoured from her trek to the bar and, instead, headed in that direction to make sure they weren't there to make trouble. If they were, she'd have them escorted out and refund their tickets.

It didn't matter if the dancers were men or women, she didn't want anyone on her stage heckled or harassed. Or made fun of. If they wanted laughs, plenty of comedy clubs could be found around the greater Pittsburgh area.

She stopped in front of their table and faced them, slapping on her best customer service smile. "How are things tonight, gentlemen?"

All six eyeballs took a slow roll down her body from hair to heels. Their action was nothing out of the ordinary, since working at a strip club, it came with the territory.

With a smirk, the one with the most severe haircut and broadest shoulders answered, "Eye opening."

Her gaze sliced over all three. "Are you enjoying your evening?"

"The evening just got better." The man sitting in the middle, with dark hair and just as dark eyes, pushed out an empty chair from under the table by using his foot.

She pushed it back in so it wouldn't block anyone's path. "While I appreciate the offer, I have to politely decline since I'm working."

A mature-looking man with salt-and-pepper hair and a matching beard sat to the left of the other two. "Are you the manager?"

"Yes."

All three of them were not only very handsome, but pretty damn hot. Even sitting down, it was hard to miss that they were in really good shape. Maybe they were part of the Peckers team and only came for support.

"Are you gentlemen enjoying the show so far?" The music and lighting changed, an indication that a dancer was taking the stage behind her to do his solo routine.

She shifted out of their way. "I'm sorry if I'm blocking your view."

"We're not here for the view."

"Then, I'm sorry if you thought it would be women dancing tonight. I can refund your tickets if you'd like. Here at The Peach Pit we only want you to have the best experience."

The muscular guy to the far right dropped his head and snorted.

Mr. Salt-and-Pepper's grin got wider. "We know who was scheduled to dance tonight. No need for a refund."

Well then...

"It's not an issue that we're here, is it? I didn't see anything limiting the show to women only. Did we miss the small print?"

Her mouth opened. Nick, the manager of the all-male revue, never said men couldn't buy tickets. And there were plenty of nights where women came in to watch the girls dance. No one had a problem with it and sometimes they could be the best tippers.

She couldn't discriminate as long as someone wasn't there with ill intentions. "There aren't any restrictions. You're welcome to stay." *As long as you behave*, she added silently.

The darker complected hunk, sitting in the middle of the man-meat sandwich stated, "You think it's strange that we're here tonight."

"No, I just want to make sure everyone is comfortable. That's all."

Mr. S & P nodded, amusement deepening the lines at the corners of his eyes. "We're only here to support Blaze. He's a good friend of ours."

Ah, so they did know one of the dancers. That was a relief. "That's wonderful. I'm sure he could use the support since he's new to dancing. Although, to watch him you'd never know it. He definitely has the right moves."

Mr. Broad Shoulders snorted again while a burst of laughter came from Mr. Dark Eyes.

"He's very dedicated to pleasing the ladies," Mr. S & P said with a smirk.

She ignored the sexual innuendo. "He did a great job doing so last week and I'm sure he'll do the same tonight." She pulled in a long breath. "Well, gentlemen, I'll leave you to enjoy the rest of your night. I'm MJ, by the way. I'll be around, so if you need anything, just ask."

Mr. S & P tipped his head and blinded her with his smile. "Great to meet you, MJ. And thank you."

She gave them a nod and headed toward the not as handsome or hot Mutt. The prospect sure didn't smell as good as that testosterone rich trio, either.

For the rest of the show, Mel ended up staying behind the bar with Mutt to make sure he wasn't screwing up the drink orders too badly. While there, she kept her eyes scanning both the floor and the stage to make sure the event was going smoothly.

Occasionally, her gaze would land on the back table to make sure Danny's three friends were behaving themselves.

She sipped at a rum and Coke she made for herself while dancer after dancer took their turn on stage, did their sexy routine and then disappeared backstage once finished. Like last week, Blaze was the last dancer to do his individual routines.

Also like last week, he nailed it. And, of course, just like last week, the women went wild and tipped him well.

She watched him carefully to see if he acknowledged his friends' attendance in any way, but he never looked once in their direction. She assumed he didn't know they were there, even though, from where she was behind the bar, it was hard to miss them hooting and hollering the whole time Blaze performed his routines.

By the time those deep voices reached the stage, they

most likely got lost in the sea of high-pitched squeals, screams and shrieks.

Maybe it was better he didn't know. That could affect his performance.

When Mel first started dancing, some guys she graduated with from high school came into The Peach Pit. They were just as surprised to see her as she them. Unfortunately, she ended up being more self-conscious about dancing that night than ever before. Getting naked in front of strangers or regular customers was one thing, friends, family or classmates was quite another.

She was relieved none of them had requested a private lap dance. If they had, she most likely would've quit on the spot so she wouldn't die from embarrassment.

The more time she spent on stage and the more experienced she became, the less she cared about who watched. More importantly, learning to give zero fucks about judgmental people was freeing.

After the Peckers' final group routine, she waited a bit to give the guys enough time to get dressed before worming her way through the throng of women leaving. She wanted to check in with Nick before the manager left for the night and maybe even have a few words with Danny.

But before she could reach her destination, he appeared out on the floor already dressed. She might not have spotted him at all if he didn't stand head and shoulders taller than most of the women completely circling him and clamoring for his attention.

He had the same type of smile plastered onto his face that she wore when she talked to his friends.

She stood out of the way and waited patiently for him to finish interacting with the women but as he was chatting, his eyes scanned the room and landed on the back corner table where his friends still sat. Since the lights had been turned up and the crowd had thinned, it was now easier for him to see them.

The manufactured customer service smile he'd been wearing while dealing with his "fans" turned into a very real grimace. Then she heard boisterous laughter coming from their table.

She decided to save him from the thirsty women and approached the pack.

"Thank you for coming tonight, ladies. Keep an eye on our website for future shows." She jutted her hand above her head and waved Sapphire over. "Sapphire will see you out. I hope you enjoyed the show and please be careful heading home."

Sapphire came over, rounded them up and herded them toward the exit, even though it took some strong prodding.

When it was finally only the two of them, she announced, "Your friends are here," as if he wasn't already aware.

"Yeah, I see that," he mumbled with a frown now turning down the corners of his lips and creasing his brow.

"I assume you didn't know they were coming."

"I... did... not," he drew out, shooting a glare across the club to his friends' table.

Taking a quick glance over her shoulder, she noticed the three men grinning and waving at Danny. The one in the middle even blew him a kiss.

It didn't seem as if they were in any rush to leave their seats. No, they were kicked back and waiting on the man himself.

When she turned back to Danny, she found him not staring at his friends, but her instead. "Do you want me to have them removed?"

He sighed. "No. While that would serve them right, I'll handle it."

She rolled her lips under at the resignation in his voice, proving his friends weren't there for support but to bust his balls. "All right, then. Once I have a few words with Nick, I'll start shutting things down for the night so I can get out of here as soon as everyone is gone."

"I'll make sure they leave here in a few."

She nodded. "I want to thank you again for dinner the other night. It was nice."

His jaw shifted and he glanced down at her, his face far too serious. "Hey, can you stick around after? I'd like to talk to you about something."

"What?"

He shook his head. "I can't talk about it here..."

Well, damn. It didn't sound like it would be another dinner invitation.

When he continued, he lowered his voice even further. "For the same reasons you don't want to bring up certain subjects in the club. After I deal with those assholes, we can talk."

"Where?"

"Where's a safe place to go?"

"The diner?"

He shook his head. "No. Not in public."

Her heart began to thump heavily. She had no idea what it could be about, especially since he was worried about being overheard. She assumed by the Demons.

A shiver slithered down her spine.

That couldn't be good.

Chapter Twelve

"I JUST NEED a few minutes of your time," he murmured, his attention caught on the tiny mole right above the left side of her upper lip. It was sexy as fuck and he had the crazy urge to taste it.

"Okay," she whispered with her brow furrowed.

Her eye color kept him guessing. One second they appeared blue, the next a light green. The color combination reminded him of the ebb and flow of the Caribbean Sea.

A surf he could easily drown in.

"How about once you're done with your friends, I meet you backstage? We can decide then where to go for privacy."

As she talked, he picked up the sweet smell of her breath, most likely from whatever she'd been sipping while behind the bar. Of course he noticed her drinking because every minute he'd been on stage, his stupid ass kept track of her wherever she went in the large room.

The struggle had been real when it came to keeping his eyes off her and concentrating on his routines instead. She was the kind of woman to catch his attention and keep it. Not an easy feat.

It wasn't only the way she looked or even the way she dressed. It was also the way she moved. The way she spoke. The way she dealt with both the public and her employees.

All impressive and attention-worthy.

Her confidence only added to the mix. Especially how she didn't tuck tail and run when the Demons infiltrated her place of employment.

The MC wasn't chasing her out; she'd walk away when she was good and ready.

All of that turned him the fuck on.

Tonight, her blonde hair was pulled up, but not in any type of severe hairstyle. The style was soft and sexy with long, loose strands framing her face. Long sparkly earrings dangled from both lobes and the matching gem in her right nostril glinted whenever she moved under the club's lights.

Her deep green blouse seemed to be nothing more than a silk scarf draped around her neck and encasing her tits. Her exposed firm belly gave him—and everyone else, including his asshole club brothers—a view of a navel piercing, also the kind with dangling jewels.

Her skin-tight white pants left no doubt she wasn't wearing underwear. Her three-inch spiked heels matched the color of her blouse. If that scrap of fabric could even be called a blouse.

He was surprised his club brothers hadn't been all over her, especially since those three were horndogs.

"I'll be in the back," she announced, her nostrils slightly flared and a sparkle in her eyes.

Apparently, he hadn't been too stealthy when he checked her out up close and personal.

"I'll find you." He remained where he stood while watching Mel head backstage.

The back of her blouse was completely open, teasing him with the tempting line of her spine. Two thin gold chains crisscrossed her smooth skin to hold the drapey fabric together. Being a former stripper, she probably knew techniques to keep everything in place since she couldn't be wearing a bra, just like she wasn't wearing panties.

Finn pulled in a breath.

Maybe he should scratch the idea of becoming her "fake" boyfriend. There was nothing "fake" about what he wanted to do with her.

He shook those thoughts free and reluctantly turned his attention to the table in the far corner. Sucking in a bolstering breath, he donned invisible armor since he was damn sure he'd need it.

He was surprised any of them showed their faces tonight. Especially after the discussion with Crew about some of them coming into the club as regular customers. He wasn't sure how smart it was to create a tie between "Blaze" and Crew, Rez and Decker.

With a quick glance over at the bar, he noticed the prospect had already split, leaving Mel to clean up after him.

Fucking dick.

The prospects had no motivation to do their jobs, or do them well, since they couldn't be fired. That could and probably did put Mel in a bind and more stress on her shoulders as manager.

Other than Mutt, Finn hadn't seen Saint or any other Demons tonight. It was like those motherfuckers had left Mel to fend for herself. Besides the young prospect working the bar, she had to pull in Sapphire and some of her dancers to help out.

She had a lot of fucking patience to deal with the Demons and how they were running the club. A lot more patience than Finn would be able to muster.

Tonight his patience was lacking for another reason...

"I hate you motherfuckers," was the first thing out of his mouth when he stopped at their table.

Laughter burst from Crew. "How can you hate us when we came to support you?"

Finn snorted and shook his head. "Is that what you're calling it? Support? How the fuck did you get in here?"

Decker couldn't wipe the huge fucking smile off his face. Finn was willing to help. "We bought tickets, genius. How else?"

He inhaled deeply in an attempt to cool his annoyance.

Still chuckling, Crew said, "You were the one who suggested we come in as regular customers. So, here we are."

Here they were. "Not tonight, you asshole. When the women are on stage and when more Demons are in the house."

"Yeah well... Since you said your performance wasn't being recorded, we decided to come in and witness your skills for ourselves."

Thank fuck they didn't allow phones past the lobby.

"Don't you think you three showing up here is a bit obvious?"

Decker shrugged, wearing a shit-eating grin. "Men don't come to these things?"

"Maybe men like Cross," Finn answered. "Are the three of you sharing a closet? Do you need help coming out of it?"

"Did the fact that this club was a sea of horny women go over your red head? After you Peckers spin their dials all the way to ten, you leave those women hanging. If more men were smart, they'd buy tickets, too. It would be like shooting fish in a barrel," Decker said.

"Then, why are you still sitting here with these two dicks?" Finn asked him.

"We're working," Rez said.

"Yeah, right. Working on my last fucking nerve. You assholes need to go. MJ needs to close up."

All three rose to their feet and carefully extricated themselves from the tight back corner.

When Crew came around the table, he leaned into Finn and murmured, "You talk to her yet?"

Finn kept his own voice down, too. "No, told her I need to talk to her after I'm through dealing with you dicks."

"Was Saint here tonight? I didn't see him."

Finn's eyebrows rose. "Do you even know what he looks like?"

"I pinned a few of his mugshots up on our board at The Plant. I also have them on my phone to verify it's him, just in case he was here tonight."

"I can verify him the next time I'm at The Plant since you don't have your phone on you." Finn grinned.

"Or you could walk out to the lobby, since that's where my phone is being held hostage."

"I could, but you guys can see yourself out. I need to go talk to Mel. She's probably waiting and wants to get the fuck out of here since it's supposed to be her night off."

Crew didn't seem to be in any rush to leave. "I guess the Demons don't give a shit about wearing their colors here. The guy manning the bar was the only Demon present from what I could see. Did you see any in the back?"

"No. The bartender's a prospect named Mutt. However, since this isn't their normal clientele tonight, I didn't see him doing any deals. I'm not sure if he would be the one to do so, anyway."

"Are you saying you were actually watching for any suspicious activity? From where we sat, it looked like you were too busy paying attention to someone else who doesn't wear a cut. Though, I have no fucking complaints about what she was wearing."

Finn ignored his dig. "Do you have info on Mutt, yet?"

Crew shook his head. "Not yet. I'll get a file started, but I'll need a picture if you can snag one."

"I'll see what I can do. If Mel agrees with this arrangement, I'll get her approval to bring in a phone to take pics. I'll assure her that I won't take any of the girls or any customers, the whole reason for that rule." Finn blew out a breath. "At least there's one bright spot with you assholes showing up tonight. You can see firsthand that me dancing here isn't going to give us anything to work with. I think we'd see more sitting in the actual seats during normal business hours when more Demons are around."

"Maybe."

What the fuck. "No 'maybe' about it."

Rez blew him a kiss. "You just want to get out of wearing that cute-assed outfit. Your ass looked so damn *fiiiiine.*"

"I know I look damn good in that shit. I just don't want to waste my time or the task force's."

Crew grinned. "I'll take it into consideration."

"You're such a dick."

"I've been called much worse," the task force leader stated.

"No shit. By me."

"And me," Decker added.

"And definitely me." Rez elbowed Finn. "Who was the

chick with long dark hair and the awesome fucking tits wrapped up in leather and lace talking to your girl?"

Your girl. He mentally sighed. "Sapphire. She's the hostess. She works both the front lobby and the customers on the floor."

"Damn. She can work me over anytime. She do private lap dances?"

"How the fuck would I know? Ask her, not me. I'm not an employee here, remember?"

"Ask your future girlfriend."

"Future *fake* girlfriend."

Decker bumped his shoulder against Finn's and said with all seriousness, "Hey, you stuff a sock down there or something?"

Or something. "Nope. That's just me in a relaxed state," he lied.

"So, you're a show-er not a grower."

"No, I'm a show-er *and* a fucking grower. Some of us are just naturally blessed like that."

Rez hooted and pointed to his nose. "Something's growing and it's not your dick, liar."

"Don't be a hater because all you have is a tiny gherkin while I have a big fat dill pickle." Finn grabbed his crotch over his jeans and shook it. "You're a snack while I'm a fucking meal. If you haven't heard that redheads are hung and you'd like proof, I'm willing to show you. Warning, you might need therapy afterward."

Decker snorted.

"We already had an eyeful of your package." Crew jerked his chin toward the exit. "You two head out and grab our phones. Need to jaw with Little Orphan Annie here for a second. I'll meet you out in the parking lot."

Once Rez and Decker were gone, Finn asked, "What's up?"

Crew's expression turned grim. "We're not going to be able to pay her as a CI."

Finn scraped a hand along his jawline. "I thought you got it approved already."

"I did. But I've got to say, I'm damn glad we crashed the party tonight. I watched her. I also watched you. Between seeing what she looks like and knowing you too fucking well, I'm sure as fuck you aren't going to be able to resist at least trying, brother."

"Are you saying I don't have any control?"

"I know what you like and she's exactly what you go for. You're going to do your best to hit that. Even if she ends up being a quick bang, it's too much of a risk for the investigation and that's a gamble I don't want to take. If we put her on the payroll and you two hook up, that has the potential to fuck us."

"The money was supposed to sweeten the deal, Crew. She wants out of here."

"Yeah, you already said that. But the money she'd get wouldn't even make a dent for what she's trying to do, brother. You know it's not some windfall. We're talking fucking peanuts."

Finn ground a hand against the back of his neck at this change of events. It might not be a lot of money but it was a little extra she could tuck away to put toward her dream. And her escape.

"So, from what I saw tonight, my gut's saying this is a no-fucking-go. But that doesn't mean we still can't use her assistance. We'll keep the fake boyfriend angle, if she'll agree to that. *Aaaand* you're going to pull out all the stops to convince her into being a cooperating witness."

He stared at the DEA agent. "I'm not sure helping to take down the Demons will be enough motivation for her to put herself in that kind of danger, Crew."

"All she has to do is keep her eyes open and report shit she sees to you. Then when you're here in the club under the guise of her boyfriend, you'll know what to look for. If you play that role right, we might not need her to testify as a witness at all. Only you." Crew slapped him on the back. "C'mon, Prince Harry, you're an expert at sweet-talking the ladies. Just do your thing. Maybe tempt her with your big dill pickle."

With a smirk, Crew headed out.

Finn stood there for a second, considering this change of plans and how to rework what he originally planned to say to convince Mel.

He'd have to just wing it.

With a muttered, "Fuck," he headed backstage to find her.

———

She studied the outline of Danny's profile. She couldn't make out the fine details of his chiseled face since the only light in the vehicle came from the halogen spotlights attached to the rear of the building.

But even in the mix of shadows, she could see both hands firmly gripping the steering wheel and his brow pulled low.

"Whose van is that?"

Huh? She glanced in the direction he was staring. An old Chevy Astro Van way past its prime was parked in one of the end spots up against the building. The hubcaps and large patches of paint were missing, leaving behind bare steel and plenty of rust.

"I don't know. This is the first I'm seeing it. I didn't notice it when I came in earlier."

"Everybody's gone, right?"

"As far as I'm aware. I did a walk-through to make sure the building was empty."

"Sapphire?"

"She was going to lock up the front and leave as soon as your friends left."

"It's not hers?"

A half giggle escaped her as she tried to imagine Sapphire tooling around town in that old rust bucket. The woman had a closet full of shoes worth a lot more than that van. "No. She parked out front tonight."

"Did you lock the rear door?"

"It locks automatically. But I double-checked it since, as soon as we're done here, I'm getting in my car and leaving."

His head twisted toward her. "Do they have cameras back here?"

This line of questioning was making her heart thunder in her chest. "Yes."

"How long do they keep the files?"

"Normally thirty days. After that they're automatically deleted unless we want to save them."

"Do you have access to them?"

This had to be what an interrogation felt like. Or someone planning something nefarious, like a break-in. "I do. Or I did. I haven't had a reason to check them recently."

"Is it an NVR system?"

"An NVR system?"

"A network video system, where the footage is stored either on a hard drive or in a cloud."

"Yes, it's stored electronically. Laura had some sort of account set up that's password protected."

"And you have that password?"

"If Taint didn't change it. But should I be worried about the van being parked there? If so, I can call the police or have the van towed."

"No."

She frowned. That wasn't the answer she was expecting with the way he was acting. "Well, no matter what, it can't stay back here if it doesn't belong to one of my employees. I don't understand your concern about it, though."

"You just said everyone is gone. So, no vehicles except for ours should be parked back here."

"Right. If it doesn't belong here, then I'll get it towed if it's still here in a couple of days. That doesn't mean you're not making me a little worried." More than a little. His paranoia about the van was ramping up hers.

"You're safe with me."

What did that have to do with the price of beans? "I'm not worried about you." She wouldn't be sitting alone with him in a dark parking lot if she was. "It's the way you're acting about that vehicle. Like someone could be in it just waiting to kidnap me or something." *Or something.*

Truthfully, she didn't put anything past those fucking Demons. They were really turning the job she loved into a job she now hated.

He pulled in a breath. "I'll explain my concern in a minute. It's partially what I wanted to talk to you about."

"The van you didn't know about until now is partially what you have to talk to me about?" That didn't even make sense.

"Not the van. The Demons. Do you want to do something about them?"

What power did she have? "Of course I do. I wish they never bought the club. But I didn't, and still don't, have a say in that. I don't have the money to buy them out and even if I did, I doubt they'd sell it to me. They worked long and hard to rip it from Laura's fingers."

"If you had a way to rid your life of them, would you do it?"

That seemed like a trick question. "Yes, but that would mean finding a job elsewhere and I'm already keeping an eye out for an opportunity. Do you know someone who could be an investor? Is that why you wanted to talk to me? Is it you? Are you independently wealthy and one day you decided you were bored and that's why you joined the Peckers?"

He huffed out a breath. "I hate to crush your hope, but unfortunately, I'm not rich and I don't know any investors. However, there may be another way to go about it."

This whole conversation was putting her on edge. From the van obsession to getting rid of the Demons.

She was a woman who put her head down and worked hard. Taking down a dangerous outlaw MC was not on her life's agenda. Especially after seeing what they did to Laura. Mel had no idea just how far they would've gone if Laura hadn't given in.

"In a legal way? I don't want to lower myself to their level by using intimidation and scare tactics. Or doing anything illegal."

"No. This is legal." He shifted in the driver's seat as much as he could to face her. Even though his face was caught in shadows, she could see how serious his expression was.

She attempted to swallow the lump stuck in her throat. "Then please get to the point. By skirting around the subject in an attempt to 'prepare' me, all you're doing is freaking me out."

He nodded. "Sorry. I don't mean to freak you out.

Listen... I have a proposition for you, but I don't want you to say no until you hear me out. I also don't want you to say no until you give me the opportunity to answer all your questions. As best as I can, anyway. If you ask me something I don't know, I'll do my best to find the answer. I want you to feel completely comfortable with this."

Mel pressed a hand to the racing pulse in her throat.

Before she could respond, he continued, "I needed to see if I could trust you before I revealed some things about me. I will also need you to trust me. Trust will be important for this to work."

She didn't know him well enough to trust him completely. He seemed nice enough, but that didn't mean shit.

"How do you know you can trust me?" she whispered.

He peeled her hand from her throat and gave it a squeeze. "I'm a good judge of character."

So was she, but that wasn't fool-proof.

Releasing her hand, he grabbed his phone from the center console. After turning on the flashlight app, he handed it to her. "Keep this low and pointed toward the floor. What I'm about to show you, I don't want showing up on the security cameras."

What the hell was going on? Her racing heartbeat now pulsed in her temples.

She accepted the phone from him and did what he said, keeping the bright light pointed at the floorboard at her feet.

He leaned forward and dug into the back pocket of his jeans. When he pulled his wallet out, he kept that low and out of view, too. He flipped it open and held it under his phone. The light bounced off shiny metal.

What the—

"I'm a cop."

Chapter Thirteen

"You're a cop," she repeated, not posed as a question, but a statement of disbelief.

"Yes." His gut instinct better be correct. It had always been accurate in the past but odds were one day it would be wrong. Finn only hoped like fuck today was not that day.

Even in the Kia's mostly dark interior, he could see the surprise, possibly even shock, in her eyes. He wasn't sure if he should be impressed with himself that he'd hidden his true identity so well, or insulted that she couldn't fathom him being in law enforcement.

"Are cops' salaries so bad you need to strip as a second job?"

"Being a cop definitely doesn't make me rich but I'm not dancing because I need the money, Mel. In fact, I can't keep any of the tips. But... I'm not only a cop."

The whites of her eyes expanded even more. "What does that mean?"

He dug into the wallet and pulled out his federal task force ID.

When she took it from him, her fingers held a slight tremor. She tilted it so she could read it under the cell phone's light. "What is this? It doesn't match the badge."

"That's correct. The badge belongs to the Southern Allegheny Regional PD, where I'm an officer, but the ID is for a special assignment I'm on right now. I'm part of a federal drug task force. My current assignment for that task force is being undercover to investigate and gather evidence against the Deadly Demons."

"Wait... So..."

He waited, giving her a much-needed minute to wrap her head around what he just revealed.

"So..."

He pinned his lips together and let her work through it. But after another long excruciating pause, he couldn't wait any longer. "I went undercover with the Peckers, but only for the two shows at The Peach Pit."

Her lips tipped downward at the corners. "Does Nick know?"

"Yes, but he's the only one."

"And your friends who showed up tonight... Are they even friends?"

"More than friends, actually. I consider them my brothers. They're law enforcement and working on the same task force, too, but that's not how I know them. We're all members of an MC."

"An MC? Like the Demons?" she squeaked.

Not even fucking close. "We belong to the Blue Avengers, a club exclusively made up of law enforcement."

Her brow furrowed. "MCs like that exist?"

"Yes. Firefighters have MCs. Former military. Lots of brotherhoods form motorcycle or riding clubs. It's one type of bonding and helps cement their brotherhood, their community. Especially since they all have something in common."

"Do you all ride Harleys?"

"Most of us, yes."

"Do you wear those leather cuts, too?"

"We do, but only when we ride. Our MC isn't a way of life like the Demons. It's only one piece of our life, even if an important one."

She turned to stare out the passenger-side window. Her chest slowly expanded and contracted for a few seconds. "Okay, so... Why are you telling me all of this?"

"I need your help."

She turned to face him again. "You or the task force?"

"The investigation. I went undercover with the Peckers as a way to get behind the scenes at The Peach Pit. Our suspicion—and I think you have the same—is that the Demons bought this business for two reasons. As a front to sell drugs and also to cook the books."

She rubbed her forehead. "Cook the books?"

"Launder their drug money. They're buying up local businesses that deal with a lot of cash."

"And The Peach Pit handles a lot of cash," she said flatly.

"Do you have access to the books?"

With a shake of her head, she answered, "No, Laura used an accountant and I'm not sure what the Demons are doing, if anything, when it comes to bookkeeping. If they're cooking the books, like you say, I'm sure her accountant wouldn't want to be involved."

"I'm sure the Demons wouldn't want him to see the books, either. Who makes the deposits?"

"Any cash is locked in the safe a few times a night and the remainder after closing. Previously, when I'd come in the next day, either Laura or I would prepare the deposit and one of us would take it to the bank."

"Who handles it now?"

"Saint."

"Fuck," he muttered. "How are you getting paid?"

"Laura used a payroll service since they handled everything. Right now, my direct deposits are still coming from that company. But if I had to guess, the payroll is only being funded by the credit card deposits and not cash. I suspect they're pocketing any cash coming into the club."

"That could come back to bite them with the IRS if there's any major discrepancy between the amounts of cash previously deposited and what's being deposited now."

"Taint could be depositing some, but I doubt he's depositing it all."

"Or he's depositing cash from the meth sales. However, we don't have confirmation about that yet and can only assume at this point. A strip club is a perfect front."

"Isn't money laundering a RICO violation?" she asked.

"Sure is."

"That means the feds could seize the business, right?"

"Possibly, but we're trying to avoid going after any of them until we have all our ducks in a row. We don't want to tip them off—or the organization they're trafficking for—before our investigation is complete. Right now we're in the evidence gathering stage. The more solid proof we get, the stronger the case will be when indictments come down."

"You said you need my help, but you haven't said how."

"Have you noticed them selling drugs?"

"I haven't. But using the club as a front makes sense. It has to be why they fought so hard to get their hands on this business. They refused to take a no from Laura." She clamped a hand onto her forehead and gave her head a little shake. "Truthfully, I've had my blinders on since they took over. I've only been biding my time and trying to avoid stirring up trouble and dealing with Taint's wrath. I guess I should've paid better attention."

"Moving forward, I need you to be very observant."

"And then what?"

"And then you report back to me with the date, time and names of the actors involved when you see any suspicious activity. Give me whatever details you can. I need you to be my eyes and ears." At least when he wasn't at the club himself. He was about to reveal that part of the plan next.

"Basically, what you're asking me to do is observe and let you know if I see anything," she concluded.

"Yes," he drew out slowly, "but that's not all."

Her head jerked back. "Don't ask me to sell drugs for those assholes."

He huffed out a breath, both amused and surprised she thought he'd ask that of her. "No, nothing like that. I'm not asking you to do anything illegal at all."

"Then what?"

Here goes nothing... "I want to be your boyfriend," tumbled out of his mouth.

Hers hung open for a few seconds. "What?"

"Your *fake* boyfriend," he followed up quickly. "I want us to pretend we're dating."

Her eyebrows pinched together. "Why?"

"It gives me a good excuse to hang around the club and also have access to the back where the deals might be going down. If I just came in as a regular customer, I'd have no good reason to have full access to the club."

She swallowed hard as she stared through the windshield and at the rear of the brick building. Once again, he decided it was best to wait her out and let her process this unexpected proposal.

It would make his life so much easier if she agreed. Could they continue to investigate the Demons without her help? Sure as fuck could. But her cooperation would be a boon since two sets of eyes were better than one and she knew The Peach Pit better than anyone.

If she didn't agree to either requests, the task force would most likely be stuck sending someone in to sit out in the stage area, as well as be forced to set up surveillance.

And nobody wanted to sit surveillance if they could avoid it.

When she turned to face him again, a sharp uptick of tension filled the air. "Will helping you put me in danger?"

"Life in general is dangerous."

A little groan escaped her at his deflection. "Some lives are more at risk than others, especially if you willfully step into a situation as you're proposing. What if the Demons find out I'm watching them and even giving up information? And if you try to feed me bullshit about making sure I'll be protected... just don't. I've seen that movie before. It never turns out well for the informant."

He couldn't argue that. Instead, he said carefully, "Since you made it clear how dedicated you were to this club and how you still want to take care of your dancers, I figured you'd want to help excise the Demons from your life."

"Of course I would, but would there even be a guarantee of that?"

"No. I said life can be dangerous but it also has no guarantees."

She once again groaned at his lame platitudes. "You're asking a lot for little in return. I could end up being a target for those bikers."

"I am and you could. I'll be completely honest, Mel. It'll be a crapshoot. No matter what, I do plan on looking out for you, if you agree to assist. I promise you won't be doing it alone if you agree to both parts of this plan." Or, *hell*, either option but he didn't want to encourage her to pick one or the other.

She squeezed her forehead between her fingers and sat silently for several heartbeats. The woman definitely did not make impulsive decisions.

"Tell me something. Is your name really Danny? I didn't look at the name on the ID you flashed, I was more focused on the organization. I guess I should have. You just... caught me off guard with this whole thing." She flapped a hand around. "My head is still spinning."

"I get it. It was probably the last thing you expected for me to talk about. I wasn't lying when I told you my name is Daniel, but in reality, no one calls me Danny. Not even my mother. I was only using that version as my undercover name."

"What do your friends normally call you?" She lifted a finger. "People you're not trying to deceive."

Gingerhole, Heat Miser, Pippi Longstocking, Conan O'Brien, Little Orphan Annie... The list was endless but he'd keep his answer simple. "Finn."

"Why Finn?"

"Finnegan is my last name."

"Daniel Finnegan." She said his name like she was rolling a Lifesaver around in her mouth.

Crazy enough, his real name coming across her lips made his cock take notice. He'd used different versions of his name with past hook-ups. But with Mel, for some strange reason, he was relieved she now knew the truth of who he really was.

"What does your mother call you?"

191

"Daniel."

"If she calls you that normally, using your whole name when you're in trouble must not be as effective."

"It is when it's said in a mother's scolding tone and accompanied by a scorching look."

Mel's laughter lightened the thick air in the Kia. It could be a good sign. As was the fact she hadn't told him to fuck off or bolted from his vehicle. Yet, anyway. She remained in the passenger seat, listening and even asking questions.

Of course, he expected her to be worried about being a cooperating witness against an outlaw motorcycle club. That should be a natural reaction for any civilian. He'd be concerned if she wasn't.

It would be smart for her to remain cautious whether she agreed to help the task force or not.

"I assume your mother's still around?"

The personal questions could be a way for her to see if she could trust him. Normally he didn't give out personal information to anyone he didn't know well. But he also hoped to get to know her better, whether she became a cooperating witness or not. "She's definitely alive and literally kicking."

Her head tilted. "What does that mean?"

He wished he could see her captivating eyes better. "She's a dance instructor."

"Wow."

"Yeah, she's good."

"She's how you got your natural ability." She let out a dry laugh. "Normally strippers show up as fake cops. You're a real cop who showed up as a fake stripper."

"Basically, yes."

"The upside down," she murmured. "Did you take lessons from her?"

He grimaced. "Not willingly."

"You're really damn good, Officer Finnegan."

"Just Finn."

"Finn," she repeated softly.

Damn. His cock even liked her saying his nickname. But then, it liked a lot of things about her. "I need to forewarn you, if you agree, I plan on playing a very jealous, possessive boyfriend. I'll drive you to work just about every day and take you home, too. I'll be hanging around for hours in the club to keep an eye on you because I won't like you being around so many horny men. I'll act controlling as fuck, maybe even aggressive, if the situation calls for it. But by remaining close, it'll also help me protect you from Saint and all of his asshole brothers."

Her gaze sliced over to the van. "Do you think it was Taint who parked the Chevy there?"

"I do. You said you have access to the cameras. When you get a chance and if you're willing, I need you to check the footage to confirm that. My educated guess is the van being left there isn't just coincidence and was on purpose."

"What purpose?"

"As a drug drop-off."

"I don't understand."

"If they have someone dealing in the club, that person will only keep a small amount on their person. This way if they get popped, it's not enough for a distribution charge and they can claim personal use. If and when they run out, they get more from the stash in the van. It's called a re-up. Then someone else comes by and re-ups the van's supply. Since it has a license plate, I'll take a photo of it before I leave and I'll run it through PennDOT. But my guess is, it's either registered to a prospect or the previous owner. They most likely bought it from a junkyard for the sole purpose of using it as a stash vehicle. By keeping the majority of the drugs outside in the van, if the prospect is busted dealing, it's set up so it can't come back on the business. Unofficially, it'll be the prospect's drugs, not the Demons'. By doing it that way, they keep both the MC and The Peach Pit clean by making the prospect a scapegoat and pretending he was a lone wolf."

By the Demons handling it that way, it might not threaten the business itself if any of them got busted. On the other hand, if the Demons got caught money laundering, it would knee-cap the club. A RICO charge was a whole other ballgame.

"And that prospect willingly takes the fall on his own?"

Her question drew him back to the topic of drug dealing. "Yes. If he doesn't flip and does time for the crime, earning his full set of patches once he's released is usually a given."

"And if he flips?"

"What do you think?"

"I think I need to give this some thought," she murmured. "When do you need an answer?"

"Not tonight, if you want to take the time to consider it. But preferably soon."

She pressed her knuckles to her mouth.

For the third time, he kept his trap shut and let her work out whatever she needed to work out in her head. Not unexpectedly, she might be uncomfortable spying on the Demons. They weren't choir boys. They were deadly like their club name suggested.

She also might not feel comfortable playing his girlfriend.

"What are they selling?"

More interest could be a positive thing. So was her not instantly shutting him down and out.

"I'm sure they're selling weed but the investigation isn't about that, it's for crystal meth. They're trucking large amounts from Mexico to Pittsburgh."

"Wow, a whole enterprise, then."

He tipped his head. "One that pays very well."

"It makes sense now why they wanted The Peach Pit so badly. And why after getting it, they really don't give a damn about making the business successful. I knew something was off, I just didn't know the exact reasoning behind it. They're not only going to destroy the club but people's lives by providing a very dangerous, addictive drug."

"They don't care about any lives but their own. It's all about money and power."

"Power. What power does an MC want?"

"They want to control territory, mostly. Increasing their territory expands their area for selling drugs but avoids getting into war with any other MCs. Of course, selling more drugs makes them more money."

She blew out a breath. "A violent gang, that's all they are. No better than street gangs like the Crips and Bloods."

Huh. "Or criminal organizations like the Mafia. But you're right, some MCs are no better than street gangs on two wheels."

"Some aren't?"

"Some like ours aren't, no."

She turned to blindly stare out the passenger-side window for the third time. Once again, he didn't want to push her, so he said nothing. But the whole damn time, a clock ticked in his head.

"Okay," she whispered to the window.

Wait. What? "Okay..." he drew out, waiting for her to explain.

She fisted her hands in her lap and twisted her head to face him again. "I'll do it. I'll help you and your task force." Not an ounce of uncertainty colored her answer.

"Are you sure you don't want to take tonight to think about it?"

She shook her head as she glanced at the parked Astro Van. "No. Fuck them. What they did to Laura... They tried to destroy her life. They *threatened* her and her kids. Now, they might destroy the business she worked so damn hard to build. So, fuck them. They need to go down."

Well, damn. "Laura wasn't the only one who worked hard to get the club where it is, right? You did, too."

"Yes. With plans to buy it once Laura retired, but I was also working on convincing her to make me a partner in the meantime."

"Was she considering it?"

"She was." Mel sighed. "Now that dream is dashed and I'll have to start from scratch somewhere else. But that doesn't mean I can't give those assholes a parting gift."

He smashed his lips together to prevent grinning like a damn fool. Her attitude showed her strength and determination. While it was good for the task force, it was also a huge turn-on for Finn. Some men were into meek and mild, even submissive, women. Finn preferred women with a bit of fire. Speaking of fire...

"You can't tell anyone about this. Not even Sapphire." Even with the little he'd seen them interact, he could tell they were close. But confiding in the hostess about what they were doing could put Mel at risk, even unintentionally.

She blew out a soft breath and with it an, "Okay."

"Also be aware, whenever I come into the club, I'll be keeping my phone on me. Make sure Sapphire knows that. I'll most likely have to take photos for documentation and evidence."

"We have a policy—"

"I understand the reason for that policy and I promise not

to violate anyone's privacy. Both your girls and your customers."

"Unless they're breaking the law."

"That's a given. The subjects of our investigation will be the exception."

"That's fine. I'll tell her to let you keep your phone. I'll just need to come up with a good excuse. What about the prospects who work the front? They're not going to let you keep it. Even the girls can't have their phones with them on the floor. They have to store them in their lockers and only use them in the dressing room."

"I can use the employee entrance."

"Saint..."

"If he says something, we'll make other arrangements. If I have to, I'll grab a burner and hide it somewhere inside. In the meantime, text me if you see anything suspicious. I don't care how small. If you can grab a picture without a risk of you getting caught, do so. But bottom line, don't put yourself in harm's way. If they're doing what we think they're doing, we'll have plenty of other opportunities to document their activity, including sending in CIs to make buys."

"Basically, I need to pull off the blinders, pay attention and let you know what I see."

"That's it." He paused. "Well, except for the dating part. Are you okay with that, too?"

Without hesitation, she answered, "Yes. I'm willing to pretend we're dating."

Crew would be in hog heaven with that news.

"Will I have to eventually get on the witness stand and face them?"

He had to tell her the truth. "It depends. We'll avoid that, if possible, and one way would be if I witness the activity myself. If you do have to testify, we can ask the court to keep you anonymous for your safety." He reached over and squeezed one of her fisted hands. When it relaxed under his, he kept it there.

"By obscuring my face and voice?"

"Yes."

She nodded and focused on his hand covering hers.

It was time to lighten the mood. "Have you ever dated a ginger before?"

She lifted her gaze to him. "No, but I still won't be dating a ginger. We'll only be fake dating, right?"

Right. "I'll have you know, there are perks to being my pretend girlfriend."

"Oh?" She fought a grin. "I can't wait to hear them."

He didn't bother to fight his. "You get to spend time with me. That's the biggest perk of all." When she laughed, he added, "And I'll always pay for dinner."

"You or the government?"

"Me, by the way of the government. Your tax dollars hard at work, of course."

"*Mmm hmm.* Is that all?"

"Did I already say that you get to spend time with me, my sparkling personality and, of course, my good looks?" He wiggled his eyebrows.

"Can you help me find my eyes? I rolled them so hard, they popped out and hit the floorboards."

He grabbed her chin and lifted her face. "Let me see."

"Well, at least one of us can see."

He chuckled. "I could see that being your new career. A comedian who strips. You'll be raking in the dough."

"*Hmm.* Not a bad idea. Open a club that combines comedians and strippers."

He snorted. "I'd attend."

"And hosts drag queens."

"I'd still attend."

"Maybe some musical theater."

"You lost me there. Unless it's hot, naked women swinging around a pole, cracking jokes and then busting out a show tune when you least expect it. I might pay good money for that."

"Stripper variety shows."

He laughed. "You're on a roll."

"Just like my eyeballs," she huffed. "All right, well... It's time for me to head home."

As she reached for the door handle, he grabbed her arm. "Wait."

She twisted in her seat to face him.

"If we're going to play a couple, we need to practice to make it look real."

"And how do you propose we do that?"

He tipped his head toward the building, indicating the cameras. "It can't hurt for the Demons to see us doing something couples do."

Her breath shuddered. "Like what?"

Cupping her face, he swept his thumb back and forth across the soft skin of her cheek, then he slid his hand to the back of her neck, driving his fingers into her long, silky hair.

She didn't resist when he pulled her closer.

"Just a simple kiss." He leaned in and whispered, "For practice," a fraction from her lips. "And it'll look good on camera."

"Of course," her warm, sweet breath whispered over his lips, "for practice."

It surprised him when it wasn't him closing the slight gap between them, it was her.

It started out as a simple kiss. A light brush of her lips across his. Then she did it again. And again. He let her take it at her own pace, even though he was dying to deepen it. Not kiss her. Fuck no. He wanted to take her mouth, to conquer it. To taste every inch. To steal her breath, to make her groan...

But this was only practice, he reminded himself. They needed to act like a couple, to look believable. Like two people who knew each other intimately.

When her tongue traced the seam of his mouth, he opened it, expecting her to only be a tease. Do only enough to get him hard before leaving him hanging.

But she shocked the shit out of him when she gripped his face roughly with both hands. Their tongues collided and tangled. Tasted and twisted.

Even more surprising, it wasn't her groan they shared, it was his. Because... *Fuuuuuck.* The kiss was groan-worthy. She was so fucking good at it that he never wanted it to end.

In the past, he'd been with women who were awkward kissers. That was not Mel.

Fuck no.

Unfortunately, it did end a few seconds later when she pulled back slightly with her eyes wide and her breath ragged. A gleam on her lips and in her eyes.

"Was that believable?" she breathed.

She had to ask?

"It's hard to say." Literally, it was so damn hard. His erection was caught crookedly in his jeans. Only, he didn't want her to think he was some weird perv by jamming his hand down his pants and adjusting it. He'd just have to suffer through the uncomfortable angle for now.

However, a couple of things became clear... First, that short kiss with Mel had the same effect as wearing that damn elastic band around his cock when he danced.

And second, that one real kiss with her wasn't enough. *Hell,* he wanted much more than a fucking kiss. So much more. That made him say, "We can't get enough practice. Our relationship will need to look legit. For your safety and mine." Was that putting it on too thick? Did he care if it was?

Fuck no.

"Then to be safe, I think we need to try that again," she whispered. "For practice."

He was on board with that. "Practice does make perfect," he got out right before she took his mouth again.

Yes. A woman who took what she wanted.

He liked that. So fucking much.

He disliked when women acted innocent if he knew damn well they weren't. He appreciated a woman not ashamed of her sexuality or afraid to act on her desires. To go for the brass ring. To grab the world by the balls.

For fuck's sake, she could grab his balls at any time.

If she was inclined, right now would be good.

But he knew better than to push his luck or do something to push her away. She had agreed to help him out, in turn, helping the task force. That was a big win.

Granted, the kiss was another big win, too.

He'd take all the wins he could get.

This time, though, he shoved her tongue out of his mouth so he could explore hers, taking the kiss deeper and making *her* groan.

Fuck yeah. This whole fake boyfriend thing might make up for the two nights he had to get up on stage and strip.

Even though the kiss was once again over way too soon, it was a damn good start. When she pulled back, her breathing was a bit ragged, her eyes remained closed and her lips remained parted for a few seconds.

And then, *fuck him*, she sighed like she just had the best orgasm.

He cleared his throat because he had to pull her out of

whatever she was going through. If he didn't, he was going to suggest for them to climb into the tight back seat of the Kia and then they'd really give Saint a show. "I'm certain we can pull it off."

Her eyes popped open. "Pull what off?"

When she licked her lips, he bit back a groan of disappointment since there would be no back seat action. "Playing a couple."

"I'm good at faking it."

Damn.

She shot him a huge smile that lit up the Kia's interior.

Well, double damn.

"I really have to go now."

He resisted stopping her this time when she opened the door and climbed out.

In one way he was disappointed, in another he was now looking forward to seeing how this new twist in his undercover assignment went. "Mel..."

She glanced over her shoulder.

"Do you want me to follow you home?"

"To make sure I'm safe?"

No. "Yes."

"I appreciate your offer, but I'll be fine."

"I'll take you to dinner tomorrow night. We'll go over more details then."

"If Cookie shows up."

"If she doesn't, I'll bring you dinner. I need Saint and his flunkies to start seeing me around. We need to make it clear to them that you belong to me."

Her mouth opened and he swore he heard a soft hiss escape.

Fuck yeah. "I'll see you tomorrow night."

"Tomorrow night," she repeated with a nod and shut the passenger door.

He waited until she was safely in her vehicle and out of the parking lot. Before he left, he snapped a photo of the Astro Van's license plate. He wanted to get a shot of the vehicle identification number, too, but he'd have to figure out a way to get it when it wasn't so obvious. If Saint saw him doing that on the camera, it might blow both his cover and his plan.

After that, he went home to take care of his "issue" by fantasizing about a gorgeous, sexy blonde with Caribbean Sea eyes, who was kind of funny, too.

Yeah, maybe this assignment wouldn't be so bad after all.

Chapter Fourteen

WITH THE OFFICE chair tipped back as far as it could go, Finn had his ankles crossed and his boots kicked up on the third floor conference table. He had a baseball cap pulled low and his eyes closed.

He'd been up a little too late last night taking care of business. Both in the shower and in bed.

Kissing his new *fake* girlfriend had made Finn a very busy boy.

It also made him tired. After he met with Crew, he'd go back home and crash for a few hours before heading over to The Peach Pit. Either to wait for Mel to finish her shift or, if she got stuck working a double, to go get her dinner.

He opened his eyes when his boots got knocked off the table. "You think this is your place, asshole? Keep your boots off the fucking table."

He tipped the bill of his hat up and shot Crew a grin. "Got news."

"Yeah? Good news?"

Finn nodded and sat up. "I convinced her to help."

"Well, look at you, Pippi. Maybe you impressed her with your satin-wrapped, sock-stuffed package."

"That's a given, but I don't need to stuff. We already had that conversation, remember? But truthfully... Since she *really* hates the Demons, it didn't take much to convince her."

"You mean it didn't take much for her to agree to be a cooperating witness. I can't imagine it didn't take some arm twisting for her to agree to be your girlfriend."

"That didn't take much of an effort at all, either."

Crew snorted, yanked out the rolling chair across the table from him and sank into it with a groan. "Now what?"

"I'm going to head over there later and hang for a little bit so we're seen together and can show off our new 'relationship.' If all goes well, I'm taking her to dinner."

"Then what?"

"Then I'm going to play the possessive, controlling boyfriend who can be a dick about her being around a bunch of men at a strip club. That'll give me a good excuse to be extra clingy."

"That's a good angle."

"Of course it is. I know what the fuck I'm doing."

Crew snorted again, shaking his head. "Try not to stir up too much trouble with the Demons. We don't want them banning you from the club or, worse, firing her."

"I'll simply pull the same bullshit they do when they treat their women like property. I already warned her my behavior might be over the top."

"Well, redheads tend to be hot-tempered. Simply act accordingly."

"You could've just stopped at 'hot.'"

Crew grinned. "Could've, but didn't."

"Also, I cleared it with her about having a phone in the club. However, if it causes an issue with Saint or the prospects since it's against club policy, I might grab one of the burners and hide it there."

"Brains *and* dancing skills. Quite a catch there, Ginger Snap."

Finn waved a hand down his body. "Don't be hating on me because I'm the complete package. Maybe one day you, too, can achieve that illustrious status. You'll just have to work a little harder. Maybe you can take the spot I'm vacating with the Peckers so you can work on your moves."

Crew laughed so loudly that Butler, sitting at one of the desks transcribing wiretap recordings, had to pause. "Who said you were done dancing with the Peckers?"

"Yeah well, now I'm right where you wanted me *without* having to strut around on stage giving everyone an eyeful of the blessing I was born with. Anyway, I put this tidbit in my daily report, but since I doubt you've read it yet... A piece of shit Astro Van showed up in the parking lot behind the club. I'm pretty sure those fucknuts are planning on using it as a stash van. Mel's going to check the security camera footage to see if it was Saint, or at least a Demon, who dropped it off."

"Damn. They're digging their heels in deep there."

"Yeah, seems so."

"Then it's good you have your foot in the door and that Mel will be another set of eyes."

"I'll also have her check it after a couple of days to see who's re-upping the stash."

"Good. Can she grab us copies of any pertinent videos?"

"They're stored in a cloud, so I'll see if she can download any important footage for our files."

"With her being the manager, we should be able to use anything handed over willingly for our case. Even better, that'll be irrefutable evidence against the Demons."

"The best kind." Finn scraped his fingers down his beard.

"Too bad we can't rip that club from their grubby fucking fingers so she can buy it at auction like we did with this place."

"Yeah, well... You know how long that shit would take. First, the government would have to seize the property and then..."

"Yeah. Years of red tape. It wouldn't be an ideal situation for her financially."

"Wouldn't it be better for her to start her own club in the same area, steal the stable of dancers and their clientele?" Crew asked.

"If she does that before the Demons are taken down, it might put a target on her back from the MC."

"It could," Crew agreed.

"No matter what, the dancers will go wherever she goes because she was one of them and she treats them with respect. I doubt those bikers do."

"They don't respect women in general."

"True enough."

"That it?"

"No," Finn answered. "I need another vehicle. That fucking Kia will not fit my dominant persona. I can't be in the club bossing around my woman, then go out and lose my balls the second I climb into a Soul. It's a fucking joke."

Crew pursed his lips. "I'll see what I can do. The problem is, you were pretending you were broke. That's the reason we used for why you joined the Peckers."

"I don't need a fucking Lamborghini. Just a used pickup truck or something. Something more manly than that damn Kia. Driving it is destroying my soul."

Crew chuckled. "True dominant men aren't affected by fragile masculinity."

"Like you'd know, J. Crew. All right, I just wanted to give

you that update. I'm heading home to catch a little more shut-eye." He pushed to his feet and headed toward the door.

Crew calling out, "By the way, you're welcome for that cushy assignment," stopped Finn in his tracks.

"Yeah? You get up on stage and deal with that rabid pack of women while your cock is turning a scary shade of purple from a lack of circulation, then tell me if it's cushy."

"But look where it landed you. Now you get to be a hot blonde's boyfriend. If you play it right, you might get some extra perks out of it."

He only hoped so because his fist wasn't a great substitute for the real thing.

———

SAPPHIRE SIDLED up to Mel and leaned into her, warning, "Taint's here."

Great. "Thanks for the heads up. Hey... *umm*... last night..."

With raised eyebrows, Sapphire straightened and stepped in front of Mel to face her. "Last night..."

Here goes nothing... "Danny and I hooked up."

Mel winced when the hostess's squeal was so high-pitched, it could draw a pack of wild dogs. "No, you didn't! With that hot hunk of ginger spice?"

"*Mmm hmm.*"

"Well, look at you, you lucky bitch. Your dry spell is finally over. It's no surprise you picked him to do it with. He's irresistible."

"It's only been dry because I've been too damn busy since Laura left."

"What matters is you got laid!"

"Phire, lower your voice," Mel hissed.

Sapphire swatted her freshly-manicured hand in the air. "No one can hear me over the music. So, now what?"

"So," she shrugged, "I like him."

"I would hope so since you two did some dirty pole dancing."

"He's taking me to dinner if Cookie graces us with her presence tonight."

"Even if she doesn't, go. I can manage things until you get back."

Mel gave her friend and coworker a smile. "Thanks. It'll be interesting to see how things go."

"Wait, you want more with him than performing the coochie cha-cha?"

Mel shrugged. "He seems genuinely interested. Like I said, we'll see."

"If it pans out, great. If not, still great because you got laid, girl!"

"The reason I'm telling you is, he'll be stopping by later. Don't charge him a cover or take his phone."

Sapphire's head jerked back. "Don't take his phone? Waiving the cover charge is understandable. The phone, MJ..."

"He swore he won't take any pics of the girls or the customers."

Sapphire pursed her dark red lips. "And you believe him?"

"I do, but I guess it'll be a good test to see if my gut instinct is right and I can trust him."

"Maybe. But why can't he be without his phone? I figured he was dancing to make some extra cash, but is his day job important or something? Shit! Is he an emergency room doctor? *Mmm.* I can picture him wearing a stethoscope and nothing else."

Shit. "No... It's..." She needed to come up with an excuse and quickly. "His... mom is really sick and her nurse needs to be able to get a hold of him at any time."

"Wow. She's bad enough to have a nurse?"

Shit. "Yes... She's in hospice." *Shit. Shit. Shit.*

Phire slapped a hand over her mouth and her eyes went wide.

Mel hated lying to her like that. She should've come up with a better story sooner.

"Oh no! He has to be devastated."

"He seems to be taking it as well as he can. He needed to talk to someone about it, so that's what we did last night. And then..." Mel shrugged.

"One thing led to another... Wham, bam, thank you ma'am, and can I have another?"

Mel laughed. "Something like that."

"Good for you, girl. I need to get a little whammy-bammy myself. From someone who doesn't sit in those seats," she flipped her hand toward the stage behind them, "or wear one of those gross leather vests."

"Oh God, *please* don't get tangled up with any of those damn Demons."

Sapphire shuddered and fake gagged. "I prefer a man who doesn't use motor oil as a cologne."

"And keeps their facial hair trimmed neatly instead of it looking like a dead, bloated possum alongside the road."

"And smells like one, too."

"A man who showers daily is always a plus."

"I bet ol' Blaze smells *diiiiiivine.*" Sapphire sighed.

Mel smiled. "He does. He's a great kisser, too."

Her eyebrows pinched together. "Kissing? Screw the kissing. Girl, he's got that whole hip action thing going on. How was the *pop, pop, pop?*" She thrusted her curvy hips the same way the male strippers had last night. "Him doing his thing on stage had to be foreplay for you."

Mel wiggled her eyebrows.

"Damn, you *are* a lucky bitch. I'm *soooo* damn jealous. Don't mind me, I'll be out front pouting for the rest of the night. Maybe even imagining you two going at it all hot and heavy. *Mmm mmm mmm.*"

Fantasizing was exactly what Mel did last night after she got home. Once she got in bed and closed her eyes, she couldn't stop thinking about Finn's smooth moves on stage. She swore the man's joints were equipped with well-greased ball-bearings. She also couldn't get that toe-curling, panty-wetting kiss in his Kia out of her mind.

Sleep had been impossible until after she broke out her favorite battery-operated boyfriend. While her BOB did the trick in a pinch, she would've preferred the real thing. Now she was dying to know if his cock had freckles, too.

She smothered a giggle and got back to business. "Where did you see Taint?"

"Heading into the office with Tweedle-Dumb or Tweedle-Dee. I can't tell them apart unless I look at their name patch and I try to avoid getting that close." She wrinkled her nose.

"All right. I need to talk to him."

"Find me when you're through so I know he didn't corner you or anything."

Or anything.

Sapphire grabbed Mel's upper arms and gave her a little shake. They locked gazes. "Don't let him shut the door while you're in there. You hear me?"

A shiver ran down Mel's spine and she nodded. "Safety is one of the things I need to talk to him about."

"Good luck with that," Phire said dryly before heading

through the doors to the lobby area.

Mel turned and scanned the room, her gaze finally landing on the back hallway. She inhaled a deep bolstering breath and headed in that direction.

She needed a damn raise to deal with these bikers.

Plastering on a smile, she turned on her charm as she wound her way through the occupied chairs and tables, giving her regulars a nod and pausing for a few seconds to introduce herself to any customers she didn't recognize.

When she got to the hallway, she asked Popeye, standing sentry, "Is Ta— *Saint* back there?"

The shaggy-bearded prospect stared at her with dull, bloodshot eyes and shrugged. "Been fuckin' standin' here for the last coupla hours. How the fuck would I know?"

Mel beat back her impatience and took another deep breath, pushing past him and down the hallway, heading to the main office. When she got there, the door was closed and, leaning in to listen, she could barely make out two male voices inside.

Taint's and someone's she didn't recognize.

Before she could knock, the door was flung open, causing her to take a surprised step backward. Her heel caught and, with a sharp gasp, she lost her balance.

An arm snaked out, snagged hers roughly and yanked her back onto both feet. She came face to face with another young biker she'd never seen before. Her eyes flicked down to his rectangular name patch right below the one stating he was a prospect. *Chubs.*

Great. Another new, inexperienced, unmotivated employee. Just what this place needed.

Since the baby Demon was tall and lanky, she wondered how he got that nickname. Actually, it was probably better she didn't know.

"Good," she heard from inside the office. "Get in here."

She peeked her head around the door frame and asked Taint, "Who?"

"Both of you."

Great.

"We're being summoned," she muttered to the newbie.

He said nothing but followed her back into the office. As he went to close the door, she stopped him. "Please. Leave it open. I get claustrophobic."

She didn't, but it was a good excuse and better than telling them the truth that she didn't trust any of them. At all.

"Woman—"

Mel gritted her teeth at that. She was not Taint's fucking woman and never would be.

"This here's Chubs. He's gonna be workin' the front door. Sapphire's wastin' her talent there."

Fuck. Sapphire's fear might be coming true.

"Want her workin' the floor and sellin' private dances for the girls. Lookin' at the fuckin' books, I see that's where the money is. You need to concentrate on that, too."

He looked at the books? Doubtful.

"That also means if someone wants a fuckin' private lap dance from her or you, you do it. You got me?"

What? "I no longer dance."

"Want your job? Ain't askin' you to get on the fuckin' stage, woman. Just tellin' you what I expect. You need to earn that fuckin' salary we're payin' you. If that means someone's willin' to part with some scratch for you to give him a private show, then you fuckin' do it. Gonna charge a premium for you and the dark-haired slit."

Mel's nostrils flared and her fingernails dug painfully into her palms.

"Have that Sapphire bitch teach Chubs how to run the

front good. Givin' her two nights to get him squared away, then she's back on the floor full-time. Hear me?"

Mel pulled in a long breath and breathed out, "Yes."

"Good. Like a bitch who listens."

She bit her bottom lip to keep from telling him to go fuck himself up the ass with a saguaro cactus.

"Get out of here, Chubs."

"You got it, brother."

Saint scowled. "You ain't my brother, yet, motherfucker. Gotta earn it."

Chubs flicked his hand over his shoulder and disappeared out the door.

Saint turned his dark eyes to her. If eyes were the windows to the soul, that biker had a black one. "You want me for somethin'?"

Just you out of my life. "I have something to discuss with you."

He jerked his chin toward the chair in front of the desk. The desk he had his boots up on. "Take a load off."

It was supposed to be her office, too. She had previously shared it with Laura, but since Taint took over, she now hardly used it. She'd rather be on the floor and away from him as much as possible. The only time she felt comfortable using it was when there was no chance of him coming in and catching her in there. She tried to be clear of it before the club opened.

Luckily, it was rare that Taint ever showed up before four o'clock in the afternoon, if he showed up at all. He was about as dependable as his ol' lady.

"I wanted to let you know that the cameras for the rear parking lot aren't working."

Without warning, he dropped his boots to the floor and surged to his feet. After checking to make sure the door was still open, Mel turned her eyes back to him—and his hands—as he came around the desk and invaded her personal space. Not touching, but still too close for comfort.

He sucked on his teeth and jerked up his chin. "Why you lookin' at the cameras?"

Sketchy much? "I do when I have a concern or there's an issue I need to check on. Last night when I left, I saw an old van parked in the employee lot. It was still there when I came in earlier and I wanted to see whose it was. If it's abandoned, I need to get it towed."

Before she could move out of his reach, he snagged her chin tightly within his thumb and forefinger and squeezed it painfully, holding her there. "Don't worry your pretty little head about that. It ain't abandoned."

She jerked her head back, freeing herself. "Are you saying I should ignore something like that? As the manager, I'm paid to handle issues."

"Ain't an issue. When you come to me with a real issue, I'll address it. The van ain't one, ignore it."

The fine hairs on the back of her neck stood. Finn was right. They were using it to stash drugs.

Goddamnit! "Okay, but what about the broken cameras?"

"Will look into it."

"Saint, I'm concerned about the girls' safety when they go out to their vehicles at night."

"Yeah? If they're fucking scared, they can get a prospect to walk 'em out."

"Half the time your prospects are gone before the girls leave. That aside, you're not concerned with the security of the club itself? What if someone breaks in?"

"This is a Demons owned business, woman. You think anyone's gonna fuck with it?"

She bobbed her head when she shot back, "And if you

think every criminal is aware of that fact, you're foolish."

His nostrils flared and a muscle in his bearded cheek jumped.

His bushy black beard had a few stray grays in it. As did his long, stringy hair. Worse, the man stunk. A unsavory mix of unwashed pussy and stale pot.

She fought the curl of her lip.

"Said I'm gonna check it out."

"I hope so."

"Don't like that fuckin' attitude and don't need you tellin' me what to fuckin' do," he growled.

"As the manager, it's my job to point out any issues."

He jabbed a finger at her. "*Your* job's to make this club scratch. To keep those girls on stage and rakin' in the dough. Don't you fuckin' forget that. Let me worry about the safety. Got it covered."

Sure he did.

She answered with, "Okay," because how else was she going to answer? She knew he wouldn't fix it. She doubted it was even broken. He probably shut it off somehow. Maybe even cut a wire, since what she saw was nothing but static.

"That's the way a woman should always be. Agreeable and no backtalking."

Asshole.

When she got to her feet to hightail it out of there, he blocked her way. She tried not to panic but her pulse thumped in her neck. "Yeah, you should be bringin' in a pretty penny for private dances. It's a waste you lookin' like that and not earnin' your keep."

She narrowed her eyes on him. "I more than earn my *keep*." And she would not be actively offering herself up for any private dances. He could go fuck himself.

He licked his lips. The ones difficult to see through his

unkempt beard. "Might hafta get one of those lap dances myself. Make sure you're up to the club's standards."

Dread tightened her chest. "I doubt Cookie would appreciate that."

"She's my ol' lady, she ain't my boss."

Great. "Okay, I need to get back out on the floor."

Her breath seized when he reached out and slid his fingers down a strand of her hair until the backs of his knuckles brushed over her bare cleavage. "You a real blonde?"

Taking a step back, she ran into the chair. She kept going, shoving it out of the way so she could escape his touch, but he snatched a fistful of her hair before she could step out of his reach. "Yes."

"Prove it," he said softly.

"I'm not going to do that."

One side of his mouth pulled up and he finally released her hair. She couldn't get away from him fast enough. Her heartbeat was racing out of control and she was creeped out with how bold he was.

"Tell Sapphire about Chubs, yeah?"

She nodded and power-walked out of that office all the way to the lobby to break the bad news to Sapphire. She only hoped that her hostess didn't quit on the spot. She didn't trust Chubs or any of the prospects to do their job right. Or do it at all.

As soon as she pushed through the double doors to the lobby, she didn't see Chubs, but Sapphire stood behind the counter, making change for a customer. It was something they did often so the men would have enough tip money for the dancers.

She waited until they finished, then just as she was stepping up to the counter, the front door opened.

Chapter Fifteen

FINN CAME to an abrupt halt just inside the door of The Peach Pit and took in the two women. One blonde, one brunette. Both beautiful as fuck.

Since the gun on his ankle would set off the metal detector, he didn't go any further. To avoid that, he would've entered through the employee door but when he tried it, it was locked.

While that was a good thing for the women's safety, it wasn't so good for him.

"I'm so sorry about your mom!" exclaimed the dark-haired hostess, rushing over from behind the counter and through the metal detector to give him a breath-robbing hug.

He blinked. *What?*

From over Sapphire's shoulder as she continued to squeeze the stuffing out of him, he saw Mel come over to stand slightly behind the hostess. She bugged out her eyes at him in a silent message. One that made him realize Mel must have made up some sort of story. Unfortunately, he had no idea what it was.

His eyes sliced from Mel back to Sapphire as the woman pulled away.

"Oh... Thanks. It's been... difficult." A warning, even by text, would've been nice so he wouldn't have walked into an unknown situation.

Mel gave him a thumbs up and a grimace.

"I can only imagine. Well, hopefully she's not in too much pain."

For fuck's sake. "Fortunately, she's not."

"Oh, that's a relief."

As soon as Sapphire went back through the metal detector, Mel swapped places with her. She grabbed him by the elbow and turned him toward the door. "Phire, can you keep an eye on things for a few minutes? I need to grab some fresh air."

"Of course. Take your time." She gave them an exaggerated wink.

He raised his eyebrows at Mel and only received a slight shake of her head in response before she shoved him out the door. She kept them moving until they were far away from the entrance.

When she finally stopped, they stood at the corner of the building in the shadows where no one could overhear them.

"Hello, girlfriend," he greeted, then leaned in and pressed his lips to her cheek. "So, what was that about?"

"Let me preface this by stating that I hate lying to my friend and best employee." She blew out a breath. "To set up the whole dating scenario, I told her we hooked up last night and we're going to see where things go between us. I also instructed her to not confiscate your phone when you come in. However, when she balked at that, I had to quickly come up with an excuse. Other than the real reason, of course. I explained your mother's very ill and her nurse needs to be able to contact you at a moment's notice."

He narrowed his eyes on her. "How sick?"

"Like hospice-type sick."

Damn. "While that's a good excuse, my mother would most likely disagree. Did you tell her with what? I don't want to be caught off guard if she asks me any questions."

"No."

It kind of creeped him out to say this but... "Even though she's never smoked a day in her life and is the healthiest woman I know her age, let's just say she has end-stage lung cancer because she was a chain-smoker."

Mel pressed a hand to her forehead. "I feel like I need to apologize to your mother, even though I've never met her."

"If, for some reason, you ever do meet her, let's not tell her we were planning her demise."

Mel let out an awkward laugh.

"And while I'm sure you don't like lying to your friend, it's best to keep her in the dark about what's going on with the investigation. If she sees any suspicious activity with the Demons, will she come to you about it?"

"Of course. And if she does, I'll pass that on to you."

He tilted his head and studied the woman with her face half hidden in shadows. "Just out of curiosity, is Sapphire her real name?"

This time her laugh was more genuine. "No, that's her stage name. She still uses it to keep her anonymity. Just like everyone knows me as MJ. None of us use our real names while here."

"That's smart. But if anyone wanted to find out who you really are or where you live, all they would have to do is find a way to run your Chevy's registration." Just like he did with the Astro Van.

Or, worse, follow her home.

"I realize if they're that determined, nothing will stop them."

Too fucking true. Whackos always found a way. "Speaking of safety, I tried to get in the back door but it was locked."

"It's kept locked. I'll give you the code. But since Taint's here tonight, maybe it's better that you didn't come in that way. He doesn't know about you yet."

The keypad was a much better idea than handing out keys as long as the code was changed on a regular basis. "How often is the code changed?"

Mel answered, "Monthly, unless there's a reason to do it sooner."

"What kind of reason?"

"Disgruntled employee. A violent boyfriend. Typical threats."

"Is anyone other than employees given the code?" he asked next.

"The cleaning people, that's it. The employees aren't supposed to give the codes to anyone, but you know how that goes."

"And you're giving it to me."

"Right. That might not go over well."

"If anyone complains, let me know and I'll just use the front entrance. The other issue besides me not wanting to give up my phone is that I'm carrying."

"Carrying what?"

The corners of his lips twitched. "I'm wearing an ankle holster."

Her gaze automatically dropped to his feet. "Oh."

"That's why I didn't step through the metal detector right away."

"I don't think I can come up with a good excuse for you to carry your weapon into the club."

"To be expected. I'll use the employee entrance when I can and lock the gun in the car when I can't."

"That sounds like a plan." Mel wrapped her arms around herself and shivered when a cool late September breeze blew through the dark parking lot.

"You shouldn't be out here dressed like that." He shrugged out of his light-weight leather jacket and hung it over her shoulders, giving them a squeeze after doing so.

Tonight she wore a long, turquoise slinky dress full of sequins that sparkled when she moved, hugged every damn curve, framed her cleavage perfectly and made her ass look downright edible. Though hot as fuck, it was sleeveless and open-backed. Definitely not made to be worn outside in cooler weather.

"Thank you."

"You ready to go back in?"

She shook her head. "No, there's something else I need to tell you and I can't inside... I checked the cameras earlier to see who left the van out back."

"And?"

"And nothing. The footage was nothing but static. Either the cameras are broken or they've been disabled. I even went back a week to see how long it's been disabled and it's been about three days. But get this, the rest of the cameras around the building *are* working. For now, anyway. I mentioned about it being disabled to Taint. He said he'd look into it and to not 'worry my pretty head' about it."

No fucking surprise. "The disabled cameras and his response pretty much confirms my suspicion about the van being used to stash their supply. Have you seen anything else tonight?"

"No, not yet," she answered.

"Did your so-called assistant manager show up yet?"

Mel huffed out a breath. "It's too early for her. If she comes in at all, it's usually last minute."

"I'll hang out here until she does. If she doesn't, I'll head back out and grab you some dinner. Sapphire, too, if she wants anything."

"She'd probably like that."

"In the meantime, while we wait to see if Cookie shows up and since Saint's here, I think it's a great time to show off our new relationship."

"Okay."

"Can you get me around the metal detector?"

She pointed at the corner of the building. "We can walk around to the back and go in that way."

"Sounds like a plan." He glanced down at her heels. They had to be at least three inches high. "Can you manage it in those shoes?"

She laughed. "Have you seen the shoes strippers wear on stage? These are a cake-walk compared to six-inch platforms."

He shook his head. "I don't know why you women torture yourselves like that."

"For men. Plain and simple."

"Honestly, we're not worthy."

She shrugged and smiled. "But your money is."

He liked a woman who told it how it was. No bullshit. All facts.

While the truth could be uncomfortable, lies could be downright painful.

He held out his hand and she stared at it for a second before slipping hers into his. He gave it a squeeze and guided her through the dark to the rear of the building where he had parked next to her turquoise Trailblazer. Almost the same color as her dress.

Her eyes, too.

"Did you purposely match the color of your SUV to your eyes?"

"I never really thought about it until you mentioned it. I just thought the color was pretty."

Like you.

She released his hand when they got to the back door to punch in the code, repeating it out loud so he'd have it. He stored it away in his memory bank.

He hesitated before opening the door for her. "I'm going to hit the head and use it as an excuse to snoop around a bit."

"Okay, I'll go check in with Sapphire."

"I'll find you when I'm done."

She paused with her hand on the door handle. "Just be careful since Saint *is* lurking around. He was in the office when I saw him last."

He remembered seeing a closed door at the end of the hallway with an "office" plaque. "That's on the right, just inside the door?"

"Yes."

He nodded, pulled the door open for her and placed his hand on the small of her back, guiding her inside.

She shrugged out of his jacket and held it out to him. Once he took it, he stood there watching her head down the hallway, leaving him on his own. Yeah, he was right. Her ass was fucking spectacular in that dress. And the sexy, graceful line of her spine...

Fuck.

At the end of the corridor, the prospect named Popeye unclipped the red velvet rope and let her out into the main area of the club.

Finn walked past the office on his right and the dancer's dressing room on his left. The next two rooms were the VIP rooms. They were across from each other with numbered plaques next to the doors. Even though they seemed to be unoccupied, when he tried the knobs, he found them both locked.

As he continued on, he kept an eye on Popeye's back. With the DJ's music filling the club, the prospect probably had no idea Finn was wandering around backstage and he'd like to keep it that way for as long as possible.

As soon as he heard the office door open behind him, Finn beelined it toward the men's room but froze when he heard, "That stupid fuck let you back here?"

Finn assumed the "stupid fuck" was Popeye. He turned to face the man himself. Saint. "I'm looking for MJ."

The DIC—Demon In Charge—sucked on his teeth and narrowed his dark eyes on Finn. "Why you lookin' for her?"

"She's my girlfriend and I keep an eye on her."

Saint's head jerked back and he frowned. "Didn't know she was fuckin' anybody."

"I didn't know you two were besties and shared your personal lives with each other."

Even with his long, bushy beard, Finn could see the man's jaw clench. They locked gazes in a silent stare down.

Saint's dark eyes narrowed even more until they were practically slits. "Wait. Aren't you one of those fuckin' Pricks?"

Actually, that would be pretty fucking funny if it was coming out of anyone else's mouth other than the biker's. "Peckers."

"Like I give a fuck."

Finn shrugged. "You should since I figure our troupe made your club a bunch of scratch."

226

"And I figured you guys were all fags. Surprised you're hittin' that slit."

Fuck you, you motherfucking homophobic dirtbag. I can't wait to take your ass down.

Finn's chest tightened and his molars ground together. Pinning his fists to his sides also prevented him from laying that motherfucker out cold.

Getting into a brawl with one of the subjects of their investigation would be stupid and could possibly fuck up his chance at future access to The Peach Pit. Instead, he let his anger rage in his head and pulled in a deep breath in an effort to keep it contained.

Play it cool, Finn, play it fucking cool. Assholes are going to asshole.

"Name's Danny."

"You think I give a fuck? Shouldn't be back here."

"Like I said, I was only looking for my woman."

"Look elsewhere," Saint ordered, clearly not leaving any room for negotiation. "She ain't supposed to be back here fuckin' off and you ain't either."

"Didn't mean to impose. I'll see myself out."

Saint pulled on his scruffy beard. "You do that. But don't be distractin' her from doin' her job."

Finn sucked in a slow breath and nodded. "I won't get in her way." With that and clenched teeth, he headed back out into the stage area, pushing past Popeye.

It was time to settle in for the evening and start observing.

And not the girls on stage, either.

Two hands landed on his shoulders and a soft cheek pressed against his. "Hey, boyfriend," was whispered into his ear.

"Hey, yourself." He twisted his neck. "Kiss."

Mel didn't hesitate to plant one on his lips, but it was a lot shorter than he'd prefer.

She smelled so damn good. She wore just enough fragrance to get his blood racing but not enough to make it curdle.

As she rounded his chair, he snaked his arms around her hips and settled his hands on her ass, giving her firm cheeks a squeeze. "Goddamn, you must work out."

She gave him a smile that sparked a fire in his gut. "I do. And I'm glad I keep in shape since Taint informed me earlier that I have to make myself available for private dances."

"He did what?" burst from him and he sat up straighter, regretfully dropping his hands from her ass. He grabbed her arm and pulled her into his lap so they could talk without the fear of being overheard.

As if it was a common thing between them, Mel settled in and hooked her arms around his neck. Even so, she kept her head on a swivel. Most likely keeping an eye out for Saint.

"He said he looked at the books—" Mel rolled her eyes, "which I highly doubt—and determined the majority of the money made is from time spent in the VIP rooms."

"Is that true?"

"No. If the business had to rely on what's made in the VIP rooms, Laura would've had to close the club's doors years ago."

"Did you agree with going back to doing private lap dances?" Why did that idea annoy him so fucking bad? She was his fake girlfriend, not his real one, *for fuck's sake.*

"Of course not. While it's good money, I gave that up five years ago."

"You don't have a choice?"

"Not if I want to keep my job."

He ground his molars. *Jesus fucking Christ.*

"But that doesn't mean I'm going to go around advertising that opportunity. He's requiring that from Sapphire, too. Fortunately, she isn't as upset about it as I am since she still occasionally fills in on stage if a dancer calls out. It also doesn't hurt that she makes a nice chunk of change every time she lands a private dance."

"Are you totally naked when you do a private dance?" He rubbed at his chest because he suddenly had heartburn.

"Legally, I can't get totally naked, but normally the girls get down to thongs where only our lips are covered. And you know what lips I'm talking about."

He certainly did.

"What the girls charge depends on what the customer wants and for how long they want it."

"Like touching?"

"Touching. Grinding. Even cleanup."

"Cleanup?"

"Do I need to explain why they'd need cleaned up?"

"No. I've had a private dance before, but I don't remember it going that far."

"Did you ask?"

"It was my twenty-first birthday, I didn't know to ask. I probably couldn't afford it, anyway. Not when my fist is free."

She shook against him when she laughed.

"Would I get a discount? Being you know... your boyfriend and all?"

"If you're my boyfriend, wouldn't you see me naked for free?"

229

"Would I?" She was sitting on his lap and if they continued to talk about her giving him a lap dance, she might get an unexpected surprise.

And maybe have to do a little cleanup afterward.

"Well, if you want to practice, I'll be glad to give you my best critique. Especially after you've seen me bumping and grinding in only my skivvies. It's only fair."

She combed her fingers through his hair, and leaned in until her warm breath swept over his cheek. "I'll keep that in mind."

"I don't like that you're being forced to do something you don't want to do."

"Did you really want to strip on stage for *your* job?"

Good point.

"And if I don't, I have a feeling if he doesn't fire me, he'll force me to go back to dancing full time. Right now, I don't have any other options. I wish I did and I'll keep looking, but..." She sighed. "Enough about that. Have you seen anything worth taking note about?"

"No. I sat here on purpose so I can keep an eye on Popeye and also on Mutt behind the bar." He pointed to his barely-touched drink. "His bartending skills suck, by the way. How hard is it to make a Jack and Coke? A toddler could make a better one."

She sighed again. "I know. Taint acts like he's so damn worried about making money. The bar brings in a ton with the right bartender, but the idiot fired them all."

Of course he did. He didn't have to pay the prospects much, if anything, and they were most likely involved in the meth dealing. The less outsiders working in the club, the better. "How about you? Have you seen anything?"

"I'm definitely keeping my eyes peeled now. The only thing to report is Sapphire's training a new prospect named

Chubs and she complained that he keeps going out front to smoke."

"He probably is."

"But is that all he's doing?"

"There are cameras pointed on the front lot, right?"

"Yes, three. Two cover the lot itself and one the front door. There's also one in the lobby pointed at the entrance, too. All of those *were* working when I checked them this morning."

"Then I need to come in here when the club's closed so I can go through some of the footage."

"When do you want to do that?" she asked.

"Tomorrow morning before any Demons get here."

"Okay. I'm usually here a couple of hours before opening. And now that you have the code, you can just let yourself in the back door."

"That should give me plenty of time to skim through some of the footage you have from the last thirty days. I might even bring a flash drive along to download the files so someone else on the task force can go through them carefully."

"I could probably just give you the direct link and password to the cloud storage."

"The only problem with that is it might record the IP address we'd access them from. I'd prefer we don't tip them off."

"Do you think Taint would know anything about IP addresses?"

Saint was probably a complete dumbass, but... "Not going to risk it. I'll grab what I can get tomorrow and then run it past the task force leader. I'm sure the feds have experts with a way of getting around that problem."

Movement caught Finn's eye. Saint was working his way

over in their direction with his eyes glued on them. *Goddamn it.* "You should get back to work. Let me know if Cookie shows up."

"Oh shit," slipped from Mel when she spotted Saint.

Finn helped her to stand before he stood, too. He didn't want to remain seated and give Saint the upper-hand.

"You'll know when Cookie shows up. With the way she looks and acts, you won't be able to miss her," she whispered, then gave him a quick parting kiss. "I'll check back with you when I can."

"He buyin' a lap dance?" Saint growled, stopping in front of them both.

Finn squared off with him. "Why the fuck would I pay for something I get for free?"

Saint jabbed a finger toward the floor. "You're standin' in my house right now and you wanna be touchin' my girl and have her sittin' in your lap, then you pay." He turned to Mel. "What'd I tell you about earnin' your keep?"

He was acting like The Peach Pit was a damn brothel and he was the pimp. *Fuck that.*

"She's retired from dancing. I'm not okay with her getting naked in front of other men."

"She will do what I tell her to do."

Finn cocked an eyebrow. "That's my job, not yours. She's a top-notch manager and you could never replace her. *That's* what you pay her for."

"Didn't hear me askin' your fuckin' opinion. You wanna be in this club, you keep that shit to yourself. If you can't, then you know where the fuckin' door is."

"When it comes to MJ, I have a say as her man. You should know how that is."

"How long have you been her man? A fuckin' second?"

"Longer than that. I'm sure you can understand what it means when I say I claimed her."

Saint stared at him, then his gaze sliced to Mel, held for a few seconds, then came back to Finn. "When she's here, her ass belongs to me. When she's out there, it belongs to you. You don't like it, you can get the fuck outta here and take her with you."

Mel slipped her right arm around his back, planted her left hand on his gut and leaned into him. She turned her face up to him and away from Saint, widening her eyes slightly, but enough for him to notice. "Honey, it's okay. I need this job." She patted his stomach.

That was a good reminder to back off. Finn was too close to getting his ass kicked out and that would defeat the whole purpose of playing Mel's boyfriend.

He shoved down his rising annoyance. "You're right, baby. I know you need that money. You just know how much I hate sharing you."

She got up on her toes and pressed a kiss to his cheek. "It's just business." She released him but didn't move away from his side.

"She'll be rakin' in a whole lot more with her time in the VIP room." Saint smirked and raked his gaze over Mel. "Might have to book a lap dance for myself."

Fucking motherfucker.

His nostrils flared and he choked down the words on the edge of exploding from him.

She isn't your real girlfriend, dummy.

"Might even be addin' some more options to the VIP room menu. The more scratch a customer's willin' to part with, the more he'll get." Saint stared at Finn, waiting for a reaction.

He struggled to keep his face a blank mask. "The girls

should have the option on how far they're willing to go."

"They got options. It's called a fuckin' door. They can stay or go. That's it."

"You're going to lose dancers," Finn warned, not wanting any of the girls to be in a situation where what they do could be considered prostitution. It could not only get them in hot water, but get the club shut down, putting them all out of work.

"Then I'll fuckin' replace them. Now," the Demon turned to Mel. "Go work on partin' these men from their money. Nobody should leave here without an empty wallet."

With a last look at Finn, Mel nodded and turned. When she did, Saint smacked her ass so hard, the slap could be heard over the music.

Mel jerked forward, but caught herself. It took her a second or two to shake it off and after inhaling deeply, she strode away.

Finn was damn sure if she had a gun, that motherfucker would have an extra hole dead center in his forehead.

He was tempted to put one there himself. The only thing holding him back was he knew karma would eventually make herself known to the Deadly Demons and he'd be the one to help introduce them.

Saint's smirk widened. "She got a tight snatch?"

Finn turned his attention back to the asshole biker. "You'll never fucking know."

The Demon's grin disappeared and he took a step closer. "Givin' you two options, too. Stay or go. You stay, you better be spendin' some scratch. You don't, you'll be goin' with some help from my bouncers. You got me?"

Finn met the asshole's eyes and held them. He counted to ten in his head before responding. "Yeah. Hear you loud and clear."

Chapter Sixteen

ONLY TWO VEHICLES were parked in the employee lot behind the club this morning. No, three. How could he forget the stash van sitting there like a sore thumb?

He punched in the four-digit code and waited for the lock to click. As soon as he yanked open the door, he heard it.

Music. Not quite as loud as when a DJ was in the booth, but loud enough to hear strains of it all the way at the rear of the building.

Tomorrow he would start dropping her off at work and taking her home, just what a controlling boyfriend would do.

The office door was open, but the lights were off. The same for the dressing room.

When he continued toward the stage area, he noticed both VIP room doors were closed, so he figured they were still locked.

The closer he got to the end of the hallway, the music became louder and the bass thumped more intensely against his chest. While not in view of the stage yet, he could see that most of the club's interior was dark.

Just as he stepped out into the main area, the song changed to *Earned It* by The Weeknd, a slow and sultry tune.

A spotlight lit up the stage and caught in that bright beam was a blonde...

Not just any blonde.

Mel. Completely lost in the music. Or in her head.

With her eyes shut and one hand holding the pole above her head, she circled it in a seductive strut by lifting her knees high and keeping her body fluid. The word *graceful* flitted through his brain.

Her wearing a black fedora was as unexpected as seeing her on stage.

After a sudden spin, she pinned her back to the pole, tipped the hat down and slid down until she was squatting on her heels with her knees spread.

When she slid back up, she removed the hat and whipped it, spun around to face the pole, grabbed it with both hands and arched backward. She was so damn flexible, the ends of her hair, a flowing gold waterfall, almost brushed the floor.

And her outfit...

Sweet baby Jesus. She wasn't naked, but what she wore was sexy as fuck.

Her black, skin-tight, high-waisted shorts had straps circling the top of her thighs, reminding him of garters. The matching skin-tight black top, at first glance, could be a fancy sports bra, but he never saw one quite as elaborate with four black straps radiating up her chest to meet the one circling her neck like a choker. Another black band hugged her under her breasts and two triangles of what could be spandex barely contained the overflowing ivory flesh.

How her breasts didn't fall out of that top while she whipped around that pole, like a washing machine set to the spin cycle, before hanging upside down, he didn't know. But then, there might be a secret to it. One like the elastic bands that kept the Peckers hard while they danced.

The difference between Mel this morning and the women dancing last night was she was barefoot and couldn't be wearing a stitch of makeup. Her ivory skin had a natural glow and a light sheen of sweat made it glisten under the spotlight.

When her eyes opened, she was still unaware he stood frozen in place, not even a foot past the end of the hallway. He needed to let her know he'd arrived, but he also didn't want to disturb her. Or his own personal show.

While the dancers last night were good, Mel was perfection. It could be he was a bit biased.

Facing the pole, she slid her arms up until they were stretched above her head as far as she could reach. Once she got a better grip, she shimmied effortlessly all the way to the ceiling. Hooking a single leg around the metal tube and only holding on with one hand, she extended her body out and spun.

Holy fuck.

An insane amount of upper body strength was needed to do some of the moves she was nailing. But then, he'd never seen abs like that on a woman. Not to mention, the powerful thighs that kept her from crashing to the stage and breaking her damn neck.

When she suddenly flipped upside down, only holding on with both legs, his breath seized.

While still inverted, she slid down until her hands met the stage and she did a move he could only call a cartwheel, even though it wasn't. It reminded him of a leg flip that a gymnast might do.

The woman was the epitome of strength and grace.

237

He'd been to plenty of strip clubs in the past and while, yes, it took a lot of strength and power to do the job right, a lot of dancers simply didn't care. They did the "bare" minimum to make their money. Show tits and ass. Flirt with the customers. Maybe sensually play with another dancer to get the men frothing at the mouth.

But some were true athletes. Their core strength insane. Their control spectacular. Their dance moves choreographed carefully. Those were the women who impressed him the most.

Powerful but still feminine.

Beautiful. Athletic. Sensual.

Impressive.

Mel was all of that. And more.

When the song changed to *Body Party* by Ciara, she whipped around the pole again, gripping it with only one hand and the back of one knee, her blonde hair fanning out around her like a cape caught in the wind. Her back arched and she flung her head back as she continued to circle.

He knew the exact moment she spotted him. A fraction of a second later, she landed hard on her ass with a grunt. He rushed over to the stage to where she was folded over, one hand pressed to her pumping chest and her hair hiding her face.

His heart had wedged in his throat. "You okay?"

She lifted her head and said breathlessly, "Holy shit, I thought you were one of them."

Them. "A Demon?"

She nodded, getting to her feet.

"Do they know you come in here early to dance?"

"No. They haven't discovered that yet. If they do, I'll be forced to stop."

"By them?"

"Yes, but not because they won't like me using the stage to stay limber and in shape."

"Because you don't trust them," he concluded.

"Yes."

It pissed him off that she had to be so damn cautious because of the club's new owners. Now he worried about them catching her on stage, dressed like that. While what she wore shouldn't matter, with them, it might. Especially when the club was closed, like it was now, and no one else was around. No witnesses. No one to have her back.

He tamped down his rising fury. The best thing he could do for her would be to help serve karma on a fucking platter to those Demons. "Do you trust me?"

He hoped her slight hesitation only meant the question had been unexpected. Then again, she hardly knew him. He no longer assumed citizens thought cops were trustworthy or good. He had seen plenty of shitty ones himself.

So, taking caution with someone new was smart, whether a person wore a badge or not.

"Yes, but I didn't think you'd show up quite this early. I thought I'd be done before you got here."

"How many times a week do you dance?"

"As many as I can manage."

His gaze rolled down her body, appreciating how toned and fit she was. Since he worked hard on his, too, he knew how much time and dedication was involved. He swept his hand out. "Then don't let me stop you."

She lifted an eyebrow. "An audience of one?"

"I can keep an eye out for any intruders." It wouldn't be a sacrifice, that was for damn sure. He tipped his head to the side. "Do you mind?"

"It's only fair, I guess, since I got to ogle you."

A smile pulled at his lips. "You were ogling me?"

Her shoulders lifted and fell. "You're hard to ignore."

Speaking of hard, he was surprised he wasn't right now. With how she was dressed, with the way she moved, with how husky her voice had become with that last statement. "The feeling's mutual."

A bit of mutual appreciation was definitely going on between them.

The song changed again, filling the space between them with *Dark Horse* by Katy Perry.

Pressing her shoulder blades to the pole, she stretched one arm up, cocked one knee and planted her bare foot on the narrow metal cylinder behind her. Arching her lower back, she pushed out her tits, then licked her lips and gave him a look that sent fire roaring through him.

Goddamn.

Normally, strippers used those types of actions to cause a reaction... A shower of cash being thrown onto the stage or a customer booking a private dance. It was a look perfected to make the man, or woman, think they were the only one in the room getting the dancer's attention, when that was farthest from the truth.

But *no one* else was in that club this morning.

And he certainly hadn't dug out his wallet to make it rain cash.

Falling forward at the waist, she swung her head and torso in an arc, flinging her hair so it caused a blonde explosion around her. When she straightened, her gaze rolled from his feet to face with excruciating slowness.

But every cell—every damn one of them—in his body stood up and took notice when she winked and crooked a finger at him.

A bass drum beat in his chest and his cock became as hard as the damn pole she was gripping.

He was in no way ignoring that invitation, so he hopped up onto the end of the stage. Walking an invisible line, he stepped heel to toe and added a roll to his hips and shoulders, the same way he had during his routines the last two Monday nights. As he did so, she continued to work the pole, keeping their heated gazes locked.

Then he was there, standing in front of her, close enough to touch.

Close enough to fill his nostrils with her scent.

Close enough to see the pulse pounding along her throat.

Close enough to see the unmistakable invitation in her Caribbean blue eyes.

Jesus. Was there any other woman more captivating than the one standing before him?

From the second he saw her across the club his first night at The Peach Pit, she quickly sucked him in without even trying. And this morning, he was giving up and going under.

Completely fucking under.

What was crazy about the whole thing was they had only kissed so far. He didn't understand this pull.

Who was he to question it? He would act on it, instead.

Starting at her temple, he dragged the back of his hand along the edge of her face, down the side of her long neck, traced the black elastic collar circling her throat, then continued across her collarbone. He skimmed his knuckles along the outer curve of her breast and down her ribcage. He paused only long enough to flick the dangling jewelry at her navel with his fingernail before dragging his fingers along the taut skin of her belly and finally curling them around her hip in a tight grip.

Letting the song *I See Red* by Everybody Loves An Outlaw flow through him, he lightly trailed the fingertips from his other hand, starting from her armpit, up the tattooed skin of the arm stretched above her head. When he reached her hand, he took it and unwrapped it from the pole and pressed it to his own chest, where his heart thundered under her palm.

Her lips parted, her eyelids got heavy. Her chest rose and fell at a rapid pace. Her nipples were shouting, "Hello! How are you?" through the black fabric of her top.

He slowly guided her hand along the side of his face, over his beard, down his throat, then hooked her arm around his neck, ready to draw her closer.

But before he could, she pulled away, breaking their connection, and with an amazing quickness and agility, once again shimmied up the pole using her upper body strength and by gripping the silver cylinder between her knees. At the very top, she spun in several circles, hanging on with just one hand and her thighs.

When she let go, she once again fell backwards until she hung upside down, the dangerous move stealing Finn's breath.

He was fearful she'd fall. Amazed that she didn't.

Staying inverted, she corkscrewed down the pole head first. Only stopping once they were face to face. Her upside down. Him right-side up.

A smile slowly grew across her face and she grabbed his head, pulling him to her and crushing their lips together.

While it was the most awkward kiss he'd ever experienced, it was also hot as fuck.

He was dying to touch her the way he wanted. Brush his fingers over her pointed nipples, curl them around her throat, drive them into her long hair, dig them into her muscular ass, slide them inside her wet heat.

But not at this moment. Not on that stage. It would have to wait for a better time, a better place.

He had no doubt it would happen. He only needed patience and a plan.

She sucked his bottom lip into her mouth and gently clamped down on it with her teeth before releasing him.

Somehow she swung her legs without kicking him and ended up standing with two feet on the stage. She pressed her back to the pole again and kept both of their arms stretched over her head, hanging on.

Using the back of his knuckles, he brushed the wild mane of hair out of her face, then splayed his fingers over her cheek and leaned in.

She met him halfway, letting him take the lead this time. He claimed her lips and invaded her mouth with his tongue. Sweeping and tasting every corner, sucking on her tongue, her lips.

With every inhale he took her in, with every exhale he gave her him in return.

While they kissed, they began rolling their upper bodies and hips in synchronized moves following the rhythm of the song. It only took a hot second before the rolling turned to grinding.

His fingers slipped from her cheek to dive into her hair and fist it. The kissing became more fevered. Until finally, he had to stop before he fucked her right there against that pole, on the stage, where anyone could walk in and see them.

Her breathless, "Wow," whispered across his lips.

His rock hard cock ached unbearably. He'd never wanted a woman as much as he wanted the one before him. His voice sounded strained when he asked, "Are you as turned on as I am right now?"

With her ragged breath puffing from between parted lips, she slid her hand down his throbbing erection and he pressed into it. "Did I leave any doubt?"

No. He could see it. The flush, the nipples, the heat in her eyes. The way she had moaned during their kiss.

He had zero doubt. "While I'm sure it would be hot as fuck to take this further here, I'd prefer to avoid the Demons walking in and witnessing it."

"That would scar me for life."

He cupped her cheeks and tipped his head down to meet her eyes. "Your place?"

"Now? I need to open soon." She smiled and planted a hand on his chest. "But... I have an idea."

"Don't say your car." It wasn't only the fact that it was a car and that was not where he wanted to fuck her for the first time, it was the fact that cameras were out there. While they might be considered "disabled" that didn't mean they were broken. He wouldn't put it past Saint to have a way to access them to keep an eye on what his prospects were doing with the stash van.

That would be smart on that asshole's part.

Not only didn't he want to be seen with his pants down by that motherfucker, he definitely didn't want Saint seeing Mel naked.

And Finn wanted her completely naked.

"Don't worry. I won't."

Now his curiosity was piqued. "Then where?"

Without answering, she rolled her lips under like she had a secret and grabbed his hand.

Was he a damn fool right now because he'd follow her just about anywhere?

Yes, yes he was, but, with her firm tug, he went with her anyway. She paused at the back of the stage only long enough to snag the fedora from the floor and drop it onto his head with a smile that lit up her face.

She continued on her mission and he let her blindly led

him to whatever she had planned next. Which was down the stage steps and back hallway, until they stood in front of VIP room number two.

The knob turned freely in her hand, surprising him, and she pushed the door open and yanked him into the dark room.

A switch was flipped and the room lit up with a red glow. For a second, he thought he stepped into a damn cherry. Everything in the room was red, not just the filtered light. A red high-backed couch sat along one wall, upholstered in vinyl. Most likely for easy cleanup. The opposite wall was completely made up of mirrors. A red armoire was tucked into the back corner. A small table sat next to the long couch, holding a lamp, a box of tissues and what looked like baby wipes.

No surprise there wasn't a pole since the ceilings were of normal height. Would he love to see Mel working the pole totally naked?

Fuck yes.

Some kind of small screen sat on another corner table and Mel immediately went over to it.

"What's that?"

"A smart system that controls the lights, regulates the room's temperature and plays music. There's also an emergency button the dancer can push if she needs help. There's a notification system at both the bar and also up in the front lobby, as well as in the dressing room. If the emergency notification goes off, an army will come running."

Smart.

She tapped on the screen and the lights dimmed a bit further. A few more presses later, music filled the room from hidden, built-in speakers. He didn't recognize the song but it had a heavy bass.

"Do you all have personalized playlists ready to go?"

"Yes."

This was no half-assed business. At least until the Demons got their grubby little paws on it. They had already started cutting corners—like replacing good employees with prospects—and he doubted they would be upgrading anything. Or even be worried about the girls' safety. He could see the club spiraling into a dark pit and everyone beginning to bail as that ship sunk.

But the Demons' lack of business sense wasn't his problem at the moment. His focus was elsewhere. "How often is this room cleaned?"

She turned and regarded him. "The cleaning crew cleans it every night after closing. From top to bottom."

"And in between bookings?"

"Girls are on their own for that. If we're available, Sapphire or I will do a quick wipe down. But on the nights the VIP rooms are busy that means the club's busy and we're hustling as much as the girls."

She moved over to the wooden armoire and when she opened it, he could see shelves full of things like towels and cleaning supplies. As he moved closer, he also spotted condoms and dental dams.

What the fuck.

"You keep condoms in the rooms?"

She licked her lips. Was she nervous? Well, he *was* a cop and getting paid for sex was illegal in the Commonwealth of Pennsylvania. Cops went undercover all the time doing stings on massage parlors and clubs for that reason.

"They're not charging for... that."

"Mel..."

She shook her head. "They're charging for renting the VIP room by the hour, or partial hour, or even by the number of songs plus any alcohol, like a bottle of champagne. If one of the girls wants to take it further, that's on her. Once the door is closed, what she does is her own business."

"That's skirting the law."

"As long as it's not breaking any laws... Again, it's up to the girls what they do and how far they take it. However, I'm worried if it's up to Saint, that might change."

"If he pushes them into prostitution, him taking a cut would make him a pimp. He could get charged for that alone."

"If that happens, the girls would get charged, too. Even if they're forced."

Of course they would. "If it comes to that, you all need to walk out."

"Easier said than done. A lot of people have no choice to stay at jobs they hate." She sighed. "Enough about that. Please. That's not why I brought you in here."

He cocked one eyebrow. "Not to have sex?"

"Well... not to have sex for money." She threw a couple of condoms on the vinyl couch, then dragged a chair over from the wall to the center of the room.

She headed back to the smart system and clicked through the beginning of several songs until the room filled with Joe Cocker's *You Can Leave Your Hat On.*

She turned and pointed to the chair.

Hell, he was no fool, so he sat.

And, *fuck him,* he left his hat on.

Chapter Seventeen

FINN STARED straight ahead and waited. He swore the pumping organ in his chest had fallen into the stiff organ between his legs, since it pounded with every heartbeat.

He scrubbed his damp palms down his jean-clad thighs to avoid touching himself as she came around the chair to stand in front of him.

He was going to self-combust if she didn't do something and do it soon. All that would remain in the chair would be charred fabric and a pile of ashes.

The condoms, out of his reach on the couch, were calling to him.

"You don't have to do this, Mel. I don't need a show."

Her husky voice swept over him. "I want to finish what we started out on the stage."

So did he, but since he had considered that foreplay, he was ready to move on to the main event.

"Just let me do this."

His mouth opened.

Don't say shit, you idiot. Just let her do whatever she wants to do for you. To you. With you. All of the above.

His mouth snapped shut.

She did the high-step strut as she circled him in the chair, dragging her nails across his collarbones, his shoulders, the back of his neck, until she stopped behind him. She tipped his head back until she could see his eyes under the brim of the fedora. They stared at each other for a moment before she plucked the hat off his head and tossed it onto his lap. She wasted no time grabbing the hem of his shirt to pull it up and over his head.

He didn't turn around to see where his Henley ended up, because he really didn't give a fuck right then and there. He had more important things going on.

She reached over, pressing her breasts to his back, snagged the hat and replaced it on his head.

"Have a thing for hats?"

"I have a thing for you."

Well, fuck... The feeling was mutual.

She once again came around to stand in front of him and, using her knee, she knocked both of his open wider until there was space for her between them.

No lie, this was going to be the best fucking morning of his life. He already knew it and he still wore his damn jeans.

Squatting at his feet, she planted her hands on his thighs, threw her head back and circled it, causing her hair to fan out around her. As she rose once more, she rolled her body from hips to shoulders. Once... twice... and if she did it a third time, he would grab her at the waist, toss her on the couch and just take her without the fanfare.

His fingers squeezed the shit out of the sides of the cushioned metal chair, similar to one used at banquet halls, and forced himself to remain seated. He decided it was best he kept his mouth shut, too, since his voice might crack like a fifteen-year-old hormonal boy.

He only hoped that what happened during his first lap dance at twenty-one did not repeat itself at thirty-four.

He was more mature now, right? He had more control?

He wasn't so sure when she climbed onto his lap, straddling his thighs and ground her firm ass against his erection, driving him to the brink.

Jesus fuck. She was trying to turn his cock into Old Faithful.

"Mel," he croaked.

She pressed a finger to her lips, gave him a warning look and a sharp shake of her head.

He blew out a breath and gritted his teeth.

She arched backwards over his knees until she could plant her hands on the floor. Then, *fuck him*, she hooked her fucking calves over his shoulders, bouncing her ass against his already volatile dick.

He bit back a whimper as he stared at her crotch only inches from his face. She dropped her feet back to the floor on either side of him, arching her agile body into a freaking bridge.

How the fuck was she so damn flexible?

Then somehow—it had to be sorcery—she rolled her body backwards off his lap—again, like a gymnast—and popped up onto her feet, plucked the hat off his head and placed it back on hers. She turned and strutted a couple of steps away, taking herself just out of reach.

With a glance over her shoulder, she gave him a slow wink.

Did he stop breathing? He might have stopped breathing.

Using her thumb and forefinger, she flicked the fedora off

her head and rolled it expertly down her arm until it landed in her hand.

After the Joe Cocker tune, he had lost track of the music because he was so focused on Mel. What sane man wouldn't be? Even so, he didn't miss when the next song started—*Partition* by Beyoncé—and she began to move to the music, her hips and shoulders swaying with exaggeration.

The woman had some fucking skills. No one could argue that. She did the world a disservice by no longer dancing in front of an audience, but on the other hand, he was happy he was the only one seeing this display.

She rolled the hat back up her arm and, by popping her bicep, it landed right back onto her head. She had to have practiced that move a million times. That did not come naturally.

Reaching behind her neck, she released the Velcro on the collar portion hugging her neck. In another effortless move, she managed to peel off her top and throw it over her shoulder, all without knocking off the fedora.

The warm, damp fabric landed in his lap and he quickly gathered it in his fist.

When she spun around, she held the hat in front of her chest, covering everything but the outer curves of both breasts. Still swaying with the song, she shifted the hat around, only giving him tiny, quick glimpses of what he was dying to see.

When she finally threw the fedora to the side, he blinked and blinked again. Not because her tits were perfect—they were—but to make sure he wasn't seeing things.

Oh hell no, he wasn't. Both nipples were pierced with silver curved barbells.

He wanted to say something, but nothing would come

out. At least out of his mouth. He was worried something would spew out elsewhere before he was ready.

Since when had any woman ever taken him so easily to his knees like this before?

He'd been with plenty of them. He'd seen plenty of tits and ass. But the woman before him was blowing his goddamn mind. And "all" she was doing was dancing topless.

"Mel..." Again, he got a stern look, so he shut up and let her do her thing.

The problem was, he was desperate for her to do *him*. And soon.

She spun around again and hooked her thumbs into the high-waisted bottoms, wiggling her hips as she slowly worked the skin-tight fabric down a bit, then back up, down a little more, then back up.

Yep, she was an expert tease and her goal was to kill him.

She continued to work her hips and those damn shorts lower and lower, slowly exposing two firm, ivory cheeks he was tempted to bite and leave his mark behind.

His gaze followed the black fabric falling to the floor at her feet. When he slowly lifted his eyes, he followed the smooth lines of her body.

She bent over at the waist, grabbed her ankles, swung her head between her spread calves, her blonde hair sweeping the floor and giving him a clear view of a glistening pink pussy that made his mouth water. From between her legs, she blew him a kiss.

For fuck's sake.

She straightened and spun, giving him a look that made him think he might have said that out loud.

He raked his gaze down her again now that she was giving him the full monty. Nothing blocked his view of her body made up of curves and lean muscle. Abso-fucking-lutely stunning.

Did he somehow sleep through the last few months and he woke up right at Christmas?

It had to be Christmas.

Or his birthday.

Or a damn dream. And if it was, he was going to be very disappointed.

He'd been with some beautiful women, but Mel was so much more than that. But then, maybe he never took the effort to know any of the others. If he searched deep enough, maybe he never wanted to.

Here he was in a "fake" relationship with this woman, even as short as it was, and they were about to change the dynamic yet again, since what they were about to do was far from fake.

And he was done with sitting in that damn chair.

Without taking his eyes from her, he leaned over and quickly unlaced his boots, toed them off and yanked off his socks, almost ripping one in his struggle to get it off.

When he surged to his feet, she moved within arm's reach. But he had an important task to do first before he touched her. Because once he started, he wouldn't want to stop.

She pulled the chair out of the way, and began to circle him, sensually scraping her nails over his heated skin. Driving him absolutely out of his fucking mind as he quickly shucked out of his jeans and straining boxer briefs.

Obviously, he didn't do it as gracefully as her. In fact, he almost fell on his ass. Of course, he was more frantic than her to get naked. Because, *duh*, he knew what came next.

And his momma didn't raise no fool.

Once totally naked, he fisted his bobbing cock and

squeezed it tight before stroking it a couple of times and using his thumb to smear the precum over the throbbing crown.

A single finger traced the line of his spine, her palm ghosted over his ass, then the air shifted around them as she came to stand in front of him.

They were both totally fucking naked.

Nothing stood between them any longer.

She tipped her head toward the vinyl couch. "Sit over there. I'm not done with you yet."

"I'm done, Mel. I'm not sure I can take any more." If he wasn't careful, he might cross the finish line without her.

He wanted to ask if she'd done this with other men—not for work, but for her own pleasure—but, *fuck him*, he didn't want to hear the answer. In his own mind, he wanted to believe he was the only one lucky enough to have this personal experience.

He glanced over at the red vinyl, not so sure he wanted his bare ass cheeks and nuts sticking to it. As soon as his gaze flicked to the stack of towels in the open armoire behind Mel, she made a dance production out of grabbing one as the song *I Feel Like I'm Drowning* came through the speakers.

And just like *Leave Your Hat On*, the song by Two Feet was timed perfectly.

He had no idea how she made a towel so damn sexy, but she did when she used it as a prop as she sashayed back over to where he waited impatiently. "I want to touch you."

The corners of her lips pulled up slightly. "Soon."

"You're killing me, Mel."

She raked her gaze down his naked body. "You look pretty damn good for a dying man." She placed the towel on the couch and pointed to it. "Now sit."

To prove once again he was no fool, he sat. As soon as he was settled, Mel turned, giving him a view of her delicious ass, and backed up, wedging her bare body between his *just-as-naked* thighs before climbing on his lap backwards.

What was she doing?

When she settled in, her slick, hot cunt pressed against his cock that leaked with impatience.

She was so damn close. *So* damn tempting.

Relieved that they were finally getting down to business, he expected her to reach for the condom. Instead, she planted her hands on his thighs and did more sorcery by bending her body in an impressive way and setting her head on the couch in between his thighs.

Well, *damn*, that would be a weird, but wild, way to get head.

Gripping his thighs for balance, she managed to flip her legs up so her knees were perched on his shoulders and her sweet pussy only inches from his face.

He stared at the beautiful sight before him, forgetting to breathe for a second. At least until his nostrils flared to pull in the heady mix of a slightly musky and salty scent caused from the exertion of her dancing.

The addictive aroma was pure woman, making him want to smother his face between her thighs. If he suffocated doing it, so be it.

Seeing her pussy and inhaling her scent was like an addictive drug. He couldn't think about anything other than the sight in front of him and all he wanted was...

More.

"Tell me when I can touch you."

Her warm breath brushed over his twitching cock.

"I need to hear it, Mel." And fucking soon.

"Touch me."

Thank fucking fuck.

He grabbed two handfuls of her ass and pulled her

toward him. Shoving his nose right into her hot cunt, he breathed that intoxicating scent deep into his lungs before sliding his tongue through her slick folds to taste her.

Goddamn heaven.

Even after her sweet tang coated his lips and tongue, he still couldn't get enough. She ground her pussy into his face even further, her moan hitting his ears before it became muffled when she grabbed his cock and circled it with her lips.

He struggled to continue, to concentrate on bringing her to orgasm as the pull of her mouth wreaked havoc on his sanity. This woman was upside down giving him a blowjob he'd never fucking forget. Better yet, she wasn't just lapping or sucking the tip and doing the bare minimum, she was swallowing the shaft almost to his balls. She made a cock ring out of her fingers and squeezed the base as her tongue traced the thick ridge from root to rim.

Mentally, he shook himself free and began to eat her pussy like he was a contestant in a pie-eating contest with his hands tied behind his back. Clamping his lips around her clit, he sucked as hard as he could, causing her body to jolt and her groan to vibrate around his length.

She scraped her fingernails over his balls and pressed a fingertip mid-perineum.

Jesus, while she knew exactly what she was doing, it could end up being a problem.

His muddled brain reminded him that they didn't have all morning. Employees would be arriving to work soon, and, *for fuck's sake*, he was determined to use at least one of the condoms waiting on the couch before that happened. If she kept doing what she was doing, it tragically might go unused. That made him more determined than ever to make sure she came before he did.

Doing his best to block out her skills with her mouth and fingers, he concentrated on the sweet treat in front of him.

Best. Cherry pie. Ever.

He separated her cheeks and stroked his thumb through her crease over and over, pausing each time over her anus as he sucked one swollen fold into his mouth, then the other. However, every time she groaned around him, it pulled at his concentration and he had to fight even harder to stay on track.

Without warning, she released him with a loud gasp and slammed back into his face, almost breaking his nose. Her fingernails dug into his thighs and she groaned, "I'm... coming..."

Thank fuck!

But he didn't need her announcement, as her orgasm was so damn intense it was impossible to miss. Her anus pulsed under his thumb, and her clit throbbed in between his lips. Her powerful thighs crushed his head like a nutcracker.

Her body went from solid to liquid a few seconds later. However, she didn't move.

So, he did.

After a kiss to each quivering inner thigh, he maneuvered her legs until she was sitting right-side up and on his aching lap.

Their eyes met, held and, as if in sync, a slow smile spread across their faces.

Donna Summer's sultry voice filled the room when the queen of disco started singing *Love to Love You Baby*.

Mel wrapped her arms around his neck and pressed her pierced tits into his pumping chest. She followed the outer curve of his ear with the tip of her tongue and sucked on his earlobe. Then a whispered, husky, "Perfect," made his cock flex, even though it was crushed beneath her.

She was right. The '70s song had the perfect tempo and lyrics for what they were about to do.

When he reached for the condom sitting at the end of the couch, calling to him like a Siren, she knocked his hand away and snagged it, tearing it open. Without a pause, she reached between them, pulled his cock from under her and rolled the condom down his throbbing length.

When she rose on her knees, he grabbed her hips and held them tight. "Wait."

She hesitated, a crease marring her brow.

"Kiss."

Her expression smoothed out and she leaned in, brushing her lips over his. Once, twice... Before she could do it a third time, he invaded her mouth with his tongue, taking the kiss deeper. After a few seconds, he pulled down on her hips in a silent signal she understood. She lined him up and slowly sank down on his length, taking all of him.

With their mouths parted, but still connected, they both took a moment to simply breathe—one inhale, then a second —but neither moved.

He closed his eyes and breathed through the urge to slam up and into her once the sensation of the hot, slick cocoon snugly surrounded his pulsing cock. "Unless you want this over in a few seconds, we're going to have to start out slow."

She smiled against his mouth. He didn't find his concern as amusing as she did, but he also didn't want to pretend he wasn't teetering on the edge.

Because that edge was sharp and narrow.

She leaned back, amusement still on her face. "Do you need a distraction?"

"Baby, you *are* the distraction. But I guess I'll suffer through distracting myself with these," he teased. Cupping the weight of her breasts in both hands, he stroked the soft skin with his thumbs.

She curled a hand around the back of his head and pulled him down. He latched his mouth around one pierced nipple, flicking the tip and barbell with his tongue.

Since he'd never been with a woman with pierced nipples, he wasn't sure how far he could go without doing damage. He lifted his head slightly. "How rough can I get with them?"

"As rough as you'd like. They're fully healed."

"Do the piercings make them more sensitive?"

"For me, yes. I can now come solely from nipple play."

Damn. Now he was tempted to test that claim, but he was already at his limit. Worse, time was running out. To him, that only meant they'd have to do this again when time and the location wasn't an issue. He only hoped Mel would want the same.

"Let me just say they're hot as fuck."

She flicked her fingers at his nipples. "I bet you'd look great with them, too."

He grimaced since he was not one for needles. It was one reason he didn't have any tattoos. "I'll just enjoy yours."

She shook against him. "I'll enjoy mine, too."

With a grin, he pulled her other nipple deep into his mouth and sucked it as hard as he could. Her back arched and she dug her fingers into his hair, holding him there. But before he had his shit packed tight, she began to circle her hips.

She was messing with a stick of dynamite.

"Mel..."

"I want to come."

"Believe me, I want you to come, too... but... *fuuuuck.*"

He turned his face away and clamped his teeth together as she began to ride him like a jockey at the Kentucky Derby.

"Mel..." he forced through his clenched teeth.

"Just let me..."

The fuck if he was stopping her, his concern was more about disappointing her. He didn't want anything deterring her from doing this with him again. Blowing his load before she orgasmed might just do that.

Motorcycles. Meth. Mafia.

He chanted those words over and over in his head trying to distract himself.

Mel.

He needed to try something else because she was not taking this slow. She was a goddamn kangaroo hopping on his lap.

He turned his head back and opened his eyes, only to see her head thrown back and her mouth parted. A flush colored her fair skin and rose into her cheeks.

He tried to block out the noises she was making, but...

Out of desperation, he sank his teeth into the flesh around her nipple, then sucked it hard and teased the piercing with his tongue. If it was true that nipple play made her orgasm, then he'd use that to his advantage.

He kneaded one breast while sucking it and, at the same time he pinched and pulled the other nipple as hard as he could.

"Finn," she gasped.

"You like that?" he barely managed.

"Yessss," hissed out of her.

He did it again. Pulling one nipple as hard as he could, then twisting it while scraping his teeth over the pebbled tip of the other. He switched back and forth, giving each breast attention by sucking, pinching, plucking and biting.

261

The more attention he paid to her tits, the faster she rose and fell on his cock. Every time she hit bottom, she ground herself against him, driving him as deep as she could.

His attempt at a distraction might have been counterproductive.

"Mel," he murmured in warning against the soft curve of her breast.

"Just... Just a few... hang on..."

He dug his nails deeper into the cliff as he swung precariously. But he was losing his grip.

She groaned, "I'm almost there."

Same.

She grabbed his face and yanked him away from her chest, sucking his soul right out of him when she took his mouth. She slammed down one more time, ground her pussy hard against him and then exploded around him.

Holy fucking shit.

Her orgasm was so damn intense, he could feel every contraction, even through the condom. While that impressed him, it did not help keep his shit together one fucking bit.

Fuck it, he was raising the white flag. Abandoning the strong front he was desperately trying to cling to.

With his heart hammering a hole in his chest, he grabbed her hips, held her down, lifting his and, with a grunt from his very core, shot powerful jets of cum into the condom.

When he finally melted back into the couch, his chest and heart still pumping out of control, Mel fell across his chest, her ragged breathing sweeping over his ear.

"That," *pant*, "was," *pant*, "fun."

Hold up. Fun? "It was hot as fuck."

She straightened and their eyes met. "That, too." She ripped her gaze away and asked, "Ready?"

For what?

Ah, the dismount.

No. "Yeah." Circling the root of his slick cock with his fingers, he secured the condom in place as she lifted up and off him.

"Now... I need to go shower and get dressed before the girls come in for the early shift." She climbed off the couch and moved around the room gathering her discarded outfit.

How could she recover from that orgasmic experience that easily?

He would have preferred she had stayed on his lap so they could linger in that euphoric after-glow. *Hell,* he could even curl up together and take a cat nap. But apparently, she had things to do.

Technically, so did he. But, unlike her, he needed to recover first.

"I... need a minute." Or twenty.

"Take your time." She glanced over her shoulder as she tugged her black shorts up her legs. "What about the videos? My employees will be here soon."

Fuck the videos. He'd worry about those later. Right now he was too busy figuring out how much money he had in his account and how big of a diamond he should buy her.

He closed his eyes and shook reality back into his head.

He loved being a bachelor. He loved the variety of playing the field.

Never... Never in his fucking life had he had the urge to put a "ring on it." Not once.

So, why now?

Ridiculous. Quite clearly he wasn't thinking straight and, during that intense orgasm, a few brain cells were ejected along with his cum.

With a sigh and before he made the mistake of going down on bended knee, he said, "Tomorrow morning I'll pick you up at your house and we can watch some of the videos then. Will that work?"

Business. Stick to business. It was safer.

"Sure. I'll text you my address."

Shit. Should he tell her he already had it?

No reason to freak her out. "Okay. What time you want me there?"

"Will this be a regular thing?"

"The sex?" He sure as fuck hoped so.

She rolled her lips inward for a second, the corners of her blue-green eyes crinkling. "Picking me up."

"That's the plan. Unless I'm needed elsewhere."

Sinking her teeth into her bottom lip, she nodded. "Okay. I'll let you know what time later."

She headed toward the door.

"Hey..."

She paused with her hand on the knob and glanced back at him. He was sure he was a sight. Skin damp with sweat, his hair standing on end, her essence still clinging to his beard and his dick still wrapped in a full condom...

"I'll let myself out after I get dressed. I'll check back in later."

She nodded. "I'll see you then."

After she closed the door behind her, he dropped his head to the back of the couch and blew out a long, loud breath.

He was afraid he might have just tumbled down a deep black hole.

One he might not be able to escape.

Chapter Eighteen

Finn pulled into the driveway of a small gray stone church. He ducked his head to take a better look at the limestone building through his windshield.

Once he rechecked the address in Mel's text, he glanced up through the windshield again and snapped his fallen jaw back into place. While he had known her address previously, he had no idea *what* was actually at that address. He certainly hadn't expected an old church.

Not just any church, either. What looked like a historic one from the 1800s. The fucking place had a bell tower and everything.

A white wooden picket fence separated what would be considered the small front yard from what was most likely a backyard and met a matching four-foot limestone wall that surrounded a just as old cemetery.

At least she had no neighbors.

Well, she did. Sort of. But they were the silent-type since they were six feet under.

He was undecided whether having your home

surrounded by a cemetery with occupants over a century old was cool or creepy.

He'd have to ask her if she believed in ghosts. Or if her place was haunted.

He shuddered at the possibility.

Last night, he had wanted to follow her home but her so-called assistant manager never showed up again, so she was stuck working until closing. He had stayed for a while, but besides Popeye disappearing several times toward the back of the club last night, Finn hadn't noticed any dealing out in the open. The prospects were definitely not exchanging meth for money on the floor.

He had kept a close eye on Mutt, too, stationed behind the bar. If the wannabe bartender was dealing, he was being slick about it. He'd talk to Crew again about sending someone undercover into the club to test the prospects.

After he said goodnight to Mel, he had sat in the dark, in the Toyota Tacoma Crew had scored for him—*thank fuck*—and kept an eye on the Astro Van for over an hour.

Unfortunately, he didn't see a damn thing. Saint, like Cookie, never showed at the club at all and none of the prospects working the club last night took a trip out to the van.

Frustrated that this undercover assignment might not pan out, he finally went home to catch some shut-eye since he was scheduled to pick up Mel bright and early this morning.

Nine might not be so early for him, but with her long hours, it was for her. He didn't know how she managed a busy club with hardly any sleep night after night. The thought of how she was forced to push through exhaustion made his blood boil.

He would have a little discussion with Saint about those late nights. But in private and without Mel around.

As her overly protective and concerned "boyfriend," of course.

The subject of his thoughts slipped out the heavy wooden door tucked inside the stone vestibule, pausing only to lock it before jogging down three stone steps and heading over to his truck. He had no fucking clue how the woman had any energy to jog to the car, forget going into work early, dancing on stage for an hour and then managing the club for the next eight to sixteen hours.

Lots of caffeine could be the answer, since she carried a travel mug.

But however she managed it, this morning he could see it was beginning to take a toll.

The closer she got to the Tacoma parked in her stone driveway, the easier it was for him to see the dark circles under her eyes and deep creases in her normally flawless face. It was more apparent since, like yesterday morning, her face was make-up free.

It probably didn't help when the last two Mondays she would've had time off, hosting the Peckers had stolen that much needed down time from her.

He jumped out of the driver's seat and ran around to the passenger side just as she got there.

"Morning, girlfriend," he murmured.

"Morning, boyfriend," she countered with a smile ghosting her lips. "What happened to the Kia Souless?"

"I told Crew to get me something that would fit my undercover persona better. The Kia only fit if I was pretending to be a gay stripper, but since I'm stepping into the role of an over-protective, dominating boyfriend, I figured a truck would be more believable." He let out an "alpha-male" grunt.

"You should've picked a Ford then. You know, a lifted

truck with the big knobby tires and big metal balls swinging from the rear bumper."

He laughed. "Hey, I didn't get a choice. Really, I'm just glad to have a truck. I even like it. Rides nice."

"I'll be the judge of that," she said, handing him her travel mug while she hauled herself into the passenger seat.

Once she was settled and strapped in, he handed back what was strong coffee by the smell of it and slammed the door shut. He power-walked around the front of the Toyota and climbed into the driver's seat.

As he pulled the seatbelt across his body, he asked, "Where did the congregation go that used to be here?"

"They built a much bigger, more modern church down the road. One of those big mega places with all the fancy shit."

He put the truck in reverse to back out of her driveway and onto the road. "At least you've got quiet neighbors."

"For the most part."

"What does that mean? Is the cemetery haunted?"

Her delicate laughter filled the truck cab. "Do you believe in spirits?"

He glanced over to see her studying him as he drove. "Do you?"

"No. But you won't catch me wandering through the cemetery after dark."

"Your place is surrounded by graves, Mel. That short stone wall isn't going to stop the spooky afterlife from floating over to your side of it."

Out of the corner of his eye, he saw her shrug. "No place is perfect, right? The truth is, I fell in love with it when it came on the market. It had been previously refurbed into a residence perfectly and, luckily, it also was in my price range. The best part is, the location is peaceful."

"When was it built?"

"Methodists built it in 1867."

"Damn." He was right about the 1800s. "I can't wait to see the inside."

"You'll have to wait for an invite first."

He glanced over at her again with a cocked eyebrow. "What do I have to do to get one, girlfriend?"

She had been staring out of the passenger window and when she turned toward him, she wore a teasing smile. "I'll give you a tour tonight when you bring me home. As long as Cookie shows up tonight. If she doesn't, I might just roll out of the truck and right into bed. I can't take much more of this."

"Did you get any sleep at all?"

She took a long swallow of coffee, then sighed. "About three hours."

"You know, you could've slept in this morning and I could've put off checking the videos one more day." He really shouldn't delay but would. For her.

She scrubbed at her forehead. "I want to hit the pole before the doors open. Dancing helps keep my head on straight, puts me in a better mood and somehow gives me enough energy to power through my shift."

He got it. Working out did the same for him and also helped him focus. But he also didn't want her dropping from exhaustion.

Keeping his eye on the road, he reached over and snagged her hand, giving it a gentle squeeze. "You need to take care of yourself."

"I also need to keep squirreling away money so I can get the hell out of The Peach Pit."

"But pulling doubles so often might kill you before you get to that point."

"The long hours are also fattening my bank account. That fact helps keep me going."

"A fat bank account isn't going to matter if you're six feet under like your neighbors."

Her fingers stiffened in his, so he let the subject go. Like he planned, he'd have a word with Saint as the "concerned" boyfriend.

When he pulled into the back lot at the club, it was empty as expected, except for the piece of shit Astro Van.

He picked a parking spot on the opposite side of the lot and shut off the engine. He twisted toward her in the quiet interior. "Did you eat breakfast, or do you want me to grab you something?"

Her blue-green eyes softened. "I ate, but thank you."

"It's the least I can do for you for agreeing to help out our task force."

"Believe me, I want those fuckers to go down as much as you."

He pressed his lips together at the intensity she said that. It made him even more determined to make that happen.

The more proof the task force got, the easier it would be for the feds to indict and convict. In turn, shutting down that whole criminal organization. Maybe even the Russos, too.

In a perfect world, anyway...

"Plus, helping you is no hardship," she wiggled her eyebrows, "since it comes with perks."

"Like?" Would she admit that having sex with him was a perk?

She waved her hand through the truck cab. "Like my own personal chauffer."

He grinned. "That it?"

"Well, you *have* bought me dinner a few times. Who doesn't like to eat for free?"

He laughed. "Damn."

As she reached for the door handle, he stopped her. "Wait." He quickly got out and went to her side of the truck. After opening the door for her, he offered his hand.

She placed her warm fingers in his. "I didn't think cops were this chivalrous."

He snorted. "We have our moments. And believe it or not, a controlling boyfriend would open the door for you on any vehicle or building. It's a subconscious way of controlling your movement."

She climbed out and stared up at him. "Really?"

Fuck. He wasn't sure if that was true, but it sure as shit sounded good. "Yep."

"Then I guess I'll have to get used to you doing it as long as you're acting as my boyfriend."

He followed her to the employee entrance.

"How about if I set you up in the office to go through some videos while I do my workout?"

He'd rather watch her. But there would be plenty of mornings for that since he was sure this assignment would last a while. "Sounds like a plan. I'll keep my phone next to me while you're out on stage. Keep your phone with you and text me if any of the Demons come in through the front. I'll keep an ear out for anyone coming in the rear."

She plugged in the security code and as soon as the lock released, he held the door open for her.

"I'll stick around until the girls start arriving and once I know you're not alone, I'll head out and come back later, okay?"

She stopped in front of the door on the right, pulled out a set of keys from her small bag and unlocked it. "You don't have to worry about me."

"Mel, you're my girlfriend. It's my job to worry about you."

"Fake girlfriend," she reminded him.

"Partner in this assignment."

After stepping into the dark office, she flipped a switch, lighting up the interior, and he followed her over to the desk. It was covered in open beer cans, dirty glasses and just plain... filth.

"He's such a damn pig," Mel muttered, pushing trash out of her way. "He can't even keep his dirty boots off the desk." She sat in the office chair, wiggled the mouse to wake up the computer screen and began typing. "I'll pull up the site where the security footage is stored and put in my password to give you access."

He came around the desk to stand behind her as she got into the club's cloud account and pointed to the screen. "There are all the folders you need, one for each camera. There will be thirty days' worth. If we want to keep them longer than that, we have to download them to our own hard drive."

"Unneeded. The past thirty days will be more than enough to sort through. Once we go through these, it'll be easier to monitor future footage. We'll just have to keep up with them."

As soon as she stood, he went to take her place in the chair but she stopped him with a hand on his arm. "Hey, boyfriend..."

Glancing down at her, he searched her face.

"I..."

His stomach did a somersault when she took a deep inhale.

"I just wanted to thank you for giving me some hope after I had lost it all."

He tipped the brim of an invisible hat. "I'm here to protect and service, ma'am."

"Don't you mean serve?"

With a wink and a cocky grin, he answered, "That, too."

She rolled her lips under, but failed at hiding her amusement.

"I'll check on you before I leave." She nodded and before she could exit the office, he stopped her with, "Hey, girlfriend..."

When she paused, he tipped his head, indicating she should come back over to him. She closed the gap between them, keeping her curious eyes on his face.

Stepping into her, he curled his fingers around the back of her neck and pulled her even closer. "Kiss."

Their lips brushed once, then a second time before he took it deeper. Tasting a perfect mix of Mel and coffee.

He wished like hell they had time to do a repeat of yesterday morning.

You have a job to do, jackass. And that job isn't named Mel.

But he *did* want to do her.

Again.

He broke off the kiss before he said fuck it and they both got their daily cardio done in one of the VIP rooms.

He gazed down into her blue-green eyes, strumming his thumb over her soft cheek.

"Was that more practice?" she whispered. "Because no one was here to see it."

"It wasn't for them."

She stared at him a few more seconds, a soft smile curving her naked lips. "I'll leave you to it."

"Text me if you need me," he reminded her.

She nodded and it was impossible to pull his eyes from

her as she walked away. Once the office door was closed, he went to work.

————

SITTING IN THE TACOMA, Finn's eyes swept the shadowed parking lot for the hundredth time, searching for any signs of movement.

He'd been sitting there for over an hour already and was about to crawl out of his damn skin from boredom. He swore if Crew had him do surveillance for any length of time, he'd quit the task force. To him, sitting surveillance was inhumane torture.

But, once again, the last hour had been frustratingly fruitless since he saw no one dealing in the rear lot or going out to the Astro Van.

"Fuck's sake," he muttered.

If the line of Harleys parked in the rear lot was any indication, at least a half dozen Demons had to be inside the club. Like Mel feared, Saint was slowly replacing all of the employees with his own people.

That left no doubt that, between the increase in prospects, the original CI's report and the recent arrival of the Astro Van, the MC was dealing out of the club. He just needed solid fucking proof.

Finn sent Mel a text, hoping she had her phone with her.

Here. Can I get thru the back door w/o Saint noticing?

While he waited for an answer, he mentally ran through his day, both here at the club and The Plant.

While in the club's office this morning, he had watched a few recordings, looking carefully for any signs of dealing.

Like surveillance, it was mind-numbing work. Especially since *each* camera feed had about seven hundred and twenty hours' worth of footage to comb through. And there were *multiple* camera feeds.

Granted, a lot of it was of an empty parking lot or a dark, deserted club that could be fast-forwarded through, but it was still a time-consuming task.

An hour and a half was definitely not going to cut it. It wouldn't even make a dent.

Wanting to avoid any questions or blowing his cover, he had to be out of the office before any of the dancers showed up. He ended up downloading all the folders available onto a 16TB hard drive small enough to fit into the inside pocket of his leather jacket.

Once he shut down the computer and checked on Mel at the tail end of her workout, he reluctantly left her to head over to The Plant and sat through a few more hours' worth of security feed until he wanted to throw himself out of the third floor window.

He left the hard drive for Crew, hoping he would get someone other than him to scour the rest of the footage for evidence. Two or more sets of eyes were better than one, anyway.

Hell, the task force leader could throw a damn watch party if he wanted to. Show it on the big screen, invite all available task force members, get a case of beer and order in pizza.

That was one party Finn wouldn't be attending if he could help it.

When his phone finally dinged, he read the text from Mel:

> He's tied up with Mutt. Now's a perfect time.

He answered with:

> Heading in now.

Climbing out of the Toyota, he took a quick glance at the cameras at the rear of the building. One pointed at the paved lot, the other was over the employee door, facing downward. But like Mel said, they seemed to have conveniently stopped working the day before the stash van showed up. That left Finn with no proof of who dropped it off, though he had a damn good idea.

He walked down the music-filled hallway and paused behind Popeye standing guard at the velvet rope with his arms crossed over his chest. Just beyond the biker, Finn spotted the person who was most likely the culprit talking behind the bar with Mutt.

From where Finn stood, he could see the bartender nodding but not saying much as Saint's gums flapped.

Seeing that motherfucker instantly made his spine tighten.

As he pushed past Popeye, the surprised prospect growled, "How'd you get the fuck back here?"

"You must have been in the bathroom yanking on your dick," Finn said, not stopping. If Popeye had more to say, the prospect could chase him down.

With a quick glance over his shoulder, he saw the biker wore a sour expression but remained where he was.

Finn scanned the room and didn't see Mel, but he did spot Sapphire sitting on some man's lap, leaning in close and talking into the guy's ear. His guess was the former hostess was working hard to get the customer to buy a private show from one of the dancers. Maybe even from her since she was now being forced to work the floor.

However, the man's hands were not where they should be... kept to himself. Hell no, they were pawing Phire's ass and edging too close to her tits.

Finn took a little detour from his path to the bar to swing by the table.

He paused only long enough for him to ask Sapphire, "You good?" and receive a thankful nod and a widening of her manufactured smile in answer.

He nodded back and continued on his trek, his attention now pinned on the man with narrowed dark eyes watching him approach.

"What're you doin' interferin' with my girls?"

First off, they're not your fucking girls, you motherfucker. They're loyal to Mel. Those words cut like razor blades when Finn swallowed them down and said instead, "Wasn't interfering. I just wanted to say hello."

"Won't take me much to ban your ass from this club."

"I can't say hello?"

"You can fuckin' say goodbye."

Finn tipped his head toward the stage. "Just here to watch the show and wait for my woman to finish her shift so I can take her home."

Saint sneered. The man was in desperate need of a dentist. "Could also pick her the fuck up outside."

"I could, but I planned on spending some money in here tonight. Got a problem with that?" He turned to Mutt to prove his point. "Give me two fingers of your best bourbon, neat."

The *wet-behind-the-ears* biker most likely didn't know what the fuck a good bourbon was or how much two fingers were. He probably only knew Boone's Farm and toilet bowl moonshine. Why he was in charge of the damn bar, Finn couldn't fathom. Definitely not a smart business decision.

But then, he doubted Saint and the Demons cared about the actual business. It was only a front for their real money-making enterprise.

Finn threw a ten spot on the bar after Mutt dropped off a glass of amber liquid over ice. *Christ*, the fucker didn't even know what "neat" meant.

He sighed, took a sip to test to see just how "top shelf" the liquor was, then met Saint's eyes. "Need a word."

The Demon's eyebrows rose in a *"are you fucking kidding?"* type of way. "Standin' here. Say your piece."

"Want me to say what I have to say in front of your lackey?"

With a grumble, Saint sent Mutt to the other end of the bar, just out of earshot. "Start talkin' now 'cause I'm already fuckin' bored with this conversation."

Dick.

Finn leaned in to make sure Saint heard him clearly. "I don't like how tired my woman is. Don't like fucking a damn wash rag because she's too exhausted to participate. Cookie needs to be replaced if she can't do her damn job. It's unfair to MJ to force her to work doubles several nights a week just because your ol' lady doesn't want to show up and pull her weight. If she can't do her damn job, find someone else who can. Or put Sapphire in that position, instead."

"Didn't hear the little blonde bitch fuckin' complain'."

Finn's nostrils flared and he barely managed to keep his fists at his sides. But he wasn't sure how long that might be possible. He unlocked his jaws to say, "That's because she's not sleeping in your bed. Unlike mine."

"She can come to me if she got a problem with it."

"*I'm* coming to you. I'm her fucking man," Finn growled, slapping a hand to his chest.

Saint stared at him with his lips pursed. "Thinkin' you need to stay the fuck outta this club. Stickin' your nose in shit you got no goddamn business gettin' involved with. Distractin' my manager when you're here, too. Not good for business."

"I'll tell you what's not good for business... You banning me from this club. If I go, she goes, because I'm taking her with me. Then you can explain to whoever you answer to why the club's going under because of bad management. MJ's worth her weight in gold and you know it. You just don't care or want to admit it."

His eyes narrowed even further until they were barely slits. "Know what she's worth. But she's worth even more naked and bouncin' on someone's lap—" he leaned in until he was almost nose to nose with Finn, "other than yours—than wanderin' around with a dress on."

A burn filled Finn's chest. "Like I said, without her this club will end up closing its doors. And I doubt you want that." *Then there goes your front, you asshole.* "Starting tonight, she leaves at the end of her shift, whether your ol' lady's here or not. If MJ wants to work longer hours, that'll be her choice," Finn caught Saint's eyes and held them when he leaned across the bar to finish with, "not yours."

Saint lifted one thick dark eyebrow. "Thought you just fuckin' said it's yours. Your woman, your rules, right?"

"Now you're getting it. I'm the only one with a say in what she does. We got plans tonight, so make sure Cookie's here before seven. If she's not, that's your problem, not MJ's." Finn swiped his drink off the bar and swallowed the remaining bourbon before slamming the glass back down. He glanced over at Mutt and pointed to his empty glass. Once the prospect grabbed it and slipped away, Finn turned his focus back on Saint. "Just need to know you heard me loud and clear."

Finn refused to be the first one to break their stare-off.

Finally, Saint, wearing a deep scowl, gave him a slight chin-lift. A second later, he turned and walked away.

As soon as Mutt brought over his next drink, Finn took it and went to find an empty seat to wait and watch.

Chapter Nineteen

IT WAS A PATTERN, but not one anyone not paying attention might notice. He'd have to tell Mel so she could keep an eye out for that same behavior when he wasn't at the club.

Whoever stood guard at the velvet rope would look at their phone, disappear for less than five minutes, then reappear in their assigned spot.

No one inside the club directly approached either Popeye or Ringo tonight, but both, whosoever turn it was to keep people out of the employee area, disappeared several times. Most likely if confronted, they'd simply use the excuse of going out back to smoke. But smoking a cigarette usually took longer than the time they were gone.

No, they were doing quick exchanges most likely. They'd get a notification, like a text once the buyer was out back waiting, then the prospect would go out to the parking lot and complete the money-for-meth swap.

When Ringo disappeared again, Finn rose from where he sat in a back corner—where it gave him the best view of most of the club's main area—and headed to the restroom. Both the women's and men's rooms were just outside the entrance to the back hallway, so he could snoop around with the excuse of having to "break the seal."

But when he got there, the only person in the hallway was Dazzle rushing toward him since she was up next on stage.

The bright pink-haired woman covered in body glitter shot him a blinding smile as she hurried past him in her sky-high platform heels. "Hey, Danny!"

"What's up, Razzle Dazzle?"

She laughed at his teasing and threw over her shoulder, "Just so you know, you look damn good with clothes on, too."

"So do you," he yelled back, but kept his eyes glued to the exit at the end of the hallway.

Fortunately, he didn't have to wait long.

The door cracked open and Ringo slipped inside. Since the prospect's eyes were focused on his phone, Finn had no problem popping around the corner and into the restroom without being detected.

He waited a few seconds to make sure he was alone, then pulled out his own phone. Keeping his eye on the closed door, he dialed Crew.

"Yeah?" came the short, gruff answer.

"What's up your ass?"

"Nothing. Watching Thursday Night Football and you're interrupting the damn game."

"All right. Fuck you then." Finn hung up and leaned back against the sink, waiting.

His phone lit up not even two seconds later. As expected.

Wearing a wide grin, he put the phone to his ear and answered, "*Helllllloooo?*" in a sing-song voice.

"Fuck off. What do you want? Hurry up, you have until the end of half-time."

"The Steelers aren't even playing tonight."

"So? Some of us watch football because we like the damn sport, not just one team, Pippi. Time's a-ticking, so spill whatever you need to tell me."

"We need surveillance set up on the back parking lot of the club."

"You see something?" Crew asked.

"Only what I expected. One of the prospects gets a message on his phone, I'm assuming by text. Right now my guess is the buyer is already out back waiting before sending the message and once received, the prospect steps outside with the plausible excuse of needing to smoke and the exchange takes place. Almost like a damn druggy drive-through. It reminds me of the old pager system dealers used, just more modern."

"The messages are likely in code, too," Crew murmured.

"I'm sure. I mean, the Demons are probably short on brain cells but still have enough to know that cell phone records and texts can be subpoenaed."

"Codes can be easy to crack," Crew stated.

"Like I said, they're short on brain cells, but what other options do they have? Customers can't just walk in and order drugs at the bar. I mean, they could, but that would be totally stupid. Another problem with dealing inside is the person would need to go through the metal detector and pay a cover charge. Not many drug users want to pay a fee to get their fix. They'd rather spend that money on getting high."

"True. But there could be club regulars who are buying, too."

"Could be. That's probably why Saint replaced the bartenders with prospects. It wouldn't be difficult to have a patron approach the bar to get a drink and a baggy of meth. Slip it under the napkin and slide it across the bar. They'd need to be slick about it since the cameras out on the floor do work. For now, anyway."

Crew chuckled. "No shit. Thanks for all that footage."

"You whack off to some of it?"

"Just to you prancing around on stage."

Fuck! He forgot they'd have the recordings from the last two Monday nights he danced with the Peckers. He should have omitted those and gone through them himself.

"I saved some of that footage for blackmail."

"Blackmail's a crime," he reminded the DEA agent.

"You willingly gave me that footage. So, basically, you're fucked, *Blaze*." Crew cackled like a bitch. "I think we'll set up a private screening with our whole MC and even invite the task force. I'll bring the popcorn."

"I'm glad I could help you figure out your sexual preferences. I figured you've been confused. You're welcome."

"Well, fuck yeah, who can resist that tight, freckled ass of yours? I'd hit that."

Even though Finn knew he was just joking, he smothered his laugh so it wouldn't echo loudly through the bathroom. He wasn't supposed to have his cell phone in the club, so he didn't want to get busted with it. Especially by Saint.

Crew went from being his typical jackass self back to the serious task force leader in a second flat. It was enough to give anyone whiplash. "I'm surprised they're not dealing in the bathroom or somewhere where it can't be witnessed at all."

"My guess? They're doing that, too. I need an excuse to hang around in the hallway. Maybe in the next week, Mel and I can pretend we're having a deep conversation or something."

"I'm sure you'll come up with something. Have you banged her yet?"

Like he was going to tell Crew that. "She's my *pretend* girlfriend, remember?"

"And your fist isn't your girlfriend, either, but you fuck that hard and often."

"But unlike you, who dreams of me while tugging on your Johnson, I don't think of you. I'm not into asshole DEA agents who sport gray hairs on their droopy, wrinkled balls."

"You only wish you had balls. Those tiny banana hammocks you wore on stage proved you don't. All right. Time's up. I've got more important things to do than talk to you."

"You mean important things like task force business?"

Crew huffed. "I'll work on getting surveillance set up. I'll let you know as soon as I have it arranged."

"That's—" He pulled his phone from his ear. His BAMC brother had hung up.

Asshole.

After tucking his cell phone away, Finn stepped out of the bathroom and almost ran smack into Mel.

She slapped a hand to her chest in surprise. "Oh! I was looking for you!"

"Something wrong?"

"No, one minute you were sitting out on the floor, the next you were gone. I got worried. Plus, you're my ride home."

She was worried about him? *Huh.*

He lowered his voice so he couldn't be heard over the thumping music. "I was trying to catch them in the act."

Mel took his cue and lowered her voice, too. "Have you seen them actually dealing?"

"No, not yet. But I just got off the phone with Crew and he'll be setting up surveillance. I just want to make you aware of that if you see another strange vehicle in the vicinity."

"Saint won't figure it out?"

Finn sure as fuck hoped not. "He shouldn't."

He glanced toward the main club area. Ringo was gone again. The prospects were busy tonight. Word must be getting around that this was the place to get a fix.

She squeezed his arm, catching his attention. "Are you ready to go?"

"Cookie show up?"

"No, but Taint told me to leave anyway. He's *never* done that before. Makes me wonder what he's up to."

Well, *shit*, maybe his little talk with Saint worked.

He put his mouth to Mel's ear. "Before we go, I need your help. Ringo's gone again. I think they're dealing out in the back parking lot. It would make sense since those cameras are disabled and that's where the stash van is parked. Even better for them, there's no traffic passing by, either."

"Shit."

"So, let's get out of here. Maybe we'll catch the tail end of a deal when we walk outside."

When he draped his arm around her shoulders, she slipped free. "I need to grab my stuff. And I normally change into street clothes before I leave."

He could see why. The short black dress she wore was so damn tight it had to be a struggle to sit in it. Plus, the spiked heels had to be killing her feet after being in them for eight hours.

"You can't take the time to change tonight. How quickly can you grab your bag?"

A crease marred her forehead. "Thirty seconds?"

He slapped her lightly on the ass. "Then, go. Hurry."

He followed her down the hallway and waited right outside the door when she disappeared into the dressing room.

The second she came back out, he pressed a hand to the small of her back and steered her toward the exit. But just as they reached it, Ringo came inside.

"Fuck," Finn muttered under his breath.

"Where were you and why aren't you watching the hallway?"

Shit. He was not expecting Mel to confront the prospect like that.

Neither was Ringo, since he stopped and frowned at her. "Don't answer to you."

Mel squared off with the biker. "Yes, you do, since I'm the manager."

Finn stepped next to her and curled an arm around her hip in solidarity.

Ringo sneered, "I only answer to Saint."

Mel shrugged. "Fine. I'll talk to Saint, then."

"You do that." The prospect pushed past them, knocking hard into Finn's shoulder on purpose.

Dickhead.

He took a deep breath to tamp down his temper at that obvious slight, then escorted Mel out the door into the late September evening and toward the Tacoma.

He kept his voice low. "You'll be wasting your time talking to Saint about him. He's more than aware of what the prospects are doing since he's the one who probably ordered them to do it."

"Of course. But those prospects leaving their posts is another way to put the girls at risk. Just like the cameras being disabled. No one is preventing a customer from just going into the dressing room to harass the girls. Or worse. I don't like it. Someone should be watching at all times. Someone should also escort the girls out to their cars when they're done for the night. Ever since Saint fired my bouncers, every safety measure that Laura and I put in place has been disregarded. If someone gets hurt..."

Her frustration was palpable and he hoped the dancers appreciated how much she cared about them.

He helped her into the truck and once she was settled, he jogged around to the driver's side and climbed in. When he had the door shut and no one was able to overhear them, he finally replied with, "Okay, tomorrow, if and when Saint shows up, I want you to complain to him about the issue of the prospects disappearing. Make sure to emphasize how it puts the girls in jeopardy. Then let me know what excuse he uses for them. Once he gives you that lie, press him on it. For example, if he says they're just going out back to smoke, tell him that smoke breaks should be limited to certain times and during them, he needs to make sure someone else is covering the hallway."

"I can do that."

He pushed the start button and brought the Toyota to life. "Good. Let's get you home. I bet you're hungry."

"I am."

He was, too. For the blonde in the black, super short, *sexy-as-fuck* dress with the killer legs. "We can pick up something on the way, if you want. Plus... I really want a tour of your haunted house." Not to mention, other places.

"I never said it was haunted!" She shuddered.

With a laugh, Finn shifted the truck into Drive.

———

MEL CLUNG to his arm as she dangerously weeble-wobbled over the stone driveway in those crazy heels.

"I could carry you, you know."

"Oh, is that a service you provide as part of your 'protect

and service' package?'"

He laughed. "Only for you."

"Once again, you've proven chivalry is not dead."

"I don't want you spraining an ankle."

"I'm sure Taint would love me hobbling around the club in a slinky dress and an orthopedic boot."

He chuckled at that vision. "I don't think anyone is really looking at your feet, Mel. Well, maybe a certain type of clientele is, but most are not."

She paused at the top of the vestibule steps and cocked an eyebrow at him, keeping a completely straight face. "Then, what are they looking at?"

"Your sparkling personality."

She released a delicate snort. "Well, that's disappointing since I spend a fortune on shoes."

Once at the door, she reached into her bag and pulled something out. He figured it was her keys until she held her hand out to him.

He frowned at whatever was on her open palm. It looked like... cookies of some sort? Whatever it was didn't look appealing to him. "What's this? An appetizer before dinner?"

"They're not for you." She jiggled her hand. "Take them."

He did and lifted them to his nose. The odd smell made it wrinkle. "Who are they for? Are they to appease the ghosts?"

Her shoulders shook as she unlocked the door and pushed it open. The second she did, two big dogs rushed forward. He quickly took a giant step back, almost falling over his own feet.

"I hope you like dogs."

"Now you tell me?"

Two large Doberman Pinschers circled Mel, whining and crying in excitement. She gave both wiggling dogs a scratch behind the ears as she bent over and planted kisses on their head. "Did you miss me, my babies?"

Their crying increased to a fevered high-pitch, making Finn wince.

"You'd think I haven't seen them in weeks."

Suddenly, one broke off and ran up to him, jamming its nose directly into Finn's crotch. "Damn." Then it circled around and jammed it in his ass. "I'll have you know, your dog just committed assault."

Misdemeanor muzzle molestation more like it.

"She's just saying hi."

"There are other methods to say hello without a nudge to the nuts or a poke in my asshole. I'm not sure if I like those big teeth so close to my junk."

"It only takes a treat to win over their hearts."

He offered a biscuit to the dog sniffing him up and down. The treat was gobbled down without even chewing. The other Doberman came over more slowly, sniffing Finn's feet first, and he immediately offered it the remaining treat. Once again it was swallowed whole. Despite that enthusiasm, he still had all of his fingers.

"Hurry up and go potty," Mel ordered.

"I don't have to go."

"Minx. Jinx. Go potty," she urged the dogs again, pointing at a patch of grass in the yard out front. They must be trained well enough not to run off.

"Oh, you weren't talking to me," Finn teased.

"If you have to go, it's best not to do it out front. By the way, despite how old this building is, I do have indoor plumbing."

After the dogs ran out to the grass, he asked, "How can you tell them apart?" They both were red Dobermans and to him, looked identical.

"The one lifting his leg has a penis, the one squatting doesn't."

"I guess that's a good way," he said on a laugh.

As they stood near the door and waited for the two dogs to finish up, he noticed while both had cropped tails, their ears had been kept natural. He didn't know a lot about dogs, but he knew there was some controversy about cropping ears.

"They're beautiful. And great protectors, right?" Though, neither had barked at him, a stranger. Being with their mistress might have made a difference. However, he would not be testing that theory by breaking in any time soon.

"They sure are. As long as I introduce a new person to them first, they're fine. But have a stranger walk in? They will make it clear this is *their* house and they'll do it loudly. I don't worry about anyone breaking in. Plus, they're the best companions ever. Super loyal and they listen intently to whatever I tell them. If I'm having a bad day, just their presence cheers me up."

"They sound like the perfect roommates. How old are they?"

"Four. I adopted them from a Doberman rescue when they were about a year old. They're littermates but the family who bought them as puppies gave them up because they were having a baby." She rolled her eyes and shook her head.

"Who's who?"

The dogs sprinted past them back into the house. Mel pointed to each one as they went. "Minx is the female, Jinx the male. Come on," Mel encouraged him. "I'll get dinner started, then give you a quick tour."

"I told you, you don't have to cook. We could've picked up something on the way." After following her in, she closed and locked the heavy wood door behind him.

"I want to. I appreciate everything you're doing and,

anyway, with my long hours, I rarely get a chance to make a home-cooked meal."

Right inside the door, she kicked off her heels with a drawn-out sigh, while he turned in a slow circle, taking everything in. "This place is fucking awesome. Did you do any of the renovations?"

"No, I bought it like this. I think it was originally converted back in the '90s. Then a contractor bought it, modernized it even more before flipping it. When it came up for sale again, I thought I'd have to fight for it, but it turns out a lot of people are freaked out over practically living in a cemetery."

She wasn't *practically* living in a cemetery she *was* living in one. "I could see that." He would think twice before living in a place surrounded on three sides by hundreds, maybe thousands, of dead people.

But that might be the only con of the place since he could see why she wanted the church. The interior, what he could see of it so far, was amazing. Even if it was small.

Being an old chapel meant the ceilings were high, but they were made of high-polished wood. Both sides of the open area that made up her main living space had the high arched windows that normally would be stained glass. Hers weren't. They looked like they had been updated with plain double-paned glass. Even so, every light fixture in the place that he could see so far, whether suspended from the ceiling, on a table or standing in a corner, was made of stained glass.

It was enough to remind anyone of the building's beginnings.

"I need to get out of this dress and get comfortable. I'll be back in a flash."

Or she could flash him. He wouldn't complain. It wasn't like he hadn't seen her naked already.

"Take your time. I'm soaking all this in." His eyes followed her as she hurried up the wood staircase with both dogs flanking her. The stairs ran along the right wall and had a modern-looking cable railing system so it kept a sense of open space needed for a compact house.

He could hear her moving about the open loft on the second floor as he studied the wide-planked wood flooring that might be original but refinished. They were gorgeous, just like the owner of the property.

"Is your bedroom up in the loft?" he called upstairs.

"Yes. And it's the only bedroom. That's another reason why I had no other buyers outbidding me on this place. Not many people can deal with only one bedroom and in an open loft at that." Her voice floated down to him. "Not ideal for families."

He let his gaze sweep the entire open living space again. "This place must suck to heat and cool with the high ceilings."

"Luckily the place isn't too big."

"Can you get up to the bell tower?"

"Yes, but I keep it closed off. There's not enough space to do much with it, anyway. Did you notice the roof this morning? It's still the original slate. Something hard to find. They last a long time but, unfortunately, it's just as hard to find anyone to repair it."

"I can imagine. That will be a lost art soon, if not already." Her bare feet padding down the steps drew his attention back to her. "No stained glass."

She was now wearing tight black leggings and an oversized, white button-down shirt hanging off one shoulder with the sleeves rolled up. Her hair was gathered into a long ponytail and her face was once again scrubbed clean.

Almost a girl next door look, but still sexy as fuck. Especially since she hadn't bothered to put on a bra. She was bouncing wild and free.

Hurray for freedom.

"No, they removed all of the original windows and sold them to help pay for the new church. At least I can open these windows. And I don't have a crucified Jesus staring down at me and judging my life's choices while I eat dinner. I would find that a little creepier than being surrounded by hundreds of people taking their eternal rest."

"Does the congregation still bury people out there?"

"No, they ran out of space."

"Packed house."

She lifted a single finger. "But the best neighbors to have. No disputes at all and the dogs can make as much noise as they want without complaints. The property and the church might be small but it's perfect for me."

He was impressed that the two dogs hadn't left her side since the second they came back into the house. He was sure, because of them, she had no worries about living out in the middle of nowhere by herself.

She tipped her head toward the back of the "great room," where only a long island counter with three more hanging stained glass light fixtures separated a small but professional-looking kitchen. All the appliances were modern and stainless steel, and it was very organized. One of the neatest kitchens he'd ever seen.

She went straight to the refrigerator and began pulling things out. As she was bent over, she was a magnet for his eyes. Especially since the black stretchy fabric hugged her perfect ass. He didn't notice any panty lines either. The woman had completely forwent any underwear.

He liked that. A lot.

Mel didn't seem to have one damn hang-up. At least that he could see.

Once she was done pulling out the chicken and some other ingredients, she closed the fridge door with her foot since her hands were full with two beers. He grabbed them from her and twisted off the caps before handing one back.

"Let me season the chicken quick and scrub the potatoes. We'll throw the meat on the grill along with some veggies and I'll throw the potatoes in my Instant Pot. We'll be eating before you know it."

He stepped behind her, where she was working on the food, and grabbed her hips, leaning into her back and pressing his lips to the side of her exposed neck. "I'm really fucking hungry."

"I'll make you a big portion."

"Not for food," he clarified. His stomach took that moment to growl loudly calling him out as a damn liar.

She turned in his arms to face him, an amused grin on her face. "I'm hungry for you, too, but my stomach is on E."

"We can eat first." He managed to keep the disappointment from his voice. "But I first need a little taste of the meal I'll enjoy later."

Her hands grasped his waist as he leaned in and took her mouth in a deep kiss. He forced himself to keep it short so he wasn't tempted to tell her to put the chicken back in the fridge.

When they parted, he stared down at her face for a few seconds before releasing her.

Apparently that simple kiss affected her just as much as him, since her voice turned husky. "I'll show you out back since I need to start the grill."

Food before fucking, he reminded himself. "I might not be

able to cook a great meal but I can sure grill a damn good steak."

"What about meat that used to cluck and not moo?"

"Passable. I might need close supervision."

"I can do that. Come on."

Behind the kitchen, a hallway ran the width of the church and seemed to be the only closed off area on the main floor. She pointed out a small laundry room to the left and a half-bath to the right. Then they continued straight out French doors to a huge slightly raised platform made out of composite deck material. A hot tub was in one corner, and white lights were strung from one post to the other, completely circling the deck.

While she lit the grill, he wandered around the deck, peering out into the dark to watch the dogs inspect every inch of the yard enclosed by the short stone wall.

"They don't jump that?"

"No. They're boundary trained. That's why I trust them to go out front, too."

"Did you train them yourself?"

"Mostly, yes. I did hire a trainer to help since I wanted to make sure I could handle two big dogs at once. I never had a dog before these two." She pointed to an outdoor couch. "Sit and enjoy your beer while I get the rest of the meal prepped."

"I didn't get the rest of the tour yet."

"I'll show you upstairs after we eat. There's a basement, too, but unless you like dark, damp spaces, I doubt you'll want to explore it. Since it has a dirt floor, I only have the furnace and stuff like that down there."

"So, basically you have the main floor and a loft that takes up less than half of the length of the church."

"Luckily, I don't need much. That's why this place is perfect."

Chapter Twenty

WITH HER LEGS curled under her, Mel sipped at the last of her beer while she relaxed on the couch enjoying the pleasant end-of-September weather. Summer was on its last legs and fall was peeking around the corner.

The dogs seemed to have already accepted Finn. He quickly won over Minx's heart by throwing a ball to the other end of the yard every damn time she brought it to him. Of course, Minx ate that up and only wanted more.

"She likes you."

"That's good. What about him?" He tipped his head toward Jinx sitting close to Mel and guarding her, but also keeping an interested eye on what Minx and Finn were doing.

"He takes a bit longer to warm up to strange men."

For what had to be the hundredth time, Minx ran up to him with the tennis ball clutched between her jaws and her tongue hanging out to the side. Finn threw it again before looking over at her. "You've had a lot of strange men over?"

While his question didn't have a judgy tone, it did sound somewhat jealous, instead.

Interesting. Especially since they were only supposed to be a "pretend" couple and they'd only had sex once.

So far.

He had no reason to be possessive or jealous unless he was at the club playing his part of "Danny the boyfriend."

"When I had more time to date, I had a few over. You don't invite women over to your place?"

"Rarely. I don't want them to think they can stick around."

"*Oof.*" When she tipped the beer bottle to her lips to finish the last swallow, his gaze practically seared her throat.

Dinner had been good, the company even better and they seemed to be content simply while in each other's company. Several times they sat in companionable silence and it wasn't awkward at all. But it was getting late and, even though she certainly didn't want him to leave yet, sleep pulled at her.

"I'm always upfront with women about their expectations."

"Meaning?"

"If they're expecting more than a night, or two, then I'm not for them."

She *oof*-ed again at his "non-committal bachelor" response.

He shrugged. "It's better than lying to them or leading them on. Or have them mistakenly look at me for a long-term relationship." He raised his beer to his lips. This time she watched his Adam's apple bob in his corded neck as he took a long swallow.

"Another beer?"

He shook his head. "I'm good. Thank you for dinner."

"My pleasure."

"I plan on getting to that next."

She raised her eyebrows at him. "Do you want to go over my expectations first?"

"We've already established we're fake dating, girlfriend."

She studied his strong profile. Even though he sat within arm's reach, he hadn't made a move yet. Maybe she should suggest heading upstairs soon. She wanted to have sex with him while she still had the energy. Unfortunately, it was waning fast.

He set down the empty bottle at his feet and twisted toward her. "What expectations do you have?"

"Besides a few orgasms and you taking down the Demons? Not much."

"*Oof*," he echoed her.

"Well, you asked. I love sex, but I don't need a commitment to have it."

"I'm not sure I've run across a woman with that mindset before."

"Then you're not looking in the right places. Plenty of us exist who don't mind having no-strings-attached sex."

"Is there a secret club you all belong to? If so, please let me know the name of it and how I can get in the door."

Her lips twitched. "Of course there is. It even has a secret handshake." She held out her hand to him and he enveloped it in his much larger one.

Instead of shaking it, he lifted it to his mouth and brushed his soft lips across her knuckles. He studied her for a few seconds before saying, "I'll take the upstairs tour now, Mel."

Him sweeping his thumb back and forth over her inner wrist, along with the deep rumble of his voice holding promises of what was to come next, shot a shock of lightning down her spine. Her nipples instantly pebbled in response.

Funny how she suddenly found a spurt of energy.

"Then, let's go in," she suggested, unfolding her legs and sitting up.

Without releasing her hand, he rose and helped her to her feet.

———

FINN GLANCED around the open loft that, like the stairs, had an open cable railing along the edge. Apparently, Mel must not have a fear of heights. Upstairs, similar to downstairs, was designed just as modern. An interesting contrast to the exterior of the church. Old on the outside, new on the inside.

The more he saw, the more he appreciated it and could see himself living in a place like this. As long as it didn't turn into a real-life remake of the *Dawn of the Dead*. If the ghosts kept on their side of the stone wall and he kept on his, everything would be peachy.

On one wall was a king-sized bed and on the floor nearby sat two large dog beds. Across the loft was a wall-mounted TV. Not quite as big as the ninety-six inch at the BAMC clubhouse, but still impressive.

In the back left corner of the loft was a huge walk-in closet. On the right, a nice-sized bathroom with not only a shower stall, but a large soaking tub. Since the ceilings were angled due to the roof line, a large skylight had been installed low enough to give Mel a view while taking a bath.

What that view consisted of he didn't know since it was dark as fuck outside. One thing about living out in the country, the nights were pitch black.

"This place is really impressive, Mel." He snagged her wrist and pulled her to him, slamming her chest into his. "Just like you."

"I'm just a simple woman trying to make ends meet."

Bullshit. "Don't sell yourself short. You see what you want and go for it. With that gumption, I have no doubt you'll one day soon own a club of your own and you'll make it a damn success."

"Maybe the Demons buying out Laura was the push I needed."

Maybe. But that didn't mean he liked the pressure put on her from that shitty deal.

It might not be in the next few months, but the MC's time was coming. Investigations of this magnitude were typically long and drawn out since the feds had to make sure their case was bullet-proof before dragging in everyone involved. Otherwise, they'd be letting them free just as quickly. In the meantime, the task force needed to identify weak links in the MC. Members willing to turn into witnesses in exchange for lesser charges.

While he was currently standing in Mel's bedroom thanks to the Demons, fuck thinking about them right now. He had better things to do.

Like the blonde staring up at him with a sly smile on her face. "Just so you know, my expectations aren't being met right now."

"What do I need to do to change that?"

She sounded very serious when she demanded, "I want to see all your freckles."

One eyebrow lifted. "All of them?"

"I think it would be fun to go on a little hunt."

"I can think of other fun things to do."

Her smile widened. "I'm up for suggestions."

Before he could give her any, she took a step back and began to thumb open the buttons of her shirt one by one with excruciating slowness. A tease of sorts, but nothing like her lap dance in the VIP room. It was not only the hottest lap dance he'd ever had, but the hottest sex.

However, that didn't mean tonight wouldn't be just as hot. It would only be different. He was fine with variety as long as it included Mel.

His heart thumped wildly as he watched her shed the shirt, circle the pads of her thumbs over each nipple before hooking them into the waistband of her leggings and making short work of removing them.

Wearing only two pieces of clothing meant she was fully naked in a matter of seconds. Once she was, she drew her hand from her pussy all the way up and over each tit before curling her fingers around her own throat. "Your turn."

He did a spin on the ball of his foot and gave her his back. Without fanfare, he yanked off his shirt, tossing it to the side. He subtly flexed his back so the muscles he worked so hard to achieve popped. "How many freckles do you see?"

"Too many to count."

"Figured."

"But that doesn't mean I don't want to try," she insisted. "Maybe I'll do it in batches."

The soft steps behind him made him hesitate and keep his back to her, waiting to see what she'd do next.

Wrapping her arms around him, she planted her hands over his pecs and pressed her pierced nipples into his back. He clenched his abs to give them definition when she ran her palms down his torso and didn't stop until her fingers hovered over his belt buckle.

At the same time, the tip of her tongue drew a line from the top of his back up the center of his neck. As she worked his belt open, she ran her soft lips from his hairline back down and across one shoulder where she softly sank in her teeth. Just enough to get his endorphins flowing and his cock flexing in his jeans.

She made quick work of unfastening his belt and jeans before sliding one hand back up his torso with a murmured, "Maybe I should count your abs, instead," and drove the other hand into his boxer briefs. His hips jerked as she circled his hard length and began to stroke.

"Fuck, Mel," he groaned.

"Yes, fuck Mel. Please."

"That's on my to-do list, but first..." He turned, dislodging her hold and capturing her face between his hands, so he could kiss her thoroughly.

With a groan of her own, she melted into him, returning the kiss, and scraped her nails down his chest and over the very tips of his nipples.

This woman made him so fucking hard that he had to force himself to slow down so he wouldn't rush this tonight. He reminded himself they had a bed. They had time. They didn't have to worry about anyone else walking in on them or catching them in the act.

Tonight, it was only the two of them.

And two nosy Dobermans sticking close to their mistress. He only hoped when they got down to business and things got noisy, the dogs didn't think he was hurting their mistress. Because that was the last thing he wanted to do.

Gripping her waist, he lifted her and tossed her onto the bed where she bounced a couple of times. She settled with a smile and intense heat in her turquoise eyes as she scanned him from his head to his hands where he worked on freeing himself from his boxer briefs and jeans. He pushed them down to his ankles before unlacing his boots and kicking them off and out of the way. When he stepped out of his pants and underwear, he left them where they landed, the dogs taking the opportunity to use their snouts to snuffle through the clothes.

He ignored what they were doing and concentrated on what the woman was doing... crawling backward on the bed. Once she was settled near the headboard, she crooked her finger at him and used her other hand to stroke between her spread thighs.

"You don't have to tell me twice." Climbing onto the bed, he stalked her on his hands and knees.

He went back and forth, using his tongue to play with the piercings and sucking one nipple deep into his mouth before taking the other. When her fingers slid into his hair and her nails dug into his scalp, she dropped her head back and released a moan loud enough to encompass them both.

He squeezed and kneaded both breasts, continuing to suck and tease. Nip and nibble. Until she squirmed beneath him, encouraging him by whispering his name.

Not Danny, but Finn.

None of this was pretend. This was one-hundred-percent real.

With a last kiss to each nipple, he worked his way lower but before he could reach his intended destination, she yanked on his hair with both hands. He paused, tipping his eyes up to her.

She shook her head. "On your back."

"Me?" he asked, surprised she would stop him from what he'd been about to do.

"Yes, you."

"Do you want to sit on my face?" *Please say yes.*

"I have other plans," she purred.

He could live with that. They switched places and once he was on his back, she settled between his legs, licking up his length and engulfing the sensitive crown in her hot, wet mouth.

For fuck's sake, yes, he *could* live with that. The woman was sucking his cock like she'd been lost for days in a desert and he was her only water source.

He would gladly hydrate her. Among other things.

She gently squeezed his sac as she practically swallowed his full length. He grabbed her ponytail in his fist and every time she took him all the way to the root, his grip had to create a harsh pull on her scalp, but not once did she stop. In fact, she sped up to the point where he had to cry mercy.

"Mel..." he groaned in warning.

Now it was her eyes tipping up to his strained face.

"As much as I'd love to let loose in your mouth, I'd rather do it deep inside you. At least this time... Another time..."

She released him with a wet pop. "Another time."

Thank fuck she would give him that. He already was afraid he'd never get enough of her. She was that addictive.

Sexy as fuck. Unashamedly sexual, too.

Independent. Smart. Driven.

Fucking perfect.

After one last lick up his thick ridge, she moved to straddle his waist. Once she did, his focus automatically landed on her pussy since her damp curls pressed against his skin and the heat of her slick pussy seared him and definitely tempted him.

His nostrils flared and his mouth watered when he picked up her warm, sweet scent. He wanted to bury his face between her thighs and get lost forever.

Another time. Right?

"I think you're the first blonde I've been with who's actually a true blonde," he murmured, stroking the tightly trimmed hairs decorating the top of her mound.

"It's in the blood."

He slipped a finger between her folds to find her slick clit pulsating. Proof she was as ready as he was. "What kind of blood?"

"Scandinavian."

He lifted his head. "Pure?"

"Half. My mom's side."

When she leaned forward, her piercings brushed along his skin, making his cock twitch and a translucent string of precum to connect the tip to his hip.

But she wasn't done with him yet.

He desperately held tightly to his patience through every brush of her lips and scrape of her nails along his heated skin. She wasn't counting his freckles, but trying to play "connect the dots" with her tongue, instead.

As much as he wanted to hurry up, flip her onto her back and drive himself to the hilt inside her, he made himself wait. Told himself to be patient. Reminded himself the wait would be worth it. That the delay would only make the moment he slid inside her even more intense.

He jerked and every muscle tensed when she nipped at his right nipple, but he was prepared when she did the same to the left.

Squeezing his eyes shut, he forced himself to suck in a deep breath to try to cool the raging fire inside him as she continued to explore.

Only he wasn't sure if he could temper his want of her. He wanted to be inside her right fucking now but he was also enjoying everything about what she was doing.

For fuck's sake, he was torn. *Patience, asshole. You'll be where you want to be soon. Just have some fucking patience. Don't make it a sprint, make it a marathon.*

When she rose to her knees again, he managed to keep his hands to himself, only touching her with his eyes, instead.

He must have missed it when she released her ponytail since her blonde hair now curtained her face as she shifted forward and tipped her chin enough to stare down at him.

A smile crept across her face and her bluish-green eyes held a naughty gleam.

Fuck yes...

Nice was overrated. Naughty was his preference.

Dirty would be even better. And he had no doubt this woman could get downright filthy.

He was here for it. If not tonight, then another night. Because he already knew this second time wouldn't be enough. A third or fourth time wouldn't be, either.

Mel was not the typical woman he normally fell into bed with.

That should worry him.

It didn't. And that should worry him, too.

Maybe tomorrow it would. But tonight?

Interlocking their fingers, she pinned his hands against the mattress, holding him down as she took his mouth. But only for a few seconds, giving him just enough to leave him wanting more.

"I need to fuck you, Mel." No truer words.

"Soon," she whispered into his ear before using the tip of her tongue to trace the outer shell. Her teeth snagged his earlobe, biting down hard enough he was afraid she'd pierce through it.

She brushed her lips down one side of his bearded jawline and up the other before heading back to his mouth.

With his lips parted in expectation of another dick-throbbing kiss, she stole his breath instead before giving it back to him along with her own.

No.

No more.

He was done with her toying with him. With her driving him out of his damn mind.

Now it was his turn to do the same to her.

SHE WASN'T PREPARED when he popped up his hip, knocking her off balance. Using that momentum, he flipped her onto her back and immediately caged her in. With his hands planted on each side of her head and his thighs squeezing her hips, he gave her just enough of his weight to pin her to the bed.

Not that she planned on going anywhere. She was perfectly fine where she was currently.

His hazel eyes simmering with unrestrained heat made her breath catch when they locked gazes. The man was so damn gorgeous that sometimes she couldn't believe he was real.

She'd never been attracted to redheads. Until Finn.

Everything about him stoked the flames swirling in her belly and caused molten lava to surge through her veins.

"I can't wait any longer, but I need to taste you first."

In truth, she couldn't, either. Every cell in her body ached for him. "I'll allow it." He swallowed his chuckle as soon as she followed with, "Even though I had so many more things I wanted to do to you."

"Same. But are we in a rush?"

"No. I assume this assignment will take a while."

His brow furrowed. "This isn't part of the assignment, Mel."

Was that disappointment she heard?

While she was well aware sex wasn't a part of his undercover assignment, she didn't expect much more out of it than them simply enjoying each other during that time. She wasn't searching for anything deep or permanent.

More than that, she doubted Finn was looking for anything other than playing pretend, anyway. In the meantime, there was nothing wrong with both enjoying the benefits of their fake relationship and their very real attraction.

When Finn crushed their lips together, she was pulled back into the moment, and the kiss turned from simple to intense the second his tongue swept through her mouth and teased hers. He explored every inch before retreating to give her the opportunity to do the same.

His thorough kisses made every part of her clench and every cell in her body sigh in satisfaction. They stole her breath. Made her moan. Made her want him to the point she physically ached for him. Everywhere.

He dragged his tongue over her bottom lip, then captured it between his teeth and tugged. When he pulled away slightly, his ragged breathing matched hers. His erection a steel pipe pressed into her thigh, the tip slippery against her skin.

After a brush of his bristly cheek against hers, his lips traveled down her jaw before he tucked his face into her neck where his tortured, "Mel," came out muffled.

His warm breath beat against her throat as his lips followed her pounding pulse and he licked the delicate skin at the hollow of her neck.

Air rushed from Mel's lungs as Finn's mouth traveled lower. Even with her head tipped back, she managed to keep her eyes on him.

Following him on his determined path.

His mouth skimmed across her chest and around the outer curves of her breasts. They swelled and ached for his touch and her nipples pebbled painfully, even before he blew lightly across each tip.

It wasn't enough. None of it was.

"Finn," she groaned.

Without a word, he continued with his pleasurable torture. Most likely payback for when she had him pinned to the bed.

He continued lower, scraping his beard down her belly, dipping his tongue into her navel for a second before going even further. His warm breath battered her skin, raising goosebumps along his path. Until finally, he reached the tightly-trimmed blonde hair at the top of her mound.

He touched her there with his tongue, avoiding her clit, where she really wanted his lips. Just a tease, but hopefully, a preview of what would come next.

Spreading her thighs even wider, he pinned them down using his broad shoulders. He dipped his head and nuzzled his nose below the small patch, his breath beating against her most sensitive spot.

But still, he didn't go further.

When she lifted her head, his eyes tipped up to hers and a wicked smile crossed his face and a gleam filled his hazel eyes. He touched his tongue to the very top of her pussy, right above her clit, which was swollen and throbbing, impatient for him to continue.

"Finn," she whispered in desperation.

If he wanted her to lose her mind, she was headed in that direction.

"Why are you waiting?" she asked with a moan and a sharp jerk of her hips, even though he had her weighted down.

After a quick press of his mouth to the top of her pussy, he was gone, continuing on with his exploration. Brushing his fingers, his lips, his warm skin down her thighs, over her knees and calves, not stopping until he reached the top of her feet. Then he made his way back up.

Her pussy pulsed with an intensity she'd never experienced before when he snagged her ankles and planted her feet on his shoulders. In anticipation, she fisted the sheets seconds before he buried his face between her quivering thighs.

The tip of his tongue flicked her clit, again teasing her, before he plucked her sensitive nub with his lips and sucked it hard. Her hips shot off the bed and she fisted the sheets even tighter, close to shredding them with her nails.

His skilled mouth, tongue and even teeth were making her crawl out of her skin, and wreaking havoc on her sanity.

She was torn between wanting to urge him to stop what he was doing and drive hard and deep inside her instead, but she also wanted to encourage him to continue on his current path and make her come with his mouth.

She chose the latter, since they'd get to the rest soon enough. She just needed patience.

And orgasms. Lots and lots of orgasms.

She had no doubt Finn was the man to give them to her. She got a taste of his skills in the VIP room and wanted a repeat.

Driving her heels into his back, she thrust her pussy up and against his mouth. He complied by both sucking both her clit and swollen folds until once again his name was forced from between her lips. On a groan, a moan and a sigh. Especially after he spread her slick folds and plunged two fingers inside to fuck her hard.

His words vibrated against her sensitive clit. "Want you to come."

No shit. So did she.

311

And she was getting there. She was so damn close.

He nibbled along her folds, down one, up the other, scraping his teeth over her clit until her hips twitched uncontrollably.

When he lifted his head and his fingers stilled, she hissed out a frustrated breath. A grin was there and gone so quickly, she almost missed it before he dropped his head and resumed his sweet torture all over again. Circling, flicking, sucking. Biting. Pumping his fingers in and out of her. Finding the spot that drove her even closer to the edge.

She lost herself in everything he was doing.

The dam was about to break...

With clenched jaws, she twisted her fingers into the sheets as the most intense orgasm rocketed through her.

Well, damn.

Not bothering to wait until the climax was over, his tongue drew an invisible line up her body until he caged her in once more. Once again face to face, he stared down at her, his lips glossy, his hazel eyes dark, his expression almost pained.

When he took her mouth again, she could taste herself. But only for an instant, before he demanded, "Condom."

"About time."

"Good things take time, Mel," he rumbled.

"I can't argue that. Condoms are in the nightstand."

He was gone and back in a second, once again staring down at her, the corners of his lips curled up. "Interesting drawer."

She shrugged, not bothering to fight her smile. "A girl's gotta do what a girl's gotta do."

"It looks like you like to do a lot of doing."

She laughed. "That I do."

"We might have to take out some of those toys and do some playing."

"I'm up for that."

"But not tonight," he finished.

"Not tonight," she agreed. Dragging her nails down his back, she grabbed two handfuls of his ass and squeezed in unspoken encouragement. "Suit up, officer."

He tipped his head, "Yes, ma'am," and sat up on his heels, his eyes never leaving hers as he tore open the wrapper and rolled the condom down his hard length.

When he was done and back on his hands and knees, she grabbed his face and pulled him down, capturing his lips and taking control this time. To show him how much she wanted him. How much she was ready.

While she kissed him, he settled his broad body between her thighs and slid the head of his latex-covered cock through her wetness, from her clit all the way to the crease of her ass and back up to where it needed to be. Exactly where she wanted him.

He positioned her arms straight over her head, then slowly ran his hands from her armpits up, and when he got to her wrists, he not only drove them into the bed, he drove his cock inside her with a grunt. Once he was fully seated, his eyes shut and he stilled, waiting while her body stretched around him, accepted him. Squeezed him tightly.

He pressed their foreheads together and, though too close to focus, his eyes locked with hers. For one pounding heart-beat. And another.

Then he began to glide in and out of her with each smooth thrust of his hips.

His whisper was rough. "You feel... so damn good."

She agreed, this was so damn good. *He* was so damn

good. Especially when at the end of each long, full stroke, he would grind himself even deeper inside her.

Wrapping her legs around him, she dug her heels into his thighs and lifted her hips, meeting him thrust for thrust. His pace stuttered before it quickened, and once it did, he began to power into her harder and deeper. With abandon and more recklessly.

Then she was rising, climbing, her climax building.

He released her wrists, gripped both sides of her face, driving his fingers into her hair as he took her mouth hard and slammed into her even harder.

With a fevered pace, he drove the air from her lungs with each thrust, then he gave it back to her. Until finally she was right there.

Right. There.

She struggled to keep her mouth on his when an orgasm ripped through her like a whirlwind from her head to the tips of her toes. She knew he felt it because he groaned into her mouth, even though he didn't let up. He continued to pound her relentlessly. Not slowing down even for a second. He was on a mission to follow her on this journey.

She cried out in surprise as another orgasm came out of nowhere, causing her toes to curl, forcing her to rip free from his mouth in an effort to catch her breath.

He held her head in place and stared down at her with a look in his eyes she didn't recognize or understand. But she didn't have time to analyze it because a second later he drove deep once more and, with a guttural grunt, let go.

Chapter Twenty-One

MEL STOOD near the bar and even though she faced the stage, she didn't see Chyna, or even the customers on the floor all intently watching the dancer. Instead, she was reliving what happened last night after sex.

After cleaning up and climbing back into bed, she had turned her head and studied Finn's profile for a few steady heartbeats before saying, "Stay."

With his arms folded under his head on the next pillow, he appeared totally relaxed and didn't seem to be in any rush to roll out of her bed or house. He turned toward her with both his eyes and expression unreadable. No surprise, no panic, no reaction at all. "All night?"

With what he said earlier that evening, he most likely didn't linger afterward with any of his conquests.

"Yes... but no pressure. Only if you want to." She would never beg a man to do something he didn't want to do. Just like she wouldn't want to be pressured to do the same.

He licked his very kissable lips while mulling over her

words. "Well, it *would* be more convenient since I'm taking you to work tomorrow morning."

"Well," she repeated, "there you go."

"If I stay, how about not going into the club so early? You can work up a sweat here on another type of pole, instead."

Even though she laughed, what he proposed sounded like a good plan to her since she could do with a repeat. It was nice to find someone capable in bed. Someone knowledgeable on locating both her G-spot *and* her clit.

He was a unicorn, that was for sure.

"Just so you know, I've never asked anyone to stay." He wasn't the only one who didn't like clingers.

He rolled onto his side and slid his knuckles along her jawline before nestling his fingers in her blonde rat's nest spread over the pillow. "I'll take that as a compliment, then. And... Just so you know, I've never stayed even when asked."

No surprise. "Then, if you stay, I'll take that as a compliment, too."

He did end up staying and despite not being used to having a man sleeping next to her, she slept better than expected. Better than she had in quite a while, all because of the Deadly Demons.

But the man lying next to her could be the solution to her problems and that possibility had somewhat settled the worry gnawing at her.

This morning she'd made him breakfast and while she showered, he cleaned up the kitchen. Another surprising move.

Yep, a total unicorn.

He didn't drop her off at the club until right before the girls began to arrive. She did skip dancing on stage this morning since she ended up riding his pole, just as he'd suggested last night.

Unfortunately, their attempt to have sex before feeding her four-legged fur-babies made them impatient. It also didn't help that they normally slept in bed with her and last night her poor dogs had to *suffer* by curling up in their plush dog beds, instead.

In revenge, they squeaked their toys in a passive-aggressive fashion through the majority of their morning sex. Worse, she swore they were doing it in time with each thrust and creak of her headboard.

It turned into an obnoxious symphony of sex and squeaky toys.

Eventually it got to the point where Finn had to stop. He closed his eyes and dropped his head, shaking it. "Can... they... not..."

She tried to smother her laugh but it bubbled from her anyway. "Honestly, I'm so used to them doing that, I no longer hear it."

"Unfortunately, I do."

"Is it putting you off your game?"

He grimaced. "It's... distracting..."

"Sorry. They normally sleep in bed with me and only sleep in their own beds when forced to. However, their breaking point is a late breakfast." She and the dogs had a routine, Finn being there was screwing with it.

"Should we call a time-out so you can get them fed?"

"Will that help?"

"Fuck yes, if it gets them to stop cock-blocking me." With a groan, he slid off and out of her.

"Don't you move," she ordered, wagging a finger at him.

"What... do I look like a fool?" he asked in surprise as she got up and tugged on her robe.

She glanced back at the bed before heading downstairs.

No, he definitely didn't. He looked damn good in that spot.

She sighed at the memory and mentally shook herself back to the present until she could once again hear the DJ's music and see Chyna doing her much beloved moves for her loyal fans. Mel needed to concentrate on her job, not float off into la-la land, distracted by a sexually-skilled, hot as hell redhead.

Watching one of her top-earning dancers once again drove home the fact she needed to get the hell out of The Peach Pit and take the girls with her.

Her eyes scanned the floor, making sure the customers appeared content and satisfied. Most had drinks forgotten on the table, or in their hand, since they were mesmerized by Chyna doing her signature upside down splits on the pole.

The agile woman took her routines seriously, as did most of Mel's dancers. Their dedication was one reason the club had been so successful before the Demons hijacked it. But if the MC began pushing them to do things they were unwilling to do just so they could remain employed, then Mel had no doubt those attitudes would change. For the worse.

A supportive workplace made for happier employees. Bullies created the opposite. It was Management 101.

Movement at the back of the room caught her eye.

Speaking of bullies...

Keeping her head pointed toward the stage, she let her eyes slide just enough to the left to watch Taint without him noticing. Standing behind the red velvet rope, he leaned into the newest prospect and "employee," another winner named T-Bone.

As soon as Taint was done whispering sweet nothings into T-Bone's ear, the prospect gave a single nod and disappeared toward the rear of the building.

Mel's heart began to thump almost as hard as when she and Finn had sex earlier and her brain began to spin with the possibilities of what the prospect might be about to do.

Did Taint "re-up" the drug supply in the van and was telling the young recruit to re-up his own stash?

Look at me thinking in those terms. A regular detective.

Honestly, she wished she had no reason to know them and that she never knew the Demons existed. Unfortunately, that horse had escaped the barn and her only choice was to find another ride.

She waited a few more seconds to see if Taint would replace T-Bone by standing watch at the hallway. When he also disappeared, she headed in that direction.

While she knew the task force might be setting up surveillance, she didn't know when. Finn had mentioned last night getting that arranged wasn't a simple or quick process. It took detailed scheduling and organization. Unfortunately, she also wasn't sure when Finn planned on returning to the club this evening.

She could *casually* wander into the back and see if she could catch T-Bone in the act. Maybe even snap a few pics for evidence since the sooner those assholes got out of her life, the better. If she could help nudge that along, she would. *Hell*, she'd help shove those bastards right off a steep cliff with zero regrets.

When she headed down the deserted hallway toward the exit, she noticed the office door was ajar. She slowed down and crept past it, sneaking a peek inside to see Taint leaning back in the office chair with his filthy boots propped on the desk and a cell phone to his ear.

With a shake of her head, she paused at the back door to pull up the hem of her dress just enough to reach her cell phone. Her new black lace garter "purse" was genius. It was the perfect solution to carrying her phone in the club without any of the Demons, or even the customers, knowing she had it. She also bought one for Sapphire and instructed her to keep her phone on her at all times.

With the direction the club was headed and especially with the current lack of safety precautions, she wanted them both to be prepared in case of an emergency. All of the women needed to look out for each other, especially since none of the Demons gave a shit about them.

Property. They were nothing but property to make a profit.

Once she quietly slipped outside into the waning daylight, she again paused, taking a second to scan the back lot for T-Bone or any strange vehicles in the area there to buy drugs.

She saw absolutely nothing and blew out a frustrated breath.

Then she heard it. The unmistakable sound of a door sliding open on the opposite side of the Astro Van from where she stood.

T-Bone.

Whether he just did a deal or not, she didn't know. But what she could do is catch him in the act of taking drugs from the van for upcoming deals. She had to guess that the prospects never went into the van when their meth customers were around. If those same customers knew where the drugs were hidden, she had a feeling the van would be broken into or even stolen.

Why pay for drugs when you had an opportunity to get them for the five-finger discount?

Stepping carefully and quietly around the van, she stopped at the back corner to peek around it. T-Bone had to have climbed inside since she could hear but not see him.

She positioned her phone so it looked like she was texting when in reality her camera app was open and ready for action. Dropping her head to pretend she was typing on the screen, she kept her eyes tipped up just enough to see as she moved closer to the open door of the piece of shit on wheels.

Inside the van, she heard a grumble and something fall, followed by a searing curse. She leaned her head in and asked with feigned concern, "Everything all right?"

Whatever the asshole had dropped, T-Bone quickly snatched back up and stuffed it into the inner pocket of his cut.

The whole time she stood just outside the van, she did her best to snap pictures without looking like she was doing so. Or at least she hoped she was pulling that off.

Because if she got caught...

"Get the fuck outta here," the prospect growled.

"I thought you hurt yourself. I only wanted to check on you."

Instead of answering, he gave Mel his back and blocked her view of whatever he was messing with. Most likely putting away the remainder of the stash back in its hiding spot. She continued to snap photos, hoping they would turn out worthwhile and not just be of her own feet. Or T-Bone's ass. Or the rusty floor of the POS-mobile.

"Is this your van? I was wondering whose it was."

"Get lost, bitch."

Mel's head jerked back and she corralled her instinctive response of telling him to kindly fuck off. Instead, she straightened her invisible manager's hat and said, "I'm the manager here. Don't speak to me like that."

"Just fuckin' did. Whatdya gonna do about it? Run to Saint? Go 'head and see where that fuckin' gets you."

What a dick.

When he began moving toward the open side door, she quickly took a good look around the van, trying to take as many pictures as possible without setting off T-Bone's alarm bells.

"Back up, bitch."

Okay, her manager's hat just became skewed. "My name isn't bitch, you fucking dickhead."

This time T-Bone's head jerked back.

Good. The asshole needed a rude awakening. If he thought she would simply take his verbal abuse...

Hell no. She would match his energy. "First off, you're new here so you might not know that my name is MJ and you need to use it. Second, and without exceptions, you need to respect me."

"Don't need to do shit."

She pointed toward the employee door. "What you need to do is go back inside and stay where you're assigned."

Climbing out of the van, he pushed past her when she refused to move and slammed the door shut, effectively ending her secret snooping.

Pulling himself up to his full height, he turned and went nose to nose with her. "And *you* need to fuck off."

Mel did not "fuck off" but wrinkled her nose, instead. "And *you* need to brush your damn teeth. Your breath smells like three-day-old roadkill. Have you been sucking off one of your buddies? Do you like to swallow?"

Jesus, Mel, do you have a death wish?

Apparently, she did. She had poked the mangy bear enough that his hand snaked out and, before she could step out of reach, he gripped her by the throat, whipped her around and slammed her back into the van. All the air rushed from her lungs and her phone tumbled out of her fingers and hit the pavement. For the few seconds after her head made impact, all she saw was stars and all she heard was a ringing in her ears.

Her groan lodged in her throat where his fingers circled her neck. His lip curled up in a sneer when she clawed at his wrist in her attempt to get free.

She winced as the sharp shards of pain shot through her rattled noggin and along her spine from the jarring impact. "Let... me... go..."

"Don't work for you, bitch. *You* work for the Demons. *You* belong to us. Guess you need a fuckin' lesson on how that works."

With as much power as she could behind her words, she forced out, "I don't belong to you. I don't belong to anyone. So, shove that lesson up your fucking ass."

T-Bone's eyes narrowed on her and she did *not* like the slow tobacco-stained smile that crossed his tattooed face. "Feisty as fuck. I like it." He then grabbed his crotch with the hand not choking her.

His fingers squeezed even harder, closing off her throat and making her wheeze in desperation to draw in air.

As her vision began to darken around the edges, she heard a female voice scream, "Oh my God, MJ! Get off her, idiot!"

It sounded like Raven. Mel didn't want her getting caught up in a mess she created.

"MJ!"

"Get—" She was screwed because she couldn't tell Raven to go get a bouncer. She no longer had employees who weren't Demons. None of them would help her. Not a damn one. They had zero respect for women. Especially for women who talked back. "Get... inside, Raven... I'm okay."

"You're not okay! Let her go! Saint! Get that asshole off of her!"

Oh shit. Taint was now outside?

Even when T-Bone's fingers flexed on her neck, he did not loosen his hold. However, with his attention on the head Demon, she managed to barely nudge her phone under the van with her toe.

She doubted it was enough for them to not spot it, but hopefully the screen had automatically locked by now so they couldn't see she'd taken pictures. If they did, she was afraid her problem would no longer be a bruised neck, but a broken one.

"What the fuck's goin' on here? Let her fuckin' go, T-Bone."

"She's bein' a fuckin' bitch."

Taint shook his head. "You ain't yet figured out they're all bitches?"

"This one was bein' a cunt more than normal."

Taint grabbed T-Bone's shoulders and yanked him off her. As soon as she was free, her hand automatically went up to her sore throat and she gulped in air.

In that moment, she discovered two things:

Breathing was *not* overrated.

And she enjoyed doing it.

"If you can't handle a sliver of a slit like her, you might not be earnin' your fuckin patches."

"Then lemme handle her the way I wanna handle her."

"What the hell does that mean?" Raven yelled, somewhere behind Taint.

Taint shot a scowl at Raven and pointed at the door. "Get the fuck back inside and back to fuckin' work."

"But—"

"Raven, go," Mel croaked, again not wanting the dancer to sink knee deep in the shit she stirred.

"Come with me," Raven urged, stepping around Taint to get closer to Mel, her dark eyes full of worry.

Of course Mel wanted to go back inside with Raven, but her phone was still under the van and she didn't want to risk leaving it behind. Especially if it had important evidence that might help Finn's case.

She wouldn't know that until she scrolled through the barrage of photos she took.

Sucking in a bolstering breath, she told Raven, "Go. I'll be in shortly."

Taint warned the dancer, "Go back inside now or find another stage to flash your fake tits."

Raven's eyes met hers, her eyes now full of hatred instead of worry, and Mel gave her a slight nod. The dancer only hesitated for a few more seconds before turning and leaving Mel out there alone with Taint and T-Bone.

As soon as the door clicked shut, Taint spun on her. "Didn't I fuckin' tell you to mind your own goddamn business?"

"This club *is* my business!" Mel's yell caused her to cough from the strain on her bruised throat. As soon as she caught her breath, she said, "That's what you pay me for, but you're trying to run a formerly successful business into the ground."

"Ain't runnin' shit into the ground. Stick to doin' your fuckin' job of managin' the dancers and makin' sure customers are happy. That's it. You don't like how things are goin', then fuckin' leave and take that other cunt with you. Ain't gonna tell you again about keepin' your nose out of Demon business."

"Demon business? You're putting the rest of us at risk by doing sketchy shit on this property."

His jaw turned to concrete and the twitch in Taint's cheek was easy to see, even under his long, unkempt beard. She was clearly pushing his buttons like she had T-Bone's.

She didn't care.

Fuck him and fuck his MC.

"What *sketchy* shit d'you see?"

Shit. Now she had to backtrack a bit. She did not want Taint aware that she knew they were dealing drugs out of the club. "Both the cameras being disabled and this van sitting here abandoned in the lot are suspicious. It was parked there before T-Bone started working here, so why was he climbing inside it?"

Taint's nostrils flared. "Told you to ignore the goddamn cameras and the van. Ain't your business. It's mine."

"The first one is a safety concern and the van's hard to ignore since I have to pass it every time I arrive or leave here and it's been sitting here for days. Not only is it an eyesore, Saint, it takes up valuable employee parking."

"Ain't hurtin' shit. Last time I'm tellin' you to mind your fuckin' business. Do your fuckin' job or bounce. Don't give a shit what you decide to do, just do it."

The hell if she was backing down. That was what Taint wanted. However, that wasn't what he would get. "I want assurances that you're not doing anything illegal that'll get this club shut down. If that happens, all the dancers will be out of work. They have families to take care of. Tuition bills to pay. They rely on that money and you're risking their livelihood."

Taint bared his teeth and gritted out, "Last. Fuckin'. Time—"

Tires chirping nearby caught their attention and Mel

heard the roar of an engine when a vehicle shot into the back lot.

A quick glance over her shoulder confirmed her suspicion that it was Finn.

Great. His arrival could be either good timing or bad depending on what happened next. "That's my boyfriend pulling in now. He's not going to like that T-Bone slammed me around like that."

"Boyfriend." Taint huffed sharply and spit on the ground barely missing her stilettos. "He ain't your boyfriend. We all know how you slits are. You're just workin' him over for some scratch. Seen it before. You pretend to like him and he showers you with money and gifts. Typical stripper whore."

Mel didn't have to hear Finn's approach, she could feel his energy. It was snapping and popping, making the air crackle around them.

"What the fuck happened?" He stepped between Saint and her, his eyes inspecting her from the top of her head to the tip of her high heels. He lightly touched her throat, his eyes as sharp as shattered glass. "Did he fucking choke you?" Finn spun on Saint. "You touch her?"

Taint's spine snapped straight and he pulled back his leather-clad shoulders. "You don't fuckin' belong here."

Finn stepped toe to toe with the biker, getting right in his face. "You fucking touch her?"

"Danny," she breathed, worried fists would start flying.

"Answer me," Finn demanded.

"Fuck off." Taint sucked loudly on his teeth. "Don't answer to you."

"Anyone who touches my woman without my permission answers to me. And I expect a fucking answer. Did you hurt her or," his head twisted toward T-Bone, "was it you?"

T-Bone's chin tipped up and cockiness oozed from him

when he said, "She was stickin' her fuckin' nose where it don't belong. Need to keep your pussy on a short leash."

Oh no. Finn was already on the warpath and now...?

Mel lost her breath and her heart took a tumble when Finn rushed the prospect. Before T-Bone could take a defensive stance, her fake boyfriend swung.

Chapter Twenty-Two

MEL'S SCREAM OF "DANNY, NO!" managed to permeate his brain as he cold-cocked a prospect he hadn't seen before. The biker, whose patch said his road name was T-Bone, was maybe in his early twenties, and, apparently, needed some life lessons on disrespecting women.

Finn would gladly teach him one or two. But not with his words.

He tuned out Mel's panic and hyper-focused on the baby biker in front of him, while making sure he wouldn't be ambushed by Saint from behind.

Two bikers against one undercover officer would suck. Without a doubt, he would end up on the losing end of that fight. For that reason, he needed to make this a short lesson so he could protect himself from the prospect's leader.

While T-Bone was still trying to shake off the first hit, Finn put all his weight behind the right upper-cut he delivered next. With satisfaction, Finn watched the young biker crumple like a dropped accordion before face-planting on the parking lot pavement. Out fucking cold.

With that fucker out of the way, he spun toward Saint. Despite the sharp pain in his knuckles, he kept his fists up, his body loose and his boots spread just in case the older biker wanted a taste of what Finn was dishing out.

If he did, Finn would serve it with pleasure.

Once again seeing the darkening marks on Mel's neck fanned the flames of fury burning inside him. But what convinced him to beat back the burn was the handgun Saint held.

That was a stark reality check and a good reminder of who the task force was dealing with. Plus, only a fool brought fists to a gunfight and Finn's temper wasn't at the point he'd be stupid enough to pull his own weapon.

He liked his job.

He liked his life.

And he really liked the woman who stood nearby watching with a hand clamped over her mouth and her eyes wide with worry.

No, getting shot would not only fuck up Finn in more ways than one but would also leave a mark on Mel, too.

He sucked in air in an attempt to control his impulses.

"Take one more fuckin' step toward me and that'll be your last one," Saint warned, pointing the Beretta at Finn's chest.

Finn believed him. The man didn't have his finger along the trigger guard. Fuck no. He had it on the trigger itself.

One twitch of that finger and Finn would be on the ground, bleeding out. A combination of common sense and street smarts had him lifting his hands in surrender and taking a few steps away from Mel so she wouldn't be caught in any crossfire.

He didn't trust Saint not to shoot him.

Hell, he didn't trust Saint. Period.

But he did hold his ground when the biker took another step toward him. "Hey, man, fists are one thing, bullets another. If someone knocked around your ol' lady, you'd be straightening that asshole out, too."

"See your lips flappin' but don't give a shit what's comin' outta them. You got no say here."

Finn's breath seized when Saint jabbed the gun's muzzle in Mel's direction. That was enough to fan the embers burning in his gut.

"She don't, either. I'm the fuckin' boss here. She needs to get that through her thick head or get the fuck out."

Finn's lungs began to pump again when the pistol was turned on him once more. If someone was going to take a bullet today, he'd rather it be him than Mel. He'd never forgive himself if that happened. She was an innocent in all of this mess.

Taking another step closer to Finn, Saint's gaze dropped briefly to T-Bone when the prospect groaned and began to resurface from the dark space where Finn sent him.

Saint raised his eyes back to Finn. "You're banned from this club. Get the fuck off this property."

Fuck. Fuck. Fuck. Crew was going to be pissed about Finn losing access to the club. Worse, he wouldn't be able to keep an eye on Mel. "Or what?"

Saint cocked an eyebrow at him. "You really wanna find out?"

From the corner of his eye, he saw Mel rush toward him. "Fi— Danny, please... just go. For now."

"I'm not leaving you here."

"Then take her with you," Saint told him. "I'll get the dark-haired piece to take her place."

"He's leaving right now," Mel quickly assured Saint,

tugging on Finn's arm. "Come on. I made this mess, let me clean it up."

Finn reluctantly let her lead him to the other side of his Toyota Tacoma. But mostly to get her out of the line of fire. They stopped where the truck could be used for cover and no one could overhear them talking.

"Listen, just go for now and come back at seven to pick me up. In the meantime, I'll try to smooth things over with Taint." She dropped her voice to barely a whisper. "Plus, I have to grab my phone. It fell when T-Bone slammed me against the van. I took as many pictures as I could while he was inside it."

His brow pinched together. "Pictures of what?"

She shook her head. "I have no idea. Sorry. I had to hide what I was doing so I took random shots. They might show something," she sighed, "or they might be garbage."

He ground his teeth together, tucked a thumb under her chin and tipped her face up. He dropped his and held her gaze. "I don't like you putting yourself at risk."

While he was impressed by her bravery, her safety came first.

She planted a hand on his chest. "Didn't I agree to that risk when I said I'd work with you?"

Finn pulled a long breath in through his nose and covered her hand with his, giving it a gentle squeeze. "Tell me... And I want the truth, Mel. Are you okay? Do you need to go to the hospital?"

She rubbed the back of her head but nodded. "I'm fine. No blood or loss of limbs. I cracked my head against the van and my back is a bit sore, but I'll take some aspirin or something. I'll be fine. Don't worry."

Every time she insisted that she'd be fine, it had the opposite effect on him. It didn't reassure him, it made him more worried. "How the fuck won't I worry when I can see the bruises already forming on your neck?"

Her fingers fluttered over her throat. "Listen, just let me deal with this. I'll cover the bruises with makeup once I go back inside and once Taint's cooled off, I'll try to smooth things over with him."

"I'm going to say this again, Mel... I don't want to leave you here. You could walk away."

She dropped her voice even lower. "Do you *really* want me to walk away and leave you without anyone on the inside? It's bad enough he just banned you from the club."

He pinned his lips together. He'd have to have a meeting with Crew so they could figure out another angle.

His silence was answer enough for Mel. "Of course you don't. I'll be fine. I promise."

That wasn't a promise she could give. Her safety was conditional on more than only herself. She had to deal with an outlaw MC with everything to lose. And that made them dangerous.

He closed his eyes for a few moments in an attempt to breathe out the tightness in his chest. Tension that would only get worse once he got into his truck and left Mel behind. When he opened them again, he ordered, "Phone on you at all times. Give Sapphire my number and have her keep her phone on her, too. Also give it to the girls. Tell them that if any of them see you in trouble, they need to call or text me immediately and I'll be here as fast as I can, or I can send in the locals."

"What if he changes the code? You won't be able to get in."

"Then you tell someone to let me in. I'm not going to let them manhandle you like that again. Never again, Mel. I didn't pull my weapon this time, but next time someone might end up with an extra hole in their fucking head."

"Then that will not only blow your cover, it might blow your investigation."

She might be right but he didn't care.

Then it hit him. He cared more about her than his damn job and the task force.

When the fuck did that happen?

It couldn't be because he slept with her. He'd never gotten attached so quickly to a woman he'd knocked boots with. If it wasn't the sex, how did she get past his carefully maintained armor?

Did he somehow step in quicksand, like Fletch?

For fuck's sake. He had to be imagining it. "I'll be back at seven sharp. If you're not out here, I'm going inside."

She rose on her toes and planted a kiss on his lips while squeezing his bicep in assurance he did not feel. "I'll see you at seven."

"Stay safe," he murmured. Dread filled his entire being as he watched her walk away.

If any of those motherfuckers touched or hurt her again, he would burn that club to the ground, along with anyone wearing a Deadly Demons cut.

As Dirty Harry once said, *"Don't fuck with me, buddy, or I'll kick your ass so hard you'll have to unbutton your collar to shit."*

Just call him Dirty Fucking Danny.

———

GRINDING his teeth and curling and uncurling his fingers into fists, Finn took long strides across the third floor of The Plant.

Maybe he should've headed home and went a few rounds with the heavy bag hanging in his condo's garage instead of showing up here. But he needed to meet with Crew and give him an update, so here he was...

However, every inch of his skin itched with the thought of leaving Mel behind at the club.

He reminded himself that managing the club was her job.

It was her job.

It was her goddamn job!

He needed to get over it. She worked there long before him and would probably end up working there after him. She was capable of handling herself. Proof apparent was when she didn't break down into a quivering, crying mess after T-Bone—that fucking motherfucker—manhandled her.

"Settle down, Ginger Snap. You getting all red in the face isn't going to change anything. It'll just give you heartburn."

"One of those motherfuckers hurt her, Crew. Fucking hurt her."

"She knew getting involved was a risk, so why's your panties in a wad?"

Once he ran out of floorspace, he spun on his heel and headed in the opposite direction.

He no longer saw Crew leaning against the long table with his arms crossed over his chest. Or Rez and Decker transcribing wiretaps. Or even seeing Nox sitting at a computer, typing up a report. No. He only saw Mel wincing when she rubbed the back of her head where it struck the van, and the marks on her throat T-Bone left behind. "Yours would be, too, if you saw her damn neck. She was slammed against the stash van because she was snooping around in an attempt to help us."

"Did you ask her to do that?"

"No."

"Well, there you go. She took a risk of her own accord. She can't expect to light the match to burn down an outlaw MC and not get a few heat blisters in the process."

Finn slammed to a halt. "Are you fucking serious right now?"

Crew shrugged. "Here's an easy solution that might unjam your thong: tell her to do nothing but observe unless we approve it first."

"Yeah, right." He scraped his fingers through his hair. "She hates those assholes and would love to see them go down sooner than later."

"She's not the only one, brother. But as you know, an investigation like this takes time and once that's complete, the wheels of justice grind even slower. If they even grind at all."

Finn ground his hand against the back of his neck and began to pace again. Yeah, he needed to hit something or maybe even go to the range. Blasting some paper targets with Saint and T-Bone's names written center mass over the silhouettes would relieve some tension.

"Yo, Carrot Top, you're going to wear a path in the newly refinished floor," Nox shouted from the other side of the room. "I worked hard on that fucker."

"I'm not worried about these fucking floors. They can be replaced. I'm worried about Mel, who can't."

"Holy shit," burst from Crew. "Did the man who rarely sticks his dick twice in the same woman actually catch some feels? Is that even possible? I expected you to fuck her—hell, we all did—but not fall for her."

The room became dead quiet. No talking. No laughing. No typing. Nothing.

All eyes had turned toward him. *Fuck!*

"I didn't fall for her," he insisted quickly before they began busting on him for something other than his red hair.

"That's impossible since I haven't even known her very long."

"Brother, right now you're acting like a protective boyfriend, not a fake one."

"I'm protecting our asset," Finn insisted.

"Protecting our asset? Tapping her ass more like it." Crew lifted a hand. "Not that there's anything wrong with that and that's the whole reason we didn't make her a paid CI."

Was he that fucking predictable?

Finn's fingers curled into his palms even tighter and he wanted to wipe that shit-eating grin clean off Crew's face.

The task force leader grimaced. "Truthfully, I'm a little concerned that little fat fuck Cupid might be flying around Rockvale like a damn blood-sucking mosquito. First Fletch, and now you?"

"Now nothing." Tucking a finger into the collar of his shirt, he tugged at it, trying to keep it from choking him. It must have shrunk in the dryer.

"Sounds like Little Orphan Annie escaped the orphanage only to end up on a boat headed down *d'Nile*," came from Rez, sitting at one of the wiretapping stations near the front windows, his headphones now hanging around his thick neck.

Finn shot him the bird.

Rez winced, slapped a hand over his heart and fell backward into his chair, laughing. "Anyway... if someone sees that chubby fucker flying around here with his arrow, shoot him first, will ya?"

Finn ignored Rez and stopped in front of the DEA agent. "I don't give a fuck how you take this... Even though the investigation isn't over yet, I want Saint gone. She's not safe there with him in charge of that club."

"See, asshole? This is how I know you've tripped and

fallen over Mel. You're not using your fucking head right now. You're using your heart. When you tripped, the Tefloncoating must have chipped. You know how fucking dangerous not using your brain can be in this line of work, Finn. And anyway, they'll just replace Saint with someone else. Someone possibly a lot worse. At least you already know what you're dealing with when it comes to this Saint guy and can take heed."

Crew was annoyingly right. Taking Saint out as a player wouldn't change the game, it would only put one Demon behind bars out of many. Finn was damn sure that jail was Saint's home away from home and most likely the man wasn't afraid of being incarcerated, anyway.

"But... if it'll keep you from busting a cap in his ass, maybe we can secure him in a cage for a few days until things cool off."

Finn shot a scowl at the task force leader. "Bust a cap in his ass?" He never expected that to come out of Crew's mouth.

"At least that proved you're actually listening. We *could* have a Uniontown PD officer pull Saint over—with probable cause, of course—and ask for a vehicle search. When he refuses—because we know he will—we'll get a dog out there. Once the dog hits, we'll have enough PC to search his vehicle and if he's transporting, we can take him into custody. That will keep him out of Mel's hair at least until he gets bailed out."

While that sounded good, it was only a temporary solution. Once Saint got released, he could return to the club more aggravated than ever.

"I don't want him blaming Mel for that stop-and-search in any way. And he just might since she keeps challenging him. She doesn't hide the fact that she doesn't like him. She's also made it known that she's not happy with the way he's running things. And after what happened today, he might know she suspects they're dealing drugs. I haven't had a chance to go over everything that was said or done before I got to the club, but he was definitely not happy about her being nosy."

Crew stroked his bearded chin as he considered Finn's words. "Even though we couldn't prove it in the security footage, my best guess is that Saint's the one transporting drugs from the Demon's clubhouse in Uniontown to the stash van behind the club. That alone puts him at risk for a random search and seizure. For him, the vehicle *and* the drugs. I'm not sure if he would pin that on your girl."

"While that's my assumption, too, that doesn't mean he won't blame her. It's not like these bikers are reasonable people." Finn asked, "You don't think he's the one transporting from the mother club to Uniontown, do you? If we decided to pop him to put him away for a short, but forced, vacay, it would be easier and safer to have someone intercept him farther away from The Peach Pit. It's possible if he got snagged in West Virginia, he might not suspect Mel at all."

"Good thinking, but no. Group one already identified the transporters from West Virginia to Pennsylvania. It's not one Demon. They rotate and switch the schedule up to prevent a pattern. But since group one now has at least two task force members on the inside with the mother chapter in Moundsville, their mixing shit up to throw off the task force doesn't matter. However, we still don't know where they're stashing it yet in PA. My guess is that they have it secured somewhere in that gas station in Uniontown."

"Another good reason for at least one of us to prospect with that chapter," Nox murmured, still facing the computer.

"I'm working on that, but in the meantime, we still need

Jeanne St. James

to keep gathering evidence since shutting down the Demons needs to be a coordinated effort. That means we need enough so all three chapters—Uniontown, Moundsville and New Philadelphia—can be hit at once so they don't have time to get rid of the evidence."

"Also so they don't have a chance to scatter," Rez added.

"What about the Russos?" Decker asked from the front of the room.

"What about them?" Crew asked with his brow furrowed.

"They're a major player in this whole thing. Are we just going to let them skate?"

Crew answered, "I sure as fuck hope not. From what I understand, the FBI will work with the DEA on indictments after we shut down the Demons from the three active chapters. We might be able to get some of the bikers to testify against the Pittsburgh Cosa Nostra for a reduced sentence."

"Don't bet on it," Finn said. "Bikers don't bend easily. For them, doing time is a rite of passage. They probably get a special tattoo every time they go inside. Just like gang members get a teardrop tattoo for each murder they've committed."

"Or a kindergartener getting a gold star," Decker huffed.

Rez whacked Decker in the arm. "Aww. Does your Valee Girl love getting gold stars, Daddy Decker?"

"In fact, she does. Would you like me to bring you some? How about a nap mat?"

"I could use a nap," Rez laughed.

The second his cell phone vibrated in his back pocket, Finn pulled it out. It could be Mel.

No surprise, it was. "Shit."

Crew's gaze swung from Rez and Decker back to Finn,

his amusement quickly dissipating. "What? Is she in trouble?"

Her first text stated that she was fine—just like she had insisted earlier—and she was staying out of Saint's way. "No, it doesn't seem like it."

Before he could text her back, a photo came through. He squinted at the confusing picture.

"Then what? Is she sexting you? Why are you squinting? We saw her tits the other night at the club. No reason to squint."

Finn sighed and continued to swipe through every picture as she sent them. "She took some photos during the incident after catching the prospect in the van. Or should I say she tried to take photos. They're complete dog shit. Well... except for this one."

Crew quickly moved behind him and peered over his shoulder. "Which one? Let me see."

Finn tilted the phone away from the DEA agent to hide the photo, but Crew almost knocked it out of his hand.

Before Finn could stop the phone from falling, Crew caught it and walked away, wearing his signature smart-ass grin and peering closely at the picture. "Damn. Those are Mel's feet?"

"Yeah."

Crew laughed. "Didn't know you were into feet."

"I'm not, but look at them in those *sexy-as-fuck* stilettos. Actually... don't. Give that back to me. I don't want you rubbing one off to it."

When Crew darted out of arm's reach, Finn followed him with his hand out. The task force leader pinched the photo with two fingers and zoomed in closer. "Okay, that's fucking hot even though I'm not a foot man." He swiped through the rest. "Any better photos?"

Finn snagged the phone from his fingers and immediately locked the screen. "No."

"Can I see the pic of her feet?" Decker asked.

"Also no."

Crew pointed his obnoxious grin at him. "You're definitely not acting like she's your fake girlfriend."

"We have a mutually agreed upon arrangement to make our relationship look real, that's all." He quickly added, "To protect her and our investigation."

"Uh huh. Let me suggest this: before it gets more serious between you two, make sure she hears you sing first."

"One, I doubt she'll ever hear me sing since I have no reason to invite her to karaoke and two, clean out your fucking ears because I sing great. I'm so good I could go on tour."

Decker slammed his hand on the desk and fell over laughing.

"Despite the fact you could be his doppelgänger, you're no Ed Sheeran," Crew told Finn. "If you haven't noticed, your singing voice makes glass shatter and pussies yowl."

Finn shook his head. "Yowl?"

"Yeah. Dogs howl. Pussies yowl."

Finn huffed, "Okay, Dr. Crewlittle."

"More like it makes pussies dry as the Sahara Desert," Decker huffed. "And your singing is one reason why I named my ginger pussy Finn."

Finn did not need a reminder that Decker named his orange cat after him.

Before he could respond, Rez yelled out, "Christ almighty! If I have to go undercover, do not partner me up with someone for a fake relationship, Crew. Apparently that's a gift that keeps on giving. That's more likely the cause of Finn and Fletch's downfall, not that stupid flying cherub."

"Fletch seems happy with Wilder," Nox mumbled over at his desk.

"That's because Wilder is a kick-ass bitch," Rez said. "Who wouldn't want a woman like that? She's probably taught Fletch a thing or two."

"Monty's a kick-ass bitch, too," Decker suggested, wiggling his eyebrows.

Rez grimaced. "Monty's like a sister despite being part of our brotherhood. I can't even begin to imagine her naked."

Neither could Finn. "Enough talk about Monty since she's not here to give you a smackdown. And, newsflash, she doesn't want to see you naked, either, Alvarez."

"Hey, you don't know that and I look good naked!" Rez exclaimed.

"Nobody cares. Anyway... all the photos Mel took seem to be useless."

"You know what wasn't as useless?" Crew started. "Those videos. Tell Mel we need the most recent security footage."

"Has someone already gone through everything I gave you so far?" Finn asked, surprised.

"We're still slogging through them. We found some video of what we suspect is one of the prospects dealing out front but it isn't conclusive enough to make a difference for our case. They're slick about it. We need footage that clearly shows them dealing or what could be perceived as dealing. Enough to convince a grand jury."

"Yeah, most of the dealing is out back. The whole reason the cameras back there were disabled."

"Speaking of the club's rear parking lot, Rodgers took a drive-by to check the logistics of having a team sit surveillance."

"And?" Finn prodded.

"Unfortunately, there's no good spot to sit undetected. Not the way the property is set up. There's nowhere to hide. We might as well sit there in a marked unit with the emergency lights flashing and the sirens blaring."

"Yeah, I was afraid of that, but confirming it just makes it worse now that I'm persona non-grata."

Crew dropped his salt-and-pepper head and stared at his boots for a few moments. When he lifted it again, he said, "We've got two other options now that you've been banned from the premises. One, we can send someone else in to do undercover buys or... we can install our own cameras."

Finn's ears perked at that idea. Could they pull that off? If so...

"We'd need probable cause and a court order to do that," Decker called out from his seat.

"No shit. I'm a *senior* special agent, remember? That senior designation proves I know some shit. It's also why they have me leading this group." Crew scrubbed his fingernails on his chest, then blew on them. "I've got mad skills."

Nox snorted over at his desk, shook his head and went back to typing.

Rez spun his office chair around to face Crew and Finn. "How about we break into the van after closing to confirm it's a stash van first and not just an abandoned piece of shit?"

"We'd still need a court order for that search, the same as for installing cameras," Finn reminded him.

"Abso-fucking-lutely. Otherwise, any evidence we find would be tainted because it would be fruit of the poisonous tree. And rotten fruit is useless." Crew slowly drew a hand down his short beard as he continued to work a plan out in his head. Finn was waiting for puffs of smoke to escape his ears. "How about this... Let's hold off on pinching Saint and instead, I arrange for a drug dog to sniff around the exterior of the van. If it hits, that should give us enough PC to get a court order to install our own camera system. That'll be more efficient than sitting surveillance. Better on the budget, too."

"Can we get away with installing our own system?" Finn asked. "That would be so much fucking better than someone sitting in a van nearby and pissing in a bottle." Anything was better than that.

"No shit," came from Decker.

"I second that 'no shit,'" said Rez. "The only thing I hate more than transcribing wiretaps is sitting in a fucking vehicle for hours and hours until I want to eat my fucking gun."

Finn bugged his eyes out at Rez before sliding his eyes over to Nox and back in a silent message.

Rez grimaced and silently mouthed, "Fuck."

Finn risked a glance over at Nox. Their BAMC brother was still typing away with his back to the rest of them. Maybe he didn't hear Rez. Though, that was doubtful since Rez had a big fucking mouth.

Crew huffed out a breath and shook his head, glaring at Rez.

"Where would we put those cameras?" Decker asked, trying to move past Rez's fuck-up.

"Definitely one or two facing the back lot since that's the area where we have zero visibility. We should put one inside the van, too, so we can capture whatever's going on in there. Also one in the office for the hell of it. Your girl will have to give us access afterhours to install them."

Your girl. "I'll have her give me the new security code if Saint changed it." His educated guess was, to keep Finn out, Saint immediately changed it after the earlier incident.

"We'll need to make sure whoever installs the system isn't caught on the cameras that are still functioning. That would fuck up everything," Crew announced as if none of them knew that. "And from the footage you got us, it looks like there are a bunch of cameras on the inside."

"Yes, there are. In the lobby, pointed at the bar, the tables, the hallway, the stage. They're everywhere except the bathrooms, the dressing room and the..." *Fuck*, did the VIP rooms have hidden cameras? If they did, he hoped Mel would've mentioned that before they had sex in there.

Finn glanced at Crew. No, there couldn't have been. If there was, he would've never heard the end of it. In fact, he wouldn't put it past his brothers to put that performance on the big screen downstairs after making a vat of popcorn.

He continued, trying not to think about that possibility. "As of now, Mel still has access to the security footage. Maybe she can shut it off for the time it'll take us to set up the cameras. Somehow make it look like a glitch."

"I might know someone who can assist us with that," Crew murmured, deep in his thoughts.

"What about Rodgers? Does he have skills in that department?" Finn asked about Crew's fellow DEA agent also on the task force.

"Possibly. I'll ask him. If not him, then I'm sure I can find someone to manipulate the footage or at least instruct us how to make it look like the gap in time is a glitch and not on purpose."

"Mel will also have to ensure the security cameras facing the rear lot are still disabled before we go in." As long as Saint didn't pull her security access. If he did, that would put a huge kink in their plan.

"Let me see how quickly I can get a drug dog out there and right before the handler goes out, we'll get Mel to check to make sure those cameras are still disabled. See? As much as you'd like her out of there, we need her."

Once again, the jackass was right. But that didn't mean Finn had to like it.

Crew whacked him hard on the back, making him lurch forward. "Brother, I can still see how fucking tense you are about this whole thing with her. Dr. Crewlittle suggests you straddling your original love and take her out for a long ride."

"Are you talking about Mel or his Harley?" Rez asked with a snort.

"A long ride on either would do him some good," Crew answered.

"Let's plan one for Sunday," Finn suggested, since he was road captain. "We have to get as many in before it gets too cold. Will that work?"

"Count me in," Rez answered.

A long ride would do Finn some good. It would be even better if he could convince Mel to be his backpack. She'd probably love it. He wondered if she owned any footwear other than *fuck-me* pumps.

"You just have to be careful that going along doesn't blow your cover," Crew said.

Another reminder he didn't need. "Yeah. I'll do what I did last time or wear my full-faced helmet with the dark tint."

Decker stood and, with a loud, obnoxious yawn, stretched his arms over his head. "Damn shame Fletch has been missing out. Never thought I'd hear myself say that the MC isn't the same without him."

Crew laughed. "Right? But he can't ride with us until he's no longer wearing an Angels' cut. 'Til then he needs to either ride strictly with Wilder or in formation with the DAMC."

Nox glanced over his shoulder, his fingers paused over the keyboard. "Are they still letting him ride on their runs?"

Crew answered with, "They are. Even if reluctantly. Good

thing the prez of that MC has a reasonable head on his shoulders. That's our only saving grace for Fletch and Wilder remaining undercover with them. He's now done over thirty major buys from the Demons. That's a nice chunk of meth off the streets."

But the Demons still remained walking free. Finn was more determined than ever to speed this investigation along to change that.

"Those buys hardly make a dent," Decker said, "when they're transporting five kilos a month from Mexico."

"And it's our job to cut that down to zero. But we need to do it right and not rush the process."

Finn sighed impatiently and scraped the tip of his thumb across his forehead. "Okay, soooo... What am I going to do now that I'm banned from the club?"

Don't fucking say surveillance.

"You'll be assigned to watching the camera feed once we get them installed." The task force leader grinned. "What else?"

"Christ," came out on a groan. That was almost as bad as surveillance, which was like watching paint dry. Or watching golf.

"Well, since you lost your fucking temper and K-O'd a Demon prospect, you no longer have physical access to the club, so, lucky you, you're now stuck with digital access."

"You would've done the same thing."

"You're probably right. Men who abuse women need their asses handed to them. But you still have a job to do, so you're going to suck it up and do it. Especially since the sooner we wrap this investigation up, the sooner your girl will be out from under the Demons' thumb. That's what you want, right?"

For fuck's sake, he hated when Crew was right.

Chapter Twenty-Three

HE KEPT MOVING and never lingered in one spot, his feather-light touches whispering over every inch of her heated skin. Add in the teasing flicks of his tongue on the sensitive tips of her pierced nipples. The fleeting brushes of a fingertip across her pulsing clit.

All in an attempt to drive her out of her freaking mind.

He was succeeding.

Planting a hand on the mattress, Finn lifted his torso but dropped his head until his parted lips hovered over hers. With their mouths only a hairsbreadth apart, their warm breaths merged into one.

Breathe in. Breathe out.

Finn was in no hurry tonight. He was traveling a slow path to push her to the very edge of her sanity.

"I can't take anymore," she groaned, rolling her head from side to side.

She wanted him to hurry up, to be inside her. But, *damn it*, she also wanted him to continue on this torturous path of pleasure.

Frustrating for sure, but it also fanned the fire in her belly, causing flames to sweep through her from the top of her head to the tips of her toes.

He slid his lips lightly up her jawline and pressed them to her ear. "Are you telling me to stop?" His voice, whether he meant it to be or not, was soft but firm. An intoxicating mix of both a commanding cop's, but it also held a lover's promise.

"Don't you dare," she warned him.

"Are you sure? I don't want you to suffer needlessly."

"Of course you do."

Shaking with laughter, he skimmed his lips along her arched throat, only pausing for a heartbeat at the hollow of her neck before moving on... across her right shoulder, around the outer curve of her breast, down her belly.

Digging her fingers into his short hair, she clung to her wits as best as she could as he continued lower...

Lower...

When she tipped her head down, his darker than normal hazel eyes locked with hers while he took his time settling his muscular bulk between her spread thighs.

She could only imagine that if him taking his time was torturous to her, it had to be excruciating for him.

Even so, she wouldn't feel bad for him. Not one bit since he caused it.

Every night and again every morning for the past few days, he hadn't gone slow. *Hell*, she hadn't, either. It had been more like a sprint than a marathon.

As soon as they'd walk through her front door after he picked her up from work, they'd be on each other like two animals during mating season. Kissing, biting, clawing at each other's clothes. Leaving a path of shoes, jeans and underwear behind them like bread crumbs.

Last night he had even carried her upstairs naked with

her arms hooked around his neck and her legs wrapped around his equally naked waist. Amazingly enough, when he reached the loft, his panting wasn't from exertion but from his impatience to be inside her.

But tonight was different. He had switched from the left passing lane to the right cruising lane and drove like a ninety-year-old behind the wheel.

His murmur against her skin drew her from those thoughts but she was unable to make out whatever he said. His eyes lifted, catching hers once again and holding them.

Him eating her pussy while watching her reactions might make another woman self-conscious, but not her. All it did was turn up the dial from hot to scorching.

Her clit was already swollen and throbbing when his warm breath enveloped it, making her groan in frustration.

"I know what you're doing," she accused him when he teased her there with only a flick of his tongue. She wasn't sure how much more she could take.

He paused and lifted his head. Totally opposite of what she wanted. "What am I doing?"

"Edging."

"I don't even know what that is."

Right. "Liar."

He had the nerve to chuckle. "I take it you're not enjoying it?"

Oh, she was. But she also wasn't. "I'm about to shatter but not in a good way. Make me come."

"I plan on it. Why are you in such a rush?" The corners of his lips twitched.

"Finn," she growled, digging her nails into his scalp and pushing his head down. "Stop talking and get back to work."

With his upper body pinning down her thighs, when he shook with amusement this time, he made her shake, as well.

Jeanne St. James

"Oh my God! You're enjoying this way too much!"

Ignoring her outburst, he sucked on her clit, but just as she was getting into it, he lifted his head again. "Was that torture?" He then ran his tongue from the bottom of her pussy back up to her clit. "Was that torture?"

"It was so fast I couldn't tell. Try it again."

He dropped a soft kiss to the top of her mound. "Like that?"

Out of frustration, she began to scramble from under him but he only put more weight on her, thwarting her attempts to get free.

Without another word, he began to eat her pussy in earnest. Like he hadn't eaten a meal in a month.

Yesssss. Finally!

Her head dropped back to the pillow and her back arched when she drove her hips up, encouraging him to give her more. She couldn't get enough of his mouth toying with her clit. His lips sucking, his tongue circling. The light scrape of his teeth against her sensitive nub and over her slick folds.

"Finn," she groaned, her fingers flexing as she got closer and closer to the elusive edge. She only needed a little more. She was so damn close.

He dragged a finger down through her wetness and back up before slipping one finger inside her, then a second...

And... he was gone. Gone! Leaving her hanging. His breath, his lips, his fingers only a fleeting memory.

As she opened her mouth to complain, he was back, his knees separating her legs even wider and the thick head of his latex-covered cock taking the place of his fingers. He slid it back and forth through her slick folds, opening her up to him.

Sliding his chest along hers, his skin brushed over the hard points of her nipples and dragged over her piercings, giving them a delicious pull. Capturing her mouth, he stole both her breath and her moan.

She fought the instinct to close her eyes, to lose herself in what would happen next. Instead, she kept her gaze glued to his as he filled and stretched her inch by inch. Still not in any kind of rush.

It hit her then. The reason he had gone slowly and took his time. By doing so, he was savoring every moment of this time together. It allowed her to do the same.

What was happening between them was now past the point of him only being a fake boyfriend. Or of this only being about sex. Along the way, a connection had grown. Even in just the few short weeks they'd know each other.

Did he realize it and want her to discover the same? Possibly.

Or was she overthinking this whole thing and making more of their relationship than it was? Simply a working one.

But what started as him staying over the first night he came to her place, quickly turned into him staying every night in her bed. Fake boyfriends didn't do that.

Sometimes real boyfriends didn't, either.

None of this was about his job. It also wasn't about hers. No, this went beyond them joining forces to work with the task force and against an outlaw MC.

With each roll of his hips, they came together and moved apart like they were both on stage doing body rolls. It was smooth and coordinated. Finn knew how to control every muscle. He could move his hips during sex as expertly as he could on stage.

Gliding his fingers along her rib cage, he flicked a curved barbell with his fingernail before trapping a nipple and rolling it roughly between two fingers. His mouth traced her pulse along her throat before moving down to suck on the other puckered nipple.

His powerful and broad back flexed under her nails, as she scraped them over his heated skin, most likely leaving marks behind as they continued the dance of two lovers.

But it wasn't a fast-paced salsa, it was a sensual bachata.

On one hand, she was anxious for the explosive finish to their routine. On the other, she wasn't ready for it to end. Because it was that damn good.

What made it even better was he didn't make sex all about himself like some men did. He not only knew how to please her, but cared about how he went about it.

Suddenly his hips stuttered, then paused. And when he released her nipple, a shuddered breath escaped him.

The look in his eyes and the sharp cut of his jaw all screamed that he had reached his limit of taking it slow. Of making it last longer.

"Mel." Her murmured name on his lips almost sounded like a plea. Or an apology.

Maybe even a warning.

The man was done.

But then, so was she.

Her answering, "Finn," told him she was okay with whatever he needed to do next.

The tension in his jaw loosened and he blew out a breath. With a single nod, whether to her or himself, he bared his teeth and began to fuck her harder and a hell of a lot faster, circling his hips at the end of each thrust. She lifted her own over and over to meet his, encouraging him with her movement, her words, and by driving her nails into his muscular ass cheeks.

Because if he slowed down again, she would scream.

Luckily, he didn't. As if a switch had been flipped, he

pounded her over and over. Never slowing down. No longer teasing, but all business.

Wrapping her hands around his head, she pulled him down, but avoided his mouth and instead, buried her face against his throat. The deep grunts accompanying each thrust vibrating against her lips.

She licked along his pulse line and traced the strained cords of his neck. But it didn't take long before he broke free so he could brace his hands on either side of her head and continue to drive into her without mercy. His grunts become louder as each thrust powered by his muscular thighs slammed the air out of her lungs.

His name fell from her lips over and over. She begged him not to stop and pleaded for him to keep going. She wanted everything he was giving her and more.

Her orgasm approached like a slow moving storm. Shocks of lightning, crashes of thunder surrounded her, swallowing her whole. Making her muscles twitch, her toes curl, her heart race until...

She was done.

Done.

So damn done.

Her back arched and her body twisted when a climax ripped through her, dragging Finn along for the ride. With his knees anchored into the mattress, he powered up and into her once... twice...

She might have imagined her name spilling out of him because she wanted to hear it and not because he said it. And when he stilled deep inside her with the root of his cock pulsing, she also wished the thick jets of cum filled her and not the condom.

The first might have been reality and not only in her head, but the second was pure fantasy. At least for now. If they continued down this current path, that could possibly change.

Would she want it to? Could she envision Finn remaining in her life once her part in the investigation was over?

With a groan, he collapsed on top of her, his skin hot and damp, his breathing irregular and his heart knocking against her chest.

Their bones must have turned to liquid since both were incapable of moving.

Or it could be that neither wanted to be the first to burst the bubble of contentment they were currently cocooned in.

They lay quietly, the only sounds to be heard were of their still unsteady breaths and the soft snores of her dogs curled up in their beds.

It wasn't long after cleaning up, they were also curled up together and softly snoring, too.

———

As soon as she fed the dogs, she had climbed back into her warm bed and tangled herself up with Finn. Even though she needed to get up soon to make them breakfast and get ready for work, she wanted to delay it as long as possible.

That hammered home the fact she'd never been so attached to a man before. It should disturb her but, surprisingly with Finn, it didn't. If any man would be the reason for losing some of her independence, at least she picked a good one.

One that respected her, despite her line of work.

One that treated her like a partner, and not a lesser.

One that recognized her savvy business sense, and didn't

consider her a brainless twit because of how she looked and dressed.

One who seemed to support her desire to start her own strip club and didn't try to steer her toward a more public-perceived "respectable" profession.

Finn didn't seem to care she'd been a stripper for years. He didn't seem to care she managed a strip club.

He didn't seem to care about what she wore to work.

Some men would have a hard time dealing with at least some of it, if not all. They might lie and pretend it was okay when in fact, they secretly hated it.

But maybe she was giving him too much credit.

He might think differently if they were in a real relationship. Because besides the awesome sex, the rest of it was supposed to be fake.

His heavy arm lay across her body under her breasts, his muscular, lightly-furred thigh pinned her legs to the mattress. His breathing was soft and steady where it was tucked into her neck, his thumb gliding lightly back and forth over the fading bruises.

They both had slipped into lazy mode.

The last couple of men she'd been with, she had felt restless after hooking up with them. She couldn't wait for them to leave, or she made excuses for her to escape their place.

With Finn, she was content and comfortable and had no urge to put space between them. She assumed since he was in no rush to leave her or her warm bed, he felt the same.

She brushed her fingers mindlessly through his thick shock of red hair, studying his very relaxed expression. She liked his weight on her. It wasn't smothering at all but more like a weighted blanket that bathed her in calmness.

She would enjoy every second with him for as long as it lasted. Like her, none of his past relationships had been long or serious. It wasn't like she had been avoiding them, she just never met anyone she wanted to spend more time with, instead of less.

Funny how this fake relationship turned out to be more fulfilling than any of her previous real ones.

It could be that he was only staying over since he insisted on taking her to work every morning and picking her up in the evening, despite the fact that Taint had banned him from inside The Peach Pit.

She thought it was no longer necessary, but when she mentioned it, he insisted on continuing to play the part of her controlling, possessive boyfriend. Even though he might not be allowed inside the club, by him taking her to and from work, Saint would be reminded that Finn was still in the picture.

"What are you doing tomorrow afternoon?" rumbled from him and vibrated through her chest.

"Like every other Sunday, I'm working." Normally she didn't mind working on the weekends. It wasn't like she had other plans. But she had a feeling wherever he was going with this was going to make her regret having to work this Sunday.

"Bang off."

She frowned. "Do what?"

He pressed a quick kiss to her nipple. "Call in sick."

Oh sure. "I need the money, Finn. Otherwise, I'm never going to escape that place. Can whatever you have planned happen on Monday, instead?"

He pursed his lips. "That won't be possible, but... Maybe you can get Sapphire to cover for you for a couple of hours? You can just go in late."

If Laura was still the owner, sure. She could've taken the whole day off, but things had changed.

Before she could dig deeper into whatever idea he had,

he rolled off her and snagged his phone from the nightstand nearest him. He tapped on the screen before putting the phone to his ear, then rolled onto his back, tucking one arm under his head. "Yo, prez, got a favor... Yeah... Well, fuck you, too... I'm moving the run to an earlier time... I don't give a shit. Nobody's going to bitch. Just two hours earlier. Eleven instead of one." His gaze lifted to the ceiling. "Yeah, whatever. Do me a favor and let everyone know. Blame me. Also, no cuts. I'll explain later." Without a goodbye, he pulled the phone from his ear and stabbed at the screen before tossing it onto the bed next to him.

Mel waited for him to explain all of that since she still had no idea what was happening on Sunday. Besides him mentioning it was some kind of run. "By the way, I hate running. I'd rather stare directly into a solar eclipse."

His rich chuckle washed over her. "It's not that type of run."

"What type is it?"

"A type that involves straddling, not strides." He rolled into her and brushed a strand of her loose, messy hair out of her face. "It's when my MC gets together and rides in formation."

She blinked and stared at him. "And you want me to go along?"

"I wouldn't have asked if I didn't. The only thing is, we'll both have to disguise ourselves on the slim chance a Demon would spot us. That would bring up questions we don't want to answer. I'll borrow a full-faced helmet for you and I'll be wearing one, too. Dress as plainly, and warmly, as possible. You'll need boots if you have them. If not, closed-toe shoes. Have you ever rode on the back of a bike?"

"No. But maybe you should have first asked me if I would

like to before assuming." She raised her eyebrows in emphasis.

"Do I need to ask that?"

Of course not. He already knew the answer. "Have you ever taken a woman on one of your runs before?"

"Do I need to answer that?"

Of course not. She already knew the answer.

And she didn't need to hear it to confirm their relationship was no longer fake. It had taken a turn and they needed to figure out what to do with that.

Chapter Twenty-Four

It could be any given Sunday during football season. After the Blue Avengers finished their club run, any members not working, or not scheduled for a later shift, settled in to watch NFL games.

Today the Ravens once again filled the big screen. No one sitting around the U-shaped TV area was rooting for them since the Baltimore team was a much hated division rival of the Steelers. Finn's BAMC brothers, and lone sister, only watched to cheer for the opposing team.

With a lazy sigh, Finn leaned back on the middle couch with an open beer in his hand and his feet propped up on the low center table.

He was having a hard time concentrating on the Ravens turning the Cleveland Browns into mincemeat. Instead, he couldn't shake the memory of Mel being a backpack on his Harley.

He almost didn't recognize her when she trotted out of her little stone church and down the steps.

A silk scarf did double-duty by both hiding her long blonde locks and protecting them from the borrowed helmet. A white leather jacket covered her narrow shoulders, and strategically torn jeans encased her toned legs. More surprising, she wore hiking boots.

He had been wrong assuming she only owned a closet full of neck-breaking pumps and stilettos. Along with a single pair of sneakers and flip-flops.

If he didn't know any better, with the way she was dressed, he would've thought she was some bad-ass biker chick. Especially when she didn't hesitate to throw her leg over the seat and settle in behind him, automatically wrapping her arms around his waist to hug him tight.

She had loved every damn second on his bike and said so several times, with a genuine smile on her face and a sparkle in her eye.

And though he might not admit this out loud—especially when surrounded by his MC brothers who would torture him relentlessly about it—he loved every damn second of her riding with him.

They weren't the only "couple" on the run. Jamison's wife, Bella, had joined them like she normally did. North also had his fiancée along with him.

As usual, Miller's wife stayed home with his litter of kids and Cross rode without his husband. No surprise that Nash, even when not on tour, wasn't really keen on riding with a bunch of badges.

It has always been said that opposites attract. Cross, a corporal with the Southern Allegheny Regional PD, and Nash, a member of the Dirty Angels MC, were living proof of that.

Right before they arrived back at The Plant, Finn peeled

away from the formation so he could take Mel home to get ready for work. While she did that, he went to his place to switch out his Harley for the Tacoma before returning to get her and drop her off at work.

Monty had also cut away early from the run to head to SCI Greene for her ten-hour shift. She had thanked Mel for being the reason the ride was scheduled early enough for her to participate since she rarely got a Sunday off.

Both of the women had gotten along well. But then, Monty wasn't what Finn considered a typical woman. The prison guard saw zero competition in Mel. And Mel was used to dealing with a bunch of women because of her job. Because of that, there was no cattiness and they instantly fell into a natural and easy camaraderie.

Although, Finn didn't appreciate Monty and Bella telling Mel some of his secrets. Like how terrible his singing was. And how he never stuck around after banging one of his conquests.

Oh yeah, the women had been lobbing hard-hitting truths like grenades before the run and during the mid-ride pitstop.

A piece of popcorn bounced off Finn's cheek. He glanced over at the culprit.

"While I'll reluctantly admit that you're not a complete ugly fucker... How the hell did you manage to score a woman like that?" Frasier asked. "Despite how down to Earth she was dressed today, she naturally exudes class, while you're just a simple ass. Make it make fucking sense."

"We're a *fake* couple, remember? It's only an arrangement," Finn answered the liquor enforcement officer.

A few huffs and snorts rose from around the couches.

"Someone is *still* floating down *d'Nile*. He must have lost his paddles," Rez huffed and lifted a beer bottle to his lips.

"There was nothing fake about the way she clung to your back like that. Or the smiles on your faces every time you two talked. Or the way your eyes tracked her every move, brother," North said with an arm flung over his fiancée's shoulders. Naomi was the only woman left at the clubhouse this afternoon since Jamison and his wife had a family dinner they had to attend.

"Or the constant touchy-feely shit going on between you two," Cross added with a smirk.

"He's oblivious." Crew came over and dropped onto the couch next to Finn. "I think the question is: what the hell does she see in Prince Harry here?" The DEA agent slapped Finn's chest hard, making him fold forward and grunt.

Finn rubbed the point of impact. "Fuck off."

"It has to be those double-jointed hips." Decker, sitting to Finn's right, lifted his own hips off the couch and humped the air a few times. "I gotta say, I'm a bit envious."

"If you need help, I'm sure my mom can teach you to move your hips like a pro."

"Are you saying your mom's a cougar?" Decker growled like a big cat and clawed the air.

"You're not her type."

"How do you know?"

"Because she likes men more intelligent. Not muscle-bound meatheads like you."

"She's been a dancer most of her life. I bet she's *really* flexible." Decker's expression turned smug as he wiggled his eyebrows and laughed.

Finn fake gagged. "Dude, seriously. Stop. That's my mother you're talking about." He grimaced.

"Nothing wrong with an experienced, mature woman, especially when she can hook her heels behind her neck."

"Now I need brain bleach. You're such a motherfucker."

"Maybe instead of Daddy Decker, you'll have to call me Stepdaddy Decker." Decker winked at him.

"There isn't enough fucking booze in the world for me to call you that," Finn shouted.

A muffled ringing in someone's pocket had them all checking their phones.

Crew went from amused to serious in a second flat when he glanced at his screen. He rose from the couch. "It's mine."

With the phone to his ear, he left the TV area, wandering over toward what they considered the club's "bar." Which was no more than a counter with shelves hidden behind it that held alcohol, glasses and other shit needed to get pickled. Also in the corner was a fridge stuffed full of unhealthy food and drinks.

Finn tipped his head back and called out, "Grab me another Molson while you're up."

Crew turned away and pressed a finger to his other ear to block out the noise.

The call must be important.

Not even two minutes later, Crew called out, "Yo, Finn."

Finn glanced over his shoulder. "What? Is there no more Molson? Then just grab me—" He swallowed the rest when the task force leader's gray eyes locked with his and he tipped his head, indicating that Finn should get his ass off the couch and come over to him. With a groan, he rose and headed over to the counter where Crew was waiting. "What's so important you're interrupting the game?"

"You're not even paying attention to it."

"Because we already know how it's going to end. The Browns won't ever turn this game around."

"And that surprises you?"

It shouldn't. "I was holding out hope they could pull a W out of their asses."

"Speaking of wins, we sort of got one, though it shouldn't be a surprise... The dog hit on the Astro Van."

Finn's eyebrows pinched together. "Damn, that was quick."

"That's because I cashed in on a favor," Crew explained.

"When did the handler go out?"

"About four this morning while the club was closed and she could use the dark for cover."

She. Of fucking course. Crew might ride the rest of them when it came to avoiding commitment, but after his ugly divorce, he turned into the king of post bust-a-nut bolting.

"Tomorrow morning I'll write up an affidavit for the judge and have him sign the court order for the camera system. As soon as I have that in hand, I'll get our Black Box team to go in and install them before coming over here to set up the live feed."

"Just live?" That would mean someone would need to watch twenty-four/seven.

"No, it'll be digitally recorded, too. It'll be a slick system and much better than The Peach Pit's."

Naturally. The federal government's budget ran circles around a strip club's. "How soon will that happen?"

"I've already lined it up, we just needed the probable cause for the affy. I'll push them to get in there and get it done the second the ink dries on the judge's signature. Right before they do, Mel will need to provide the latest security code. But listen... I don't want you or her there when the team's installing it. They're going to be as stealth as fuck going in and getting out. If, for some reason, the team gets caught, I don't want you or her tied to them in any way."

"Understandable." If Mel got tied to the investigation, it would put her in harm's way.

"I'll let you know when it's on the schedule."

"But you don't care if Mel knows about the cameras, right?"

"I think it's better she does since she's a part of this. Plus… It might give her a sense of security since you said she's worried about the dancers' safety. Now she'll have working cameras again. It just won't be the Demons who have access to them."

"Could we have gone this route from the get-go?"

"We didn't have enough PC at the beginning. Now we do." Crew slapped him on the back and, as he walked away chuckling, he threw over his shoulder, "Be thankful we did it the way we did, brother. Otherwise, you wouldn't have had the opportunity to meet and fall for your new girlfriend."

———

FINN WANTED to pound his head on the desk.

It had been two weeks straight of watching the camera feeds. Almost fourteen days of more than eight hours each watching the footage. He'd skim through any "dead air," like when the club was closed and empty, but he'd still keep an eye out for any unexpected activity. Since he was damn sure the Demons didn't give a fuck about doing illegal shit only during official business hours.

Every morning he'd drop Mel off at work first, then come over to The Plant and sit for those long, torturous hours. He'd only quit when it was time to pick her up from the club again.

While he kept one eye on the screen showing multiple live streams from the task force's cameras, he'd search the recorded video from the hours he couldn't watch in real time. He was surprised he hadn't gone cross-eyed yet.

In addition to the task force feeds, Decker was almost finished searching the thirty days' worth of video from the club's cameras.

Were they finding what they needed? To a point, yes. Were they both ready to stab themselves in the eye with a sharpened pencil? No fucking doubt.

The camera hidden in the Astro Van had confirmed that as soon as Saint graced The Peach Pit with his presence in the late afternoon, he'd head directly to the stash van, climb in, pull both meth and pot from a saddlebag and stash the small, easy-to-sell baggies in their hiding spot. He'd climb back out, lock up the van and glance around to make sure no one saw him.

One by one the prospects working at the club that day or night would head out back for a "smoke break," unlock the van, climb in and stuff a mix of individually packaged weed and meth into the inner pockets of their cuts.

The MC's operation wasn't complex. It also wasn't anything unexpected. The task force simply needed documented proof of who was involved, what they were selling and the quantity.

In truth, at this point they'd seen enough. They'd documented enough illegal activity to arrest everyone involved and even raid the club itself. Finn hoped Crew would soon pull the plug on investigating this location so they could concentrate elsewhere.

It was time to move on from The Peach Pit since they didn't have anyone on their team making buys there. Unlike with Fletch's undercover deals with Wolf and his Demon crew.

The task force needed that important connection as long

as they could keep it. They relied on the DAMC's tentative good graces on allowing Fletch and Wilder to remain among their midst, especially since law enforcement were considered enemies. The Dirty Angels president could easily tell them to fuck off tomorrow and shut down that leg of the investigation.

Luckily, Fletch and Wilder managed to fit into the biker life without making too many waves since they were both pros at undercover work. Chameleons would be a good descriptor for both the state trooper and FBI agent.

Because of his hot temper, Finn hadn't been as successful. If he'd been able to keep his cool, he wouldn't be stuck sitting at a desk for hours at a damn time, bored out of his gourd.

Also while he watched, he had to make sure he wasn't solely focused on whatever small square on the screen included Mel. He forced himself to keep an eye on the bar, the lobby and the back lot, as well.

But when the prospects weren't active and Saint or Cookie were nowhere to be seen, his eyes naturally found Mel wherever she was.

She was aware their cameras covered the complete interior of the club, but she didn't know their exact placement. However, one morning when he dropped her off at the back door, he had pointed out the two facing the back lot to ease her worry about the girls' safety when they left for the night.

Whoever Crew's Black Box team was, they were experts at wiring and hiding cameras. Mel said she never would've noticed them if he hadn't pointed them out and even then, she had a hard time seeing them. Of course, that was the goal. The last thing they wanted was Saint or his fellow flunkies discovering they were being watched.

That would end up as a master class on "how to fuck up your federal investigation."

When his eyes scanned the live streams, he saw nothing out of the ordinary. Dazzle was currently dancing on stage. Sapphire and Mel were working the floor and checking on customers. A few men sat at the bar talking to each other and Mutt, the prospect bartender. Some of the girls were doing their best to separate patrons from their money by talking them into a private dance.

When the club was open and hopping, most of the time he didn't have a chance to watch the recorded footage, so he solely concentrated on the live streams.

Like tonight. While the club wasn't packed solid tonight, being a Thursday, it was busier than earlier in the week.

He tracked Mel heading over to Sapphire, leaning in and saying something to her before winding her way back through the tables.

Every time a customer would reach out and touch her, Finn would grind his teeth and scream internally for them to release her. Even if the touch was innocent enough, like them grabbing her arm or wrist to get her to pause at their table. No matter what they did, she always gave them a warm smile and treated them with respect.

The other night while they recovered in bed after having a vigorous round of sex, the conversation turned toward her job and that touching. "Why do you let them get away with that?"

"What you're seeing is mostly harmless. If something is inappropriate, I handle it differently."

"How?"

"Well, if they mistreat me or the dancers in any way, they get banned from the club. If they do anything worse, I call the police.

We do have limits, Finn. Just because the girls get on stage and strip or do private dances, or Sapphire and I show a lot of leg and cleavage, does not give *anyone* the license to touch us, to make us feel uncomfortable or do something without our consent."

However, one disturbing fact she admitted to was that since Saint had fired all her former bouncers and replaced them with prospects who didn't give a fuck, the customers had become more handsy than ever. The prospects' lack of response when someone tried something inappropriate only allowed those same people to push the envelope.

That meant, not only were the women dealing with the Demon dickheads, they were now on their own to protect themselves from disrespectful men in the audience.

It was a catch-22. The task force needed her on the inside for now, but Finn wanted her the hell out of there.

Finn watched Mel make her way over to the velvet rope where that motherfucker T-Bone stood. She had no choice but to pass him if she needed to go into the back.

He held his breath as she skirted the rope while ignoring the prospect. Only she didn't get by him unscathed. Quicker than shit, T-Bone's hand snaked out and he snagged her wrist, yanking her off balance and causing their bodies to slam together.

Finn quickly clicked on the hallway camera feed so it opened up to full screen. He leaned in closer, every muscle in his damn body turning to stone. The damn cameras might not have sound but he could see Mel's mouth moving and her pissed expression as she tugged on his hold, struggling to free herself. All without success.

"Let her fucking go," Finn growled under his breath, his fingers tightening into fists. "Get away from him, Mel!"

When he surged from his seat, the wheeled office chair

shot from behind him and crashed into the meeting table. His outburst caused a rush of footsteps in his direction.

Crew, in the middle of typing up another affidavit, popped out of his chair and rushed over. "What? What happened?"

Before he could explain to the group now gathered behind him, the task force members got to witness in 4K Mel's knee jerking upward in a blur and making direct contact with T-Bone's sac.

"Damn!" Decker shouted behind him.

"*Fuuuuuuck.*" Finn winced but watched with pride as her action caused the prospect to crumple to the ground in slow motion, effectively causing him to release her.

"*Oof.* Someone got their testes tested," Nox grumbled.

"For fuck's sake, that won't make life at the club any easier for her," Crew announced dryly.

Probably not. But seeing the agony on the prospect's face was so damn satisfying. Finn only wished he was there to get a little satisfaction himself.

Without taking his eyes from the monitor, Finn explained, "That's T-Bone, the goddamn prospect who hurt her last time. I should've—" He bit back the rest of it. What he wanted to do and what he could do in reality—without landing behind bars himself—were two very different things. Unfortunately.

But he didn't have to say out loud what he was thinking. Everyone behind him could read between the lines.

Crew gave Finn's shoulder a reassuring squeeze. "If only it was that easy, brother. A punch is one thing, a bullet is another." The task force leader nudged him over slightly so he could see the monitor better. "Does she look okay?"

"Looks like it... Oh fuck," he groaned as Saint came

rushing out of his office, using long strides to quickly eat up the space between him and Mel.

Proctor left the desk where he was transcribing wiretaps to join them. "Why is she still standing there?"

Because she was not the type of woman to back down. Though, the woman needed to learn how to pick her battles. And right now, Mel was going toe to toe with Saint, pointing at the downed prospect and yelling in the head Demon's face.

"I wish we could hear what the fuck was going on." While Finn appreciated her bravery, he wished she wasn't taking Saint head-on. Not alone like that. Or at all.

Saint stood there with a hard look on his face, but wasn't saying shit. And because he wasn't responding to whatever Mel was saying, it was only winding her up even more. Clearly apparent by the way her head was jerking and her arms were being flung around.

"She needs to get the fuck out of there," murmured Nox right behind him.

No shit.

"If you call or text her, will she answer?" Crew asked.

"Probably not. She doesn't want him to know she has a phone on her." Finn sucked on his teeth out of frustration.

"At this point, who fucking cares if he finds out? Right now she's like a dog with a bone. Someone needs to toss that fucking bone to distract her and get her away from Saint. Try calling her," Crew ordered. "If she answers, tell her to get the fuck out of there."

"I'm her ride, remember?"

"For fuck's sake. Call her anyway and tell her to back off before she gets seriously hurt."

Finn reached past Crew to grab his phone off the desk, but before he could call Mel, his whole body turned to concrete. His heart seized, his lungs emptied, and his blood froze in his veins as he watched Saint reach for Mel.

With two hands he shoved her so hard, she slammed into the wall. When he went after her again, Mel somehow managed to lift her leg high enough in her skin-tight dress to kick at him. But instead of making contact, he caught her ankle, throwing her off balance enough for her to fall backwards and land hard on the floor.

"Oh fuck no he didn't," Decker growled.

"Oh fuck yes he did!" Nox yelled.

"That motherfucker!" Finn shouted.

As she scrambled to get up, he grabbed her hair and used it to start dragging her down the hallway.

"Jesus fucking Christ!" Finn screamed at the monitor. Where the fuck was he taking her?

Mel was clawing at his arm, trying to free herself, but Saint never even paused, ignoring his arms being shredded by her nails. He continued down the hallway to the rear door and slammed the push bar with his boot. The door flew open and he continued yanking Mel outside.

"Switch the camera feed!" someone yelled behind him.

Fuck that. He'd seen more than enough. Watching wasn't going to end this. Only action would.

"I'm going!" Finn yelled.

Nox immediately blocked his way and so did Crew, getting right in his face. "You aren't. Not yet. That'll blow your cover. You're supposed to be her damn boyfriend, remember? You're not a cop. You're definitely not a fucking federal task force officer watching a secret camera feed. You're Danny the Dancer. Remember that, brother. Don't worry, karma's a cunt and Saint will get his."

"I'm on the phone with my sergeant right now. He's

sending multiple units that way code three," Proctor announced with his phone still to his ear.

Code three meant a priority response. But that still didn't mean they'd get there in time to prevent her getting hurt worse.

Even so, thank fuck Proctor was an officer with the Uniontown PD and could go directly to the source instead of dialing county dispatch and wasting time. Even better, since his sergeant knew the basic details behind Proctor's special assignment, Finn's fellow task force officer wouldn't need to explain how they knew about The Peach Pit incident when they weren't even there.

Proctor came over and placed a hand on Finn's shoulder. "My PD will get her out of there. Since I told them the victim is the girlfriend of another officer, they'll break the speed barrier. Once they do and arrest Saint, you can either pick her up at the club or they'll have someone transport her to the station."

"As long as she doesn't need medical," Crew added, peering at the monitor. When Finn practically shoved him out of the way to see what was happening, the DEA agent warned him, "Keep your shit together. You going off the rails isn't going to help anyone."

"Jesus fuck," he breathed at what he saw.

The four other men closed in behind him, forming a human cage around him, in an attempt to contain him.

Watching the monitor, Finn bared his teeth, ready to snap at anyone who tried to stop him. He struggled not to start shoving and hitting, so he could rush over to the club and check on Mel. Despite everything Crew said.

His brain was only focused on one thing. Making sure Mel was safe.

His heart thumped in his throat. His gut burned. His brain screamed at him to do something. She needed his help.

She needed him to save her.

He needed to save her.

He could do nothing. Absolutely fucking nothing but watch.

Mel now lay on her back on the pavement and Saint stood over her, his face a mask of fury. Every time Mel tried to get up, he'd plant his boot on her chest and push her back down.

She began to use both her feet, now shoeless, and her bare elbows to crab-walk backwards on the pavement to create space between her and that motherfucker.

A howl of rage rose from deep inside him and he couldn't contain it. Just like he couldn't stop his fist from flying and making contact with the monitor.

The screen spidered from the impact and part of it turned black, effectively disabling it.

Fuck. Fuck. Fuck.

"Dumbass," Crew grumbled and quickly switched the feed over to the unbroken monitor sitting next to it. "How the fuck are we going to observe what's going on if you're going to take out your frustration on the damn monitor?"

He immediately focused on the working screen and, even though Finn couldn't hear the sirens through the camera system, he could hear them screaming in his head as flashing lights filled up the screen.

Three marked units tore into the employee parking lot and, seconds later, a half dozen officers surrounded Saint with their weapons drawn.

Finn held his breath to see if Saint would pull any shit. Like the gun he kept on him. If he did, he hoped the officers opened fire. That would be one loss of life that wouldn't be an actual loss.

Now that Mel had protection, Finn spun on Proctor. "Make sure someone evaluates her to see if she has any injuries."

"They know what to do."

Of course they fucking did. But to keep his sanity he still needed to say it. Otherwise, he was just standing there like a helpless fuck.

"He's done," Crew murmured next to him, pulling Finn's attention back to the working screen.

When he saw Saint's hands raised above his head, Finn wasn't sure if he was disappointed or relieved that the biker gave those cops no reason to take any action other than take him into custody.

The Uniontown officers met no resistance when they spun the biker around and slapped the cuffs on him, patted him down or escorted him to the back of a cruiser to take him in for processing.

Not one damn taser used, no come to Jesus meeting with an ASP baton, not even a tussle for resisting arrest. The motherfucker cooperated because he *knew* the cops were just looking for a reason to rough him up.

Finn had a damn good reason, though.

"I want that fucker," he growled.

"You can't have him," Crew told him point blank.

"I want him, Crew. He's mine."

Crew pointed at the screen. "Jesus fucking Christ, Finn. You want to fuck up your career..." He shook his salt-and-pepper head. "No, fuck up your *life* for that piece of shit? I won't let you do that. You're not thinking straight. She's upright. She's okay. She didn't curl into a ball and give up. She fought back. The woman has a spine of steel."

He stared at the woman on the live stream being assisted by two uniformed officers.

Decker bumped his shoulder against Finn's. "And I thought Wilder was a badass. I think you might've met her match, brother."

It shouldn't even be close. Nova Wilder was a highly-trained special agent for the FBI. Mel was a strip club manager without any kind of hands-on defense training. Despite that, Mel stood up to a much bigger biker who carried a gun and wouldn't hesitate to take out a threat. One obviously never taught that real men didn't hit women.

So, yes, her tenacity was impressive.

But that didn't mean he wouldn't plan his revenge.

Chapter Twenty-Five

SHE WAS FINE.

She was breathing.

She was upright.

She was fine.

Luckily, she escaped with only scrapes and bruises. And, of course, she'd be sore from being dragged around.

But she'd survive.

She always did.

The only issue was, being banged up wasn't her worst problem. She was now unemployed.

Sapphire leaned her head against Mel's shoulder and gave her waist a tight, reassuring squeeze. Her friend had rushed outside, pale and wide-eyed, just as the police cruisers sped into the lot with their blinding lights and blaring sirens.

Someone had called the cavalry just in time. Mel glanced up at the hidden cameras.

"Wherever you go, I go, sister." Sapphire's words were thick and her eyes had a shine to them.

Shit. If Sapphire started crying, Mel would end up

crying, too. And, so far, she hadn't shed a single tear during the whole scuffle with Taint.

"You just have to let me know where we're going."

Mel pinned her lips together and sadness enveloped her like a cloak as she stared at the back of The Peach Pit.

Ten years. She'd worked here ten years. It had become her home away from home and the girls had become her family. Laura, too.

She had loved her job.

Until some drug-dealing, pot-smoking, motorcycle-riding assholes came along and destroyed it all.

She swallowed down that bitter pill because there was nothing she could do about it. "I don't have enough money to start my own club, Phire. I wish I did. I wish I could take you all with me, but I have nowhere to go."

Jesus, she sounded pitiful.

"You will," Sapphire assured her. "If anyone can do it, you can."

A squeal of tires had her glancing toward the narrow street that ran behind the strip club.

A Toyota Tacoma.

She should be relieved he came, but right now her stomach was twisted into too many knots.

Her life changed once the Demons bought the club.

Her life changed again the day Finn walked out onto that same club's stage.

And now it was about to change again.

All in a matter of a few months.

Finn's eyes were on her when he climbed out of the truck. They didn't waver even when one of the officers approached him. And they remained locked on her when he exchanged a few words with the cop.

His focus on her was so intense as he quickly strode in her direction, she swore he could see deep into her very soul.

As soon as he reached them, he pulled her from Sapphire's arms and into his own, rocking her back and forth and resting his chin on top of her head. Of course it was easy to do that right now. She'd lost her heels along the way and stood barefoot on the cold, rough pavement.

She caught herself in time before she slipped and didn't use his undercover name. "Danny, loosen up. I can barely breathe," she wheezed. His hug was crushing.

After a few seconds he finally released her and, with both hands on her upper arms, he held her away from him, inspecting her from head to toe. "Do you need to go to the hospital?"

That was the last thing she needed. "No, I have some minor cuts and bruises. I'll be fine."

A muscle jumped in his cheek when she assured him she was fine.

What wasn't fine was her dress after the pavement acted like a cheese grater. But a dress could easily be replaced.

One of the remaining Uniontown officers approached Finn. "Do you want one of us to escort her inside the building to retrieve her personal items?"

He kept his eyes locked on her when he answered, "I can do it."

"I'll do it," Sapphire insisted. "And I'll try to find your shoes."

"Thanks, Phire."

"Anything for you, MJ," she said softly, before heading inside.

"I'll give you two a few minutes, then we'll need her statement. Do you want to do it here or at the station?" The cop was once again addressing Finn and not her, the actual victim.

While that was a bit aggravating, the reason could be that they knew each other.

"Here. And when you do, you'll make it quick. I want to get her home."

The uniformed officer nodded before drifting away to give her and Finn a few moments alone.

As if a switch was thrown, Finn's whole demeanor softened.

"Jesus Christ," he whispered, splaying his hand over her cheek and pressing his forehead to hers. "Jesus fucking Christ, Mel. I lost my damn mind while I watched that whole thing. I wanted to reach through that damn screen and I couldn't. Seeing it and not being able to do anything made it so much fucking worse."

"I'm fine," she breathed.

"While I'm glad you're fine, I don't ever want to hear that particular assertion again." He enveloped her in his arms once more. "You're done working here."

The gruffness to his demand didn't go unnoticed. What happened to her had affected him deeply.

It wasn't surprising, but more of a confirmation on how he felt about her. When they agreed to become a fake couple, neither expected a real relationship to develop between them.

But then, as with everything in life, it was smart to always expect the unexpected. Thinking life was under control was an illusion easily broken.

"Apparently so, since I was fired. I consider being dragged out the door by my hair as an official pink slip."

"As you should." Sweeping her mess of hair out of her face, he lowered his voice until only she could hear him. "We have plenty of evidence now to take Saint and his prospects down."

"While that's great, it doesn't pay my damn bills, Finn." The hope to buy The Peach Pit had been dashed once Finn explained that a large investigation like this took months, even years. And there was no guarantee she'd be able to buy the club after the Demons were all indicted. The business could be strangled in red tape for even longer.

She was now out of time and had no choice but to move on, leaving behind the club she had invested so much time in.

"You're resilient enough you'll find something else."

"If it was that easy, I would've left already." She added, "Long before the Peckers showed up," to make the point she might not have met him if she had bailed as soon as the going got tough.

"The arm of the law is long. I'll put out some feelers."

While that would be a sweet gesture, the cop network probably wasn't the best or easiest way to find a strip club manager position. But if that made him feel helpful, she'd let him have it. "And in the meantime?"

"We'll figure it out."

"Will *we?*" Mel pulled back a bit and tipped her eyes up to his stony face. "Tell me, Finn... Are we still pretending?"

"Pretending?"

"That our relationship is fake." She had a few realizations while Taint dragged her outside by her hair. She would now share those same hard truths with Finn. Facts neither of them had addressed. "You stay at my place every damn night, Finn. You've been taking me to and from work for weeks now, when you really didn't have to. Your reaction every time a Demon put their hands on me was more than someone only defending an acquaintance." No, he took those incidents as a personal affront. "You should've seen your face when you got out of your truck."

His tight jaw shifted. "You should've seen my face when I had to stand there watching Saint drag you out of the building."

She sighed. "I'm sure. But would your reaction have been the same if I had simply been a paid informant?"

He pressed his lips together until his mouth was nothing but a slash.

"I know this is your job—"

"You're not my job," he said gruffly.

She ignored his interruption and kept going. "And you weren't looking for a relationship. Neither was I."

She was never one to avoid difficult, but necessary, conversations and she certainly wasn't going to do that right now. Finn was too important to her.

When he swallowed, it was hard to miss his Adam's apple hanging at the top of his throat for a few seconds before it dropped like a rock back into place. "Yeah."

"But here we are."

"We'll figure it out."

"Of course, since I have no choice but to figure out my future. I need a job. I have a mortgage, a car payment and I want to avoid dipping into the savings I put aside to buy a club of my own."

He dropped his chin to his chest and met her eyes. "Not about that... About us."

Her tongue swept across her dry lips. "Finn..." If he was going to avoid the truth, maybe it would be better to go their separate ways. She no longer had a reason or the access to continue helping the task force.

And while walking away from him at this point would certainly hurt, if she did it now it would be easier to recover and move on with her life. If she let herself fall any deeper and he didn't feel the same, it would be devastating.

She stood at a crossroads. She could deal with an uncomfortable pinch now or a hard-hitting sucker punch later. It was up to her to protect herself. Both her heart and her future.

He stared at something over her head for a few long moments. Real or imagined, she didn't know. But when he finally took a deep inhale and released it, "You're right," came along with it.

"About what?"

"It's not fake."

"What isn't fake?" She needed to hear him say it. To admit the truth to not only her, but himself.

"What's between us." His hazel eyes locked with hers again. "It never was."

Holy shit. Her hope went from tumbling to her feet to soaring above the clouds. "So, now what?"

He dropped his arm around her shoulders and steered her toward the waiting police. "Now you give them your statement so I can take you home."

Home. That would be one discussion of many when it came to "figuring it out." But not tonight.

Tonight she only needed Finn. No heavy discussions or decisions had to be made. In fact, "A soak in the hot tub would probably do me some good."

"Whatever you need, girlfriend."

Despite biting through her bottom lip when Taint slammed her into the wall, she gave him a big, even if painful, smile. "Your *girlfriend* needs her not-fake boyfriend to join her in that hot, bubbly water. Preferably naked since I have a lot more hidden freckles to discover."

"He might need to inspect you for hidden injuries first."

"Dr. Daniel Finnegan has quite a ring to it."

"My medical license, found at the bottom of a Cracker Jack box, qualifies me to do both thorough internal and external examinations."

Did he just crack a smile? Even a little one?

"Well, if in your professional opinion you think that's needed..."

"The doctor always knows best. And he thinks it's best you don't walk over the parking lot in your bare feet." Without warning, he swung her up and into his arms and didn't put her down until they reached the waiting officer.

And even then, he kept her hand interlocked with his the whole time she answered questions.

He held her hand the whole way home, too.

She never once wanted him to let go.

———

AFTER MAKING BAIL, Saint sauntered out the front door of the county jail with his Demons cut in hand and a cocky grin on his face. Finn tracked the fucker as he crossed the parking lot to an early '80s Mustang with one of his biker brothers in the driver's seat.

It was easy to follow the Ford, with black smoke billowing from its exhaust pipe like a steam locomotive, all the way back to the Uniontown chapter's clubhouse.

He had borrowed the Kia Soul tonight without Crew knowing, since Saint would most likely recognize the Toyota Tacoma. He parked down the street far enough not to be spotted but close enough where he could see Saint disappear inside the converted gas station.

He settled in for a long wait, but not even ten minutes later, he was surprised to see the man head out on a Harley.

Shifting the Soul into Drive, Finn pulled out as soon as the motorcycle roared past him.

He had no idea where the fucker was going, but the destination didn't matter. He would deal with wherever it was since he had waited for this day and obsessed about this opportunity.

Finn was about to serve Saint a little bit of rough justice before the courts served him theirs.

He trailed the bike at a distance for a few miles before it pulled into a convenience store. Luckily, because it was late, the lot was empty. After Saint parked by the door, Finn slipped the Kia into one of the spots along the side of the building and out of sight, then climbed out.

To keep from being recognized, Finn had a plain black baseball cap pulled low, a baggy sweatshirt with the hood pulled over the hat, the loose, paint-splattered sweats he'd worn while working on renovating the BAMC clubhouse, and a pair of old, *ready-for-the-garbage* boots. Even though the sun had finished falling behind the horizon, he wore his darkest sunglasses and had even used some of Mel's foundation to cover his freckles.

Without her knowing, of course. His woman would've had a shit fit if she knew what he was up to.

So would his BAMC brothers.

Not to mention, his fellow task force members.

All of those reasons were why he had told no one his plan.

Some might have tried to talk him out of it. Some might have insisted on assisting. He couldn't risk either. If his plan went sideways, he didn't want anyone else dragged into it.

Picking a spot at the very corner of the building, he leaned back, cocked his leg and planted his boot against the brick wall to wait.

Anticipation, along with the sharp thirst for vengeance, simmered just under his skin.

Finn's jaw tightened when Saint walked out of the store with his head down, tapping a pack of cigarettes against the heel of his palm.

Showtime.

Disguising his voice, Finn threw out a fishing line. "Yo, can I bum a smoke?"

The man stopped in his tracks, lifted his head and turned it toward Finn.

Finn hoped prison slang would work as bait to draw Saint over. "Brother, need a smoke really fuckin' bad and I don't got enough scratch for a whole deck. I can give you a coupla bucks for one or two sticks."

Saint's eyes narrowed on him as he tore open the pack and dug out a cigarette.

Finn jiggled the hook by jerking his chin toward the parked Harley. "Sweet sled you got there."

Saint's Neanderthal-shaped brow dropped low. "You got a sled?"

The motherfucker was nibbling at the bait.

Finn forced out a dry laugh. "Hell no. Hope to one day. Just got outta the joint and need to find a way to make some scratch first."

Not wanting to lose his catch, Finn carefully reeled in the line as Saint approached him. "What were you in for?"

"Possession. Of fuckin' course those pigs didn't believe me when I told 'em it was only for personal use. Fuckers." Finn twisted his head and spat on the ground beside him.

"Never do," Saint grumbled and held out a cigarette.

Instead of grabbing the smoke, Finn latched onto Saint's arm, yanking the biker off balance and around the corner where no one would see them.

"What the fuck!" Saint shouted but before he could get his feet under him, Finn did a leg sweep and knocked the man backwards, introducing him to the pavement. All up close and personal-like.

Just like he had Mel.

As the Demon scrambled to rise, dropping F-bombs left and right, Finn grabbed his stringy hair and dragged that motherfucker farther away from the front of the convenience store.

Just like he had Mel.

Finn fought the urge to shout in Saint's face and to tell the biker why he was about to be served a fresh slice of karma. Unfortunately, the man would still be breathing after Finn was done with him, so he needed Saint to think the attack was random or from a rival club. He didn't want the Demon tying this back to him or Mel if that could be avoided.

When Saint reached under his back, Finn pinned his arm with one boot while using the heel of the other to kick the man hard in the head.

While the man's bells were still ringing, Finn confiscated the Beretta from the back of Saint's waistband and tucked it into his own. Later he'd unload it and make sure it was never found again. Once he wiped it clean of any prints.

Technically, Finn could bring charges against him for the weapon—he was damn sure the gun wasn't obtained legally and with his rap sheet, Saint was prohibited from carrying one, anyway—but all that would do was splash shit back on Finn.

It was simply better to get it off the street once and for all. He only wished he could do the same for Saint. But he couldn't, so this was the next best thing.

When Saint tried to get to his feet again, Finn slammed

his boot into his chest, knocking him back down, his head smacking against the pavement with a dull thud.

Just like he had Mel.

However, Finn was done playing. He needed to take care of business and get the fuck out of there before someone saw them or tried to stop him.

Or called the police, creating an awkward situation.

Using both hands, he grabbed the biker by his leather cut and yanked him to his feet, then whipped around and slammed Saint against the wall.

Just like he had Mel.

But Saint's head hit the brick harder than the pavement, causing him to float in and out of consciousness.

A slurred, "What... the... fuck," came out of the dazed man as he began to slide down the wall.

Finn quickly pulled him back up to his feet.

He *so* wanted Saint to know who was doing this to him. Why he was here. Why he was dolling out revenge on his ass.

But like the gun, doing so would come back to bite him hard on the ass. Instead, he locked his jaws to keep all the words wanting to burst from him contained and drove his fist squarely into Saint's face, causing his nose to explode and blood to fly.

Finn followed that first punch with a hard left jab, and then a powerful right cross. When the man began to slide down the wall again, Finn finished with a right uppercut.

With a sliver of satisfaction, Finn watched Saint collapse into a lifeless, bloody heap on the pavement.

After delivering a wad of spit as a parting gift, paired with a hearty "Fuck you," Finn walked away.

Not once looking back at the trash he left behind.

Instead, he focused ahead on his future with Mel.

Chapter Twenty-Six

FINN SANK into the office chair and glanced around at everyone gathered at the long table.

Hold the fuck on...

His head whipped back in Decker's direction and his eyebrows pinched together. "Did you forget to shave?"

The man was anal about shaving. Was he ill?

Decker scrubbed a hand down his stubbled cheek. "Not shaving anymore."

"Ever?"

"I'm growing out my hair and beard."

"Oooooh shit." Could that mean...?

Crew circled the conference table and settled at the head of it. "Big Deck's going undercover with the Uniontown Demons."

Finn stared at the task force leader for a few seconds before sticking his finger in his ear and wiggling it. "Sorry. What?"

"He has to ditch the cop cut and smooth face to fit in."

No shit. "Decker's going undercover as a biker?" That

would be a feat since it wasn't only his clean-cut look that screamed law enforcement. The man was *in shape*. And not in the shape of a potato, either.

Sitting next to Finn, Rez rapped his knuckles on the table. "I would've taken the assignment but my Venezuelan blood isn't pure enough for them."

"But you'll still be able to do buys," Crew told him.

"Right. Dark enough to sell me drugs, but too dark to join them."

"If those MC members actually took a bath once in a while and did a little grooming, they'd be so damn white they'd glow," Fletch's voice came from the conference phone set up in the middle of the group.

"They'd be translucent," Reynolds added on a laugh.

"Hey, you're in the same boat as me," Rez told the Black state police corporal. "They'll take your money, they just won't take you."

"No fucking loss," Reynolds said with a shrug and a grin. "At least we don't reflect the sun when we take off our clothes."

"Crew, you're not concerned that the prospects working at the club the night you came to see me dance might recognize Pencil Deck?" Finn thought it was a dumb idea then, but now that move might make Decker going undercover as a Demon prospect even riskier.

"I considered that."

"I doubt they will," Decker said, unfazed. "They've proven time and time again they're not the best and brightest. Plus, once I grow out my hair and beard, change my wardrobe and adopt the way they speak, I should have no trouble pulling it off."

Finn wasn't so sure of that.

Wilder's voice came from the speaker phone. "Fletch and

I can give you some tips for blending in, if you need them, Decker."

"I'll probably take you two up on that."

"Better stop hitting the gym, too, brother. More beer, less reps." Rez said exactly what Finn was thinking.

"How's that going to work out with Val?" Finn asked the single "father."

"My mother agreed to continue to watch her until I find a live-in nanny. But I need to find one soon. She can't keep up with an active four-year-old all day, every day. My girl's too much."

Rez snorted. "If you weren't such a fucking cheap-ass, you would've had someone full-time from the first day you took custody."

"You know I don't trust Val with just anyone. Anyway, this assignment's a good push for me to finally find one."

"Will she easily take to someone new?" Crew asked.

"I sure as fuck hope so since she won't have a choice."

"Good luck with that, brother," the task force leader said, smacking Decker on the back. "Kids are both a blessing and a curse."

"Yeah, just ask Miller," Rez agreed with a laugh. "No matter how much he bitches about them, he keeps knocking up his wife."

"All right, let's get this meeting started," Crew announced. "I've got better things to do than stare at your ugly mugs."

"Sure you do." Rez jerked his fist back and forth in the air and grunted.

Crew cocked an eyebrow. "Are you volunteering?"

"Got a magnifying glass and a tweezer?"

"What the hell is she doing there?" Powers' tone of voice had all of them swallowing their next words and

Jeanne St. James

looking over at the only other Black member of the task force.

Ice slid down Finn's spine since, instead of sitting at the table with the rest of them, the state trooper decided to watch the live camera feed of The Peach Pit while keeping one ear on the meeting. "Who?"

When Powers' dark eyes found Finn, that sliver of ice quickly became an iceberg wedged in his gut. "Fuck, brother, it's your girl. She's in the back parking lot. I thought Saint fired her."

"He did and even if he didn't, she would've quit." His heart thumped heavily at the idea of Mel going back to the club by herself. And without telling him. "What's she doing?"

"You might want to come see."

Jesus Christ, did he, though? His temper was already spiking at the thought of Mel putting herself in danger. Again.

Crew jumped out of his seat and joined Powers at the desk. "Fucking motherfucker."

Fuuuuuuck.

Finn quickly followed, shoving Crew out of the way so he could evaluate the situation himself. He leaned in closer and squinted at the monitor.

Even though Powers had expanded the back lot's camera feed to full screen, the man had a damn good eye. Finn slept with Mel every night and wouldn't have recognized her right away with the way she was dressed.

For fuck's sake, she had taken a page right out of his playbook by wearing one of his plain hooded sweatshirts. However, she also wore a long overcoat, that not only hid her womanly curves, it swallowed her whole, making her appear even tinier than she was in reality. A baseball cap pulled low,

394

with the hood pulled over it, hid her blonde mane. Of course she finished off the *I'm-about-to-pull-some-shit* outfit with dark sunglasses, baggy jeans and sneakers.

Crew crowded behind him, pointing at the monitor. "Do you want to get your woman the fuck out of there? Is she *trying* to fuck up our investigation?"

He sighed. "I have no fucking clue what she's doing."

"Well, find the fuck out," Crew ordered, "before we have to send Uniontown over there again to rescue her ass."

Finn ground his teeth together as he pulled his cell phone from his pocket and quickly dialed her number.

Everyone on the third floor now hovered behind Finn and Powers. And every damn one of them watched Mel pull her phone out of a coat pocket and glance at the screen.

"Pick up the damn phone!" he yelled, his fingers gripping the phone so tightly they ached as badly as his clenched teeth.

"What the fuck?" Crew shouted as Mel ignored his call and tucked the phone back away.

Finn quickly sent her a text but knew she'd ignore that, too. But what she did do was glance up into the camera, jerk her chin up in an unspoken message and then head over to the Astro Van.

For fuck's sake.

"What's she doing, Finn?" Crew asked.

Finn was damn sure they were going to find out any second now. He grimaced and squeezed the back of his neck out of frustration.

Oh fuck!

"Is that *your* ASP baton?" Crew bellowed.

Of course it was. She must have grabbed it from his duty bag. He had finished moving into her church a few weeks ago. Since he didn't need any of his uniforms or equipment—except for his service weapon—while working on the task force, he had shoved his duty bag toward the back of his half of the walk-in closet.

With a sharp flick of her wrist, the metal baton expanded to full length and without even a goddamn slight hesitation, she used it to smash the back window.

"Well, damn!" came from someone behind him.

The next thing she pulled from under that coat looked like a can of lighter fluid.

Was she about to...

Oh fuck, yes she was.

"Holy fuck!" came from someone else.

She squirted the highly flammable liquid inside the smashed window, chasing it with a lit match.

Of course she fucking did!

A collective groan rose up around him as she made her way over to the passenger side next and shattered that window, too. She shook the can making sure to get every last drop out of it and then chucked it in the window.

With a flick of her wrist, she lit another match and tossed that inside the van, too.

Smoke began to billow from both broken windows. Light at first, then with every passing second, it became thicker and darker. Within seconds, the flames spread enough for the task force members to see them on the screen.

But Finn wasn't watching that.

He was watching Mel as she slammed the tip of the ASP baton against the pavement to collapse it before tucking it back inside her jacket.

He was torn on whether he was impressed or horrified. But what he was sure of was, he never should've shown her how the expandable baton worked.

Never.

Then, she turned to face the camera and in an exaggerated motion, she dusted off her hands.

Of fucking course she did.

With a tip of her head and a flash of a smirk, she disappeared off screen.

Finn remained frozen in place, still trying to process what his woman just did and what he should do about it.

"Goddamn," Reynolds hooted, "that van is lighting up like a Viking's funeral pyre."

"Someone grab some popcorn," Powers said.

"Fuck the popcorn, grab the marshmallows," came from Reynolds.

Rez drew an invisible cross by touching his forehead, below his chest, his left side, then his right, finishing the ritual by bowing his head. "May that piece of shit Chevy go with God."

Somewhere behind Finn, Decker asked, "Should we call the fire department?"

"Fuck no," Crew said with a sigh. "Any evidence in there is already destroyed, let the fucker burn. But what you can do, Powers, is document the system glitch."

"System glitch?"

"Yeah, the glitch that caused that section of footage to be corrupted."

The trooper grinned and gave the DEA agent a thumbs up. "You got it, boss."

———

As MEL SLID her key in the lock, the front door was flung wide open.

Finn, his face an unreadable mask and flanked by Minx

and Jinx, stood with his legs apart and his hands on his hips blocking her entrance.

She waited for him to say what was on his mind but he only closed his eyes and shook his head. Then with a drawn-out sigh, he stepped back and let her inside her own house.

She glared at the two traitors. "Since when are you two more loyal to him than me?"

"Since I explained what a bonehead move their mommy made when she torched a van involved in a federal investigation. That's when."

She pursed her lips and kicked off her shoes by the front door.

He slammed the door shut and spun on her. "That's not the same outfit you were wearing on your ridiculously reckless mission."

"I changed."

"No shit. What did you do with those clothes?"

There was no point in lying. "Burned them."

"Completely?"

"Yes. They're nothing but ashes out in a field of weeds."

"Unlike the stash van that's now nothing but a burned-out metal skeleton."

"You said the task force had all the evidence needed for The Peach Pit and the Demons who work there." Simply saying that MC's name left a bitter taste in her mouth.

"We do. But that didn't mean we stopped monitoring the Demon's activities there since we already have the cameras installed. Until they're rounded up and charged, they're still committing daily criminal acts we can document. The more we can pin on them, the less likely they'll be able to beat those charges."

"Not having the van won't stop them from selling drugs."

She groaned silently. Nothing like telling a trained cop and federal task force officer something he already knew.

"No, but burning that van along with their drug stash is guaranteed to piss them the fuck off. Now they'll be extra cautious and may even be looking for revenge."

"Did they call the fire department?"

"Hell no, because the fire department would've reported it to the police. And the fuck if the Demons want the cops and a fire marshal involved. Even in a case of arson."

That was what she hoped when she threw her plan together.

She knew setting the van on fire wouldn't be more than a hiccup to the outlaw MC's operation. It wouldn't stop them from selling drugs or continuing to run the club into the ground, but still...

Lighting that match had been extremely satisfying. She had even written the word *karma* with a marker on the pack of matches beforehand and that made the calculated risk all the sweeter.

"Mel," he breathed, pulling her into him and holding her tight, "you could've gotten caught."

Technically, she did. By the task force. But she understood his worry about one of the Demons catching her. "The girls kept Taint and the prospects busy for me."

His high-pitched, "They were in on it, too?" made her realize she should've kept that little tidbit to herself.

Too late.

"Will I be charged with anything?"

A loud rush of air escaped him. Hopefully he was blowing out some of his annoyance with it.

"It was recorded."

"I figured that. But will it be used against me?" she asked.

"Only if forensics has a reason to spend the time and money to repair the corrupted video footage."

She glanced up and met his eyes. Her heart swelled at the lengths he went to protect her.

"I hope you can bake like a freaking fiend because you owe everyone on the task force a shit ton of cookies, at least a dozen pies and a truckload of beer."

At that news, she relaxed a little. Unless someone snitched, she wouldn't be feeling the cold bite of handcuffs on her wrists any time soon. "I know a good bakery and a beer distributor."

He pressed his cheek to her temple and murmured, "Jesus, Mel, that was dangerous and just plain dumb."

Was he expecting her to disagree? "Of course it was."

"If you don't want to put me in an early grave, stay the fuck away from both the Demons and any security cameras I have access to." He leaned back slightly to stare down into her face. "Do you feel better now you got some revenge?"

She countered with, "Do you?"

His head snapped up and he stiffened against her. And not in the way she preferred him to be stiff. "What does that mean?"

She raised both eyebrows. Was he going to play dumb? "Sapphire told me Saint got the shit beat out of him."

Finn, his face a careful mask, huffed, "A damn shame."

"Do you know anything about it?" When he didn't answer, she asked point blank, "Was it you?"

"And if it was?"

Of course it was. The day Taint was released from jail, Finn came home with a few busted knuckles. When she asked him about it that night, he mumbled something about how he was helping Nox with the framework in his apartment.

At the time she didn't think much of it. After finding out about Taint's injuries around the same timeframe, she put two and two together.

"You could've lost your job," she reminded him. If he did, they'd both be unemployed.

Instead of renewing his condo lease, he moved in with her so he could help her out financially. At least until she found a new place of employment or a way to open her own club. She was actively working on both by scouring online job listings and also building a solid business plan.

"And you could've lost your life, Mel. I only recently found you, I don't want to lose you."

That declaration made her eyes sting. She gave him a shaky smile. "I don't want to lose you, either. Maybe we both need to stop doing stupid shit. Agreed?"

"Agreed."

"Now, I'm going to make dinner and after we're done eating, we can spend a nice, quiet evening together watching a movie. No fires. No fights. No MCs or security cams."

"I could use some quiet. I'll take the dogs out."

She grabbed his arm, stopping him. "Hold on. There's something I've been meaning to tell you."

He groaned. "Should I be scared?"

She rolled her lips under. "With this? Possibly. But my best guess is, you'll survive."

"What is it?"

"On my way home, I realized something..."

He groaned again and pressed a palm to his chest.

"Look, if you want to be overly dramatic, I can tell you another time." She began to head toward the kitchen.

This time Finn grabbed her arm to stop her. He swung her back around to face him. "What is it?"

"While I'm sorry I worried you, I'm not sorry for torching

that van. I'm sorry you felt the need to clean Taint's clock because of what he did to me. I *truly* appreciate everything you've done for me in the past and what you plan on doing for me in the future. Normally, that's not something I'd easily accept since I prefer to do things for myself and not rely on anyone else."

"I'm aware of that, Mel. But I wouldn't do it if I didn't want to and I don't plan on stopping any time soon."

"Me neither."

His brow wrinkled. "Stop what?"

She'd been wanting to tell him for a few weeks now but the timing never seemed right. Plus, she'd been worried he might freak out and possibly even bolt with what she was about to reveal.

However, now that his clothes took up half her closet and he seamlessly made her little church his home, too, she was ready.

She hoped he was, too.

Here goes nothing... "Stop loving you."

She swore he morphed into a statue. She wasn't even sure if he still breathed. Should she get a mirror and put it under his nose to check?

When he finally jerked into motion, like his "reset" button had been pushed, he grabbed her face and crushed his lips to hers.

That didn't taste anything like panic to her. In fact, it tasted like relief.

After a few seconds, he murmured against her lips, "Thank fuck because I never plan to stop loving you, either, girlfriend. And I expect that would become awkward if you didn't feel the same."

She smiled. "Why didn't we tell each other sooner, boyfriend?"

"Did we need to? Saying it out loud doesn't make it any more real."

He was so right. "No, but it removes all doubt."

Without warning, he squatted, hooked her around the thighs and when he straightened, tossed her over his shoulder. The sudden move made a squeal and a peal of laughter escape her.

"How about if I remove all doubt that I want to fuck you so damn badly right now?" He carried her toward the stairs. "You can also remove any doubt I have of you loving me when you tell me over and over while you're naked."

"Being naked makes it more believable?"

"I think that's on page twenty-three in the *How Not to Fuck Up a New Relationship Handbook*."

"Ah. Well, if it's in the handbook..." Even with her head hanging upside down, she spotted the dogs trailing each step Finn took up to the loft. "What about the dogs?"

"They can use the doggy door."

She couldn't argue with that. "What about dinner?"

"I just found something better to eat."

She couldn't argue with that, either.

So, she didn't.

Epilogue

A year later...

"HEY, GIRLFRIEND."

The very familiar, deep voice pulled a smile from her.

Without turning around, she purred, "Hello, boyfriend. Or should I call you partner now?"

"Either will work," he said as he pressed a kiss to her cheek and palmed her ass.

"What's your preference?"

"Husband."

Her smile widened and she turned to face the man she wasn't sure she'd survive without. She never thought she'd need to rely on a man and, while she still didn't, this particular man did make her life so much better. She hoped she did the same for him. "I didn't think you liked commitment."

"Yeah, well... A sexy blonde vixen has bound me in her spell and refuses to release me."

"Oh, sorry to hear that," she teased. "Sounds tragic."

"I've learned to live with the atrocity."

She laughed and bumped her hip against him. "*Hmm.* So, husband, huh? Then, is that a huge engagement ring in your pocket?"

Her nipples pebbled at his low chuckle. When he ran a line of kisses down her neck, she tipped her head back to give him easier access. "Sorry to disappoint you. That's just my dick."

Nothing "just" about it.

"Though, it does get as hard as a diamond," he added with a smirk.

"That sounds painful."

"Luckily, I have someone to relieve the discomfort."

"She sounds like a keeper. Better hold onto her tightly, then."

He wrapped his arms around her and pulled her against him. "I plan on it," he murmured against her lips.

She clung to him while he gave her a more thorough kiss. Unfortunately, she had to cut it short. Otherwise, they might end up in one of the VIP rooms working on a new "dance" routine.

"How are the new guys working out?" Finn asked in her ear so his question wouldn't be drowned out by the DJ's music.

"Great." She patted his chest lightly and teased, "Sometimes you actually have good ideas."

Finn had found off-duty and retired law enforcement to hire as bouncers and, surprisingly, a couple as DJs. Since they all could conceal carry, it gave the club an extra layer of security, just in case the Demons decided to pull some shit.

It was a good gig for them as a second job or career. Plus, they appreciated the "perks" since Mel only hired the best dancers. All professional and put-together women. And of course, beautiful inside and out.

Any employee who was toxic, or had a bad attitude, was quickly let go. She only wanted to hire people who took their profession seriously. To avoid a rotating door, she wanted skilled dancers dedicated to building a loyal fan base.

That mindset not only helped Mel's new club quickly become successful, but the dancers who loved coming to work and entertaining customers made a very lucrative living.

"Well, of course I have good ideas. I have a stake in this business, too."

That was true. He was always coming up with suggestions from a male point of view.

With the money she had stashed away for her own club, along with a majority of Finn's savings, they were able to put down a deposit on a building that was reasonably priced due to needing a complete renovation.

Even though he was a major investor, he insisted on only claiming thirty percent ownership, making sure she held the majority with fifty percent. Rez and Crew had also kicked in enough cash to each grab a ten percent slice of the pie.

Luckily, those two were silent partners and had no power to make any major decisions. Though, Finn's MC brothers still voiced their opinions, loudly and quite often. Usually about something for their own benefit.

Of course, she waived the cover charge for all members of the Blue Avengers and anyone working on the task force. It was the least she could do after they had her back when she torched the Demons' stash van. Plus, she considered it a professional courtesy.

In addition, emergency responders, as well as active and retired military, only paid a half-price cover charge and half-price drinks. A suggestion made by Nox, of all people, but definitely a good one.

"I do make a perfect partner, don't I?"

She couldn't disagree with that. Not only in business, but her life. "I couldn't have done it without you."

"Untrue. You didn't need me. I have no doubt you could've and would've done it on your own."

Maybe, but it would've taken a lot longer. Plus, with him as part owner, she truly believed it helped solidify their relationship and their future.

When she showed him the empty building she stumbled across, he experienced the same dread as when his MC president, Axel Jamison, first showed them the rundown building they now used as the BAMC clubhouse.

The amount of work needed to make the abandoned building her dream adult entertainment club had been extensive. And, of course, it had cost a boatload of cash on top of all their own blood, sweat and tears. But in the end, it was worth every drop shed and every dollar spent.

To be able to pay the high monthly mortgage payment, The Pink Pearl offered so much more than dancers stripping down to their G-strings. With Sapphire as her manager and Raven as her assistant manager, Mel was able to keep the club open seven days a week and offer specialty nights when it would otherwise be closed.

Once a month they held a karaoke night—on Finn's insistence—and on other nights they hosted comedians, drag shows, local bands, and traveling all-male revues, like the Peckers.

In the mornings, before the club was open for regular business, the girls taught private pole dancing lessons for extra cash. Those classes had become extremely popular with the fitness crowd, as well as women—and even men—wanting to learn an enticing dance for their partners.

Even Finn's mom helped promote the pole classes with her students.

Beyond the Badge: Finn

The Peach Pit was still open but only hanging on by a thread. The business had pretty much dried up after Mel poached all their dancers, forcing the Demons to scramble to replace them. Of course, with less than satisfactory results.

Because of that, Mel also pinched most of The Peach Pit's clientele.

The Pink Pearl was so much cleaner and classier. The atmosphere between a strip club run by bikers versus one run by someone experienced—and backed by law enforcement—was like night and day.

However, the Demons didn't buy The Peach Pit to make it a success. Their main source of income came from the meth and pot they still dealt out of that building.

At least for now.

Mel looked forward to the day she could drive by that location and see a "closed" sign on the door. She had no doubt that would happen once the task force's investigation was complete.

But for now, she ignored them and concentrated on her own business. The more successful it got, the more satisfying it was.

She wasn't the only one happy with that outcome.

She drew her hand along his bearded jawline. "I'm surprised you stopped in." While he was at the club regularly, tonight the Peckers All-Male Revue was taking over the stage. Their monthly show was once again sold out.

Finn shrugged. "I want to go say hello to them and thank Nick."

"For what?"

"For allowing me to go undercover with them as a stripper. It not only helped the investigation but, without his cooperation, I never would've met you."

Sometimes the sweetness that came out of him surprised

her. Especially since, for the most part, Finn wasn't a very romantic type of guy. "Well, then thank him for me, too."

"I will. I'm heading back there now. I'll find you before I leave." He gave her a quick kiss and disappeared.

As she waited for Finn to return, she watched Pecker after Pecker take a turn doing their individual routines, and when the last one ran off stage, she expected the whole group to return for their closing act.

What she wasn't expecting was all the lights to go out, the club to go pitch black and the music to stop.

When gasps and worried chatter from the audience rose around her, she pulled out her cell phone, using it as a flashlight, so she could find her way toward the back to check the fuses.

She stopped dead in her tracks when a single spotlight hit center stage and the music started again, this time to a song she never heard anyone use during a strip routine.

And when another solo dancer stepped out on stage, she lost her breath.

———

PERFECT by ED SHEERAN was his cue to step out onto the stage.

Finn wasn't lying when he told Mel he was going backstage to meet up with Nick and the guys. But what he didn't tell her was he was only heading back there to change into a white button-down shirt, black suit pants and a matching jacket. He left a few buttons open at the top of the dress shirt since he needed to be able to bust a few moves in it.

As he stepped under the spotlight, the women in the audience screamed so loudly he could hardly hear the music.

He spotted the chair the previous dancer used during his

routine just outside of the bright circle of light. Finn had asked Nick to leave it there since he would need it.

A wild mustang galloped in his chest and his temples had turned into a bass drum. The amount of sweat beading across his forehead was more than expected for a slower routine.

Tonight, he didn't plan on doing any crazy moves since he didn't want to split the seams in his suit. Instead, he kept it simple and sensual by doing a high-knee strut down the stage, stopping here and there to do chest pops, hip rolls and a few spins. Just enough to draw the women to the edge of their seats.

Out of the corner of his eye, he noticed Sapphire standing near the stage giving him a blinding smile and a quick thumbs up. Besides Nick, Mel's best friend was the only other person who knew of his plan.

One he hoped didn't backfire. On stage, under a bright spotlight and in front of a big audience.

Continuing to lip-sync to the song's perfect lyrics, he did a few more smooth, sexy moves before dragging the chair center stage. He turned and crooked a finger at Mel.

Even though she bugged her eyes at him, most likely in exasperation, she approached where he stood at the very edge of the stage. He leaned over, offering her his hand. When she took it, he lifted her up on stage with ease and escorted her to the seat.

"What's going on, Finn?"

He put a finger to his lips, then pointed at the chair. "Sit. This dance is only for you."

She sat. "In case you're unaware, those women believe otherwise."

He didn't care about those other women, he only cared about the one that belonged to him.

Circling the chair, he continued his routine with the

moves he learned right before going undercover with the Peckers. Only tonight he wasn't doing them to rile up the crowd or earn tips, but to woo his woman.

After a few more teasing touches and another rotation around the chair, he stopped in front of her, did a full body roll as he ran a hand down his torso, only stopping to grab his crotch and add a couple of hip rolls. When he turned around, he dropped to both knees and arched backwards until his head rested on her thighs.

With a wink, he grabbed her hands and guided both up his chest, earning him a wiggle of her eyebrows and an answering smile. As soon as he released her wrists, he straightened and spun on one knee.

When he came to an abrupt stop facing Mel, he extended an open hand. Balanced on his palm was a small, black velvet-covered box with the lid open.

In that box wasn't a pink pearl, but a diamond.

Not just any diamond, either. The one his father put on his mother's finger decades ago.

One night over dinner, his mother confessed she didn't think Finn would ever settle down with one woman. And now that he had, she was more than happy with his choice since she had fallen in love with Mel, the same as he had.

And when Mel was out of the room, his mom offered him the ring. Of course, it was an offer he couldn't refuse.

The stage lights caught the sharp lines of the emerald cut, making it sparkle. Just like Mel's eyes.

Once she realized what she was looking at, her smile disintegrated and her lips began to tremble.

Suddenly, no one else existed in that room. Nor did the spotlight or the loud music.

It was only the two of them on stage.

"Melina Jensen, I was serious when I said I wanted you to call me husband."

She pressed a shaky hand to her gaping mouth and her stunning blue-green eyes held a shine. "That's your mom's ring."

"It is. She said she'd beat me with a ballet slipper if I bought you any other ring. She also said she can't wait to call you daughter."

Blinking quickly and sniffling, she whispered, "Finn..."

"That has four letters. The answer I'm looking for only has three."

She fell from the chair right into his arms, pressing her lips to his. When she was done claiming his mouth, she whispered, "My answer is..."

He lifted his eyebrows.

"More than three letters."

That was a relief, since the word no only had two. "So, will you marry me?"

"Absolutely. There's nothing I want more."

He accepted that answer, just as she accepted the ring he slipped onto her finger.

Tonight was proof that life could be so damn unpredictable.

Especially when a simple undercover assignment managed to change the rest of his life...

For the better.

The adventures with the Blue Avengers MC and the Tri-State Drug Task Force continue in **Beyond the Badge: Decker (Blue Avengers MC, book 3)**
Turn the page to read chapter one!

Sign up for Jeanne's newsletter to learn about her upcoming releases, sales and more! http://www.jeannestjames.com/newslettersignup

---

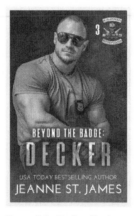

Beyond the Badge: Decker

Two similar paths colliding turns into one inevitable outcome...

As a state police corporal, Owen Decker is no stranger to working undercover. Now, as a member of the Tri-State Federal Drug Task Force, his latest assignment is to wear a prospect cut and infiltrate the Deadly Demons MC.

Unlike previous undercover assignments, this one is personal. After his sister's fatal overdose, Decker was left to pick up the pieces and raise his young niece as his own.
However, he's not the only one determined to help take down the meth traffickers.

Out of desperation, Sloane Parrish finds herself going head to head with the notorious MC when her drug-addicted sister, Sadie, gets tangled up with them. Despite being in over her head, Sloane's still willing to risk everything—including her own safety—to save her baby sister before it's too late.

Unfortunately, the Deadly Demons have no limits when it comes to protecting both their club and very profitable enterprise. So when the people Decker loves end up in the outlaw MC's crosshairs, he regrets the day he volunteered for this assignment. But he vows not to be the only one, he'll make sure they regret that day, too.

TURN THE PAGE TO READ CHAPTER ONE...

Beyond the Badge: Decker
UNEDITED Sneak Peek

CHAPTER ONE

THE RUNDOWN FARMHOUSE would not be featured on the show *Million Dollar Listing* any time soon.

Or ever.

He originally thought the party would be held at the Deadly Demons MC's church in Moundsville, West Virginia. While they *were* in West Virginia, he had no fucking clue where they were exactly.

It was safe to say he didn't like that.

He also wasn't thrilled with the fact he stood in the midst of a one-percenter MC trying to blend in.

But here he was.

To prepare, he had gone on a shopping spree at a thrift store to get some clothing to help him fit in. And to fit his weight gain.

He pressed a hand to his gut under his worn leather jacket.

Beer, pizza and cupcakes—the last baked by Axel Jamison's wife—had done the trick. Every day he'd stand naked in front of the full-length mirror and watch the muscle definition he'd worked so hard to achieve, slowly disappear.

He had gone up a size in both his shirts and jeans. He only hoped when this assignment was over, the extra weight he packed on would disappear just as easily.

But he'd run out of time and the weight gain hadn't been enough, so one afternoon a week ago Crew walked into a task force meeting at The Plant and threw a fake, but realistic-looking, silicone belly in the middle of the conference table. The idea was fucking genius—though, he'd never tell Crew that—since it made him look like he sported a beer gut without actually having one.

However, he drew the line at fake tattoos. True bikers would be able to tell the difference between the *lick-'em-and-stick-'em* body art and real tattoos done by an ink slinger. While he was dedicated to his job—and the task force—there was no damn way he'd volunteer to sit in a tattoo chair to get some random prison or biker tats for a temporary assignment.

Not even a permanent one. Any tattoos he had or would get in the future would be for him and him alone.

Thank fuck it was long-sleeve weather, so most of his body would be covered, anyway. As long as this assignment ended before next spring when the weather got too warm, he'd be golden.

He only volunteered for this undercover work after Crew couldn't find anyone else to do it for one reason or another. Plus, jumping on the opportunity to go under as a prospect got him out of doing surveillance and transcribing wiretaps.

Would he rather take another undercover assignment other than being a prospect for the Deadly Demons? Hell yes, but unfortunately, this was the only one currently available.

He didn't mind the clothes. Or riding an older Harley not nearly as nice as his own. Or even getting into the habit of using sloppy English and biker slang. What he hated most about it was the untrimmed scruff on his face. And being unable to hit the gym five days a week to maintain his hard-earned physique.

His nostrils flared. Add in the unwashed stench mixed with weed filling the air. Not to mention, the filth in and around the farmhouse made his skin crawl.

He imagined his younger sister had ended up in plenty of dumps similar to this *off-the-beaten-path* farmhouse in her search for her next high. Probably surrounded by the same type of people, if not worse.

Joining the Tri-State Federal Drug Task Force had been a no-brainer when Crew threw the opportunity out there to him and his fellow Blue Avengers. He didn't think twice about fighting the onslaught of drugs coming into the area, especially with an operation this large and this dangerous.

The task force was made up of three groups of fifteen members each. He belonged to group two that covered south-west Pennsylvania. While group one covered the mother club's area in West Virginia and group three was handling the outlaw MC's recently formed Ohio chapter.

To get his foot in the door as a potential prospect with the newer Uniontown chapter of the Deadly Demons, he had hooked up with a task force officer from group one to arrange a meet with the president.

This particular task force officer had been undercover with the Moundsville chapter in WV for over a year now. He'd gone under as soon as the task force was formed and had been only recently become a fully-patched member.

Group one actually had two TFOs undercover with the mother club. And if successful, Decker would be the first

TFO from his group to go undercover with the Pennsylvania chapter.

If he was successful. The biggest issue was passing their scrutiny despite being in his late thirties. An older prospect wasn't completely unheard of but it wasn't the norm. Most bikers Decker's age were past the point of wanting to be a bitch for an outlaw MC. And being a prospect meant just that. To pass muster, he would need to do shit he most likely wouldn't want to do. Worse, it could be illegal shit, whether selling drugs or even getting violent.

Basically, prospects were patched members' slaves for about a year. They couldn't say no, even to the stupidest shit, and if they did, they could be stripped of their prospect cut, if not worse.

Becoming a recruit for the Demons might be more difficult at this juncture since the members were overly paranoid. Rightly so, since the club was trafficking five kilos of uncut meth every month by picking it up from a Mexican cartel at the southern border and delivering four of those kilos all the way to La Cosa Nostra in Pittsburgh.

As payment, they took one kilo for themselves, then turned around and took that pure "ice," broke it down by mixing it with filler, packaged it for street sales and made a killing for the club and its members.

It was quite an enterprise.

One the feds wanted to break up.

And, of course, the main reason Decker was currently standing on the unmaintained property out in the middle of Bumfuck doing his best to blend in.

He'd met with Fletch and Wilder to go over language and mannerisms, since they'd now been undercover and living with the Dirty Angels MC for about a year now.

He held his hands, palms out, closer to the blazing

bonfire, trying to warm his numb fingers. Riding a "sled" in November was not his idea of fun. But then, most diehard bikers rode into the start of winter and some were crazy enough to ride all year round.

No fucking thanks. He preferred to keep his extremities and not lose any of them to frostbite.

While he rode the sled assigned to him by Crew to meet up with Rowdy, the undercover TFO—first to go over their story, before following him over to the party—he hoped like fuck Crew found him a four-wheeled ride with working heat before it truly turned into blue ball weather.

Though, tonight he could hardly feel his damn nuts as it was. It would only get worse as the weeks went on.

Rowdy, Decker's task force contact, appeared out of the dark to stand next to him. "Viper ain't here yet."

Viper was the Demons' president and Decker was damn sure he was a stand-up kind of guy. Of course he fucking was.

The Deadly Demons MC was set up differently than the Blue Avengers. Or even the Dirty Angels. The Pennsylvania-based BAMC was made up of regional charters, not chapters. Each charter had their own executive committee and was run independently.

Decker was a member of the Southwest Regional Charter with Axel Jamison as current president. Fletch was their VP, Rez their sergeant at arms, Cross their secretary, Miller the treasurer and Finn was the road captain.

In contrast, the Demons chapters—both Uniontown in Pennsylvania and New Philadelphia in Ohio—did not have their own officers. They answered to the executive committee of the Moundsville-based mother chapter.

From what Rowdy relayed, Viper along with his VP named Screw held on to their power with an iron fist. No one messed with them but they sure messed with everyone else. And not in a fun way.

They were ruthless.

If only took a whiff of a prospect or member stepping out of line or fucking the club over, and that Demon was handled with a quick fierceness. As in, they no longer existed. Or if they did survive, they probably wished they hadn't.

Abracadabra, make this biker disappear. Only instead of a magic wand, they used tire irons or whatever else was handy.

Decker scratched his itchy as fuck beard and leaned heavily into his newly acquired biker-speak. "He gonna show up, yeah?"

"If he don't, gonna track down Screw. Want a beer?"

"Why the fuck not?" In truth, he'd rather have a massive mug of coffee to warm him up, but sipping coffee wouldn't fly at one of these shindigs. Booze, beer, pot and whatever else was more this club's speed. And he needed to fit in, even before shrugging on one of their prospect cuts.

Right now he wasn't even considered a hang-around and he hoped like hell it wouldn't be required before he'd be allowed to become a prospect. Some clubs had that stipulation. Worse, that informal "evaluation process" could take months or even years. Decker didn't have time for that. Neither did the task foce.

While they hadn't required that of Rowdy and Goose, that didn't mean shit. He hadn't seen the Demons by-laws and it could very well be the club didn't have any. How they handled shit could change every day if Viper wanted it that way. He couldn't imagine that the DDMC gave a flying fuck about rules.

So, yeah, if Viper require Decker to hang with the club awhile before they'd even consider making him a prospect, it could fuck up everything. He doubted hang-arounds had the same access or insider info as a prospect.

Rowdy elbowed him. "C'mon, it's best you wander around and be seen. The more you talk to them, the better." He jerked his chin up at a member wearing a Demons cut. "That's my buddy, Goose, over there grabbin' a beer. We got patched in at the same time."

Decker took those words as meaning Goose was the second undercover TFO with the Demons.

As they approached him and the keg floating in a barrel full of melting ice, Decker was impressed with how well Goose blended in with the rest of the Demons.

His long dirty blond hair was greasy, his raggedy beard reached halfway down his chest and he had a huge beer belly spilling out from between the flaps of his cut. But then Goose, like Rowdy, had been undercover for a year.

A lot could happen in a year.

Fuck me if I'm still in this assignment in a year and I've gone that far down the rabbit hole.

Rowdy introduced him to Goose with a knowing look. The UCO's gaze sliced from Rowdy to Decker. "Beer?"

"Yeah."

Goose lifted a Harley-Davidson travel mug. "Got a cup?"

"No, I need one?"

The "biker" jerked on the end of his bushy beard and when he laughed his beer gut bounced. "They got 'em. Just don't recommend usin' 'em."

Jesus fuck.

"'Less you need help buildin' your immune system."

Beside Decker, Rowdy chuckled. "Yeah, learned early on to bring our own shit. Just look around and you'll see why."

He didn't have to look around the yard edged with overgrown weeds and grass to know what they were saying was fact. The area around the bonfire that included some disgusting couches and both broken and unbroken lawn chairs, was only made walkable because the vegetation had been crushed down by boots. He doubted this property had seen a lawnmower is at least a decade.

When they arrived earlier, they had also hoofed it through the farmhouse to get to the backyard. That gave him a good firsthand view of what that looked like inside. It was the kind of house that made you rethink eating at company parties or potluck dinners.

"That typical?" Decker asked, making a mental note to throw some shit in the leather saddle bags on his borrowed bike. Just in case he found himself at more of these gatherings.

"For some. Others don't give a shit. 'Specially the ones that are fucked up on drugs or booze. Once they're at that point, tainted food or drink ain't gonna do shit."

"Ain't that the truth," Rowdy agreed.

"Heads up, bogey at two o'clock," Goose warned under his breath, glancing over Decker's right shoulder.

Here goes nothing.

The president of the Deadly Demons stepped next to Rowdy, whacking him hard on the back. "Yo. Heard you're lookin' for me. What the fuck you want?"

Using the light from a single spotlight shining down onto the yard and glow of the huge bonfire full of old tires and who knows what other toxic shit, Decker turned and checked out the man he needed to impress. Or at least not piss off.

Decker's best guess was that Viper was in his fifties. He could be younger but if so, he'd lived a hard life.

A black skullcap covered his long hair, he wore a stained Sturgis Bike Week sweatshirt under his black leather Demons cut, as well as the typical biker boots and worn jeans. Tattoos covered the back of both hands and the section of neck Decker could see past his overgrown beard. The man also had a snake tattooed along the side of his face. Starting at his hairline, the reptile's body curled along his temple, with the head of the viper disappearing somewhere in his beard.

Classy shit right there.

Rowdy jerked a thumb in Decker's direction. "My man here's interested in prospectin' for the club."

An eyebrow hiked up Viper's forehead as he turned to stare at Decker. "Yeah? Why the fuck you wanna do that?"

"Guess the question is, why the fuck not?" Decker answered, meeting the head biker's shadowed eyes.

"Ain't an answer."

"Best one I got," Decker countered.

Decker could barely see Viper's pursed lips through that wiry mess on his face as he studied him some more.

If Viper was trying to intimidate him by simply staring at him, he was going to fail.

"Got a sled?"

"Sure do. Parked out front."

"Know how to keep your mouth shut?"

"Done time, so yeah, know when it should be open and when it should be shut."

Viper turned to Rowdy. "How long you know him?"

About ten minutes.

"Must be about ten years now," Rowdy lied.

Jesus.

"Yeah? Why didn't you bring him 'round sooner?"

Decker rushed to answer before Rowdy did since he wanted to be the "director" of this undercover assignment, not anyone else. This way he'd remember the details of his character and lessen the chance of fucking up. "Just recently got out after doin' a nickel inside."

Viper's bushy eyebrows and he turned to take a closer look at Decker. "Yeah?"

"Yeah," Decker answered, making his voice gruffer than normal.

"Where at?"

Decker once again hurried to answer before Rowdy since he didn't work in PA so he might not know that prison system. "Mercer."

"For what?"

"Possession." Drugs were right up the Demons' alley.

Viper raised his chin and stared Decker down. "Got a nickel for possession? Or for fuckin' up?"

"Fuckin' up. Had to survive somehow," Decker answered, jerking up one shoulder.

Viper considered him for a few more seconds before reaching into his cut and pulled out a fucking joint.

Great.

Goose rushed forward to light it for him, surprising the shit out of Decker. What, did Viper need to be treated like a king and the Demons were his subjects?

With the joint tucked between Viper's barely visible lips, the lit end flared, giving his rough face a ruddy glow. After a second deep inhale, he held it out to Decker.

Fuck.

Forget that it was pot. He was more worried about putting his mouth on the same object as Viper. Hygiene wasn't a top priority when it came to the Demons.

Taking it reluctantly, Decker put it to his lips and sucked the smoke into his mouth, pretending to inhale it.

He handed it back to Viper but the prez shook his head, indicating that Goose or Rowdy should take it next. Goose snagged it and took a long hit.

Decker blew the smoke out of his nostrils before he

started coughing on the trash weed. He knew having to do drugs would be a strong possibility, he cursed himself for not being better prepared. Especially with his virgin lungs.

Rowdy took a small hit similar to Decker before passing it back to Viper who asked, "What were you possessin'?"

He guessed this was sort of like a twisted job interview. "Blow."

"You know your ass ain't gonna be your own for at least a year? Gonna be ours. One of us tells you to do somethin', you gotta do it. No negotiation. No backtalk. No questions. You do it. You up for that?"

"Rowdy told me all about it. Sounds like freedom to me after livin' the last five fuckin' years in a fuckin' cage."

"He tell you how much it's gonna suck?"

Decker chuckled. "Yeah. Know it. Can't be worse than bein' behind bars."

"You'd be wrong," Viper said. "Inside, you got screws protectin' you. Out here, we don't even got your back 'til you're handed your patches and are one of us. *If* you make it that far. 'Til then you're nobody. You're a part of the club but ain't a part of the club, if you get my meanin'."

"Got it."

"Not sure you do. Most don't. Most prospects start out strong then decide this shit ain't for them. It ain't worth it. They run home to Mommy."

"Ain't gonna run home to my mommy. Rowdy assured me any shit I gotta eat's gonna be worth it."

Viper shot Rowdy a look. "Guess we weren't rough enough on him, then."

"Bah," Rowdy huffed. "Just ain't a pussy."

The Demons' president reached out and wiped his finger behind Rowdy's ear. "Still wet back there. You willin' to put your ass on the line to sponsor him?"

"Fuck yeah," Rowdy said with confidence. "Never woulda brought him tonight if I wasn't willin'."

Viper took a hit from the joint, and while he held the smoke deep down in his lungs, he stroked his long beard, once again staring at Decker.

Maybe he was trying to get Decker to break. Decker made sure to meet his eyes and not look away.

"Anyway," Rowdy started, "At the last meetin' you mentioned gettin' more prospects for both Uniontown and New Philadelphia."

"Yeah?" Viper spat on the ground.

Decker didn't react. He acted like he was used to people spitting at his feet.

"Yeah. Or did I hear wrong."

Viper turned his attention back to Rowdy. "Didn't hear wrong."

Rowdy slapped Decker's chest. "Then Jake here's gonna be perfect for Uniontown."

Viper squinted at Rowdy. "Why's that?"

"'Cause he's shackin' up with some bitch near there."

The prez's head swung back toward Decker. "You got an ol' lady?"

He shook his head. "Nah. She ain't my ol' lady. Just a slit I'm fuckin'. Keeps a roof over my head, food in my gut and my dick wet."

"They ain't worth much more than that." Viper sucked loudly on what teeth he had remaining. "Alright. Gonna think about it. Will let you know, brother. But remember," Viper leaned in and jabbed Rowdy's chest with his index finger, "that means it's *your* ass on the line if he fucks up."

Rowdy stood his ground and gave the DDMC president a single nod. "Aware of that. He ain't gonna fuck up."

Viper took a step back, dropped his bearded chin to his

chest and gave Rowdy a warning look, "Better fuckin' hope not."

There was a lot more said in that look and behind those words than hit Decker's ears. He figured it had to do with their drug enterprise.

This club was not simply a brotherhood that lived a biker lifestyle, they wanted to build an empire.

One that the Tri-State Federal Drug Task Force wanted to crush before it was done being built.

After the prez wandered away and was out of earshot, Rowdy turned to Decker. "Don't fuck up."

———

HE THOUGHT he was a smart guy.

Now Decker was questioning that, among other things, as he pulled his borrowed '84 Harley-Davidson Softail up to the Deadly Demons' church in Moundsville, WV. Rowdy called him three days ago and told him that to become a prospect it needed to go before the Demons' officers for a vote.

That vote was happening quicker than any of them expected.

The front lot was full of Harleys, both older and newer. If the number of bikes equalled the number of Demons inside, then he'd be walking into a lion's den while wearing a meat suit.

He shut down the bike and sat staring at old car dealership. It was a hell of a lot bigger than the gas station in Uniontown, that was for damn sure. Actually it was a lot larger than he expected.

The glass windows in what would've been the original showroom had been replaced with brick. Probably for good reason. He had no idea if the Demons had enemies, but if they didn't before, they might now due to them expanding their territory.

And bullets meeting glass could be deadly. A fact they considered when his own MC renovated The Plant. Plus, not having windows kept whatever was happening inside their church hidden from curious eyes.

A barb-wire-topped chain-link fence with solid plastic slats extended out from both corners of the large brick building and then encircled the rear of the building ensuring even more security and privacy.

While the sprawling building itself was pretty nondescript, the number of Harleys and the huge Demons logo painted on the front of the building gave the building's purpose away.

Like the gas station in Uniontown, the Demons weren't hiding that this was their church and this area was their territory. A not-so-subtle warning to other MCs and maybe even nomads.

Decker pulled his cell phone from the inside pocket of his lined leather jacket and shot Rowdy a quick text:

Here.

His answering message came a few minutes later:

Stay there. Will come get you when they're ready for you.

Decker assumed only the officers had to vote on whether he'd get a prospect cut tonight, not the whole membership. But, like considering himself as smart, he might be wrong.

Either way, he hoped shit went smoothly and he was handed his prospect rocker without a hitch. If he wasn't, the task force would have to figure out another way to get their foot in the door of the Uniontown chapter.

He got off the borrowed bike, approached the building, leaned back against it and propped his boot on the wall.

Then he waited.

Get it here: Beyond the Badge: Decker (Blue Avengers MC, book 3)

If You Enjoyed This Book

Thank you for reading Beyond the Badge: Finn. If you enjoyed Finn and Mel's story, please consider leaving a review at your favorite retailer and/or Goodreads to let other readers know. Reviews are always appreciated and just a few words can help an independent author like me tremendously!

Want to read a sample of my work? Download a sampler book here: BookHip.com/MTQQKK

Also by Jeanne St. James

Find my complete reading order here:

https://www.jeannestjames.com/reading-order

* Available in Audiobook

Standalone Books:

Made Maleen: A Modern Twist on a Fairy Tale *

Damaged *

Rip Cord: The Complete Trilogy *

Everything About You (A Second Chance Gay Romance) *

Reigniting Chase (An M/M Standalone) *

Brothers in Blue Series:

Brothers in Blue: Max *

Brothers in Blue: Marc *

Brothers in Blue: Matt *

Teddy: A Brothers in Blue Novelette *

Brothers in Blue: A Bryson Family Christmas *

The Dare Ménage Series:

Double Dare *

Daring Proposal *

Dare to Be Three *

A Daring Desire *

Dare to Surrender *

A Daring Journey *

The Obsessed Novellas:

Forever Him *

Only Him *

Needing Him *

Loving Her *

Tempting Him *

Down & Dirty: Dirty Angels MC Series®:

Down & Dirty: Zak *

Down & Dirty: Jag *

Down & Dirty: Hawk *

Down & Dirty: Diesel *

Down & Dirty: Axel *

Down & Dirty: Slade *

Down & Dirty: Dawg *

Down & Dirty: Dex *

Down & Dirty: Linc *

Down & Dirty: Crow *

Crossing the Line (A DAMC/Blue Avengers MC Crossover) *

Magnum: A Dark Knights MC/Dirty Angels MC Crossover *

Crash: A Dirty Angels MC/Blood Fury MC Crossover *

In the Shadows Security Series:

Guts & Glory: Mercy *

Guts & Glory: Ryder *

Guts & Glory: Hunter *

Guts & Glory: Walker *

Guts & Glory: Steel *

Guts & Glory: Brick *

Blood & Bones: Blood Fury MC®:

Blood & Bones: Trip *

Blood & Bones: Sig *

Blood & Bones: Judge *

Blood & Bones: Deacon *

Blood & Bones: Cage *

Blood & Bones: Shade *

Blood & Bones: Rook *

Blood & Bones: Rev *

Blood & Bones: Ozzy *

Blood & Bones: Dodge

Blood & Bones: Whip

Blood & Bones: Easy

Beyond the Badge: Blue Avengers MC™:

Beyond the Badge: Fletch

Beyond the Badge: Finn

Beyond the Badge: Decker

Beyond the Badge: Rez

Beyond the Badge: Crew

Beyond the Badge: Nox

COMING SOON!

Double D Ranch (An MMF Ménage Series)

Dirty Angels MC®: The Next Generation

WRITING AS J.J. MASTERS

The Royal Alpha Series:

(A gay mpreg shifter series)

The Selkie Prince's Fated Mate *

The Selkie Prince & His Omega Guard *

The Selkie Prince's Unexpected Omega *

The Selkie Prince's Forbidden Mate *

The Selkie Prince's Secret Baby *

About the Author

JEANNE ST. JAMES is a USA Today, Amazon and international bestselling romance author who loves writing about strong women and alpha males. She was only thirteen when she first started writing. Her first published piece was an erotic short story in Playgirl magazine. She then went on to publish her first romance novel in 2009. She is now an author of over sixty contemporary romances. She writes M/F, M/M, and M/M/F ménages, including interracial romance. She also writes M/M paranormal romance under the name: J.J. Masters.

Want to read a sample of her work? Download a sampler book here: BookHip.com/MTQQKK

To keep up with her busy release schedule check her website at www.jeannestjames.com or sign up for her newsletter: http://www.jeannestjames.com/newslettersignup

www.jeannestjames.com
jeanne@jeannestjames.com

Newsletter: http://www.jeannestjames.com/
newslettersignup
Jeanne's Down & Dirty Book Crew: https://www.facebook.
com/groups/JeannesReviewCrew/

TikTok: https://www.tiktok.com/@jeannestjames

facebook.com/JeanneStJamesAuthor

amazon.com/author/jeannestjames

instagram.com/JeanneStJames

bookbub.com/authors/jeanne-st-james

goodreads.com/JeanneStJames

pinterest.com/JeanneStJames

Get a FREE Sampler Book

This book contains the first chapter of a variety of my books. This will give you a taste of the type of books I write and if you enjoy the first chapter, I hope you'll be interested in reading the rest of the book.

Each book I list in the sampler will include the description of the book, the genre, and the first chapter, along with links to find out more. I hope you find a book you will enjoy curling up with!

Get it here: BookHip.com/MTQQKK

Made in the USA
Las Vegas, NV
12 March 2023

68986354R00261